P9-CQC-695

Best Intentions

ALSO BY EMILY LISTFIELD

It Was Gonna Be Like Paris
Variations in the Night
Slightly Like Strangers
Acts of Love
The Last Good Night
Waiting to Surface

Best Intentions

A NOVEL

EMILY LISTFIELD

ATRIA BOOKS

NEW YORK LONDON TORONTO SYDNEY

ATRIA BOOKS
A Division of Simon & Schuster, Inc.
1230 Avenue of the Americas
New York, NY 10020

This book is a work of fiction. Names, characters, places, and incidents either are products of the author's imagination or are used fictitiously. Any resemblance to actual events or locales or persons, living or dead, is entirely coincidental.

First Atria Books hardcover edition May 2009

ATRIA BOOKS and colophon are trademarks of Simon & Schuster, Inc.

Designed by Jaime Putorti

Manufactured in the United States of America

10 9 8 7 6 5 4 3 2 1

Library of Congress Cataloging-in-Publication Data

Listfield, Emily.
Best intentions : a novel / by Emily Listfield.
p. cm.
1. Man-woman relationships—Fiction. 2. Murder—Fiction.
3. Psychological fiction. I. Title.
PS3562.I7822B47 2009
813'.54—dc22 2008037967

ISBN-13: 978-1-4165-7671-6
ISBN-10: 1-4165-7671-1

For my mother

The worst, the most corrupting lies are problems poorly stated.

—GEORGES BERNANOS

PART ONE

PROLOGUE

nypdcrimeblotter.com
October 27th, 7am . . . The body of a 39-year-old woman was found early this morning in her downtown Manhattan apartment. There were no signs of forced entry, leading detectives to believe that the victim knew her assailant. The police are withholding identification pending notification of the victim's family.

ONE

I lie in bed watching the numbers on the digital alarm click in slow motion to 6:00 a.m., 6:01. My right hand, curled tightly beneath my head, is cramping, but I don't want to risk moving it. I lie perfectly still, listening to the birds chirping noisily outside, a high-pitched chorus wafting rebelliously through the harsh geometry of Manhattan. Nervous I would oversleep, I had tossed fitfully until dawn. Now, as with most missed opportunities, the only thing I long for is another chance at the night.

The lightness of the chirping fills me with a yearning I can't quite place, for unabridged land, for air, for my own childhood forty miles north of here, though I wanted desperately to escape the precisely gridded suburbs with their overriding promise of safety. Still, it's hard not to feel nostalgia for a time when I thought predictability was the worst fate imaginable.

I shut my eyes, willing the thought away.

It is a morning for fresh starts, after all.

Sam grunts softly in his sleep and rearranges his long legs, his left thigh brushing against mine under the sheets. I flinch unconsciously at the brief interlude of skin on skin and hold my breath, trying not to disturb him—he has been up most of the night. He settles into his new position, letting out an aborted sigh from somewhere deep within his dream, and I exhale, secretly disappointed that he hasn't woken, turned to me. I look down, studying his face in the pale sunlight. Always handsome, he is more defined now, his edges sharper, as if everything soft and extraneous has been carved away, leaving his most essential self exposed. I run my fingertips gently through his matted dark-blond hair—I've always loved him best this way, disheveled, unguarded.

His skin is warm, almost moist.

I try to remember the last time we made love in this fragile sliver of time before the girls wake up. I try to remember when we stopped trying.

I reach over and shut off the alarm so it won't wake him. All through the night I felt his agitation roiling his attempts at sleep, infiltrating my own. I'd turned to him once around two a.m. and asked what was bothering him.

"Nothing, just the story I'm working on. The pieces don't jibe, a source won't call me back," he said, curving away from me, though whether it was to avoid disturbing me further or a desire to be left alone, I wasn't sure. I've seen him like this many times before at the beginning of an assignment, waiting for a clear narrative to form in his head. He is a man who likes order and grows steeped in anxiety until he can impose it. Perhaps that's all it is.

For months, though, all through the summer, Sam has seemed restive for reasons I can't quite place. It has grown contagious, a malaise that has metastasized between us into a desultory low-level dissatisfaction, nothing I can touch, nothing worthy of accusation or argument, and yet. I hope the cooler season will wipe the slate clean, bring a new semester for our marriage.

I miss him.

There are moments, unexpected, unpredictable, when there is a sudden flash, a brief illumination in a look or touch, and we are us again, connected. They are hard to manufacture, though, no matter how hard I try. Sometimes I can feel him trying, too, missing me, too.

I slide carefully out of bed and pad barefoot down the hallway, bending over to pick up a crumpled gum wrapper, poorly hidden evidence of Claire's latest habit, the cloying sweet smell of imitation strawberry, grape, watermelon, vanilla emanating from her like cheap perfume, the noisy snapping and chewing deeply annoying, even more so because it is surely interfering with the six thousand dollars' worth of braces that encase her teeth, correcting a supposed crookedness that only an Upper East Side orthodontist can discern. Seizing the parental high road, I've taken to hiding my own gum-chewing habit, one of the pretenses I've recently felt it necessary to assume. I open the front door carefully, hoping its creak won't wake the children, take the papers into the kitchen and make a pot of coffee.

I can feel their breath, Sam's, the girls', in their separate corners of the apartment, surrounding me, grounding me even as they sleep. I have twenty minutes before I have to wake them and make breakfast, which, as per first day of school tradition, will involve pots and pans rarely seen on weekday mornings, scrambled eggs with chives snipped from the shriveling strands of the window herb plant, toast slathered with strawberry rhubarb preserves from the farmers' market, hot chocolate made from unsweetened cocoa and sugar rather than packets, ballast for whatever schoolyard intrigues, new teachers' quirks, algebraic conundrums, vertiginous swings in popularity lie ahead. I turn on the radio and listen to the weather report, which predicts a humid Indian summer day, the temperature threatening to hit the high eighties.

I dip my finger in the jam and lick it absentmindedly. Long ago, when the girls were still young enough to need supervision at the breakfast table, Sam and I developed a tag-team approach. I would get them up, put the food on the table and then dress while he ate with them. Though Phoebe is eleven and Claire thirteen, the habit remains, one of the unexamined rituals of family life that you realize only later are its very glue.

I take one last sip of coffee and walk into Phoebe's room first, stepping carefully over the huge shopping bag of new school supplies from Staples that have spilled across the floor, a kaleidoscope of colorful binders, highlighters in seven colors, six of which are totally unnecessary as far as I'm concerned, a new hole punch, index cards for book reports, neon-pink Post-its in the shape of hearts and arrows. Phoebe possesses a unique blend of laserlike focus and forgetfulness—she can concentrate on an assignment for hours but will leave it on the bus. It is one of the things—not just the forgetfulness, but her lack of concern about it—that she has promised, albeit halfheartedly, to work on this year, though when I suggested buying a memo pad for to-do lists, she refused. "I'm eleven," she reminded me indignantly, as if lists were one more odious thing waiting for her in adulthood, along with mortgages, insurance claims, cholesterol readings. "Writing things on the back of my hand works just fine."

I lean over to kiss her cheek and she rolls sleepily into me, burying her face in the crook of my neck, her eyes fluttering open and then closing again.

"You have to get up, sweetie," I whisper as I run my fingers under the blanket and tickle her, her body at least nominally still mine. The softness of her neck, her arms makes the walls of my heart constrict. No one really tells you how much it is like falling in love over and over, how physical and encompassing it will be. Or that you will never feel completely safe and relaxed again.

"Not yet." Her breath is heated, musty but sweet.

Since they got home from camp, the girls have grown used to lounging in bed till noon, especially in the last few weeks, when, like a final indulgent binge before a diet, we all lost the will for discipline of any sort.

"I hate school," Phoebe groans.

"It's too soon to hate school."

"It's never too soon to hate school."

I smile, knowing the words are hollow. Phoebe is by nature an easygoing child who, despite her carelessness, is generally anxious to please her teachers and popular with her friends. "Get up, my little misanthrope."

She looks at me suspiciously and is about to ask what the word means when she thinks better of it, knowing I will tell her to look it up, something she has absolutely no intention of doing. "It's not too soon for me to get a cell phone, either," she calls after me.

I leave without answering. I have decreed, repeatedly, that twelve is the age of consent for that particular piece of technology, my desire for being in constant touch, for being able to place her, outweighed by my certainty that Phoebe will lose at least a dozen phones within the first month. I make my way to Claire's room, where every available surface is lined with ornate boxes, jewelry cases, embroidered journals, the artifacts of her life stashed in tiny drawers, a Chinese puzzle of secrets and mementos. There is no one on earth quite as sentimental as a thirteen-year-old girl. In the rare moments when I am alone in the house I sometimes go through her drawers, scan her Internet history, her notebooks, looking not for evidence of crimes but for clues to who she is becoming. When I lean down to wake her, Claire shrugs away, curling deeper beneath the stained pale blue quilt she refuses to part with. It takes three increasingly strenuous shakes to get her to at least raise her head temporarily, her face hidden by a tangle of thick brunette hair almost the exact color as mine. If Phoebe is Sam's daughter, lighter in coloring and temperament, Claire, with her olive skin, her broodier nature, is mine. Claire's chosen outfit for the day—a loosely knit pale-pink cable sweater, denim mini and leggings—is carefully laid out on her desk chair. She spent a few days last week in East Hampton with a school friend shunning the beach to shop on Main Street and Newtown Lane, Claire suddenly one of those tanned, long-legged girls of indeterminate age still so alien to me with their giddy sense of entitlement apparent in every avid stride. I wonder if strangers, seeing Claire, assumed she was one of them, with an enormous shingled house and a credit card of her own.

"Honey, I think you may need to rethink your outfit," I say gently. "It's going to be too hot today."

Claire shakes her head at the ridiculousness of the notion. The outfit can't be rethought—the skirt is too short for the school's restriction that hems be within four inches of the knee to wear without leggings and the sweater is, well, perfect. Any dolt can see that.

"I'll be fine," Claire insists. Under the best of circumstances, she has a certain rigidity that, though frustrating at times, I nevertheless hope will serve her well later in life when self-doubt, frankly self-reflection of any kind, has a tendency to impede progress, if not happiness. I have come to see the benefits of having blinders on. Anyway, when it comes to clothes Claire is particularly ironclad. It's useless to fight, though that doesn't always stop me from trying. It's a hard habit to break—thinking you can control your own children.

The girls are dressed, Phoebe in capris and an Urban Outfitters T-shirt she pulled out of her dresser at the last minute, Claire in precisely the outfit she had planned, and at the table, pushing their eggs around with the tines of their forks when Sam stumbles out. He looks momentarily surprised at the presence of actual cooked food before recognition dawns on him. "Ah," he says, smiling, "the first day. The anticipation, the dread, the scramble for good seats." He bends over and kisses the top of the girls' heads. He has an informal, easygoing manner with the kids, who accept the undertone of irony as part of his makeup, like one's particular scent or way of walking. It is the same relaxed, loping charm I fell in love with nineteen years ago when we sat next to each other in the back row of a class on Hawthorne and James during our junior year in college: the smile that even then creased the sides of his cheeks, the tatty burgundy wool scarf draped casually around his neck in a way that only prep-school boys can ever truly pull off, his sly running commentary about professors, his baritone that entered my pores and stayed there like smoke. Sam seemed to have an innate sense of belonging and yet not take it seriously—a lethal combination to someone like me. My own family had struggled into the middle class, there was nothing effortless about it, every move, every emotion was splayed out, picked over, vociferously debated. The very notion of privacy was alien, suspect. Sam's cool distance was as deeply attractive to me as my lack of it was to him. Then, anyway.

I watch Sam, yawning as he takes his first sip of coffee, breaks off a piece of Claire's toast and gets his hand slapped, a shopworn routine that nevertheless tangles me up with comfort and affection.

This is what we have created, this family.

Sam flips through the stack of newspapers in front of him, quickly scanning the front pages of *The New York Times, The Wall Street Journal* and *The Washington Post* before turning to the business sections. There is an unmistakable testosterone-induced anxiety—has anyone gotten a juicy story he has somehow missed?—and poorly concealed relief that there is only the usual stock market pabulum and speculative opinion. An observer by nature, he has a talent for intuiting shifts in mood and influence, the way power moves around the city. It's what makes him a good business journalist. Still, two weeks ago, Sam's latest competitor at the magazine, Peter Borofsky, a reporter six years younger and ten times as hungry, broke a story about how the board of a Fortune 500 company spied on its own president, bugging his phone, getting his financial records. The report made it onto the evening news and Sam can't help but grit his teeth every time he hears it mentioned. This morning, at least, he is safe. So far. I know that the moment I leave he will race to his laptop to check an ever-expanding list of Web sites and blogs. There are so many more ways to be bested now.

"What kind of day do you have?" he asks, glancing up from the paper.

"Some forms to fill out at school . . ."

"What forms?" Claire demands, suspicious.

"Nothing, just the class trip consent things."

"Didn't you do that? They were due weeks ago."

"I thought I had, but apparently not. I got an e-mail from the school on Friday."

Claire looks at me disdainfully.

I shrug. There are so many forms, a new batch every day, and newsletters and invitations and updates and e-mails, as if the school is worried parents won't feel they are getting their money's worth if their mailboxes aren't constantly overflowing. "It'll be fine," I insist. I turn back to Sam. "Then I'm having breakfast with Deirdre."

Sam nods and as he flips the page of his newspaper the corner dips into his coffee and threatens to fall off into soggy little islands of print. The three of us went to college together on an upstate campus so snowy that ropes stretched like cat's cradle yarn across it for students to pull their way to classes. In recent years, though, my friendship with Deirdre has come to exist largely outside of a broader social context, a skein that binds us from our early days in Manhattan, when we shared a loft in the East Village. For fifteen years we have been meeting once a week, or close to it, though what had once been late-night drinks in cheap dive bars has morphed into early-morning breakfasts. "This is the most long-term relationship I've ever had," Deirdre often jokes. I have Sam, of course, but I know just what she means.

"You'll see her at Jack's dinner tomorrow night," I remind him.

"How could I forget? The big birthday celebration."

"Who's Jack?" Claire asks.

"Someone we went to college with."

"How come I've never met him?" Any pre-child life is suspect and murky by default; neither of the girls truly believe in its existence.

"He lives in Boston."

"You're going to Boston?" Phoebe asks, perplexed.

"No. He has a job interview in New York and asked us all out to dinner," I explain. "We haven't seen each other in years."

Jack Handel was Deirdre's college boyfriend, a scholarship kid from northern California. From the start, he and I shared a special empathy; we were both outsiders on that hilly, privileged campus, though our reactions were quite different. If I wanted—a little too desperately—to fit in, Jack wore his interloper status defiantly. It's not that he had a chip on his shoulder, but his sense of direction set him apart; he was sharper, faster, more strategic, while the rest of us were still a little soft, unformed, blurry around the edges. I still remember one Christmas vacation, when the four of us met up in the city almost every night. For Deirdre and Sam, who both grew up here, Manhattan was already a checkerboard of memories: There was Trader Vic's at the Plaza, where Deirdre swore they let her drink at sixteen—we got plastered on Scorpions, with their sickeningly sweet floating gardenias and two-foot-long straws, Deirdre and I in our thrift-shop fifties cocktail dresses wobbling out into the cold night; we went to Sam's favorite jazz club downtown and were scolded for talking during the sets; we ended up at three a.m. at Brasserie, where Deirdre's father had a running tab and we could charge enormous breakfasts, though I asked repeatedly to the point of annoyance if she was sure it was okay. I was barely able to afford a diner on my own and couldn't imagine anyone being that cavalier about money. And there were the places that they avoided. Deirdre wouldn't go to Serendipity because it was where her father used to take her to drown her parents' divorce in Frozen Hot Chocolates; she centered her life downtown as much as possible. Sam had written off all of Park Avenue on principle. The city was a game of Twister to them, and if I would never catch up I would also never risk falling into one of their valleys. That winter break, though, Jack and I were along for the ride, giddy, exuberant, lucky to be chosen. For that brief moment, opportunity, the future itself, felt boundless.

We thought it would always be that way.

Sam turns another page of his newspaper. "Who is Jack interviewing with?"

"He wouldn't tell me. He signed a confidentiality agreement."

"I can't see him moving to New York."

"Why not?"

"It's easier to be a big deal in Boston. Is Alice coming?"

"I don't think so. He'll only be here overnight. His actual birthday is next weekend, so I guess they'll do their own thing up there."

Jack is the first among us to hit forty. Deirdre's birthday is in seven weeks, Sam has six more months, I have eight.

"You'd think Deirdre would be the last person he'd want to spend his birthday with."

"It was all so long ago," I remind him.

Claire listens intently. She worships Deirdre, scavenging for clues to a life so much more captivating than anything we could possibly offer.

Sam shrugs without looking up and runs his hands lazily down his flat stomach—he still runs three miles most mornings, though his knees have lately begun creaking with alarming regularity. At thirty-nine he considers this a decidedly premature development that he plans on ignoring for as long as possible. Like most men he is determined to deny the physical signs of aging to the same degree that women obsess about them. "By the way, I may be late tonight."

"Late as in don't hold dinner?" For years, Sam and I ate after the girls, but reading numerous dire magazine articles has convinced me they will be hooked on heroin by the age of fourteen if we don't change our evil ways. Lately I've been making a concerted, if erratic, effort for all of us to eat approximately the same thing at approximately the same time. There have been spurts of upstart rebellions from various involved parties ever since.

"I'm not sure. I'll call you as soon as I know. I'm hoping to meet with someone about the Wells profile. I'm waiting to hear back from him."

I study Sam, weighing my options. It would never occur to me that being late on the first night of school is even a choice. Still, I don't want to fight this morning. And I know how much he needs this profile.

Sam has recently been assigned to write a cover story on Eliot Wells, the founder of Leximark. An early innovator in Web functionality, he is supposedly about to introduce some breakthrough cross-platform first-step artificial intelligence something or other—I don't quite get it, though I pretend I do rather than suffer through one more excruciating explanation. All I know is that the most controversial thing that has been written about Wells in recent years, aside from allusions to his cataclysmic temper, is that he has a proclivity to skip showers—though it seems to me this is said about any number of Internet gurus, as if a lack of personal hygiene is in and of itself a sign of genius. Sam is hoping to uncover something grittier and has convinced himself—though not, as yet, his editor, Simon—that there is dirt lurking in Wells's background. Of course, the great inverse law of journalism is that the further you bring someone down, the higher you raise your own profile.

"All right, let me know." I get up to dress.

"Lisa?"

I turn partially around. "Yes?"

"There's something I want to talk to you about." His face, still hatch-marked with indentations from his pillow, is earnest, almost nervous.

I look at him quizzically.

He glances over at the girls. "Later. Tonight."

"All right."

As I pass, he reaches over and grazes my forearm with his fingertips.

I will feel it there for the rest of the day, he can still do that to me.

I leave the three of them in the kitchen and go to shower, letting the hot water pour down my face, thinking of the day ahead, what to wear, my schedule at work, wondering, too, what Sam might want to talk to me about and why he thinks he needs to reserve my time. I mean, where else would I be?

When I get out I notice that his cell phone, charging on the night table, is flashing with a message.

I wrap the towel tighter about my chest, shake out my shoulder-length hair, the thick, dark waves not yet expanding from the heat into the total unruliness that had me wearing a ponytail most of the summer. I open the top drawer of my dresser, consider three different versions of a white V-neck top that to the naked eye look identical but which are in fact each completely necessary for varying levels of bloat. I can hear Sam and the girls clearing their plates. I glance at the door, still closed.

I don't know why I pick up the phone. I have never done anything like this before. It would be easy to say it is intuition, but we always claim that in retrospect.

With it still charging, I push "voice mail" and listen to his message.

It is a woman's voice, she does not leave a name, she does not have to, judging by the intimacy lacing through her tone. "I'm going to be a little late tonight," she says, the words slightly muffled by the whoosh of traffic in the background. "Can we make it six thirty? Same place."

I press the button to save the message as new and sit down on the edge of the bed, a cool sweat beading along the back of my neck and trickling slowly down my spine.

TWO

Twenty minutes later, I shepherd the girls out the front door and am surprised, despite the radio, by the warm liquidity of the air. It is the kind of day that can please or hurt or both, bringing an unexpected last chance to get whatever it is you'd had such hopes for at the beginning of the summer, a day for impulse purchases, risky e-mail. Calls to restless married men.

"Can we make it six thirty?"

I shake my head. Surely, there are any number of explanations.

"Same place," she said. "Same place."

Perhaps I misheard Sam, perhaps he said the source he was meeting with about the Wells piece was a woman. But . . .

"Mo-om."

I am snapped back by Claire's insistent voice.

"What?"

"Can I go to Coach with Lily this afternoon and buy sunglasses? They have these really cute ones with butterflies."

"It's the first day of school."

"Exactly. How much homework could we have?"

"Those sunglasses cost one hundred fifty dollars. No."

Claire pauses, considering this. "How about Dolce then?"

I stare at her as if she has gone insane. "No." In her defense, Claire is not being sarcastic or even knowingly demanding but is merely spewing brand names she's heard from friends with no real conception of the cost. As we wait for the Madison Avenue bus, surely the slowest on the East Side, I pull out my MetroCard and try to flatten a dent in it, making a mental note to talk to Sam about reconsidering the public school options.

Claire boards the bus without another word, inserts her iPod's jewel-encrusted earbuds and stares out the window, safely ensconced within her bubble of sound. Every now and then she offers up a brief semi-apologetic smile; at thirteen she is still slightly uncomfortable in the nascent world of rebellion and wavers dizzyingly between affection and affectation. I smile back across the distance and debate with Phoebe the merits of various after-school clubs, from knitting to computer graphics.

The Weston School, determined to live down its reputation as a bastion of old WASP wealth, takes a newly discovered if self-conscious pride in fostering an artistic sensibility unusual for a girls' academy. It is one of the only single-sex schools that no longer requires a uniform, though it took a three-year study and much smoothing of alumni feathers to make such a bold move; it contributes to a plethora of community projects and offers up an impressive array of pseudo-experimental cultural performances at weekly assemblies—all undeniably good and important steps. Still, we are one of the few downtown families. "They consider diversity anyone who lives below Fifty-seventh Street," Sam observed. A product of private schools himself, he never truly considered an alternative, despite the enormous pressure the tuition is putting on us. He once admitted that he had never actually met anyone who went to public school until he got to college. I have in the past argued for applying to the gifted public-school programs, that single word, *gifted,* bestowing a quasi-acceptable excuse for free education in our admittedly insular world, but I didn't put up too strong a fight. Along with the tiny class size, I had—and sometimes still do—the hope that a girls' school would instill in our daughters a confidence about assuming their rightful place in the world, a lack of apology about the space they take up that would suit them well in later life. It was not simply a matter of wanting the best education for our daughters, academic or psychological, though. Sending the girls to Weston also suited the image I had of life here, so far removed from how I grew up that it still feels unreal at times. I'm not particularly proud of this, but there it is.

As soon as we get off the bus both girls peel away from me so fast it leaves my head spinning and purposefully lose themselves in the sea of children heading to the various private schools in the neighborhood, a gilded ghetto of Spence girls in pleated skirts rolled up to their crotches, St. Bernard's boys in blazers, their shaggy hair the only thing distinguishing them from little stockbroker Mini-Me's, the ramshackle Dalton kids. I trail after them, catching glimpses of the tops of their heads until they arrive in front of Weston's large brick building and join their friends clustered outside the heavy blue double doors.

The street is clogged with huge shiny black SUVs driven the five or six blocks from home by mothers who wave thin, tanned arms at each other or uniformed drivers discreetly opening the back doors to emit their munchkin passengers. When they are older, many of the children will request that the drivers stop a block or two away so they can appear to have walked, which serves only to move the domino lineup of cars to a different side street, fooling no one. To the left, half-a-dozen nannies in baggy jeans and faded print tops stand in a tight little group, reconnecting after the summer break. Now and then they glance over at a semicircle of mothers a few feet away, Starbucks in hand, their jeans tighter, their tops less worn. They all smile reassurances of goodwill that they hope will hide a nagging mutual suspicion and go back to their own conversations. Because it is the first day, more fathers than usual are present, their faces glowing with self-congratulatory bonhomie above their well-cut suits, knowing that they can use their attendance as evidence of their involved parenting if the need arises at a later date.

"Lisa."

I turn to see Georgia Hartman calling to me. The lead mother of Phoebe's class just as she was surely the lead girl at her Connecticut boarding school, Georgia stands in the epicenter of a knot of women, looking expensively dewy without a stitch of makeup, her perfectly streaked hair pulled back into a ponytail. She has three girls at Weston, which, I figure, comes to roughly $96,360 a year in tuition. Of course, I am also quite aware that Georgia does not, like me, have a running-cost calculator in her head.

"It's so good to see you," she exclaims, with an enthusiasm out of proportion to our actual relationship. She is one of those women who treats everyone with an equal degree of intimacy, a habit quite possibly meant to put others at ease but which carries an unmistakable whiff of noblesse oblige. Then again, I may be overly sensitive on this score. Just the idea of her makes me feel hopelessly clumsy. Terrified that I will say or do something irrevocably gauche, I tend to become weirdly stilted around her, which only makes matters worse. "How was your summer? Did you go someplace fabulous?" she asks.

Fabulous is a relative term, but under any definition I am pretty certain that our vacation wouldn't qualify. Aside from a few long weekends at Sam's brother, Henry's, house in the Hamptons with his new wife, Abbie, a former ballet dancer who, I suspect, remains a borderline anorexic, our main sojourn was five days at a resort in Puerto Rico. We had sold it to the children as a good idea because it would be less crowded (read: cheaper), but it had proven to be almost painfully hot and, as it was close to the rain forest, riddled with mosquitoes. Claire counted eighteen bites the first day, though the resort record was apparently held by a woman we met on the boat ride to the beach who claimed a whopping ninety-two due to a severe allergy to the only repellent the hotel stocked. Phoebe got dehydrated on our second day and, lying in bed, her head spinning, looked up plaintively at me and asked, "What's happening? Am I going to die?" All in all, the glories of the Caribbean off-season are highly overrated.

I quickly dispatch with the trip, leaving out the infestation and Phoebe's existential crisis. "How about you?" I ask, anxious to change the focus. Georgia and her husband famously take their entire brood to a different country every vacation, averaging three a year. They have already been to India, Russia, France, Kenya, the lesser-known Greek islands and Istanbul. "There's no education like it," she assured me last year, as they prepared for spring break in Beijing and Shanghai. A Chinese tutor came three days a week to teach them all rudimentary Mandarin. "Don't you agree?" Of course I did, though that wasn't quite the point. Once, I made the mistake of confiding to another mother that I was worried about money and she told me to stop obsessing and just take my nanny and the kids to St. Barth. Seriously. "That's what I always do when I'm feeling anxious," she confided. There were so many things wrong with that sentence all I could do was nod mutely.

The funny thing is, I don't even think they recognize that we inhabit different universes. Perhaps their imagination doesn't stretch that far—anyone in the Weston community must surely reside in the same stratosphere. Except, of course, for the scholarship girls from the outer boroughs who are treated with determinedly nonchalant yet outsized kindness. I suppose there is the chance that they are simply too polite to acknowledge it; like having a friend with cancer and being uncertain whether it is best to inquire about her health or pretend that everything is normal. I can't blame them, really. The veneer of Sam's and my life is in many ways indistinguishable from theirs. It is only when you dig a little deeper, look at the forensic details, that the variables become apparent. The fact is, we are in their world on a visa.

"We took the kids hiking in Scotland," Georgia replies. She takes a sip of her latte. The tiniest speck of foam clings to her pale, thin upper lip and slowly evaporates. "The soggiest country I've ever been to but absolutely gorgeous." I imagine her writing the benediction in a ledger, putting a check mark next to "Scotland" and running her finger down the page to see what country is next on the family to-do list.

There is some discussion of various trips before conversation moves on to the merits of a new Pilates studio that has recently stolen its competitor's best teachers. Everyone agrees that they want to give it a try but are worried that, if discovered, they will be banned from the original studio and thus risk being homeless. Like breaking up with your hair stylist, it is an extremely dangerous proposition and a course of action has not yet been communally decided upon.

I accompanied Georgia just once to the original studio, where Birkin bags lined the splintery wooden cubbyholes like lunch boxes for Madison Avenue grown-ups. I had never felt so poor, fat and uncoordinated in my life. Luckily, my office is too far from either of the studios and I don't have the time midmorning to work out anyway. There's only so much insecurity I can handle in a single day.

I glance down at my watch. "I should go." I leave them drinking their coffee and plotting their Pilates exit strategy.

There was a time when I prided myself on how busy I was, rising to vice president of the PR firm I work at. Sometimes I would count the number of phone calls and e-mails I got a day, tangible proof of my place in a world I had fantasized about since I was a teenager. It brought a certain thrill, a verification. At some point, though, the excitement began to wane. Now I can't help but look at the other, wealthier, nonworking mothers at Weston and envy them the gift of time, the afternoons spent with their children, most of all their freedom to choose. Of course, Sam and I are blessed by any standards other than those within Weston's immediate radius. Chances are I wouldn't opt for a different life even if I could. I have everything I've ever wanted, more. I know that. And I'm truly thankful.

It's just that I realize, particularly lately, that it might all collapse in an instant, throwing us into an endless financial free fall with no net beneath us. The prospect, growing ever more likely, terrifies me.

It's not Sam's fault. I knew precisely who he was, what he wanted, when I married him. And I admired him for it. When he first started out he quickly made a name for himself breaking some big investigative pieces. Magazines vied for his allegiance, he gained acclaim for doing something he valued, tearing back corporate curtains to expose the seaminess within, and his choices, while not vastly remunerative, were commendable. I have always loved the stubborn, unswaying goodness in him.

I know, too, that I went along with the near-disastrous choice six years ago that landed us in our current predicament. After his early flush of success there came for Sam the inevitable settling in as the excitement of having his name bandied about, his phone calls returned, became rote, and he was left with the ongoingness of simply showing up for work every day. As most of us are. When the initial Internet boomlet began to simmer in lofts throughout the city, he was happy to have a fresh panorama to report on. But as more and more of the people he started out with defected to various dot-coms, he grew restless and, worse, began to suspect that he was a chump for staying in print.

That was the mood he was in—vocally defensive, secretly open to persuasion—when we went out to dinner one night with Deirdre and the man she was dating at the time, Gerard Neiporent, the scion of a once-wealthy, now somewhat frayed, Canadian newspaper family. Gerard, fast-talking, crackling with the kind of energy you only later realize reeks of ADD or cocaine or both, had dreamed up the archetype for a new Web site that would provide instantly updated information to media professionals on the deals being made in television, books, movies, fashion and beauty. New York is a city jet-fueled by an insatiable need to be first; he assumed that companies would pay hundreds of dollars in subscription fees for the privilege. It was close enough to Sam's purview to be intriguing without making him feel like a total Internet whore. We invested most of our savings (worrisome, yes, but all that pre-IPO equity was so very tempting), and Sam left the magazine. Fourteen months later, the venture went bust. The model was flawed, no one was actually willing to pay for information after all. And we were broke. Even our 401(k)s were gone. I don't blame Sam, I don't even blame Gerard. I certainly don't blame Deirdre, who, by the way, did not put any of her own money in and split up with Gerard five months after that dinner. But there it is.

Fortunately, the magazine was happy to take Sam back. Even those who had resented the dot-com defectors were too polite for I-told-you-so's. They considered themselves lucky; they had not made a fortune but neither had they lost one and they were content to pass their lack of nerve off as prescience. Sam settled back in and we embarked on our fretful course of economic catch-up. We debated pulling the girls out of Weston but in the end we didn't have the heart to take them from a place they loved and felt at home in. After being denied financial aid, we refinanced our apartment and cut back where we could. And then the stock market crashed.

I head south on Lexington Avenue, maneuvering around people hurrying to the subway, women wheeling double strollers, deliverymen with beefy tattooed forearms already glistening with sweat. I've loved walking the city streets from my very first summer here, when, exhilarated by the initial rush of independence, I would stroll home at all hours of the night, past bars spewing out people, outdoor cafés closing up, unafraid, free, every neighborhood a revelation, every man a potential lover. Sam and I had broken up—after endless nights of red wine and Marlboros, that's how long ago it was—three weeks before graduation, and I knew that somewhere in the city he, too, was walking the streets, perhaps eating in the same restaurants. I could feel him sometimes just around a corner, though by chance or design we never actually bumped into each other.

I thought of him more often than I cared to admit. It had been so easy at first between us. It seemed to be always fall then, the sloppy, cozy messiness, the warmth of our hands sliding beneath sweaters as we lay together on dank campus lawns, the musty smell of books as we sat in the library, our legs sneaking up against each other until neither of us could see the words, make sense of anything but each other, late nights spent confiding the nooks and crannies of our lives, skin, most of all skin, discovering the curves of my own body beneath his touch so that later, alone, I would retrace his path with my fingertips. I had made love with only one boy before—and that was not borne out of passion, but simply my desire not to be a virgin when I went to college—so in every way that mattered Sam was my first. We were both so porous, so unguarded in our love. Maybe that can truly happen only once, that unbruised optimism, that total lack of reserve or doubt. I still have, someplace, the notes he used to slip in my backpack, under my door, in my coat pocket when I wasn't looking, adorning them with quirky little line drawings and proclamations of love, unembarrassed, fearless. It seemed the most natural thing in the world.

Sometimes in the beginning, we would lie in whatever narrow dorm bed we could appropriate and indulge in a luxurious worry about that very ease, wondering if it—we—could be real. But we were just playing with the concern from the self-congratulatory distance of requited love, deep down we believed we were invulnerable. After almost two years together, though, we both began to test, to stretch the skin of our bond. Because it was the only serious relationship either of us had been in, it was normal, I suppose, for some curiosity to fester, if only so we could reassure ourselves that we truly did belong together. But trying to prove a negative when it comes to love is a dangerous proposition. In London for a semester during my senior year (which, thankfully, my scholarship covered) I made the mistake of sharing a snippet of uncertainty in a letter to Sam, whose response was to embark on a brief and, he later insisted, thoroughly meaningless affair.

When I returned, there were teary confessions, though Sam refused to tell me who the girl was other than that she was a junior majoring in philosophy, of all ridiculous things. For years I've pictured a spindly, neurasthenic girl in a moth-eaten sweater talking about Kierkegaard while she fucked my future husband. I admitted to a single night with a Moroccan exchange student I met in a Muswell Hill pub. (In fact, I had run out on him before anything really happened, but I was angry with Sam and wanted to even the score.) In the end, we decided to forgive each other's transgressions and pick up where we left off, but it wasn't that simple. The difference between what we had been and what we were now, flawed, suspicious, resentful, proved too jarring. We moved to Manhattan within weeks of each other, but by then we were no longer speaking.

Within a couple of years, I grew weary of the single life, trying on personalities, trying on men, the bass player in an eighties band making an all-too-brief comeback, the corporate lawyer who taught me to play poker with his friends but pouted like a spoiled two-year-old when he lost, the restaurant owner who brought me massive amounts of leftover food every night that I threw out as soon as he left—no one seemed to fit. What had at first seemed a landscape of infinite possibility came to feel aimless and disorienting. The city constantly shape-shifted around me; there were so many potential groups of friends, alliances, neighborhoods, so many people you could be. Deirdre was better at it than I was. After a cataclysmic breakup with Jack when she refused to move to Cambridge with him no matter how much he reasoned, pleaded, banged on her door in the middle of the night with entreaties and threats, she reveled in the freedom. But I missed a sense of belonging to a person, a place. Most of all I missed Sam—the way he cupped my hip bone in the palm of his hand, the esoteric quotes he used to send me, the calm solidity he possessed that allowed me to relax in a way I never could with anyone else, the feeling of being known, truly known. When I ran into him at a party given by a mutual friend on a frigid December night—okay, actually I had asked my friend to be sure to invite him—it was like landing on familiar ground. He phoned the next morning. He, too, had come to think of our separation as a rebuke that had outlived its purpose. He refers to it now as our "period of exile" when he tells the story to friends, to our children. How foolish we were, everyone agrees, smiling because there was, after all, a happy ending.

We were married within the year.

We moved into a cheap studio apartment in Chelsea with a slanted splintery wooden floor that mocked us whenever we went barefoot and furnished it with pieces we picked up at thrift shops and the local flea market. I loved watching Sam on Sunday afternoons bare-chested in his tattered khaki shorts sanding away—his ability to refinish furniture a revelation to me—the radio blaring, his broad back, his muscles and his shoulder blades all the more erotic because he was truly mine. Even now, all these years later, a reverberation of that early desire passes through us both whenever we walk by that block and remember that compressed time when it was just us and we had so much to look forward to.

"Can we make it six thirty?" she said. "Same place."

I turn up Forty-second Street and weave through a parade of women dressed as if from different hemispheres; some are wearing summer outfits that are not quite as fresh as they had been in June, others have impatiently pulled out their new fall clothes and are already trying to hide the inevitable wilting.

When I first moved to Manhattan I studied other women's habits of dress, of grooming, of speech and manners as closely as an anthropologist, anxious to pass as one of them. It was all I had dreamed of, coming here. Now, years later, I know that I do, most days, anyway—my hair is cut in a studio on lower Fifth Avenue favored by beauty editors, though I stretch out appointments for too many months, I know that pleated pants are the devil's handiwork and if, at thirty-nine, I am endlessly battling the same five pounds, it is never more than that (well, rarely)—but I am constantly aware of the effort it takes. I sometimes wonder if everyone else in the city is passing, too.

I used to think I could tell who was, who wasn't.

But I am beginning to think that I was wrong.

THREE

I walk into the pseudo-French bistro across from Grand Central Terminal and scan the room crowded with men and women hunched over their croissants and their spreadsheets, looking for Deirdre. I finally spot her in a back booth, her head turned away from me to avoid the flash of annoyance she knows she will find on my face. Either that or she is so immersed in Ben she has forgotten all about my arrival.

I watch them pry reluctantly apart when they notice me, peeling inch by inch off of each other as if their skin is covered with duct tape. They both smile a little too enthusiastically as I approach. Ben's presence is breaking an unwritten rule barring intruders from our breakfasts. Under the best of circumstances it would make me feel slightly dispossessed. And I wouldn't exactly call this morning the best of circumstances.

I bend over, kiss them both hello, Deirdre's dusky Creed perfume, at once familiar and exotic, filling my nostrils, and sit down opposite them.

"Don't worry, I'm not staying," Ben says lightly. "I just came for a quick cup of coffee." His face is slightly ruddy, his angular features just asymmetrical enough to make his good looks intriguing, open to interpretation. At forty-one, he is lean and muscular—he still rides a bike everywhere he goes.

"Don't be silly. How have you been?" I ask casually. I haven't seen Ben since last spring, when Deirdre broke it off with him. In fact, Deirdre and Ben have broken up and gotten back together so many times over the past two years, their desire for each other chronic and insoluble, that I no longer believe in either state and thus refrain from offering judgment or encouragement. A photographer, Ben flies all over the country on assignment, often disappearing for days at a time with no word, a nomadic man with a nomadic heart. Famous for his black-and-white portraits that highlight every line, every pore, every sorrow and vanity, he is a master at exposing a subject's innermost self while maintaining a formal aloofness. The juxtaposition is his trademark, a lure to everyone who thinks he can conquer it, win him over, everyone who thinks he will be the exception.

"I've been great," he says. "Busy. Traveling too much, but that's nothing new. How about you?"

Before I can answer, Deirdre rushes in. "Did you see Ben's portrait of Branson in yesterday's magazine section?" she asks, anxious to score points for him.

He smiles at her indulgently, too confident in his own talent to need her public praise, but basking in it nonetheless.

"Yes." I vaguely recall glancing at the full-page image of the mogul's stark, aging face. It was certainly not what I would call a flattering image. "I can't imagine he loved that picture," I remark. This is not at all how I thought this breakfast would go and it is hard to shift gears.

"Maybe not," Ben replies, pushing his auburn hair off his high forehead. "Most people are too embarrassed to admit that what they really expect is an airbrushed version of themselves. Then again, I don't think they quite know which is the more accurate reflection, the one they see in the mirror or the one they are confronted with in black and white." While he speaks, Deirdre leans into him with the eagerness of one who cannot take possession for granted. Some part of their bodies has been touching since I sat down, their hips, their elbows; I cannot see their legs beneath the table but I am sure they are intertwined, in play. It's hard not to feel extraneous around them, as if you are simply a dull and distant background, a bas-relief to highlight their intransigent attraction.

"I'm always surprised people agree to sit for you. I don't think I want to see myself that clearly. I need a little bit of denial to get out the door."

"It's a mixture of curiosity and conceit. Most of the people I photograph are used to being in control. They assume they'll be able to exhibit only the public version they want seen. But it's actually harder than they realize to hide your true nature. I just have to be patient. The trick is to offer up a little piece of yourself and wait for them to respond in kind."

"So it's an act of calculated confession. Don't they feel betrayed?"

"It's been said all journalism is seduction and betrayal. I'm sure Sam would agree. Photography isn't all that different. My responsibility is to the finished product, not to the subject. Only second-raters and sentimentalists get the two confused. The other person knows the game going into it. If they choose to pretend otherwise it's not my fault." Ben talks the way he photographs, observing everything from a distance. He was on the debate team at Yale, he likes the give-and-take. Sometimes I think he takes a contentious position just to keep things crackling. Then again, I find him awfully hard to read. Perhaps he believes everything he says.

"That's rather cynical," I remark.

"It's just how it works," Ben says. "All relationships are based on a deal. Sometimes it's verbalized, sometimes it's not, but it's always there."

Deirdre rolls and unrolls the corners of her napkin, hyperalert to his words.

He smiles. "I'm sure you two have far more interesting things to discuss than the sordid workings of photography. Deirdre made it quite clear that I was supposed to leave right after hello. Say hi to Sam for me."

"I will."

Ben rises and leans over to kiss Deirdre good-bye, lingering on her lips. I jiggle my spoon between my fingers, uncertain where to look.

Eventually, they separate. “It was good to see you,” Ben says, resting his hand on my shoulder.

“You, too.”

Deirdre watches him walk out and then turns to me. “Sorry. I thought he was just going to walk me over.” There is too much subterranean pleasure in her look for me to think she is sorry at all.

“I take it this means you two are back on track?”

“I guess.” She shrugs. “I know this sounds crazy, but it feels different this time. We’re in touch almost every day, we’re seeing each other more often.”

“What does ‘in touch’ mean?”

“E-mail, mostly. He doesn’t like the phone.”

I can’t help but wonder why even the smartest women are so often willing to contort themselves around a man’s predilections. Myself included. “Does he still want to date other people?”

“We haven’t talked about it. Frankly, I think he just likes holding it out there as an option. He travels so much, he has his kids every other weekend, how much time does he actually have?”

This seems mildly delusional to me but there is nothing to be gained by pointing that out. “What’s up with his divorce?”

“You are in a bad mood, aren’t you?”

“Sorry.”

Deirdre shakes her head. “Nothing. She’s still refusing to sign the papers.”

“Why?”

“I don’t know, she won’t tell him. She’s some goddamned oil heiress, so it’s not about money.”

“Oil heiress? I didn’t know there was such a thing anymore.”

“It’s old money.”

“Apparently.”

“She and her brothers seem to have a penchant for ending up in rehab in Arizona. They should put their name on a clinic instead of that ridiculous arts center in LA. They certainly spend more quality family time there." Deirdre's voice, throaty, rich, seemed, even at seventeen, especially at seventeen, hopelessly sophisticated in its perpetual weariness. We are, in many ways, opposites, but we recognized something essential in each other from the very first: Neither of us has the slightest sense of entitlement. An only child, Deirdre shuttled between the two warring camps her parents had set up twelve blocks from each other on the Upper East Side and in the end was left largely alone. Her father moved in with his latest mistress when Deirdre was fourteen. Her mother, sobbing, broken, shameless, sent her two, three times a week to beg him to return. Deirdre still cringes when she recalls the distaste she spied in his eyes, the set of his mouth.

It left her with a deep-seated abhorrence of appearing needy, as if the very act of asking for anything, ever, is a sign of weakness. Even now I don't think she can differentiate between justifiable need and neediness. Any amateur shrink—and she has seen umpteen nonamateurs over the years—could tell her that explains Ben, her entire roster of brilliant, ambitious, semidetached men. I've told her so myself. She knows, of course, but knowing doesn't change a thing. It rarely does. The only man I have ever known her to be with who wasn't completely elusive was Jack. And that did not end well.

I stare at the menu, trying to decide between a cranberry scone and oatmeal. "Not to change the subject, but are we doing carbs this week?" I ask.

Deirdre is always one step ahead of me when it comes to diets. She got a head start, after all, growing up in this city where all forms of beauty maintenance start a good ten years younger than in the rest of the country. I remember how she came to college with some esoteric black soap that you had to lather your face with and then rinse off using exactly thirty splashes of lukewarm water every night. Which she did. Religiously. No matter what. It does seem, though, that the list of what constitutes the bare minimum keeps expanding from manicures and blowouts to Brazilians (judging by my informal poll in the gym locker room, there is not a single female pubic hair left in Manhattan) and year-round spray tans. Nevertheless, I have always followed Deirdre's advice when it comes to this sort of thing. She once admonished me not to wear gray because it saps the sexuality out of you and I never did again. She instructed me how to make up my deep-set eyes that are just a hairsbreadth farther apart than most people's, something she convinced me was an asset though I had never even noticed it before.

"I'm trying these seaweed capsules," Deirdre replies.

"I thought we agreed, no diet drugs."

"They're not a drug. They're completely natural. They're from Germany," she emphasizes. The European origin adds to their cachet, much like this past summer's rampant use of a certain SPF 60 sunblock from Sweden whose ingredients are not yet FDA-approved and thus has to be brought back from Europe, serving the dual purpose of announcing where you have been and that your skin is far too sensitive for any lotion America can come up with.

"You take three before every meal," Deirdre continues. "They're supposed to expand in your stomach and make you feel full. The only potential side effect, according to the box, is the risk of choking to death if one accidentally expands in your throat on the way down."

"That would certainly prevent you from overeating. Do they work?"

"Who knows? My stomach is so bloated from them that I couldn't zip my jeans this morning."

I glance at Deirdre, who is, in fact, wearing jeans. White jeans. And looks quite thin. As always. With her lankiness, tangle of long, blond hair and strong bone structure, she has the kind of effortless style that appears unthinkingly thrown together and is impossible to deconstruct. Trust me, I've tried. But what works for Deirdre comes off as merely disheveled on me. I console myself with the notion that it is because at five-feet-eight she is a good three inches taller than me, though deep down I suspect there is more to it than that. "You have that hourglass kind of figure men love," she has assured me whenever I point out our differences. I appreciate her kindness but remain unconvinced.

"These are a different pair," Deirdre explains. "My fat jeans."

I roll my eyes. "There is no such thing as 'fat' white jeans. It's a complete oxymoron."

She ignores me. "I'm assuming this is a temporary setback. I'll give it a few more days."

"You didn't answer my question."

"What question?"

"Carbs or not?"

She shakes her head. "Too risky."

We both order scrambled egg whites.

"So how are you?" she asks.

I shrug. "Okay." I take a sip of coffee, which manages to be both tepid and burnt. Deirdre is having green tea, two bags, and is feeling rather virtuous about it. "I hate this weather."

"Tell me about it. I made the brilliant decision over the weekend to devote the entire front of the store to cashmere sweaters and boots and it's ninety goddamn degrees outside."

Four years ago, when her father died and left her all of his not insubstantial estate, Deirdre, who had drifted through various corners of the fashion business, never quite settling in, signed the lease for an eleven-hundred-square-foot boutique in the Flatiron district. She had studied the market carefully and knew precisely what the store would look like, its feel, its tone—though she didn't mention she was even thinking about it until the day she took it over. Despite how close we are, Deirdre rarely tells me of any decision until it is already made. She is not a woman who likes to show her work. Convinced that, faced with too many choices, women end up anxious and confused, she settled on a deceptively simple strategy, classics with a twist, a hem that dipped when it shouldn't, an asymmetrical neckline, just enough to make each piece unique but wearable, a formula that, if not exactly cutting edge, withstands the vicissitudes of trends better than most. Deirdre champions young designers, some of whom leave her at the first whiff of renown, finds others who have been overlooked and keeps the prices relatively affordable. After a slow start, Aperçu gained word-of-mouth momentum that tipped when *The New York Times* did a quarter-page feature on it in the Sunday Styles section. Despite ebbs and flows as new boutiques opened, her business has settled into a steady groove, though lately she, too, has felt the effects of the economic pall descending on the city.

"Claire is still planning on coming in this Saturday, right?" she asks.

"Are you kidding? It's the only thing she's talked about for days."

When Deirdre offered to let Claire help out in the store in exchange for clothes her face lit up as if the heavens had opened. Not only did it promise close proximity to her idol, but as far as I can tell shopping is Claire's sole extracurricular interest these days, though she doesn't have an eighth of the allowance some of her classmates do. She and her buddies have taken to going to Bloomingdale's and spending the entire afternoon trying on evening gowns, though why on earth the saleswomen put up with this is beyond me. Then again, there are probably some thirteen-year-olds who whip out their credit cards at the first good fit. Though I do worry that Claire's main area of expertise is the subtle differentials in designer jeans, seeing her look of pure glee at Deirdre's proposal convinced me. I am not above trying to win points with my daughter these days.

"You will of course report any tidbits you pick up on boys, drugs or other illicit activities," I add.

Deirdre rolls her eyes. "Relax. Deep down, Claire's a straight shooter just like you."

"You make me sound so unimaginative."

"I can't help it if your idea of acting out is using your Rose Day Cream at night."

"Just keep in mind she's a minor. With a strict budget. I can't afford for her to develop a taste for accessories."

"Yes, ma'am. So. What did you do this weekend?"

"Not much. Sam went in to work on Saturday and I took the kids back-to-school shopping. A frustrating time was had by all."

"Was he closing a story?"

"No. Trying to find one is more like it. He's doing a profile on Eliot Wells."

"Really? I've always thought he's kind of hot, in that weird Silicon Valley never-seen-the-light-of-day kind of way."

"Actually, he's based in Chicago, as odd as that is. Sam is convinced he had some shady financial doings when he was starting out. Something about predating options. This is, of course, confidential."

"I take that as a given."

"The thing is, Sam doesn't have any actual proof. I can't tell if he's deluded or if he really is on to something. But if he's wrong, he's fucked."

"Why? Reporters follow leads that don't pan out all the time. What's the big deal?"

"He needs a major story. He's apparently not the flavor of the month anymore."

"Who is?" Deirdre pushes up the sleeve of her boho chic Indian tunic absentmindedly. "Christ, can't they turn the air-conditioning up in here?"

"Good Lord, what is that?" I lean forward. Pale blue bruises in the shape of fingerprints peek out from beneath the navy and fuchsia paisley silk.

She quickly pulls the fabric down to cover them. "Nothing."

"That didn't look like nothing."

She smiles sheepishly. "Sex injury."

"Can I assume that's Ben's handiwork?"

She nods.

"What the hell were you two doing?"

"Nothing."

"We obviously have different definitions of nothing."

I stare at her, waiting for details. Our friendship was forged on dorm beds, late-night phone calls, two a.m. bathroom rendezvous where we traded the most intimate minutiae of our nascent sex lives, the fine and not-so-fine points that gained true currency only in the retelling.

"I bruise easily," she says dismissively.

"Do you know how long it's been since I had sex like that?"

"You have other things."

"Yes, but they don't leave fingerprints behind. Listen, you're not doing anything I should be worried about, are you?"

"No."

"Deirdre?"

"No," she reiterates. Then, considering, she adds, "It's strange. The sex with Ben hovers on the edge but it never goes over. At least not yet. I can't quite figure it out."

"The edge of what?"

"I'm not sure. Everything is always just a touch—more. Harder. Let's just say he's enthusiastic." She laughs. "He once told me that a girl he was sleeping with in college used to make him wear mittens when they had sex. I could never figure it out." She nods to the bruises. "Maybe this is why." She smiles back at me. "Don't look so worried. He said he just likes something to grab on to. It's fine."

"Deirdre, are you sure getting back together with Ben is a good idea?"

"Of course I'm not sure. But look, even if I'm wrong and Ben hasn't changed, would that be so terrible? I have a great time with him. And he's been totally honest with me."

"Honesty is not a get-out-of-jail-free card."

"Why can't I use him as a placeholder while I look for something better? Men do that all the time. Besides, other men always find you sexier when you're sleeping with someone else. It's like they can smell it."

"I have nothing against it in theory. I just don't happen to think it works. You care about him." I am certain that Deirdre is lying, that she does hope for something from Ben, a sign, forward movement. Women always do.

"Maybe he's right, maybe monogamy is against human nature."

"That's a convenient excuse. Besides, even if it's true, it's a recipe for disaster. Doesn't it bother Ben if you go out with other men?"

"I wish it did," she admits. "I've never met anyone so totally lacking in jealousy. It's impossible to get a rise out of him. He told me the only thing that would really hurt him is not seeing me at all." Her voice sinks. "I'm not saying you're wrong. All I know is that no one makes me feel as good as he does when I'm with him. When we're together, he's totally present. He actually listens, and remembers everything. He makes me laugh. He's not intimidated by me."

"And when you're not with him?"

"All right, so maybe our relationship is not always the healthiest one. I do wish he was more invested," she concedes. "Sometimes I wonder if I'm with Ben because there's no one else or there's no one else because I'm with Ben." She looks up. "Aren't there any divorced fathers at Weston you can introduce me to?"

"Since when is fatherhood on your list of dating prerequisites? Haven't you heard of alimony, child support, psychotic ex-wives?"

"One of the things I like best about Ben is what a good parent he is. You have to at least give him that."

"Yes," I agree. I have to admit that Ben is one of the most involved fathers I know, not out of show but from a genuine desire and delight in his children's lives. He volunteers at school fairs and potluck dinners, he helps decorate pageants and spends hours with art projects. It is hard for me to reconcile his fierce paternal attachment with the slipperiness of his other affections.

"How many kids am I going to have at this point?" Deirdre continues, playing with a strand of hair. "One if I'm lucky. I like the idea of a man who already has children."

"You realize that you are probably the only woman in New York who feels this way?"

"Good, that leaves the field open."

"You're only thirty-nine," I remind her.

"For seven more weeks. Besides, thirty-nine is young if you're married with two children. If you have a boyfriend who can't commit and you want a family, it's geriatric. Right now I'm someone who happens to be single. It's my situation, not my identity. It's not set in stone. But there's a line. Once you cross it, people don't even bother to ask if you're seeing anyone anymore. Your singledom is ingrained. I'm terrified of that," she confesses. "Turning forty is the goddamned Rubicon." She pauses. "You have no idea how lucky you are."

"I'm not so sure about that."

"What do you mean?"

I play with the edges of my napkin.

"Lisa?"

"I think Sam may be having an affair." Saying the words out loud transforms what was a whispery suspicion, a cloud that existed in my mind alone, into something concrete, with its own shape and weight; once launched into the external world it is impossible to dismiss.

"What?"

I tell Deirdre about the phone call, the woman. " 'Same place.' She said, 'Same place.' " I can hear the panic in my voice and try to push it down.

"I can't believe you listened to his messages."

"You're missing the point here."

"Have you done that before?"

"Can we please get past that?"

"Lisa, he told you he was meeting a source. I'm sure that's all it is."

"Sam said the source was a man. He said 'he.' "

"You're not sure of that."

"I'm pretty sure."

She considers this. "I once went on a date with a guy who refused to use pronouns. You know, 'I' did this, 'we' did that. I kept trying to trip him up and I couldn't. I finally asked if he was divorced or separated and he told me he was married but they had a don't ask/don't tell policy. Can you imagine?" She plays with her eggs, making patterns with their unappetizing border. "I wonder how many relationships have been done in by pronouns."

"We're off-point here," I remind her.

She looks directly at me, her gold-flecked eyes steady and sure. "Sam loves you. He always has. It's who he is."

"Maybe I don't know who he is anymore."

"C'mon, you two are closer than any couple I've ever known." Deirdre has always been dismissive of the vicissitudes of my marriage. She needs to believe in us for some reason, or perhaps she, like other single people, assumes that a marriage once formed is monolithic, not given to the drama of their own romantic lives, a fact it is more convenient not to have to reconsider. "You could just ask him."

"I'd have to tell him I listened to his messages."

"You're right. Not a good idea. He'd never trust you again."

"Trust me? He's the one meeting a woman and lying about it."

We sit in silence for a moment.

"There's more," I add.

"What?"

"He said there's something he wants to talk to me about later. Nothing good has ever followed a sentence like that."

"Oh please. He probably wants to switch dry cleaners."

"Why aren't you taking me seriously?"

"Because I don't think it is serious."

Of course, if Deirdre did take me seriously it would only make me feel worse. "You haven't touched your breakfast," I remark glumly. She has, in fact, spent the entire time poking at it as if it were toxic waste.

Deirdre smiles and for the first time all morning, she looks almost embarrassed. "I haven't seen Jack in so long. It's a basic law of human nature—you must look as thin as possible when having dinner with an old boyfriend."

"Are you nervous?"

"About tomorrow night?"

"Yes."

She considers this. "Not exactly nervous."

"Really? I am."

"You mean because of our history?"

"Among other things."

"Don't be. All has long since been forgiven. I'm sure it will be a perfectly peaceful evening."

"Funny, that's not the first word that comes to mind when I think of you and Jack."

"Actually, I'm kind of excited. And curious. Do you think chemistry has an expiration date?" she asks.

"I've been wondering the same thing. In my case I hope not."

"And in my case?"

"Christ, Deirdre. It's been seventeen years. Jack's married, you're . . ."

"Not."

"You're with someone. Even if there is some leftover ember, what good will it do you?"

"Ember, I like that." She smiles, pushing her uneaten food resolutely out of reach. "On that note, I should get going. I promised some East Village ex–rock star wannabe I'd look at her line of leather-free shoes. I can't believe she gets up before noon but it's part of her whole new 'commitment' thing. It's a perfect setup, even if the shoes are hideous, I'll look like an environmental ignoramus if I refuse to carry them." She shakes her head. "I'll give you a call later. In the meantime, try to relax about all this nonsense with Sam." She nods to her upper arm. "Look at it this way, at least you don't have to wear long-sleeved shirts all week."

"The price of love."

"Not love. I don't know what it is, but I'm pretty sure it's not that."

We get the check and head out, kissing good-bye in front of the restaurant. I watch Deirdre walk a few yards, then stumble on her three-inch heels before righting herself. Her clumsiness is like a punctuation mark to her innate panache, a dent, and I love her for it. I wait until she and her disturbing fingerprints disappear into the eddy of commuters pouring out of Grand Central Terminal and then I begin to walk up Park Avenue to work, the murky coffee, the suspicion, still clinging to the back of my throat.

FOUR

I walk into the lobby of 425 Park Avenue, swipe my ID card and ride in a crowded elevator up to the twelfth-floor offices of Steiner Public Relations, nodding hello to the two front-desk receptionists who are expertly juggling six phone calls between them—PR is a business of constant pitching and placating. As I hurry down the long corridor of open cubicles people look up, smile politely and self-consciously return to their work. I pretend not to notice the eBay and Style.com windows they rush to close as I pass. There was a time when mine was the office everyone gathered in to vent about boyfriends and bosses and failed diets or to debate whether black nail polish was hideously Goth or crazily chic. But that was two promotions ago. I miss it now, the easy camaraderie, the feeling of being in the trenches, and try to resurrect it with a smile, a gossipy interlude, though there is a strained note underneath. Frankly, it does annoy me when I see eBay up, when people wander in two hours late complaining of spats with lovers or bemoaning their hangovers and expect sympathy on my part.

My assistant, Petra, looks up from her three-inch-thick September issue of *W*. "Morning." She smiles broadly, anticipating approbation for being on time.

I smile back but refuse on principle to compliment her on the mere fact of her presence.

Twenty-four, with endless legs, no hips, a Russian accent and a brightly hennaed bob, Petra has a cheerful disposition, a father who imports God knows what from Russia—one month it's cars; the next, baby grand pianos—and entrée to every nightclub in Manhattan and Miami. For the past couple of years, the city has been overflowing with Russian models, hungry young teens who come over with little more than a plane ticket and some names scribbled on a slip of paper, girls with such bad teeth they can't smile in photographs, giving them a surly look that the uninitiated interpret as evidence of their dark Russian souls, though by the time they hit the bigger fashion magazines they are smiling broadly, either at their newsstand placement or simply because they can, having finally earned enough money to have their teeth fixed. Petra, on the other hand, has perfectly good teeth and lives in Short Hills with her family, though her father recently promised to buy her an apartment in Manhattan, which, she assures me, will help with her tardiness.

I head into my office and shut the door.

Deirdre is right. Why shouldn't I just ask Sam who he's meeting, or at least insist that he tell me what it is he wanted to talk to me about? I pick up the phone and am halfway through dialing his number when Petra buzzes me.

"Yes?"

"Carol just called. She's going to be late. She wants you to handle the Rita Mason meeting on your own. Rita and Barry are on their way up."

"All right," I reply, annoyed.

Carol Steiner is in her early fifties, petite, well-preserved and given to low-cut tops beneath fitted jackets that display an impressive amount of ripe cleavage, which, on anyone else, would have been deemed inappropriate. Divorced, she has a daughter who was kicked out of Chapin for her starring role in a blow-job soiree that ended up on YouTube and is now safely ensconced in boarding school. Carol has a new boyfriend (is that the word at her age?) and has not been turning up in the office as much as she used to. Carol, who started the business from scratch in her living room fifteen years ago and grew it, through hard work and relentless determination, to thirty-six employees, seems to have grown bored. Her newly laissez-faire attitude makes decisions hard to get signed off on but it also means that I, as her number two, am effectively running the firm most of the time. Unfortunately, no raise has gone along with this, but I am hopeful that will come. I've just been waiting for the right moment to bring it up.

"Should I show them into your office?" Petra asks.

"Yes." I hang up and hurriedly straighten up my desk. The phone call to Sam will have to wait.

Rita Mason is one of our newer and more difficult clients, a cooking maven who started out on cable and now has her own network show five mornings a week, two books on the best-seller list and a recently launched line of kitchen accessories at Wal-Mart. She also has a huge temper, a huger ego and surprisingly little common sense that seems to diminish further the more successful she becomes. Four days ago, she threw a hissy fit in a restaurant, supposedly smashed her plate on the floor, where it shattered on the waiter's foot, and then left no tip, all of which was gleefully reported on a blog and festered across the Internet with such force it hit the mainstream media. It was, unfortunately, a slow news week. For Rita, whose success has in large part been built around her carefully honed persona as the unpretentious suburban underdog, no more of a perfectionist than any other working mom (though she does not in fact have children), this is particularly damning.

Petra shows Rita and Barry Nielson, her manager, a short, shiny man with a suspiciously omnipresent tan, into my office, gets them bottles of water and shuts the door. Rita, in a navy Armani blazer, hunches over the small, round table by the window, her near pitch-black hair fanned out across her shoulders. Her body is perfect for her job, as if she focus-grouped it, with just the right amount of softness to imply she enjoys eating her own food but not enough to make one think doing so will cause sticky irreversible flab.

"Hello." I smile and hold out my hand. Rita's palm is moist, doughy. I let it go and take a seat. “Unfortunately, Carol had an emergency and won’t be joining us.”

I see the disappointment play across their faces as, quick to sense a demotion, they calibrate their response. I’ll have to ask Carol to send them both a note later. I’m getting a little tired of covering for her.

“I was just telling Rita that the drop in book sales is nothing to worry about,” Barry begins.

Rita ignores him. Just a few short months ago, she was thrilled that he agreed to represent her, but good ratings go a long way toward erasing the uncomfortable memory. “What is it with this blogging shit anyway?” she demands. “Who the fuck cares what a bunch of pasty-assed twenty-year-olds who can’t score real jobs think?”

I nod sympathetically. We, like most established old-school media companies, ignored the blogosphere for just a little too long and are now frantically trying to figure out who’s important, who isn’t, if we should advise clients to start their own blogs or link to others, how to leverage them to move product, make money, create buzz, or at the very least not be destroyed by them. We spend much time explaining to our clients—from the high-end French cosmetics firm to the twenty-four-hour gym chain—that they have to court those pasty-assed twenty-year-olds as assiduously as they court *Vogue*.

“Your fans care,” I say carefully. “The report had a lot of traction.”

“It wasn’t even true. The plate fell, it just fell,” Rita says petulantly.

“I’m sure. The unfortunate thing is, at this point the truth no longer matters. Perception is what counts.”

“You’re telling me my book sales dropped eleven percent because of one whiny klutz of a waiter in a lousy West Village restaurant?”

There is a long pause. I refrain from reminding her that the waiter needed seventeen stitches.

“It’s your job to control that kind of crap,” Rita insists.

It's your job not to pull crap like that in public, I think. "Celebrities don't get in trouble for bad behavior, they get in trouble for confusing fans with extreme personality shifts," I explain. "If Martha did it, people would just shrug, but you are the anti-Martha." More like the Antichrist, but whatever.

She glares and doesn't say a word.

"We have a plan," I continue.

"Go on," Barry prompts.

I begin to outline the strategy we devised after three brainstorming meetings with various breakaway groups within the firm. We have lined up soup kitchens in seven key media markets that have all agreed to have Rita lead celebrity cook-ins. Four prominent politicians and one ex-president are already interested in using it as a platform to discuss the homeless situation.

"Rita is not political," Barry interrupts.

"No, of course not. But she is charitable. Or at least she will be when we're done with her." It takes so much energy to smile, to appease, to spin when sometimes all you want to do is slap your clients silly.

Barry looks over at Rita, who nods imperceptibly.

There is some talk of timing and possible sponsors before the meeting comes to a close. After seeing them out, I sit at my desk staring at my computer, depleted. I look up to see Petra standing in my doorway.

"Yes?"

"Carol wants to see you."

"Can she wait a minute? I need to make a phone call."

"She seemed pretty insistent."

"All right."

When I walk into her office, Carol is seated on her couch, her thin, bare legs crossed at the ankles. A Band-Aid is peeking over the edge of her new black pump where a blister is forming on her heel. "Have a seat," she says, smiling with an uneasiness I can't quite place. "How did it go with Rita?"

"Fabulous. As long as she doesn't spill boiling soup on a homeless mother of three, we're good."

Carol nods distractedly, hardly listening. Her face seems particularly taut. Maybe too much Botox. She clears her throat. "You know how incredible I think you are," she says.

I look at her blankly. I have no idea where she is going with this.

"I couldn't have done this without you. Your contributions have been invaluable," she continues.

These are words that no employee wants to hear. Like a man who begins a relationship talk with "You know how fantastic I think you are," there is sure to be a *but* that will break your heart. I race backward, looking for something I might have done wrong, an expense report error, a phone call promised but not placed.

"I don't know if you've noticed, but for some time now I've lost the thrill," Carol continues. "Maybe it's burnout, maybe I just need a new challenge." She looks down, suddenly engrossed by a piece of lint on her skirt. "Lisa, I've sold the company to Merdale Communications."

"What?" Merdale is one of the largest PR firms on the East Coast, known for its large war chest and its conservative ethos. It is impossible that I have not heard anything about this. So much for thinking I'm connected. "Aren't they based in Philadelphia?"

"They have decided to create a toehold in New York."

"That's what we're going to be, a toehold?"

Carol ignores this. "This will be great for you. People make the mistake of writing them off as provincial but they're huge. The company will have scale. You'll have room to grow."

Scale—that great clarion cry of the city, you can hear it echoing through streets, boardrooms, corporate pep rallies, in schools, media companies, banks. Scale is survival. Scale sells. Of course, it can also swallow you whole. I suddenly feel dizzy, weightless. "I thought scale was passé, right up there with synergy," I mutter.

"Scale is never passé."

I look over at Carol but she is already someplace else. I am what she is leaving behind.

As soon as I get back to my office, I shut the door and try to reach Sam, but there is no answer at any of his numbers.

FIVE

The kitchen window is stuck open two inches from the ledge, just enough to prevent the air-conditioning from having any noticeable effect and trap the odor of the vegetarian chili I am cooking—okay, reheating—inside. Sometime during the nutrition unit her class did last spring, Claire decided to banish meat from her diet. The children kept a food diary for a week, had it analyzed by a computer and were handed back a detailed sheet listing their numerous deficiencies. Weston takes its mission of preparing students for life seriously. They will have no part in the soda-fueled rise of childhood obesity. I have to say that the school's approach worked brilliantly. Claire is now obsessed with reading nutrition labels, can rail against artificial sweeteners for an inordinate amount of time and has developed a generally negative feeling toward butter. Whenever I drink a Diet Coke, she lectures me on its supposed carcinogenic effects in much the same way I once lectured my mother about her morning Pall Malls. Claire still devours chocolate chip cookies at Starbucks and keeps a stash of Hershey's Kisses in her upper desk drawer, but her righteous convictions at the family dinner table are legion. I double-check the box of short-grain organic brown rice—the necessity of using only food produced under fair trade agreements has also recently reared its head. Any day now, I'll need to put an ethical, political, geographic and nutritional checklist of my daughter's requirements on the refrigerator.

When I finally reached Sam earlier in the afternoon and told him about the sale to Merdale, he was suitably outraged on my behalf that Carol hadn't given me a heads-up. "It's going to be okay," he reassured me. "You're great at your job, they'll love you." I shut my eyes and listened to his voice. It has always been my soft spot to rest. I used to love for him to read to me in bed at night, even if it was just a magazine. The words didn't really matter, it was his timbre, his deep, steady tone that made me feel safe, soothing me to sleep.

Sam didn't mention his meeting with a source, male or female, and I didn't bring it up, but he promised to try to get home by seven, maybe a little after. If nothing else, at least Carol's missile gave me an excuse to lay claim to my husband.

I take a sip of wine and stare out the filmy window at the alleyway below. The light is almost completely blocked by other buildings, making it impossible to get an accurate sense of time or weather; it is always the same dusky hourless gray. Everything I was certain—well, almost certain—of just twenty-four hours ago, job, husband, the intrinsic netting of my life, is suddenly flimsy, insubstantial, everything I have taken for granted now seems up for grabs. I lean over the counter and, cupping my hands beneath the window, try to force it open. The right side slides up a quarter inch and I have a brief, thrilling moment of victory before it wheezes and falls below where it was originally.

"Fuck."

"What?" I swivel around to see Phoebe standing in the doorway.

"Nothing, sweetie."

Her eyes narrow. "I'm hungry."

"Dinner is in half an hour. We're going to wait for Daddy."

"Do we have to?"

"Yes."

Phoebe doesn't budge. I am tempted to plead with her; I may be out of work, your father may be having an affair, I don't feel like cooking dinner, please just be nice to me tonight. But parents who practice true transparency with their children are usually those on the verge of a nervous breakdown—it is something to be guarded against. I turn partially around. "Have a yogurt."

"I already had a yogurt."

I take a deep breath. "All right. One cookie. Just one." I distrust any mother who says she never bribes her children.

Suspicious, Phoebe nevertheless grabs a double-stuffed Oreo, the triumph magnified by the knowledge that her sister has not scored a similar treat. I watch her turn and hurry out. Her hair is pulled up into a ponytail on top of her head and even from a distance I can see the growth pattern at the nape, an exact scalloped replica of Sam's. When she was a baby, I used to trace it with my fingertips, kiss its peaks and valleys. Now, except when she is sick and feeling particularly vulnerable, she shudders away with a single, "Gross."

I push aside a crumb left from breakfast. The apartment is always slightly tattered around the edges, so different from the spotless home my own mother kept, my brother and I sprawled out on the kitchen table with our textbooks and our loose-leafs under her too-scrupulous eye. She had never gone to college, which deeply embarrassed her. Her family couldn't afford it, and she had worked as a receptionist from the age of sixteen. If she pushed us a little too hard at times, it is understandable, especially from this distance.

A half-hour passes, forty minutes.

I peel the polish off my left index finger. I stare at the second hand of my watch as it jerks forward, pauses, jerks forward once more. I think of changing into sweatpants but don't. Surely whoever Sam is meeting will not be wearing sweatpants. I picture long, glossy legs, impossibly high heels . . .

6:30.

6:40.

This is what you do when you think your husband may be having an affair: You become a keeper of minutes.

"Same place?" she asked.

I finish my glass of wine, pour another and wander aimlessly about the apartment. I look in on Phoebe, entranced by a computer game that seems to involve some form of pirate ship. Last week I found her playing the same game with a girl from Sweden and gave her yet another lecture on not entering into dialogues with cyber-strangers. "How do you know she's not really a thirty-seven-year-old man in Peoria?" I asked. Phoebe stared back with a deep reservoir of superiority. "You act like someone can jump through the computer and kidnap me."

"They can," I replied.

Behind the closed door of her bedroom, I can hear Claire on the phone with her best friend, Lily. I stand outside, trying to make out what she is saying, but it is just a low murmur of girlishness, a muted language I cannot decipher. I knock gently—a formality—and walk in. Claire covers the mouthpiece with her hand and looks up at me.

"Finish up and start your homework," I say.

"It will only take me fifteen minutes."

"Fine, but you still need to do it. And I'd like to see it when you're done."

"Mo-om, you're not going to start that, are you? You never check homework."

There is some truth to this, but in spite of that—or maybe because of it—a righteous indignation wells up. "That's not so."

Claire rolls her eyes.

I can't remember my mother ever checking my homework, or even asking what it was. She trusted the teachers to do their job, as she was doing hers. Frankly, I think there's something to be said for that, though I'm loath to admit it publicly. At last year's science fair on electricity, it was evident that there had been engineers hired, architects employed, lighting experts paid off on the sly. One girl had built a minutely detailed replica of Yankee Stadium with a home-run sign that lit up every time the toy batter took a perfect swing at the push of a button. I mean, don't those parents ever get tired, don't they ever just feel like hiding in their bedrooms watching reruns of *Law & Order* while their kids do their homework? Of course, I don't have the courage of my convictions. Instead, I am deeply erratic; I don't check the girls' homework for weeks and then a sudden wave of guilt will envelop me. Convinced that I am a selfish, lazy parent doing my children irrevocable harm, I demand to see every essay and math problem, though I stopped understanding the answers once they got past fourth grade. Not surprisingly, Phoebe and Claire barely tolerate this onslaught of maternal oversight, knowing it will quickly pass. Still, I promised myself I would start off this year on the right foot.

"I want to see your homework," I reiterate.

"Whatever. Mom, I'm on the phone." Claire stares at me, waiting for me to leave.

I walk into my bedroom and turn on the laptop Sam and I share. All afternoon, once word of the sale to Merdale leaked out, e-mail poured in from friends and business acquaintances. On the whole they assume a cautiously optimistic if reserved tone, unsure if I am on my way out or up. I glance at a few that I haven't read yet and check a couple of media gossip Web sites but I am really just biding my time, as if my true purpose will be more acceptable if it comes disguised, even from myself, as an act of impetuousness.

I double-click on Sam's personal folder to open it.

But it is, for the first time, password-protected, locked away from me.

Then again, perhaps it always has been. I've never tried to open it before. I never thought I had a reason to.

Piqued, I type in various likely passwords, his mother's maiden name, my maiden name, his birthday, Phoebe and Claire's first and last initials combined, but each time an "error" message pops up. Annoyed, I type in "fuck you." Needless to say, this gains me access to absolutely nothing.

I go back to the kitchen. It is seven forty-five and I am about to call the girls to dinner when I hear the keys in the front door. Sam walks in holding a bouquet of yellow roses from the Korean deli tucked under his arm. "Sorry I'm late." He kisses me on the back of the neck.

I bend my head, feel his lips on my skin, slightly chapped. "It's okay."

"Here." Sam puts a manila envelope on the counter in front of me.

"What's this?"

"I did some research on Merdale for you. It's not a deep dive, but at least it will tell you who the main players are." Sam, like most men, is profoundly uncomfortable meandering around in a world of uncertainty. He craves facts, things he can fix. This is his gift, his offering.

I thank him and unwrap the flowers, sawing off the thick ends with the serrated bread knife Deirdre brought back from her last buying trip to Paris. "So what happened with your meeting?" I ask, trying to sound disinterested. I put the knife down and break off the last stubborn stems with my hands.

"What meeting?"

I fill the vase with warm water, put the flowers in. "You said you were getting together with a source for the Wells story."

"I saw her."

I stand completely still. Her.

The tectonic plates of doubt and distrust shift, creak.

I had it wrong, of course I did.

I rest my hands on the manila envelope, its edges growing soggy from the splattered chili it is resting on, exhaling fully for the first time all day. "I thought you said your source was a man?"

"I never said that. You must have misheard. Anyway, I don't know how helpful she'll be. She claims Wells was granted close to four-point-two million options without the board's approval but she doesn't seem to have any hard proof. At least not any she's offering up at this point. There's a chance she's stringing me along but my gut says there's something there. I just have to find it or get someone else to talk."

"Is Simon going to give you the time you need?" Sam's editor is notoriously impatient and the recent slump in advertising is not helping him in that department. Business magazines are always reliable early indicators of how bad the economy will get. After all, not many people want to read about investments when they are worried about their monthly mortgage payments. All over town, budgets and head counts are being slashed, victims are piling up, the death watch is on.

"That remains to be seen."

Claire and Phoebe, who heard Sam's voice, wander into the kitchen. He reaches over to kiss them both hello and the three of them sit down at the table, waiting to be fed. For a moment I forget about the morning, about Merdale, grateful for the simplicity of their expectations.

"Okay," Sam says once we all have bowls of chili before us, "let's hear about the first day of school. What's the lowdown on your teachers?"

Claire, fully immersed in the "everyone" stage of reportage, begins: Everyone hates the math teacher, everyone says that the art teacher is a lunatic, everyone thinks the Spanish teacher she has gotten is nice but doesn't explain things well while the other one is a total bitch (I shake my head in warning, which she pointedly ignores) but you learn a lot. I am somewhat reassured that "learning a lot" is the coin of the realm at Weston. It is what I appreciate most about the school. The flip side is that half the kids have SAT tutors by the age of seven.

"Who exactly is everyone?" Sam asks.

"Everyone," Claire reiterates, frustrated.

"Don't you think you should wait and judge for yourself?"

"Da-ad." I take perverse pleasure in the fact that he, too, can be subjected to the stretched-out syllables indicative of teen displeasure, though admittedly it's not as frequent. Often, I catch the girls trying out their budding female personae with him, rounding off the harder edges they sometimes jostle me with. He is, already, The Other. All I can do is sit in the shadows, watching as he accrues their gifts unbidden, almost unnoticed, leaving me both pleased—this is how it should be, after all—and slightly envious.

Sam shrugs it off, reaches over, ruffles Claire's hair and smiles. "Suffice it to say the reporting bug does not run in the family." He turns to Phoebe. "And you, my little ink-stained wretch?" He picks up her hand, covered in indecipherable hieroglyphics scrawled in ballpoint pen. "I suppose this is your homework assignment for the night?"

One of the great by-products of having children is how they can take you outside of yourself, yank you into their world, sometimes against your will, almost always to your benefit. Tonight, though, there is a running monologue, a split screen in my head as I listen to Phoebe describe—what? Something about doing three-dimensional art the first half of the year before they switch to graphics, or is it the other way around?

"So," I say when she is done. "I have some news, too." I glance over at Sam, who nods imperceptibly. "My company was sold to a bigger firm today."

Both girls look at me, waiting for an analysis, a reassurance I can't give them. The only thing that disturbs children more than a crack in the structure of their own lives is even the hint of one in yours. Despite all of their poking and prodding, their testing of limits, they have a stake in their parents' invulnerability.

"Will you have a new boss?" Phoebe asks. She has always been extremely interested in the hierarchy of our jobs—memorizing the names of our bosses and bosses' bosses. Perhaps it gives her satisfaction to know that outside the home we do not have the final word, but I think, too, that she likes the order of it, it calms her in some way, the idea that life has a clearly delineated structure.

"Yes."

"Who?"

"I don't know yet."

"I think it's going to be a good thing, Mom," Claire says. "It's like going to a bigger school. There will be more options."

I smile at her, thankful for this keyhole into the kindness and empathy that resides beneath the layer of cool. It is the best of Claire.

After dinner, the girls withdraw to their rooms, their computers, their evening showers and nightly spats and Sam and I withdraw into the minutiae of domesticity—cleaning up the kitchen, going over upcoming schedules, phone calls—that create a landing, a distraction. We speak in snippets, but it is mostly flight instructions for the evening—I'll check on the girls, the cable people said we need a new converter box, do you want some tea? It is really just a prelude until we can be alone.

When the girls are finally in bed, we sit down in the living room at opposite ends of the shabby chic couch that is now more shabby than chic, its overwashed canvas slipcover sagging and jowly.

"Did you look at those papers on Merdale?" Sam asks.

"Yes. It was really helpful, thanks," I lie. The list of officers in the company, their affiliations and accomplishments provoked a fresh groundswell of anxiety that left me nearly breathless. I put it down before I got to the end.

"How was breakfast with Deirdre?"

"All right. Ben was there."

"Ben? I thought she broke up with him months ago." Sam has always disapproved of Ben in the disgruntled way men have of sniffing out a cad in their midst. There is nothing more galling than an unapologetic show of indiscretion when you are dutifully playing by the rules. On the few occasions when the four of us have gone out to dinner, they treated each other with a heightened politeness and interest in each other's work—they are both in the media business, after all, and know some of the same people—but I suspect Sam feels like something of a journeyman when faced with Ben's itinerant glamour.

"Maybe they can work it out this time." I have always been defensive of Deirdre, her choices.

"I doubt that."

I am about to tell Sam about her arm, the bruises that have flashed in and out of my consciousness all day, but I stop myself. Deirdre and I keep each other's secrets. "So what did you want to talk to me about?" I ask carefully, there is still that.

Sam looks up from his Brooklyn Lager.

"This morning," I remind him. "You said you wanted to talk to me about something."

He shakes his head. "It was nothing. Forget it."

"You sure?"

He nods. "Yes." He reaches over, puts his hand on my knee and we are both aware of it, this act that has gone unnoticed a thousand times before. "I meant what I said. I know this is really hard on you. And it sucks that Carol didn't give you any warning. She owed you that. But you'll be okay."

"What if I'm not?"

"What do you mean?"

"What are we going to do if I lose my job? It's a really tough market out there. More people are getting laid off every day. And we have no cushion."

"First of all, you're not going to lose your job. Even if you did, we'd be all right."

"For how long?"

"You'll find another job," Sam says.

I shift my legs but cannot find a comfortable position. I know that he is right, but rather than soothe me, it only kindles an amorphous resentment. There is a universe between "You can take care of yourself" and "I'll take care of you."

"I'm exhausted," I say, rising. "I'm going to bed."

"Okay. I'll be there in a minute."

I am curled in fetal position, three pillows carefully propping up my head, the only way to relieve the permanent pain in my rotator cuff from years of carrying a bag overstuffed with papers, phones, makeup, saliva-stained children's toys, when Sam climbs in beside me, his weight sinking the mattress until we settle into the familiar valley of our own imprints. He grazes my hip with his fingertips, the pressure light, almost tentative, and kisses me gently on the shoulder. "Lisa, it really will be okay," he whispers.

I touch his hand with mine and for a couple of minutes we lie side by side, aware of each other's breath, the in and out of our lungs spiraling into the humid stillness of the air.

Slowly I feel him turn on his side, inch in my direction, until he is curled around me, his hand moving up the curve of my waist to my breasts. Desire twinges from my lower belly through my chest, my throat. I want him suddenly with a force that too often lies dormant beneath the predictability of marital sex, all those efficient couplings when you both know what pleases the other and do it because there is no time or will for risky new enterprises that may not pay off. I want him to wipe away the day, the doubts, I want him because I have always wanted him. Most of all, I want him to want me. I turn over, pull Sam on top of me, open my mouth to him. There is a rare urgency to our lovemaking—ah, we can still feel this, this need, we can still do this to each other—which is in itself a vast relief.

Afterward, Sam falls asleep and for a little while I watch his back rising and falling until I, too, drift off.

I wake with a start just after midnight to a jagged crack of thunder careening into the streets. A white flash of lightning slashes through the bedroom like a searchlight and then vanishes.

The weather is breaking in one great clamorous late-summer storm.

I reach over but Sam isn't beside me. I lie still, listening to the torrential downpour, waiting for him to return from the bathroom, wanting only to curl once more into the perfect hollow of his arm carved as if for my head alone, but he doesn't return.

Finally, I tiptoe out to the living room.

I hover in the doorway. Sam is standing by the rain-smeared window, his back to me, his cell phone pressed tightly to his ear.

"I just couldn't do it," he says. "Not tonight. I'm sorry."

SIX

I stand rooted in the doorway, completely still, waiting, listening, but Sam doesn't say anything more.

He flips his phone shut and stares out the window before turning around, his eyes distracted, unfocused. He starts when he sees me.

"I didn't hear you," he says. The sheets of water battering the window make a speckled shadow across his bare torso.

"Who were you talking to?"

He shifts his weight from one leg to the other. "I'm sorry. I didn't mean to wake you. I couldn't sleep."

"Who was that?"

"That woman I met with about the Wells piece. She left five messages."

"It's past midnight. How can you call someone at this hour?"

"I didn't want to talk to her, that was the whole point. I'm beginning to think she's a total nut job. I thought if I called now I could leave a message without actually having to speak to her."

"And?"

He pauses. "She picked up."

He walks over to me, puts his arm around my waist, settling just above the small of my back, he always calls it "his spot," as if love has its own acreage. "It's late, let's go back to bed."

"Couldn't do what?"

"Huh?"

"You told her you couldn't do something. What couldn't you do?"

"It's nothing." His hand hovers, then presses firmly against the silk of my nightgown, guiding me out of the living room. "She wants me to confront Wells and I told her I couldn't without more proof. It would blow up in my face. Let's just forget about it."

I nod, not quite relenting, not quite sure, and yet.

What choice do I have, really?

We walk quietly down the hallway, our bare feet padding against the wooden floor, and then lie side by side as the rain pounds against the pavement until, finally, we both fall back to sleep.

The next morning I am showered and dressed before Sam stumbles into the kitchen. There are no fresh eggs, no cheerful admonitions about school as the girls finish up and gather their things. Sam and I are polite with each other in a hungover, desultory way, the air dense with that post-argument haze when you haven't quite regained your balance yet and are still eyeing each other, sniffing for clues. The fact that we never really had a fight only makes the space between us harder to navigate. I leave him eating a bowl of high-fiber cereal and flipping through the papers.

Despite the fact that I agreed to let Claire take Phoebe alone on the Madison Avenue bus this year, I'm finding the follow-through a little difficult. This morning at least I have a perfectly valid excuse to accompany them—albeit one my family finds curious, to say the least. In a moment of temporary insanity I signed up to be on the steering committee for the annual Weston fund-raiser. It's not that I haven't volunteered for things before. I've gone on my fair share of class trips to the Museum of Natural History, baked umpteen cupcakes for the never-ending stream of bake sales to benefit the homeless shelter three blocks away, breast cancer research, the middle school dance. But I have always felt more comfortable when these efforts involve being with children. The truth is, I am thoroughly intimidated by the other mothers, with their cliques and their mind-boggling efficiency and their birthday parties for the entire grade of fifty-six kids at venues I can't afford to go to with my own friends. Nevertheless, when Georgia Hartman suggested it, I found myself agreeing, realizing too late that the request was made only because I had accidentally wandered into a conversation she was having with someone else about it. She never expected me to acquiesce. Why do I always get it wrong with these people?

We head out into the cooler air, the girls registering their protest at my presence by walking a few feet ahead of me. Once on the bus, Phoebe balances her notebook on her lap, doing the math homework she forgot about last night, though she refuses to admit a causal relationship between this and her resistance to writing assignments down. I can already predict the conversation at the first parent-teacher conference, where it will all be framed as a fatal flaw in parenting skills destined to consign my daughter to a second-rate college, a dead-end job, a slacker husband.

Claire, who has been tormented for the last twenty-four hours over whether or not she should get bangs, is tugging at her hair and studying her reflection in the grimy window. She has conducted an overnight poll of all of her friends and, to her consternation, they are evenly divided over whether it would be "super-cute" or "total, like, catastrophe."

"What do you think, Mom?" she asks, without taking her gaze off of her own diffuse image.

I try not to betray my shock—and pleasure—that my advice is actually being solicited. I think the idea is disastrous but I know better than to go on record in case she decides otherwise. "Your hair's like mine," I say carefully. "It's going to get poofy if it's too short."

Claire considers this. "Well, Lily thinks I should."

I wonder if children ask your opinion with the express purpose of ignoring it, or if, after the glint of vulnerability, they need to regain their pride with a show of stubborn disinterest. I'm clueless about what surreptitiously sinks in, what is sloughed off.

"Whatever," I say, muttering the outlawed word.

"What?"

"Nothing."

As soon as we get to Weston the girls meld, guppylike, into their own groups and, stranded, I feel a wave of jealousy for their easy sense of belonging. I head up to the boardroom on the second floor, a sedate wood-paneled oasis more suited to Wall Street than a bustling school. I often try to arrive a little bit late to this type of thing to lessen the time I will have to struggle through awkward chitchat or, worse, sit silently while others talk around me. It is not lost on me, by the way, that it is ludicrous for a professional woman and mother of two to be this insecure about a school meeting. I have not, in the past, had difficulty making friends, but the sense of being an interloper here has never completely dissipated. I had hoped it would be otherwise. Early on, I realized that many of the women I chalked up as trophy wives and fourth-generation former debutantes I would have nothing in common with are actually hardworking lawyers and architects, designers and journalists. I hovered around them at parent nights and socials, anxious to become friends, but they rarely put in appearances at morning drop-offs or committees like this. The women I was most interested in I saw the least. Like me, they had come to cede this territory to the nonworking mothers with a blend of relief and resignation.

Six women, including Georgia, are already seated around the long mahogany table, their bags at their feet, leather-bound notepads at the ready. On the sideboard, there is a platter of minibagels, freshly squeezed orange juice in a glass pitcher from the Museum of Modern Art and a huge polished silver urn of coffee. Needless to say, no one is eating. I settle into a chair and surreptitiously check my BlackBerry before turning it to mute. I wonder briefly if in the entire 110-year history of Weston a single father has ever sat on this committee, but the answer is obvious. I am the only one dressed for a job and I feel hopelessly overdone in my black pencil skirt and top. Then again, the casual-chic-running-around-town thing the other women have going on is actually far harder to pull off. They probably came out of the womb wearing ballet flats.

I try to enter into a conversation about our children's first day of school and think I might actually be doing okay when the woman at the head of the table calls us ever so gently to attention. "Shall we begin?" she suggests. "For those of you who don't know me, I'm Samantha. Class of ninety-one. As you know, this fund-raiser is the main Weston event of the year and there's a lot of work to be done before February. The auction is our single biggest moneymaker and much of our energy will be spent lining up donations. To start, I thought we could take a look at last year's offerings for inspiration." Samantha, a whippet-thin brunette in a sleeveless cashmere shell that cunningly shows off her zero-body-fat biceps, hands out the creamy catalogue. As we begin to leaf through it, there are nostalgic murmurs about last year's bids on the week in Provence, the front-row season tickets to the Knicks, the various dinners with famous alumni and parents, the walk-on part on an HBO series, the Oscar de la Renta wardrobe and the spending spree at Ralph Lauren. No one seems particularly concerned that charitable giving has gone down in double digits everywhere.

"Of course, a number of these are perennials but I was hoping for some fresh ideas. Ladies?"

"I could arrange a week at our ski lodge in Beaver Creek," Tara Jamison, famous for the magnitude of her divorce settlement, offers in a low, flattened voice. Her smooth, luminously bronzed face is impassive as she lowers her cup of coffee and places it with great concentration in the china saucer. Secure, cosseted, she is a woman luxuriating in the knowledge that she will never have to rush anywhere ever again. Either that or she is taking way too much Prozac.

"That would be wonderful," Samantha remarks approvingly.

Tara nods and slowly brushes aside a lock of her glossy, honey-streaked hair. She is curvier than the others, completely comfortable with her own superbly maintained softness. This alien degree of body confidence elicits a grudging curiosity and barely concealed distrust.

"My husband should be able to get two tickets to the Academy Awards," Georgia offers.

"And entrée to the parties?" Samantha asks.

"Of course."

Everyone murmurs assent and happily jots this down.

The donations continue to pile up as each woman digs into her pocket of social connections and effortlessly pulls out a gilded offering.

Samantha turns to me. "Lisa?"

"I can get Rita Mason to come to someone's house and cook a dinner for ten." I have no idea where this came from and I cannot imagine how I will ever be able to talk her into doing this.

"Good." Samantha smiles and writes this down as if it is a fait accompli. "Why don't we say for twenty, though?"

"Of course." Ten extra guests is the least of my problems.

I barely hear the rest of the conversation. As the meeting closes, Samantha sets the time for our session next week. By then Merdale will have taken over and the thought of coming in late so soon into its reign fills me with dread. Too often I feel as if I spend half my life making excuses—at work, at home, here.

Out on the street I hail a cab and as it speeds down the West Side Highway past the few remaining trucker bars and seedy diners stubbornly nestled amid all the brazen construction I get out my cell phone and call Deirdre.

"Did I wake you?" I ask. What I really mean is, Did I interrupt some esoteric pornographic act you are currently engaged in with Ben?

"No. I'm just tired. I had a bit of a rough night."

"Why doesn't that surprise me?"

"That's not what I mean. Where are you? I can hardly hear you."

"In a cab. I have to meet with some potential client way downtown. Seems a waste to me, I mean what idiot signs on with a company that was just bought, but I promised Carol."

"You don't owe her anything."

"I know. That's not why I called."

"What's up?"

"I need a reality check." I give her the details of last night, the sex (perhaps I feel I have something to prove in this department), the mysterious phone call that Sam failed to explain. "Would you believe him when he said that it was nothing?" I ask.

"Yes."

"Really?"

"That would be my strategy."

"There's a difference between belief and strategy."

"Only if you let there be," Deirdre replies. "Sam had a perfectly plausible explanation. The worst thing you can do or say is harp on it with him. Sometimes you can push someone so much you propel them right into the thing you're most scared of."

"Isn't that a 'blame the victim' mentality?"

"Maybe. But it happens to be true. You've got to stop this," she adds firmly.

"I'm sorry. I wouldn't want to bore you."

"That's not what I meant, Lisa."

"I know," I reply grudgingly. "Listen, I meant to ask you, you're not bringing Ben to dinner tonight, are you?"

"God no," she exclaims. "Though now that you mention it, it is an interesting idea."

"Deirdre."

"Just kidding. If Jack was bringing his wife, maybe, but I'm glad that it will just be the four of us. Besides, you know Ben is against enforced integration."

"Meaning?"

"He still resists every attempt I make to get us out of the little box he has us in. He hasn't even told his children he's dating. His ex-wife is practically living with her spinning instructor, for Christ's sake. You know what I was doing when you called? Writing him an e-mail."

"Why is that so strange?"

"We got into yet another relationship talk last night. Maybe *debate* is a better word. The point is, after all this time, I still seem to have this need to send a long treatise after every date explaining myself to him or, worse, trying to explain him to himself. I always feel like I have to make a case for us." She sighs. "It's okay, I just need to be patient. Anyway," she adds, brightening, "at least it makes tonight easier. I can't wait to see everyone."

"Everyone meaning Jack?"

"Everyone meaning everyone. And Jack."

We hang up as the driver stops in front of a great slab of a glass building, a shimmering proclamation of hubris and hope a few hundred yards north of the pit where the Twin Towers once stood.

Inside, the lobby has, despite the high-tech security scanners and "smart" elevators, a tentative feel, like a hostess waiting nervously for her guests to arrive. Half the building remains unoccupied despite the municipal tax breaks offered; the residual fear and mourning have soaked too deeply into this battle-scarred neighborhood. The business world remains divided after all these years between those who believe in putting down a flag and those who see no reason to go looking for trouble, as if safety is a choice and not an accident of fate.

As I hand over my driver's license, have my bag scanned and, after some confusion, punch in my floor at the C bank of elevators, I wonder once more what I'm doing here. The potential client, David Forrester, must have heard about the takeover but been too polite to cancel. When I pointed this out to Carol, she insisted I go nonetheless, convincing me that landing Forrester as a client will be an auspicious way to introduce myself to Merdale. She had first met him a month ago at a cocktail party in Southampton to raise money for Parkinson's disease, and though we rarely take on individuals—there are plenty of others who specialize in crisis management for indicted CEOs and politicians caught in New Jersey motel rooms with hookers of indeterminate sexual identity—he broached the subject with her. A hedge fund manager, he had recently been getting roughed up quite a bit in the press. Despite my misgivings, I read up on Forrester. He is the kind of man I usually despise on principle, though I cannot say precisely what that principle is—it would require a more nuanced understanding of Wall Street than I actually possess. I only know that hedge fund money has infiltrated the city like golden silt; it lies beneath the town houses and the private jets, the personal chefs and the exotic safaris, you can see it in the women's lineless faces on the Upper East Side and their daughters with their Prada bags at age twelve. It has changed the very meaning of wealth in a city already cleaved by monetary differentiation.

The elevator lets me out on the thirty-second floor and, stepping into the vast space surrounded by wraparound floor-to-ceiling windows, I feel suspended in midair, floating weightlessly amid miles of endlessly unpunctuated sky. The receptionist, a young woman with pitch-black straightened hair and a carefully honed stylishness bordering on aggression, leads me down a hallway of offices partitioned by glass and carefully designed seating areas meant to facilitate a sense of community but which appear never to have been used. All is transparency and exposure, as if privacy has been relegated to the past, a nostalgic but failed notion. There are no corners to hide in here, no doors to shut that can't be seen through.

She deposits me at the corner office, wordlessly vanishing as David Forrester rises to greet me. "Lisa, thank you for coming. I realize this must be a crazy time for you." He smiles easily, as if I am doing him a great favor. He is over six feet tall, with a body that suggests he plays tennis or racquetball or whatever it is men like him play to offset the business lunches, the deals done over expense-account dinners replete with thousand-dollar wine bills. His longish dark-brown hair and wire-framed glasses give him the air of a New England college professor rather than a financial genius known for his moral relativity.

"I appreciate your taking the time," I reply, as we sit on opposite sides of his oak desk, blatantly out of place amid so much determined modernity.

"Carol is your biggest fan. I'd be silly not to follow her advice."

"I hope she didn't pester you into this."

"Only in the most charming way."

"You know she sold the company?"

He nods. "Yes. I realize that things are in a state of flux, but I have always believed in getting to know talent whenever the opportunity arises. If you wait for perfect timing for anything in life you will be a very old, very poor, very frustrated human being." He stops, offers up that easy smile once more. "Good Lord, I must sound like a two-bit business Buddha to you."

"Not at all," I reassure him. "But I thought timing was everything. In finance and relationships."

"Considering I've been far more successful in the former than the latter, I will defer to you on that score."

"At your peril," I reply.

David laughs. "Carol was right."

"About what?"

"You."

"Did she make a convincing argument for you signing up?"

"I believe that's your job."

I flush. "Of course. In that case, let me proceed." I begin to rattle off the benefits of Merdale, making much of it up as I go. While I speak, David rests his elbows on his desk, listening patiently. His forearms, emerging from his rolled-up shirtsleeves, are sinewy and firm. I notice he is wearing a Swiss Army watch, as much of an affectation as a Rolex and yet somehow not quite as offensive.

"Merdale does good work," David assures me when I am, to the relief of us both, finally done. "As I told Carol, we have corporate PR for most of our needs and I've never been one to seek out personal publicity."

"But?"

"I'm sure you're aware that a lot of the press about me has not exactly been glowing." An ironic smile forms slowly across his features. "As long as it doesn't impact business my proclivity is usually to let people believe whatever they damn please about me. At the moment, though, I am about to announce a new fund that I don't want to see hobbled by ill-founded rumors. There's too much at stake."

"Can you tell me about the fund?" I ask, doubtful that I will understand a single word of his answer.

"It's something I've wanted to get off the ground for a while. We will only put money into green projects, alternative sources of energy, companies trying to develop better hybrids, that kind of thing." He pauses. "In case you're wondering, it is something I actually do believe in. What I would like to avoid is having my motives questioned publicly in a way that might overshadow the project and prevent people from investing. For the record, I'm not nearly as evil as people seem to think."

"I'm sure you're not."

David glances out the window at a sailboat cutting a lazy white trail past the Statue of Liberty before turning back to me. "Do you know what mosaic theory is?" he asks.

"Kind of." It's one of those terms I hear bandied about and think I understand but am probably totally wrong about. It's not worth the gamble.

"It's the technique of gathering bits of information from various places and piecing them together to form a supposition that you wouldn't have been able to come up with from a single source. The government is using it in certain terrorism cases."

I nod.

"The point is, sometimes the conclusion is accurate—and sometimes it's totally off-base. The exact same morsels of information can be put together in various ways. From precisely the same facts you can end up with completely disparate hypotheses."

"In a way that's what we do," I tell him, "present the pieces of information you give us in a manner that will create a favorable image to the outside world."

"Yes, of course. Anyway, the reason I thought you might be right for the project is that I admire the work you've done for Upward Movement." He smiles. "I did my research on you."

"So I see."

Upward Movement is an organization that helps place highly educated immigrants, often seeking political asylum, in jobs similar to ones they had in their home countries. It has been a pet project of mine for the past two years. "That was pro bono," I remind him.

"This, of course, would not be. Nevertheless, you took an NGO no one had ever heard of and got almost every Fortune 500 company involved. I wouldn't mind benefiting from a little of that expertise. When and if the time is right," he adds.

"You mean because of Merdale?"

"Yes."

We agree to speak again after things have settled down a bit and then David offers to walk me out.

He leads me past a shimmering panorama of the Chrysler Building, the Woolworth Building, past ever-busy cranes rendered silent by the thick glass, the cacophony of the city's massive construction reduced to a stage whisper. "Distracting view," he remarks. "The funny thing is, I've never particularly liked heights."

I smile. "To tell you the truth, I've been verging on a panic attack since I walked in."

"I hope it's the view and not the company."

"Absolutely. But don't you feel vulnerable here? All this openness makes me feel, so, I don't know, unprotected."

"It has been said we are a target in the sky," he agrees. "But a little sense of danger is not necessarily a bad thing. It keeps you on your toes, don't you think?"

"I have Manolos for that," I reply, though I don't, in fact, own Manolos. Well, one pair Deirdre passed on to me after she was seduced by their sale price despite the fact that they didn't fit her (or me) and proved to be beyond even the most expert stretching.

David laughs. He is clearly someone who likes to be amused but is happy to return the favor, a man confident that whatever it is he wants will come his way eventually.

"I'll be in touch," he promises as we shake hands. With that he holds open the glass door for me to pass through. I can feel his eyes on my back as I walk and, self-conscious, I turn once to check. I catch his eye, then quickly look away, embarrassed.

Back at Steiner, I pass by Carol's office but the door is closed, the lights off. As I walk past the row of desks, I notice people polishing up their résumés, dusting photos and straightening stacks of magazines. We are waiting now, all of us.

I spend the next hour going over accounts and writing summaries (though I haven't been asked, it can't hurt). I only hope they don't turn into exit reports. I am just about done when my e-mail pings. I peer at the screen. It is from David Forrester.

In the subject line he has written: Mosaic Theory 2.0. The e-mail reads: "Despite the uses made of it by the government and, as you pointed out, PR, I am far more interested in the potential personal applications of mosaic theory. You can be my test case. I'll start. I make a mean bouillabaisse, fish-heads and all. I would like to teach full-time one day. (I know, I know, everyone wants to teach . . . after their first twenty million.) At least three things the press has said about me recently are completely untrue but I'm not going to tell you which three . . . David."

As I read it again it crosses my mind that this is some sort of test: If I come up with the right answer David will sign on with Merdale. It has been so long since anyone flirted with me that it takes me a moment to realize he might be playing a different game entirely. Sitting alone at my desk, I feel my face heat up.

I am rereading the e-mail for the third time when Petra buzzes to tell me Sam is on the line. I quickly shut it before I pick up.

"Is everything okay?" I ask. Sam rarely calls so early in the day.

"Yes, fine. Listen," he pauses and I hear him take a breath. "Wells's number two has agreed to see me."

"That's great." Actually, I don't see what's so great about it. What he needs is the elusive Wells himself.

"The thing is, he's going on vacation."

"Okay."

"He wants to meet with me today."

"Today? Is he in New York?" I am beginning to sense some sort of setup, much in the way Phoebe gives an endless litany of rationalizations before asking if she can stay up an extra hour knowing that my tendency is to agree just to stop the babbling.

"No. I checked flights. With the time difference I can get out to Chicago, meet with him and still be back in time for Jack's dinner. I'll come to the restaurant straight from the airport."

"Are you sure it's worth it?"

"Why don't you trust me to know what I'm doing?" he snaps.

"Of course. It's just . . . never mind. I hope it works out, that's all."

"I'll see you tonight."

I'm not sure if he hears me when I say, "Okay," or, a few seconds later, "I love you."

As soon as I hear the click I realize that I haven't told him where we are meeting Jack. I pick up the receiver and call his office. After exchanging a few pleasantries with his assistant, Kathy, I ask to speak to Sam.

"I'm sorry, he's not in."

"Did he leave for the airport already?"

"The airport?"

"For his flight to Chicago. The Wells story?"

"You must be mistaken," she informs me peremptorily. "There is no Wells story. It was killed."

SEVEN

Suspicion crackles and pulls, nags and infiltrates, it coils around your brain, distorting your perceptions, it is the smoke you see everything through that refuses to lift. But a lie, hard and indisputable, freezes in your lungs, its ice spreading through your pores, chilling every synapse; a lie once discovered paralyzes you.

I sit motionless, my hand still on the telephone, futilely trying to arrange my thoughts into a recognizable pattern, but it is as if I am trying to decipher an unknown dialect—the words don't attach to meaning.

A lie does this, too: It opens a door. How do you know, after all, if it is an isolated fact, a tumor still contained, excisable, or if there is more lurking in the body, silent and malignant; how do you know how far it goes?

Sam and I have had our wobbles, we have had our cold wars and our reunions, but in all of our years together I have never caught him in an outright lie. Until this moment I never truly believed that I would. Sam, I always thought, came shrink-wrapped in morality. It was one of the most alluring things about him.

But.

I exhume the pieces I had so recently dismissed, the woman's voice, the midnight phone call, and casting aside the excuses and evasions, examine them anew.

My head spins, a vortex of fear, doubt and anger, leaving me dizzy and uncertain. I feel oddly numb, as if I have gotten a dreaded diagnosis I can't assimilate yet, won't even try because I know once I do, nothing will ever be the same.

I am not ready to confront Sam, not ready to take a step off the precipice to . . . what?

I don't want to hear the answers, not yet.

So I sit here, digging my nails into my scalp, looking down off the ledge—and stay resolutely still.

Slowly, I become aware of people hovering in the near distance. I glance up to find Petra standing in the entryway with two men I have never seen before. She moves aside and the men enter with a bloated, proprietary air. The smaller of the two steps forward and holds out his hand. "Robert Merdale," he says.

The last thing in the world I need right now is a Merdale drive-by. I force a smile, too wide, too anxious to please. Beneath the guise of collegiality, they are here to assert their authority, their droit du seigneur.

As I shake his hand, I try to forcibly shift my brain away from Sam, but only fragments of my consciousness come with me.

Merdale's fingers are tiny, soft and perfectly manicured. "It's wonderful to meet you," he says. He has a slight lisp overlaid on a flat midwestern accent. He might be married with three children but I have my doubts. "And this is Mick Favata." Behind him stands a bald, barrel-chested man with a bulldog face pockmarked with the ragged scars of ancient acne. The three of us sit down at the round table.

"I just wanted to introduce myself," Merdale begins, "and tell you how happy we are that you will be part of our team. I've watched you from afar and I want to assure you that you are one of the assets we are most excited about getting," he says, as if I have been acquired along with the furniture, the database, the client list. He glances over at Favata. "Mick has agreed to come on board to help out for a while. Do you two know each other? Mick was the head of Harcourt PR for years. He can bring a fresh eye to the table."

I'm not quite sure what any of this means but I do know that it's not exactly a vote of confidence. "That's wonderful," I reply.

Merdale begins a round of getting-to-know-you blather meant to show that he cares, really cares about me as a person, and I give rote answers to his queries about how many children I have, where I went this summer, how long I've been with the company, all the preliminaries we both pretend to be interested in as we edge closer to the point, whatever that might be. I am in the middle of answering his question about how assistant duties are divvied up when my phone rings. Petra picks it up and I hear her tell whoever is on the line that I am in a meeting.

"You were saying?" Merdale prompts me.

I stare blankly at him. I have no idea what I was saying. We are not off to a good start. "Sorry."

I try to recoup but before I can pick up whatever weak train of thought I'd been clinging to, Favata begins to speak in a gruff voice. "Robert has asked me to have a look at some of the accounts, see how we're approaching them, if we can improve in any way." He pauses, leans forward on his elbows, the sleeves of his blazer pulled tight against his thick arms. He could use the next size up. "Let me assure you right off the bat that I don't want your job. I'm just happy to come in and help in any way that I can."

I was unaware until this moment that I needed help. "That's great."

I glance over his shoulder at my phone but the message light remains stubbornly unlit.

"I don't want to keep you from anything," Favata remarks snidely. "We can talk more tomorrow." It sounds more like a threat than an invitation.

The minute they leave I turn to Petra. "Who called?"

"Someone from HR. They needed your benefit info. I took care of it for you."

I had no reason to think it would have been Sam. "Thanks."

I can feel Petra watching me, waiting for a postgame analysis of my meeting, but I'm in no mood. I smile wanly, tell her I have a lot of catching up to do and return to my desk.

For the next few hours, I go through all my accounts, trying to find the weaknesses before Favata does. I vacillate between feeling defensive—they are all fine—and seeing only mediocrity.

But beneath it all, I am waiting. For a plan of action, for my own nerve to return.

For an explanation that I know in my heart does not exist.

As I pick at a salad for lunch I stare at the dress hanging from my door that I brought to change into for the evening. It seems like a lifetime ago that I pulled it from my closet, held it up before the mirror, excited about the dinner, looking forward to it.

Claire calls to tell me she and Phoebe got home safely.

I talk briefly to Marissa, the latest in our ever-changing roster of babysitting NYU students.

I call Deirdre at the store but Janine, her assistant manager, informs me that she is out for the afternoon.

I call Nina Stern, a friend in the business, and learn that Mick Favata left Harcourt just over a year ago. There were some unpleasant rumors of an affair with a woman in the London office that went seriously awry, though no one uses the term *harassment,* at least not out loud. Some say there were payoffs made, confidentiality agreements signed. "Does he want back in the game?" I ask.

"He always wants in. But Robert Merdale's the only one about to give him the opportunity. This is his last chance. A word of warning," Nina says. "Be careful. Favata's a thug. And he and Merdale are fishing buddies."

"Great combination," I mutter.

I check my horoscope online.

I stare at my computer screen, unable to concentrate.

Forty-five minutes pass, an hour.

I open David Forrester's e-mail and read it three more times.

Finally I write, "You are either a benevolent serial monogamist and benefactor of worthy causes or a ruthless loner who likes to win at any cost. Which?" I pause and then, before I can think about it, I hit "send."

EIGHT

There are times—graduating college and, I am beginning to suspect, turning forty—when there seems to be an overwhelming impulse to either blow up your life or cling to it desperately.

I smooth my dress with the palms of my hands as I near the midtown restaurant's ornately gilded front door. The fitted black sheath has been riding up with every step, creating a shelf of fabric across my hips, a visible rebuke to the good intentions I had when I bought it, determined to lose five pounds. I know, of course, that you should never traffic in the currency of hope when shopping, every woman knows that, and yet. When I was younger I was convinced that the right outfit, the right lipstick, the right attitude could change the course of a first date or sway the mind of a man I felt slipping away. I'm older now, I know better. Still. I run my fingertips through my hair. It's not that I feel a need to impress Jack, not in the way that Deirdre does, but I want to be as close to my former self as possible, perhaps we all do, to at least fit into the outlines of who we were when we knew each other best.

I push open the restaurant's heavy door.

An hour ago I sent Sam a text message with its name and address but got no reply.

I hold on to what his assistant told me like a stone in my pocket, turning it this way and that, hidden from view. I will pull it out when I am ready, or when I can no longer bear it. For now, the secret weight of it is the only comfort I have. The timing will be mine.

I walk into the hushed entryway and my eyes take a second to adjust to the purposefully faded light. It's a curious choice for tonight, the kind of place given to company dinners and out-of-town tourists, a onetime clubhouse for mayors and tycoons when cigars were still tolerated and women only barely, a ridiculously expensive place with a highly recognizable name and mediocre food. There are a zillion pricey restaurants in New York renowned for their chefs' culinary creativity that I'd love to try—this isn't one of them. Jack doesn't live here and he must think he's making some sort of statement with his selection, though I fear it is not the statement he intends. I worry that Deirdre will be snarky about it or assume it is vested in irony, though I am certain it is not.

The maître d' leads me into the darkly lit oak-paneled dining room and I spot Jack alone at a corner table, sipping a drink, his eyes on the door, steady, vigilant. He is wearing an expertly tailored suit; his dark hair, still curly, is cut short. Even the cocktail before him—a martini, straight up—is, for some reason, jarring. But what did I expect, that he would be chugging dollar drafts from a keg? The past and the present overlap and separate like shadow puppets. We are grown-ups with all the accoutrements and the responsibilities; we are not.

Jack smiles broadly as I approach and as he comes into sharper focus I can see the early etchings of lines fanning from his eyes. He stands in the self-conscious way of a man with perfect but assimilated manners. "Lisa." He kisses me on the cheek. "You look wonderful."

"You, too."

"For someone my age," he jokes.

"Oh please, no qualifiers tonight. At least not before I've had a drink."

"That can be arranged." Jack motions for the waiter, assuming the role of host like a mantle.

I forgo my usual glass of white wine in favor of a martini, too. I have never had the world's greatest tolerance for alcohol but this seems as good a night as any.

"Is Sam meeting you here?"

"Yes. He's flying in from Chicago. He said he'd come straight from the airport."

"What was he doing in Chicago?"

"A story."

Jack nods and doesn't ask anything further. His ready acceptance, his apparent disinterest are a relief to me. "It's nice to have a few minutes alone together," he says.

I smile. "Yes." In some ways we had the easiest connection of the zigzagging loyalties that once bound the four of us and eventually sent us lurching apart. Our link was the least fraught and when it frayed it was due to the natural effects of time and distance rather than a conscious break.

Now, sitting beside him, I can see that he has lost none of his earlier tensile muscularity. After hours of predawn practice, days, nights on rickety buses, Jack had gotten a tennis scholarship to come east, as far away as he could get from a small northern California town and a family life he rarely explicated beyond alluding to an ill-defined roughness. At five-ten he wasn't as tall as some of the other players, nor did he have their natural grace and ability, but he made up for it in intensity. Jack wanted, needed, to win more than the country club tennis boys who populated the Ivy campuses then. The one thing I never sensed when I watched him play, accompanying Deirdre during their early courtship, sometimes even going alone to his matches, was joy. Rather, it seemed that he had looked around, assessed his abilities, weighed them against the competitive landscape and calculated that this was his clearest advantage. He knew the value of his talent, but I'm not sure it ever really made him happy. I don't suppose that was the point, though. Jack, at nineteen, twenty, had an unambiguous understanding of what it meant to win, there was none of that theoretical, wifty new-age stuff for him; it was elemental, winning meant you had a better score. He never lost his temper on the court the way others did, spurred by testosterone and the McEnroesque fad of vitriolic outbursts; whatever volatility he possessed, and it was there, I'm sure of it, was turned inward. Jack, when he erred or lost, turned silent. I wonder, sitting in this outdated, stuffy restaurant, if he is still infused with that absolutism or if, like me, he has discovered how much harder it is to be certain of anything now.

"Thank you," he says, touching my hand lightly with his fingertips.

"For what?"

"For coming tonight."

"Of course." I smile. "I'm so glad to see you. Five years is too long."

After a number of embryonic post-graduation years with no contact—why, after all, would he want to be in touch with the best friend of the woman who had so thoroughly rejected him?—there came a gradual détente. I sent Jack a note telling him of my marriage, we began to call each other every now and then, and eventually the advent of e-mail made curiosity and nostalgia so much easier to indulge in. Sometimes I feel like an emissary, keeping him updated in carefully managed snippets of Deirdre and Sam's doings, and vice versa. But I don't really mind; there is a way in which I am able to let down my guard with Jack that is hard with more recently acquired friends. We know who we were, where we started from. There is no need—or ability—to pretend.

Until now.

I feel the stone, turn it in my hand, cold and hard and smooth.

Anyway. Five years ago, when Jack married a perfectly nice young woman named Alice eleven years his junior—annoying on principle—Sam and I went up to Cape Cod for the wedding. I was surprised by his choice, but then again, I had never seen Jack with anyone but Deirdre; I didn't know if she was a precursor or an aberration, I didn't know his pattern. On paper at least Alice and Deirdre seem like polar opposites, Alice a quiet, somewhat ethereal academic working on a PhD in, I can't remember, something to do with Renaissance literature, and Deirdre, who is, well, not. When Jack and I danced in the billowy white tent redolent of wet grass and spilled Champagne, he quizzed me about Deirdre directly for the first time and, safe from the harbor of his new marriage, asked that I send along his regards.

"Who the hell gets married at twenty-four?" Deirdre remarked when I got back to the city. "I did," I reminded her. She rolled her eyes. "Well, you. You're different." I wasn't quite sure what she meant by that but I figured it was better to leave it alone. "Let me rephrase the question," she continued. "Who the hell marries a twenty-four-year-old?" I was about to say, Jack. Men. But being reminded of the male prerogative in this regard is never pleasant, especially not when it is an old boyfriend, even one you gave up years ago and have barely thought of since. (And yes, I know women are doing it, too, but please, spare me the chapter and verse, it's not the same.)

Still, when I told Jack the following year that Deirdre's father had died, he called her and they have been speaking and e-mailing intermittently ever since. She and Jack had such a combustible breakup that it is strange to think of them sliding into this kind of easy cordiality. Deep down I'm not convinced that first love can be rendered so even, so free of the tentacles of memory and regret. Then again, I may have a tendency to overestimate the effect of a college romance after nearly twenty years. Though for many it becomes a lingering obsession with the one that got away, for others it is apparently little more than an anecdote, a curious if dim moment frozen in time, the feelings no longer accessible or even comprehensible once the erotic fog has lifted. Who knows? I'm certainly no expert. I married the one who got away.

"It was daring of you to arrange this," I say.

Jack laughs. "Well, turning forty calls for a grand gesture, don't you think? It seemed, I don't know, symmetrical to spend it with you. We were together for my twenty-first birthday, after all. The age of consent meets the age of decrepitude. And since I was in the city . . . ," he adds, taking cover in convenience as if he needs to be a little less naked.

"Oh God, I remember your twenty-first birthday. We went to that truly horrific Chinese restaurant out on the highway. I remember your twenty-second, too. I don't think I've ever been so drunk in all my life." Things were already unraveling then; Sam and I entered our period of doubt; Jack, accepted early to Harvard Law, had proffered Deirdre the invitation to go with him that had morphed into an ultimatum hovering between them like a double-edged blade. That night we raced toward each other because in each of our hearts we knew that it was ending. "It feels like a lifetime ago," I say.

"Sometimes it seems like yesterday to me. In some ways it feels more real than anything that followed."

"I'm not sure if that's a good thing or a bad thing. So. How did your interview go this morning?"

"Pretty well, actually."

"You still won't tell me who it was with?"

He shakes his head. "I can't."

"C'mon, I'm good at keeping secrets."

"Since when?"

"What's that supposed to mean?"

"You always did have a fatal tendency toward honesty. Maybe it's those earnest big brown eyes of yours."

"Earnest? Is that how I look? Not exactly the compliment a woman is hoping for."

"I meant what I said. You look wonderful." He smiles. "All I meant was that it's an endearing quality but there are times when a certain amount of discretion is called for."

"People change."

"Do they?"

This is not a line of conversation I'm in the mood to pursue. Besides, I don't know the answer. I wish I did. "After all your years in Boston, why are you thinking of moving here now?"

In truth, I suspect that he had given Deirdre Manhattan, deeded it to her and was wary even to visit.

"I don't know, I guess I woke up one day and realized that if I stay there I will be doing essentially the same thing for the next twenty years. The thought gave me the chills."

"That's what this is all about, a midlife crisis? Thirty-nine is too young for that."

"I'm turning forty."

"Haven't you heard, forty is the new thirty?"

"Thank you for reducing my life to a cliché."

"Sorry. That's not what I meant. You know what your problem is? Too much early success. You shouldn't have made partner so young. It didn't give you anything to aim for."

"There's always something to aim for. Sometimes it presents itself and sometimes you have to go looking for it, but there's always something more."

"I suppose. But the problem with that way of thinking is that it makes it impossible to ever be satisfied with what you have. How does Alice feel about it?"

"I haven't told her."

"What do you mean, you haven't told her?"

"This afternoon's meeting was merely a preliminary conversation. I don't want to get into a big argument over something that might not happen."

"Would it be an argument?"

"Probably. Look, it's no big deal. I just don't like dealing in hypotheticals."

"For all you know she's dying to move," I reply. "It's easy to assume you know what the person you love is thinking, but what if you're wrong?" I am shadowboxing with the wrong shadow, I know that, but still. "Where does she think you are?"

"What is this, twenty questions?" He takes a breath, exhales. "I told her I was here to see a client."

"Jack, that's awful." And then, only sort of kidding, "Do all men lie?"

"What's that supposed to mean?"

"Nothing." I feel the martini coiling around my defenses, loosening them, a dangerous solvent on a loaded night.

"Is everything okay with you and Sam?"

"Yes. Of course."

Jack nods but he is suddenly distracted and I know without turning around that Deirdre is walking toward us.

It is what he has been waiting for.

Deirdre looks, quite simply, gorgeous. Her long hair is loosely blown out into soft waves; she is wearing a jewel-toned dress with a draped neckline that shows just enough to be enticing, and its billowing sleeves keep Ben's fingerprints safely under wraps. I watch Jack and Deirdre hug, step back an inch, reassess and smile deeply as they sit down.

"I can't believe you remembered this place," Deirdre exclaims. "I forgot all about it until I walked in the door."

"I don't remember us being here," I interject.

"We weren't. I mean, you weren't," Deirdre says. "Jack and I were."

"Really?" I don't know why I assumed I was privy to all of their memories.

Deirdre laughs. "We didn't have enough money to eat here, but we certainly managed to drink more than our share. Jack had heard rumors that there were some racy murals in the men's room left over from the twenties so we snuck in and well, you know."

"No, clearly I don't know."

"Let's just say we got kicked out."

"Quite decisively," Jack adds, smiling.

"Caught with our pants down."

They both laugh.

"How could I not know this?" I demand.

I was worried about awkwardness, jagged conversation, a night coated in scar tissue. The last thing I expected was this air of instant complicity.

"I love that you chose this place," Deirdre adds.

Jack smiles, mission accomplished.

"Here," he says, handing both of us a beautifully wrapped rectangular box.

"What's this?" she asks.

"Presents."

"But it's your birthday, we're the ones who give you presents."

"Consider them party favors, then."

"Can we open them?"

"Don't you want to wait for Sam?" Jack asks.

Deirdre turns to me. "Where is Sam?"

It is a marital habit not easily relinquished to cover for your spouse, to polish the veneer, sand off the corners. Even now, I cannot let it go. "I'll try calling him," I reply.

While they reminisce about their bathroom escapades, I dial Sam's cell but get his voice mail. I hang up and turn my attention back to them. Or try to.

"So how is life with your child bride?" Deirdre asks. She always did like to stir things up, as if only trouble can make her feel fully alive. It is so often just the two of us now that I have forgotten about this mischievous social tic of hers. "Are you happy?"

"I'm not unhappy," Jack says.

"That's not the same thing."

"What about you?"

Deirdre smiles. "I'm not married."

"I realize that. I mean, are you happy?"

"Christ, Jack." She leans back. "Who knows? Give me some ground rules, here. Are we telling the truth tonight or making ourselves look good?"

"You're assuming there's a difference."

Out of the corner of my eye I see a man approaching and look up, but it is a stranger, not Sam. The chair beside me remains empty.

Jack turns to me. "How are the girls?"

"They're great." I want to tell him how children change your stake in the world, certainly in your marriage, how it sometimes feels—this afternoon, tonight—that you are in a fragile boat together and every instinct is to right it, keep it afloat no matter what, how the fear that you will make the wrong move, tip it over, can still the breath in your lungs. But I don't. Instead, I tell him about Phoebe's sweet forgetfulness and Claire's impending teendom, about their quirks and their attributes. Still, I can tell they are abstractions to him, these children, these heartstrings of mine.

"What about you?" Deirdre asks Jack when I have bored them enough. She picks up her tangle of meticulously layered hair and lets it cascade down, an unconscious habit that surfaces whenever she is nervous or hesitant. Once, in our early years in New York, she cut it into a short, asymmetrical bob, a style that was enjoying a thankfully brief vogue for about five weeks one spring; her hand would unconsciously reach for the missing locks and then fall, dejected, to her side, her fingers twitching longingly. She hasn't had short hair since. "We keep waiting for a birth announcement," she says, with a coyness that doesn't quite hide her genuine curiosity.

"Deirdre," I warn.

"Relax. It's just us."

"It's fine," Jack reassures me. He turns to Deirdre. "No, no kids. It's not that I don't want them, I do. Very much. But Alice wanted to finish her PhD first and now . . ."

"Now what?"

"Let's say it's up for discussion."

"How romantic," Deirdre remarks.

We start in on another round of martinis. By now, Sam is forty minutes late; his absence has solidified into a fact we are all dancing around.

I begin to think about what I will do, what I will say, if he doesn't come. I begin to think about what it will mean.

"I think we should open presents," I announce defiantly.

"Are you sure?" Jack asks.

I nod and Deirdre and I tear at our boxes. Inside each there is a heavy silver frame with an identical photograph: the four of us on Jack's twenty-second birthday. It was taken with his clunky old Minolta set on timer and we had the hurried, too-close faces that come when you are rushing to outrun the shutter. We were tumbling onto each other, our heads bent at lopsided angles, our eyes glassy and wide. It would be easy, looking at the picture now, to mistake all frantic energy for happiness.

"God, we were so young," I observe.

Deirdre glances at the photo again, then leans forward on her elbows, her head resting heavily in the palm of her right hand, her sloe eyes tipped up. "Jack, can I ask you a question?"

"Of course."

"Why were you so absolute? All those years ago. Why did it have to be all or nothing? I never really understood."

"You mean about moving to Cambridge with me?"

"Yes."

I have vanished from the table, a forgotten witness on the other side of a two-way mirror.

"I loved you. I wanted to be with you," Jack says simply. "Why couldn't you have just moved with me?"

"The fashion business is here."

"You had no interest in the fashion business at the time," he reminds her.

Deirdre nods, acknowledging the truth of this. "What would I have done there? Besides being your girlfriend, I mean."

"You would have found something. I would have helped you."

"You backed me into a corner."

"I was scared of losing you," he admits quietly. "I thought if you were in another city you'd just drift away. Find someone else."

She smiles sadly. "You know what I was scared of? Turning into my mother. Completely dependent." She looks away for just an instant. "The irony is that I seem to be turning into my father instead."

"What's that supposed to mean?"

"Never mind." She raises her head, brightens. "Okay, your turn." She reaches into her bag and pulls out a small box wrapped in pale green rice paper and hands it to him. "Happy birthday."

He smiles, already pleased, no matter what it might hold.

"Go on, open it," she prompts.

He unties the bow carefully and removes the paper. Inside there is an ornately embroidered box. It occurs to me that the box itself might be the present, exquisite but empty, but Jack undoes its golden latch. Inside, there are two luminous glass marbles of swirling cat's-eye sitting in navy velvet beds. He picks one up, its concentric spheres of opacity and light shimmering in his hand. He places it back in the box as tenderly as an infant and leans over to kiss Deirdre. "Thank you."

"Do they have some significance I'm not privy to?" I ask.

Deirdre smiles. "Don't you remember how Jack always used to roll marbles about in his hands whenever he was nervous or trying to make a decision? It drove me crazy, actually." She turns to him. "Do you still do that?"

"It was tennis balls, mostly, not marbles."

"Really? I seem to remember there was some marble action going on."

He smiles. "Maybe."

"Well," I say, pulling out the gift I have brought, "my present has absolutely no significance whatsoever." I was totally stumped, after all I know Jack and yet I don't. The best I could do was throw money at the situation and hope for the best. Jack unwraps the mahogany leather billfold and thanks me with perfect if uninflected cordiality.

Jack turns back to Deirdre. "Your birthday is coming up next month, isn't it?"

"Don't remind me. It's still seven weeks away."

"What do you want?" he asks.

"Eternal youth."

"Don't you have to bargain with the devil for that?"

"I'm willing to negotiate," Deirdre replies.

The detritus of the wrapping paper and ribbons lies on the table, our glasses are once more empty.

"Let's go ahead and order without Sam," I say. "His plane must have gotten delayed."

"Are you sure?"

I nod.

We are studying the menus in silence when Deirdre's cell, buried in her bag, begins to ring.

Jack frowns in disapproval, he does not want interruptions, her attention scattered away from him. He was never someone who liked to have his carefully plotted orchestrations altered. Jack was, is, many things—but easygoing isn't one of them. Deirdre glances at him and sees this in the furrow of his brows, considers it for a second, and flips open the phone with a slyly rebellious grin. Perhaps the blueprint, the essential tenor of our relationships, is set from the first established syncopation, no matter how many years have passed.

He leans back and listens as she begins to speak. It is impossible not to.

"Ben, hi."

Jack scrupulously studies the wine list without looking up.

"Sorry, it's kind of noisy in here," Deirdre says, a bit too loudly. "I'm out with an old college friend. My college boyfriend, actually, Jack." She looks up and smiles at Jack, touching his arm conspiratorially. "No. It'll be too late. I'll call you tomorrow."

She hangs up. "Sorry."

"Who's Ben?" Jack asks.

"Someone I see."

"Is it serious?"

"Seriously dysfunctional," she answers with a dismissive laugh. "But you don't really want me to regale you with tales of my romantic misadventures."

"There's nothing I'd like more."

"I'm not falling into that trap, buddy. I still remember the time you didn't talk to me for a week when you thought I was flirting with the psych professor. I'd like for us to at least make it through dinner."

"You were flirting with the psych professor."

"Maybe I was. But you certainly didn't have to stick your fist through a wall."

"The folly of youth. Luckily we outgrow that kind of behavior."

"Yes, now we have reason and antidepressants and pass it off as maturity."

Jack smiles. "I would like to hear about Ben," he says. "If you want to tell me. I want to know what's going on in your life."

"At the moment I don't seem to have the vaguest idea what's going on in my life. At least not that part of it. Maybe we should call Ben and ask him."

"I'm not that curious."

The waiter, who had gotten his hopes up when he saw us open the menus and is looming sourly a few feet away, clears his throat.

Chastised, we place our orders.

"Shall I remove the other place setting?" he asks peremptorily while taking our menus.

"No," Jack answers. "Leave it for now."

I stare down at my napkin, mortified, while Jack discusses matters with the sommelier in a lingo I suspect is meant to impress but is largely Chinese to me. Business taken care of, he returns to Deirdre. "Tell me about your store."

"I'm not getting rich but it's great to have something of my own," she replies. "I'm sure this comes as a shock to you but I hated answering to other people."

He laughs. "Well, you never really did."

"Of course I did. You just didn't see it."

While Deirdre goes on to describe Aperçu, its layout and sartorial point of view, I spot Sam, making his way to us.

My fingers, which I had unconsciously been clenching beneath the table until they ached, relax as an immense relief washes through me.

But the overriding anxiety that had filled up every cell is quickly replaced with a burning resentment.

"I'm sorry. I circled LaGuardia forever. Flying these days is a nightmare." The words rush out as he leans down to kiss me. I dutifully offer up my cheek, but I do not, cannot, look him in the eyes.

Jack rises and they do that weird male pat-on-back, not-quite-a-hug thing before sitting back down. Sam leans across the table and smiles hello at Deirdre. "Miss Cushing."

"Mr. Barkley."

The two have a sardonic relationship that I have grown used to over the years despite wishing it were otherwise. They challenge and often amuse each other, I'm just not sure how much they actually like each other, though they are both too savvy to make those feelings explicit to me.

Jack calls the waiter over and Sam hastily orders, barely looking at the menu. An awkward silence ensues as we struggle to reestablish a rhythm, creakily widening the circle to include him.

"So," Jack says, "Lisa said you were in Chicago for a story."

"Yes. A profile on Eliot Wells."

I jiggle my foot up and down beneath the table while I listen to my husband lie.

"Interesting guy. Have you met him yet?"

"No. I've talked to a lot of his people, but he's still giving me the runaround. We can't agree on the terms. He has a lot of ridiculous demands, including veto power over his quotes, which I have a policy of never granting."

"Well, surely once he realizes your impeccable journalistic integrity . . ."

"Journalism and integrity are not mutually exclusive," Sam counters. "Which, my friend, is more than I can say for corporate law."

They are teasing each other, smiling as they jab to soften the intent, and yet.

The evening is punctuated with land mines left behind years ago; even now, the war long over, they could explode at any moment.

Jack and Sam never really chose each other; they were thrown together because of the women they were with. There were flashes of almost unintentional camaraderie and eventually there was the thread of shared experiences but there remained an undercurrent of, if not precisely distrust, then watchfulness. It wasn't always that way. It seemed at first that they would be good friends. I know that Sam would have liked that, but Jack, the ambitious scholarship kid, had a tendency to poke at him, subtly prodding at his ease and his belonging, so seemingly secure in his blueblood background, which surprised and wounded Sam. In fact, Sam had watched his family's fortunes shrink irrevocably before his eyes. His father had lost most of their money not in some great operatic downfall of bad investments but through the slow deterioration of wealth that happens through generations of benign neglect, a gradual reduction that is politely ignored for decades until, finally, it can't be. The pedigree is still there and informs every step, a hidden code that lack of cash cannot erase, but it is like a chocolate Easter bunny that you only realize is hollow once you've bitten into it.

Jack does not pick up the gauntlet. "Seriously," he says, "I get a kick out of it whenever I see your byline. I realize I'm just an outside-the-Beltway plebe but I still find it impressive. You've done some terrific stories."

Sam cocks his head to the side. "You weren't a plebe even when you were a plebe. But thanks. So, do you still have the ability to go days without sleep and ace everything that comes your way?"

"I'm not exactly taking tests these days."

"Some of your courtroom summations might count as oral exams." Sam turns to Deirdre. "Did you know that Jack has a reputation for shredding the opposition without ever raising his voice? He's so soft-spoken and polite, they don't realize what's happening until it's over."

"I'm not sure if I should be insulted or flattered," Jack says.

"Flattered," Sam replies. "I mean it. You've gotten convictions for a lot of corporate scum."

"And I've gotten others off the hook."

"I thought in the interest of harmony I'd ignore that," Sam replies.

When the food comes, we speak of politics and movies, steroid scandals and real-estate deals, but we keep circling back to us, as if our past selves are looming in the background, waiting to crash the party. Do you remember the time, I wonder whatever happened to, I never told you but, a magic carpet transporting us back in time, eclipsing the rock-strewn present with all that we don't know about each other, all that we don't ask, all that we would rather forget. And while we talk, we drink. If in the beginning the high alcohol content served to ease our nerves, it has, by this point in the evening, spread over us like a sticky syrup, dulling the inhibitions and sharpening the needs. There will be a price to pay, I know that, but it does not change the course.

We are back where we once were, in the past, reliving the endless cheap spaghetti dinners and the dizzying all-nighters, the classes we cut and the tests we crammed for, the professors, some stellar, some wasted, and the marathon bouts of conversation when everything we said seemed to matter so very much. We turn the kaleidoscope of recollections and turn it again, savoring fragments from all those times that the four of us were together as well as the times we split off into various duets forged from friendship and desire.

"Do you remember that trip we took to the Adirondacks?" Jack says. "What was the name of the guy with the lodge there? You know, the one whose family made all that money in elevators?"

"Michael, Michael Parsons." Deirdre pulls the name out of the shrouded ether of stonewashed memory.

I groan, knowing what is coming.

"I can still see you sitting buck naked on the rocks, refusing to jump," Jack nudges me. They are all laughing now.

"I'm crazy but I'm not suicidal. And it wasn't rocks, it was a forty-foot cliff."

After hiking all morning, we had come across a ravine and, in a fit of collegial daring, stripped off our clothes. That was risky enough, as far as I was concerned. While everyone else plunged into the icy water below I remained on the edge, my arms wrapped tightly around my knees, getting eaten alive by black flies but immobilized by fear. They have found this visual hilarious ever since. Needless to say, I don't.

Sam reaches over and squeezes my shoulder affectionately, but I recoil. He tries once more to reach me, to connect, and then, perplexed, he stops. This, of course, annoys me further; I don't want him to touch me but I don't want him to stop trying, either.

"Yeah, well, shall we discuss your reaction when that snake fell out of the ceiling onto your bed?" I retort, aiming my words at Jack and Deirdre. "Seeing the two of you naked twice in one day was more than I could bear."

After they went back to bed, Sam and I took our sleeping bags out to the vast lawn and lay there until sunrise, Sam pointing out all the constellations while I pretended to see them. At dawn, chilled and starving, we hijacked our host's car and drove to the fishing supply store in town, the only one open, where we devoured bags of stale peanuts and kissed with salty, chapped lips.

"I can't imagine why Parsons never invited us back," Deirdre says. "Snotty bastard."

The laughter, the memory, slowly trickle away from us.

"It was good then, wasn't it?" Jack says quietly.

We are each, for a moment, lost in our own thoughts.

When the dessert plates littered with half-eaten cakes are cleared, Deirdre stands up. "I have to pee desperately," she announces.

"I always did love your impeccable manners," Jack remarks, amused.

"Really? I seem to remember it was other things."

"Please," Sam says. "There's been quite enough oversharing for one night."

Deirdre looks at me. "Are you coming?"

I rise a bit unsteadily. I can feel my legs wobbling and I move slowly, with a self-conscious determination to appear at least semi-sober. I'm sure I fail miserably.

"What's up with you and Sam tonight?" Deirdre asks when we are standing side by side, washing our hands and staring at ourselves in the mirror, or the expressionist versions of ourselves we have become.

"What do you mean?"

"You've hardly looked at him all night."

"Don't be ridiculous."

"You're not still obsessing about that phone call the other day, are you?"

I glance over at Deirdre. I am about to tell her about Sam's incontrovertible lie but abruptly change my mind. I love Deirdre but I don't trust her, not tonight, when she seems hell-bent on provocation. I change the subject. "Why did you do that with Ben?" I ask as I apply lipstick, getting a gooey slash of "Sugarspun Mauve" on my front tooth.

"Do what?"

"Make it sound as if you were alone with Jack."

"Did I? Well, a little jealousy would be good for him."

"Yesterday you were all over him. Tonight you are . . . well, I don't know what you are. You're making my head spin."

"I believe it's the martinis and three bottles of wine that are making your head spin."

"They're certainly not helping," I admit.

"I told you we got into one of our great relationship debates last night." Deirdre sighs. "It's just so exhausting. I'm beginning to think we're better off not talking. I'm much happier with him when I'm totally deluded."

"Now there's a workable relationship strategy," I mutter.

"He drives me crazy," she continues. "Basically, he's not seeing other women right now but it sounds more like an accidental occurrence than an actual policy. He refuses to say he won't. It's like we're having an affair, even though we're both single. The pathetic thing is when I said that to him, he liked the idea. He found it exciting. I'm terrified of spending years waiting for him to want me, really want me, just me, and waking up one day to find out he never will. Or that it's someone else he wants. Someone younger. I just don't have that kind of time to waste. Not now. Not anymore." She smooths the neckline of her dress around her pronounced collarbone and turns her eyes away from me. "The problem is that I still want him."

"I know."

"Lisa?"

"Yes?"

"What if I made a mistake all those years ago?"

"What do you mean?"

"With Jack. What if he was the one I was meant to be with?"

"Don't do this, Deirdre."

"Do what?"

"He's married."

"I know." She studies herself in the mirror. The only damage the evening seems to have caused is a narrowing of her eyes, tipping her usually even features the slightest bit askew. Somehow this manages to make her appear quirky and endearing. "I know. But I can't help but wonder."

"It's just that kind of night."

She looks down, away from me. "Maybe."

When we get back to the table, Jack has signed the bill and is carefully folding the receipt around his platinum AmEx. We are about to rise when he motions the waiter to come back. "Do you mind?" he asks, pulling the slimmest of digital cameras from his pocket. We squeeze in next to each other, our heads touching, our smiles lopsided and smeary. "I'll e-mail a copy to all of you tomorrow," Jack promises.

The four of us make our way through the near-empty dining room and out into the cool September evening.

"God, I miss New York," Jack says, glancing down the block at the softly lit restaurants and expensive shops shuttered till morning. He returns his gaze to us. "Would anyone like to go for a nightcap?"

"We have to get home for the babysitter," Sam replies, before checking with me—not that I want to go, but it would have been nice to have been consulted.

Jack nods. He is watching Deirdre, waiting.

She smiles. "Sure, why not?"

I kiss Jack and Deirdre good night and then watch as they walk slowly away down the darkened street.

"No good is going to come of that," Sam says, watching, too.

I turn to face him.

The night is not over—for any of us.

NINE

The city is suddenly still around us, the very air sinking into a deeper shade of night. Jack and Deirdre have wrapped up the best part of the evening and taken it away with them. We are left with only each other.

The words, the questions, that have been pricking my skin push to the surface. But just as I am about to speak at last, Sam begins walking east, his usual fast and loping gait unaffected by the eighty-proof dinner. Like most native New Yorkers, he weaves and slices around people without thinking, while I have a tendency to hang back, tentative about boundaries only I can see. I do a little two-step to catch up with him, the sharp coolness of the air bestowing a momentary if false illusion of clarity.

"You realize that entire show was for Deirdre's sake," Sam remarks, glancing up the street for a cab while he talks. "Jack has always been like a little kid playing dress up. It's not real. Nothing about him is real. I can't believe she falls for it every time."

I have no interest in a post-prandial assessment, I have something else in mind. Still, I get sidetracked by a surge of annoyance at Sam's transparent jealousy of Jack, a puerile blend of superiority and insecurity. "Every time? That's ridiculous. They haven't seen each other in years."

"You know what I mean." His arm hovers midair, futilely trying to wave down a cab that is not only off-duty but has a couple making out in the backseat.

"No," I reply angrily. "I have no goddamned idea what you mean."

He whips around to me, stung.

His eyes narrow as they always do when he is bracing himself. These are the things you know about someone after so many years; their warning signs, their tells, the tics that once charmed you and are now irritants, stumbling blocks to affection. "I don't know what the hell your problem is tonight but I'm getting pretty sick of being on the receiving end," he spits out.

Adrenaline pumps through me, making me think I am braver than I am. "Where were you today?" I demand.

"What do you mean? I was in Chicago. I told you that."

"Really?"

"What is this about, Lisa?"

"I called your office. I had a very interesting little chat with Kathy."

Sam says nothing. Like any good journalist, he is trained not to volunteer information before ascertaining precisely what the other person knows. His strategic use of silence has, through the years, given him the upper hand in our arguments, those marital spats that seem so inconsequential, so miniaturized in retrospect. He switches his weight from one foot to the other and glances back to the street for a cab, like the unconvincing piece of busywork a novice actor indulges in.

"Tell me," I continue. "How's that Wells piece coming?"

His shoulders tense but before he can answer—before he has to answer—a taxi screeches to a halt beside him. Relieved, Sam opens the back door, motioning for me to climb in.

I do not move.

"Get in," he says.

I remain frozen.

"Lisa, get in the cab."

I do not want to give in to even this simple request. Nevertheless,

I exhale in protest and step reluctantly forward, jerking my legs angrily as I slide in with an ostentatious show of displeasure.

Sam gets in beside me, closes the door and gives the driver our address.

"You didn't answer my question," I say when the cab lurches forward.

He turns to me. "Why don't you just come out with whatever it is you want to ask me?"

"I wouldn't know where to begin."

"What?"

I turn to face him. "Okay, let's start with this. Kathy told me the Wells piece was killed."

"I see."

"Do you mind telling me what the hell you've been up to?"

Sam slumps against the backseat. "All right, yes, the Wells piece was killed. I'm sorry. I should have told you."

"Where were you today?"

"I was in Chicago. Simon was wrong about killing the piece. I can feel it. But the only way to convince him is to get more proof, so I've been working on it on my own. If I can just get one of the board members to lose their amnesia, I'll have a chance at cracking this."

"Why didn't you just tell me this?"

"I was going to tell you this morning but then Kathy walked in and I didn't want her to overhear. I've got enough trouble with Borofsky being spoon-fed all the best assignments. If Simon thinks I'm spending time on this, I'm screwed."

"You could have called me from the airport, you could have found a way."

"Maybe I wanted to surprise you, maybe I wanted you to be proud of me for a change, okay?"

"I'm always proud of you."

"Really? Because it hasn't felt that way lately. I haven't exactly gotten the feeling you trust my instincts on this one."

I'm not quite sure how I ended up on the defensive here. "Why should I trust you? You've been lying to me," I retort.

"You're convoluting the issue."

"No. Trust is the issue. What else haven't you told me?"

"Nothing. Nothing else."

We ride a little bit in silence. The cabbie's radio is tuned to a French station and the announcer's mellifluous voice drifts through the scratched glass divider, soothing and incomprehensible.

I turn to my husband and look at his profile as the city moves in slow motion by us. "Sam?"

"Yes?"

"Are you having an affair?"

"That's ridiculous."

"Are you?"

He covers my hand with his large, slightly calloused fingers. "No, of course not," he answers softly. "Lisa, I was wrong. I should have told you. I should have told you all of this. But with everything going on, I didn't want to make you more anxious than you already are."

"What's that supposed to mean?"

"You're worried enough about your job. I don't need you worrying about mine, too. That's all it was. I love you. You have to know that."

The transfusion of nervous energy that rushed through me just minutes ago deserts me in one great whoosh. The heat of the cab, the alcohol, the conversation all suddenly leave me dizzy and depleted. "I'm not sure what I know anymore," I say quietly.

We ride the remaining eight blocks in silence, staring out of our separate windows, his hand still on mine like a suspension bridge across the distance. When the taxi pulls up in front of our apartment building, Sam pays the driver and we get out without a word.

The apartment is quiet as we close the front door gently behind us. I peer into the living room but there is no one there. In a minute, I hear footsteps and Marissa pads down the hallway from the bedroom, yanking down her three-inch-long white denim mini as she approaches. An art major from Indianapolis, she is, I suspect, more committed to dressing the part than actually going to classes. She is playing at New York, one of those girls who will go home within a couple of years with a deep relief she will never quite own up to.

"What time did Phoebe and Claire go to bed?" I ask.

"Around ten?" She obviously has no idea. Her rather casual relationship to time—she has a seemingly philosophic objection to watches—is surely why she is the girls' favorite sitter.

Sam pulls out his wallet to pay her.

After Marissa leaves, I walk back into the bedroom and see that she has left a half-eaten bag of barbecue potato chips by the computer. Tiny crumbs phosphorescent with grease are nestled into the keyboard like caulking.

The sight makes me more than a little nauseous and I realize that I am still very drunk. I kick off my shoes, go into the bathroom and wash down two Motrin with a large glass of Emergen-C, then look around for anything else I can take that might make the morning more bearable. I spend far too long pondering the benefits of drinking a few extra glasses of water versus having to get up to pee five times. It is rather depressing to have reached the age when you begin to regret the price you will pay even before the night has worn off.

When I return to the bedroom, Sam is sitting on the edge of the bed, his elbows resting heavily on his knees, waiting for me. "Lisa, I really am sorry," he says. "The last thing in the world I wanted to do was upset you."

I sit down beside him. "Sam, what's our deal?"

"What do you mean?"

"The other day, at breakfast, Ben said every relationship has a deal. What's ours?"

"I wouldn't exactly call Ben an expert on love."

"That's not the point."

"What's Deirdre and Ben's deal? 'I'll pretend I've changed and you'll pretend to believe me'?"

Like all couples, we have always found a certain satisfaction in defining ourselves in opposition to other, less successful unions. That doesn't seem so easy now. "Sam."

There is a long silence.

"We're not like that," he says at last. "We don't have a deal. Not the way Ben means anyway."

"I need to be able to trust you."

"You can."

I want so much to believe him.

Despite myself, I feel a softening around the edges, a malleability, my borders growing permeable, letting him in. I don't know if this is good or bad, right or wrong. It is so hard to tell when it comes to love if you are being blindly delusional or are simply accepting the flaws and compromises, the disappointments and prosaic compensations necessary to stay together.

Sam slides out of his pants and leans back, reaching for me, stroking my arm, but I am not ready to lie beside him. He stares at the ceiling until his eyes slowly drift shut. As I sit watching his chest rise and fall I feel overwhelmingly bereft, deserted by Jack and Deirdre, deserted, too, not by my husband but by my own feelings for him, by the love that I know is still strong within me but feels just out of reach.

I leave him sleeping and go to sit in the living room, the sole light left on creating a cone of near-whiteness in the otherwise darkened room. For a long while, I remain completely still, trying to sort through the remnants of the evening, but they continually shift, realign, I cannot quite grasp them.

It occurs to me that I didn't ask Sam if he found out anything about Wells, if, after all this, the trip was even worth it.

Though I hate to admit it, he is right, I don't trust his instincts on this story. I cannot help but think he is being reckless to jeopardize his job over something no one else seems to feel has one bit of merit. It smacks of desperation. Or sophomoric grandstanding. Or both.

But if I tell him this it will only confirm his argument that I have no faith in him. In a convoluted way I will be proving him right, justifying his lie.

I'm stuck.

Which annoys me further. Or would, if I felt well enough to be actively annoyed.

Instead, I dig my BlackBerry out of my bag and open the latest e-mail from David Forrester. Not one has mentioned business.

TEN

The next morning is worse than I had imagined.

Smog clogs my mouth, wraps around my tongue, there is a rhythmic pounding at the base of my skull, an oceanic sloshing in my stomach. I have, in the recent semi-abstemious years of good behavior and scrupulous observance of adult duties, forgotten what a real hangover feels like. The last time an evening's repercussions were this devastating I had the luxury of staying in bed all morning, it was that long ago. I make a solemn vow never to drink again, wash down more Motrin with a cup of coffee and go to wake the girls.

The novelty of the new school year has completely worn away in less than a week. Judging by the deep and stubborn sleep both girls are lost in I guess that they went to bed far later than anyone will admit to, an act made worse by the fact that their internal clocks have not yet reset to school time. It will take at least two visits to each of their rooms before feet hit the floor.

I leave Phoebe sitting up with a baffled look on her face, as if she cannot quite understand how the morning happened and what it all might mean, and check on Claire. She is propped up on one elbow, attempting to flatten her newly shorn bangs with the palm of her hand, a look of severe displeasure contorting her features. This is not a good sign. If Claire is having a bad hair day, the whole family will suffer.

"You know," she grumbles, barely glancing up at me, "everyone else gets to wake up at least a half hour later."

"Who is everyone else?"

"Everyone. In my class."

It is true that a good ninety-five percent of the girls live within walking distance of Weston on the Upper East Side, their routes lined with friendly doormen who have been watching their progress since they were toddlers, a built-in security system at once intrusive and comforting. They not only get to sleep later but easily drift to one another's apartments after school, their social alliances formed by proximity as much as predilection. My guess is that this irks Claire more than the discrepancy in rising time. I do sometimes worry about the geography of her world and its ramifications, torn between wanting her to fit in and distaste at the other girls' blithe entitlement. But this morning is not one of those times.

"I realize your life is totally miserable," I reply. "You can tell your therapist all about it. But right now you have to get dressed."

"I don't have a therapist."

"Of course, how could I forget? In that case, put all complaints in writing and I will consider them at a later date. In the meantime, get ready for school."

Claire scowls at me. Parental sarcasm is rarely appreciated.

I go back to the kitchen, get out one box of cereal that contains a treasure trove of sugar for Phoebe and another filled with unappealing brown twigs that Claire will pretend to eat. I quickly scan the *Times* for stories that each might be drawn in by—a review of yesterday's fashion shows for Claire, a story on the latest human attempts at flight replete with aerodynamic graphics for Phoebe—and put them at their places. Though I began the habit a few months ago to trick the girls into reading the paper, neither has shown the slightest inclination to glance at the front page. For all their connectedness—computers, Internet, texting—for all their pricey schooling, they know absolutely nothing about current events; the full extent of their global awareness seems to be occasional references to "that dude in Iran." My motives aren't entirely selfless, though: I have never particularly liked talking in the morning and this gives me a reasonably valid excuse to avoid conversation and pass it off as education.

After two more warning calls the girls finally stumble into the kitchen and wordlessly take their places, pour milk into their bowls and begin to spoon cereal desultorily into their tired little mouths.

I sit down beside them and pour some cereal but cannot bring myself to eat it. After playing with it for a couple of minutes, I carry it to the sink, dump the whole glop out and then have to dig around the drain to excise the soggy circles. My hand is filled with cereal mush when the phone rings. Startled, I drop it all on the floor, where two oaty blobs land between my toes.

"I'll get it," Claire volunteers eagerly. "It's probably Lily."

Yesterday, the two of them engaged in a pre-school fashion conference that engendered a frantic reassessment of outfits. I tap my watch to remind Claire of the time but she ignores me and grabs the phone. Her anticipation rapidly turns to grumpiness.

"It's for you."

"Who is it?"

"How should I know? Some guy."

I wipe my hands on the not entirely clean dish towel and take the phone from her. "Hello?"

"I didn't wake you, did I?" Jack asks.

"I wish."

"I figured with the girls and all. Listen, I was wondering, can you meet me for breakfast before I catch the shuttle? I'd love a chance to talk to you alone."

"I don't know, Jack. I have to take the girls to school and . . ."

"You do not have to take us to school," Claire interjects loudly enough to be heard in New Jersey.

I shoot her a look.

"Please," Jack continues. "It's important. My hotel is just a couple of blocks from your office."

"How do you know where my office is?"

"I just assumed it's midtown."

I sigh. "Okay."

After agreeing to meet in his hotel dining room, I hang up and turn to my daughters, who are regarding me with supreme satisfaction. "All right, all right. You can go on your own today."

"We'll be fine, Mom," Phoebe assures me.

"I know. But it's my job to worry about you, okay?"

"You'll get used to it," Claire says.

"You never get used to anxiety. It's the baby chick of emotions. It reinvents itself every day. I think we've had more than enough role reversal for one day. Go brush your teeth."

The girls are just finishing up when Sam walks into the kitchen. He snatches them both back for a kiss and watches them march off. He turns to me only when they are completely out of sight.

"Who was that on the phone?" he asks, pouring himself a mug of coffee. He comes close enough to make me think he is going to kiss me good morning but stops a couple of inches away, unsure of himself, of me.

"Jack."

"What did he want?"

"He asked if I would meet him for breakfast."

"Why?"

"I don't know. To catch up."

"I thought we had pretty much accomplished that last night."

The Motrin still hasn't kicked in and the spilled cereal has dried into a sticky paste on my foot. "We're friends, okay? He's hardly ever in town. What's the big deal?"

"Do us both a favor and dial back the attitude."

"Sorry."

Sam looks at me and decides not to engage further. Like chalking a wife's emotions up to PMS, there's no mileage in it. He's not a stupid man. I leave him thumbing through the newspapers and go to shower, already regretting my tone.

It's not that I have forgiven Sam for lying about the Wells story, that will take a bit more time. But I cannot help feeling relief. It could have been so much worse, his crime, his confession, it could have been something we could not find our way back from. And I do want a way back—to us, to who we used to be—I want that more than anything. I hold my neck up to the spray of hot water, letting it spread over my shoulders.

Feeling somewhat better, I dry off, pull on a dress, the easiest thing I can find, and return to the kitchen. The girls have their jackets on and are cramming the last of their homework, pens and God knows what else into their backpacks. A half-eaten Snickers bar spills from Phoebe's outer pocket.

"I'll need that to get through assembly this morning," she says matter-of-factly, as if it has been medically prescribed.

"Are you allowed to eat in the auditorium?" I ask skeptically.

This, of course, does not warrant an answer. I watch mutely as she stuffs it back into her bag, too tired to protest. "You have your MetroCards?"

"Yes, Mom."

"Phone?"

"I don't have one," Phoebe reminds me petulantly.

"Yes, I'm quite aware of that, sweetie. Claire?"

Claire rolls her eyes.

"Evidence, please." Claire has lied about her cell phone more than once. Just last week she told me I couldn't reach her because she had forgotten to turn it on. Unfortunately, Lily called an hour later to say that Claire had left it at her house. Two days ago.

We all watch as she digs around in her backpack and comes up empty-handed.

"This is not inspiring faith," I remark.

"I'll find it later."

"You're not leaving the house without it."

"Okay, fan out, girls," Sam instructs. "I'll call it from the kitchen phone."

Phoebe, Claire and I stand in different corners of the apartment, listening. The phone is finally discovered vibrating forlornly under Claire's bed along with last year's math textbook, a pair of dirty socks and a necklace she had accused her sister of stealing.

"I told you I didn't take it," Phoebe snipes.

Claire slips it around her neck, ignoring her.

"Stay together," I remind them when they are finally ready to leave.

"You make it sound like we're going to Antarctica."

"Don't be silly. The Upper East Side is far chillier." I kiss them both good-bye. "Call me when you get to school."

"They'll be fine," Sam says, standing behind me as the front door closes.

"I know."

He rests his hands lightly on my shoulders. "Listen, about last night. I really am sorry."

"Sam, you know how I said I need to be able to trust you?"

"Yes."

"Well, I want you to know that you can trust me, too. I do have faith in you."

"I know."

We embrace, careful of each other's soft spots, the bruises still tender. For now we will fit ourselves around them, touching, connecting where we can until they fade.

"You never told me last night, how did it go in Chicago?" I ask as we separate.

"You never asked."

"Let's just say it wasn't the first question on my mind. Did you find out anything on Wells?"

"Not really."

"What does that mean?"

"Don't worry, Lisa. I'm not going to run this into the ground. I might make one or two more calls but I'm not going to immolate my career on this particular sword."

I try not to look too relieved. "So, what are you up to today?" I realize this comes out all wrong. There is a subtext now, a sheet of ice beneath our feet that hadn't been there before, altering the simplest words, twisting the intent.

"I'll be in the office all day. I have to work on a story on the subprime mortgage disaster." He smiles. "I'm sure Kathy will verify, if you'd like."

"I wasn't checking up on you yesterday. I just wanted to tell you where we were meeting for dinner."

"I know. I'm teasing."

"We haven't gotten to the laughing-about-it stage yet," I inform him.

"Right. Tell me when we get there."

"You'll be the first to know."

"What are the chances of that happening anytime soon?"

"You'd like that, wouldn't you?"

"Damn right, babe."

I smile, we both do, anxious to defang the querulous tangle of misunderstandings, to hasten it into anecdote.

Fifteen minutes—and an exorbitant cab fare—later I walk into the hotel's hushed dining room. A few people are finishing up business breakfasts but most of the diners are well-heeled tourists of a certain age in the sensible shoes and brightly colored suits indigenous to non–New Yorkers. Later, at tea, they will be surrounded by glossy shopping bags filled with the day's spoils. I glance down the row of pale yellow–clothed tables dotted with heavy china pots of jams and marmalades, silver pitchers of coffee and tea. It has occurred to me that I might find Deirdre with Jack, wearing her dress from last night and an insouciant, satisfied half smile. I don't relish the prospect.

I spot Jack alone at a banquette, glancing down at *The Wall Street Journal* and sipping his coffee. He appears still dewy from a shower, and none the worse for wear. In fact, he looks downright cheerful. Obviously, we have had different reactions to last night. We kiss hello and I sit down.

"Thanks for coming," he says. "I realize it was short notice."

"Of course."

"Last night was wonderful, wasn't it?" There is an expression I can't quite place in the set of his eyes, his mouth. And then I realize what it is: optimism.

I look at him, wondering exactly how wonderful last night was. "Where did you and Deirdre end up going for a drink?"

"I don't know. Some hole in the wall."

When the waiter comes to take our order I briefly consider being virtuous and getting oatmeal but opt for French toast. With maple syrup. I don't care, I need to carbo-load this morning.

Jack and I busy ourselves with napkins, spoons, coffee. It is harder here, with just the two of us illuminated by so much bright, unforgiving daylight. I take my cell phone out and put it on the table. The girls should be off the bus in five minutes, tops. "So is Alice planning a big celebration for you this weekend?"

"I suppose."

"You don't sound very excited."

He shrugs.

"I personally plan on ignoring the entire thing when it's my turn. No parties, no presents. Valium and a face-lift is all I ask for."

"It's not the birthday," Jack says.

"Oh?"

He studies me closely before speaking. "Things are not going all that well with Alice at the moment."

"I'm sorry. How bad is it?"

"We're not about to win any awards for marital harmony."

"Everyone hits rough patches."

"I realize that." He pauses. "Do you ever wake up and feel like you're living someone else's life?"

"It seems to me you have exactly the life you set out for." Little about Jack has ever appeared accidental to me. But perhaps sadness, regret, desire always take you by surprise, knock you off your game.

"Does it?" he asks. "It's the life I found, anyway. There's a difference."

"Will Alice move here if you get the job?"

"I don't know." He looks away, then back to me. "Lisa, I'm forty years old. Or about to be."

"And?"

"I may not get another chance."

"A chance at what?"

"This. Any of it. I'm just not sure I want to get in deeper if it's not right."

"You've been married to Alice for five years. That's pretty deep."

"Did I tell you we're building a house up on the Cape? Such a cliché. Why is it when a marriage is foundering the first instinct is to renovate or build something when all you really want to do is escape what you already have?" He leans forward. "Tell me, what's Ben like?"

"Deirdre's Ben?"

"Yes. What's his last name?"

"Erickson. What did Deirdre tell you?"

"Not much. But what she did say made him sound like a total jerk."

"They've had a complicated history."

"Don't we all."

"It's beginning to seem that way." I glance down at my resolutely silent phone. "Sorry, I'm waiting for the girls to call."

He nods dismissively. "Is she serious about him?"

"Don't you think you should be asking her these questions?"

"I did."

"And?"

"She deserves to be happy."

I can feel Jack watching me, taking my measure. He is used to ferreting out information but there is, beneath the cool exterior, a tangible vulnerability I have rarely seen. Even now, after all these years, Deirdre leaves him exposed. He puts down his fork. "She cheated on me."

"Deirdre?" I am genuinely surprised. Surely I would have heard about this.

"No. Alice. With a professor in her department, the chairman, actually," he adds. "For over a year. I found her diaries."

"Oh God, Jack, I'm sorry. That's awful."

"I'm only half sorry. Maybe it was a mistake from the beginning."

"Why did you marry her?"

"I don't know. Because it was time. Because she's nice."

"No one marries someone just because they're nice."

"Yes. You do. At a certain point you do. All her head-in-the-clouds stuff, living in the fifteenth century. She seemed so gentle. Apparently I was wrong on that count, too." He shifts his weight. "I'm not saying I didn't love her."

"Past tense?"

He takes a long time to answer. "Lisa, do you believe in second chances?"

"People make mistakes. I'd like to think forgiveness is at least an option. Is that what Alice wants?"

"I meant Deirdre. Me and Deirdre. Why should we have to pay forever for a mistake we made when we were so young?"

"Jack, I'm not really comfortable talking about this," I tell him. It is past eight thirty. School has already started. The background rumble of maternal anxiety grows stronger, clotting in my veins.

"Please."

"You're married," I remind him.

"Yes, I realize that. But, if I wasn't, do you think it's too late?"

"How can I answer that? I have enough trouble figuring out my own life these days, much less someone else's. Besides, I thought you told me you don't like dealing in hypotheticals."

"Love is always a matter of speculation, isn't it?" He leans closer, his eyes fixed, intent, assessing his jury. "I told you, it's over. My marriage is over."

"Jack." I plead for an out but he remains unmoved.

"I have never been as alive as I was when I was with Deirdre. I realize that sounds ridiculously corny, but it's true. And she feels the same, I know it. Everything since then has felt like a consolation prize. I'm not ready to consign myself to that."

"You were very young."

"Yes, but it hasn't changed. I saw that last night. How many people do you connect with like that in a lifetime? Maybe the job interview, even Alice's affair, were all meant to lead me here."

Love, or at least longing, seems to turn all of us into hopeful idiots, reading tea leaves, knocking on wood, grasping at signs only we can see. "Since when do you believe in fate? I thought you were the supreme rationalist."

"You know Deirdre better than anyone in the world. All I'm asking is for you to find out if I have a chance."

"That's all?" I look at him skeptically.

"Please."

I play with the edges of my napkin, thinking of Deirdre and her dread of ingrained singledom, her narcotic relationship with Ben that I have tried to reason and plead and pry her free from, Ben with his fingerprints and the charmingly lethal hooks he has lodged deep in her psyche. I want her to be happy, safe. Maybe Jack is right that they had been blown off-course and are now blessed with that rarest of gifts: the chance to recover what they were too young and too careless to hold on to. Of course, there is also the possibility that their separation wasn't a mistake at all. Fate, like God, can be claimed by either side in a battle. Still. Alice, the cheating Alice, is a specter to me, easily relegated to the inconsequential. "All right," I tell him. "I'm not promising anything. But I'll see what I can find out."

"You won't tell her about this, will you?"

I shake my head.

"It's Loring, Marcus by the way."

"What is?"

"The law firm I'm interviewing at. But you have to promise not to say anything. To anyone."

"You've decided you can trust me after all?"

"So it seems." Jack smiles broadly. He has gotten what he came here for.

ELEVEN

The doorman, dressed in a crimson and gold uniform as if in exile from a toy army, holds the door open for me as I race out to the street, phone in hand.

It is nine fifteen.

There has been no text message, no voice mail, nothing from the girls.

I speed dial my office, hoping Claire left a message there.

But the only voice is Petra's, saying she'll be late, her excuse so ornate and long-winded that I hang up in the middle of it.

I hurry down the block deciding whether to call the school, weighing the girls' potential embarrassment against my overwhelming need for reassurance. Parental fretfulness, the ever-present chink in the armor, wins out. I call the middle school office and speak to the dean, Mrs. Conason, trying to impart that while, no, it is not an Emergency, it is at least a Situation. She promises to check on the girls' whereabouts and get back to me. Weston has swipe cards the girls tap on entry, a computerized record of what classrooms they can be found in, it won't take all that long. "I'm sure they're fine," she reassures me. She doesn't question or complain, she knows that parents paying five-digit tuition fees expect a certain degree of service and this is one of the more benign requests.

I head into my building and take the elevator to the twelfth floor.

I walk by Carol's office and peer in, but it is empty, all evidence of her erased. Even her name has vanished from the door, leaving behind a dark rectangle where the placard had so recently been, naked and waiting for replacement.

"Morning." I am startled by a gruff male voice coming from the far reaches of the room.

I step hesitantly around the door to discover Mick Favata sitting at the large desk, a neat pile of papers before him. Only the faint scent of Carol's musky perfume remains nestled into the carpet, though I'm sure they will quickly find a way to excise that, too. For a freelance consultant, Favata seems to be staking out some pretty serious territory. Of course, there's the chance that this was the only available desk, a matter of expediency rather than a land grab. But I doubt it. "Good morning."

"Come in, Lisa."

I grasp my cell phone tightly in hand as I enter and take the seat opposite him.

"I've been going through the Elan account." He picks up a sheet of paper with the cosmetic firm's logo embossed in silver script across the top. "This mission statement is incredibly meandering."

"It was only meant for internal use." I realize how lame this sounds.

"Are you happy with your chief writer on this?"

Christ. I have a megawatt hangover. I have managed to consume at least one thousand calories before ten a.m. I have no idea where my daughters are. And I haven't even gotten into my office yet. "Happy" is not exactly the first word that comes to mind. "I think with a bit more guidance she'll step up."

Favata studies me. "We are not here to provide people with a learning curve."

"I'll talk to her."

"Good. I'd also like to discuss Rita Mason with you. I spoke with her manager, Barry, last night. Miss Mason is not happy with the whole soup kitchen idea you presented her with."

"Really? She seemed fine with it."

"To the contrary, I believe she is in danger of leaving the firm. Needless to say, none of us would like to see that happen."

I am about to reply when my cell phone rings, the sound ricocheting off the walls of the near-empty office.

Favata stares archly at me, waiting to see what I do.

It rings again.

And I pick it up.

"Mrs. Barkley?"

"Yes?"

"Both girls are fine. They are in their classes."

"Thank you." Later there will be lectures and threats, there will be privileges removed, but for now I take a deep breath and feel my muscles relax. I turn my attention back to Favata, glowering at me with his viper eyes.

"I don't want to keep you if you're busy." There is malevolent amusement in his tone.

"I'm sorry. That was rude. It's just that . . ." I am about to tell him of my AWOL daughters when I stop myself. I had broken Carol in, proven over time that I can go to school plays, parent-teacher conferences, orthodontist appointments and still get my work done, but I doubt that will be the case with these people. I remember the woman who came up to me on my first day back from maternity leave at a previous job and whispered, "Let me give you some advice. If you need to run off to a pediatrician's visit, tell them you have to go to your doctor, not your baby's. Motherhood makes them nervous." I would like to believe that things have changed. I would also like to believe that at this point in my life I don't have to prove myself all over again. Unfortunately, neither seems to be the case. "Where were we?" I attempt to regroup.

"I'd like to meet with you this afternoon. Say around three. I'm assuming that works for you?"

"Of course." I smile, trying to placate him. He is a deeply scary man.

"Good. We can go over the other accounts then." He returns to his papers. I have been dismissed.

I walk past Petra's unoccupied cubicle and head into my office, wondering how many more Motrin I can take without risking a stomach bleed. I decide to hold off. I do not think this is quite the right day to risk a potentially messy medical mishap. I flip the lights on, put my bag down and settle in at my desk. As my computer boots up I stare, perplexed, as a stark blue-and-white image appears instead of my usual solid aqua screensaver. It takes me a minute to realize that it is a photograph of Merdale's corporate headquarters in Philadelphia. I rear back and glance around for—what? hidden cameras? microphones?

I reconsider the Motrin. My message light is already blinking furiously. Yesterday, there were endless requests for client contract info and budgets from various Merdale people whose names and titles remain a blur. I press "play," dreading what they might want next. Whatever it is will surely eat up my morning. Instead, David Forrester's voice, warm and intimate and more disturbing than it should be, slips into the room. "Now that we've conquered e-mail, I thought we could talk more about the matter at hand in person. Can you meet me for a drink one evening after work next week? Give me a call."

It is a perfectly crafted message, floating a balloon and providing total deniability at the same time. It is not at all clear to me what the matter at hand is. For the rest of the morning, his voice remains lodged, a splinter in the back of my mind. I do not call him back.

I dig out all the press releases we have done on Elan, the media plan, the positioning statement, and read them through. The truth is, Favata has honed in on a real weak spot, one that I have successfully managed to avoid dealing with until now, chalking my inaction up to the faith that it would all right itself rather than my spineless fear of confrontation. The chief writer, Tessa Cardwell, has been slacking off for months. I've given her hints, sent her copy back with polite but detailed notes, shot her e-mails with vague critiques couched in encouragement. All of which have had absolutely no effect, leaving me as annoyed at my own cowardice as I am at her intractable willfulness in ignoring me.

I send her an e-mail now asking her to rewrite the release and add, "I know this is tough but we all have to step up to the plate." The Business 101 platitudes that have seeped into my lexicon make me more than a little nauseous. The Merdale people are not just making me dislike them, they are making me dislike myself.

I send one more e-mail to Nina Stern, the friend who first told me Favata is a thug, albeit one who just happens to be pals with the CEO. "You weren't kidding," I write. "Favata's a total goon. I'm trying to figure out how to deal with him. Can you help me out? You said he was fired? Do you know anyone in Harcourt's London office who'd have more details?" I worry, fleetingly, about using company e-mail for this but put it out of my head.

Nina writes back almost instantly. "Get in touch with Susanna Carter in London. I don't know if she'd be willing to talk but it's worth a shot. Here's her e-mail address. After this, I'm out of it. Sorry. Just too risky."

I quickly write to Susanna Carter asking for any information she might have and promise to keep it confidential.

When Petra finally deigns to come in, I ask her to hold all calls and shut my door. After spending far too long trying to figure out how to get the goddamn picture of Merdale's headquarters off my computer, I contemplate calling the IT department for help, but refrain because of the likelihood that this will go down in some ledger as an act of insubordination. Instead, I pull out a stack of papers and get to work preparing for my three p.m. meeting.

During the next few hours, I am vaguely aware of doors opening and closing, people being called individually and in small groups into the conference room, but I manage to block it out. I pointedly ignore the blinking message light, certain it is Deirdre wanting to recap dinner. Though I am dying to hear her version of what happened after Sam and I left them, I regret agreeing to Jack's request that I become a double agent in their emotional lives. Torn between curiosity and guilt, I choose avoidance.

At five minutes to three, I gather the stack of papers I have been working on, check my lipstick in the compact I keep stashed in my desk, caked with dusty crumbles of old eye shadow, and go to Favata's office. I knock gently. There is no response. I peer in. The office is empty.

I have Petra call his assistant, but he has left no word canceling the appointment or changing the time. I check back every five minutes—worried that this is somehow my fault, though I cannot pinpoint how—but there is no further sign of him.

By the end of the day, when the conference room is finally quiet, eleven people have been fired.

TWELVE

The rest of the week crawls by in something of a trance, as if we each feel the need to withdraw into our own worlds, hunker down and get our individual jobs done. The four of us, Claire, Phoebe, Sam and I, move as parallel lines through the apartment, the act of putting one foot in front of the other, of getting through school days and homework-laden nights, workplace machinations and the normative pedestrian tasks of cooking dinner, cleaning up, paying bills absorb us. Every now and then we look up, ask a question, try to concentrate on the answer, but we are only feigning interest, none of us has the energy it would take to truly engage. We are, each of us in our own way, tilted toward the weekend, telling ourselves that we will be able to backtrack, make up for this essential lack of attention and reconnect in the coming envelope of time, as if affection can be put on hold and reclaimed at will.

Sam and I are careful with each other, waiting for the residue of recriminations and explanations, confessions and apologies to fade, blend into the fabric of the immediate past and eventually be forgotten.

We do not mention the other night again.

Instead we practice gentleness, the small wordless touches, the chance looks that form the hallmarks of marital complicity, and if they are conscious rather than organic they are no less appreciated.

Even Deirdre and I seem to be avoiding each other, playing at phone tag with a mutual lack of conviction. When Jack e-mails none-too-subtly asking what I have learned, I can honestly tell him nothing. The person I most want to hear from, Susanna Carter from Harcourt's London office, does not reply to my first—or second—request for information on Favata.

Finally Saturday morning arrives, drowsy and slow.

I go into the living room where Sam is reading the paper, his bare feet up on the cluttered coffee table, and sit down on the couch beside him. I pick up the Metro section, stare at it, the print a dyslexic blur of black and white, and put it down, waiting for him to finish his article, acknowledge me. He puts his hand on my knee but doesn't look up until he is done.

"Have you decided what you are going to do this afternoon?" he asks as he plays with the ragged edges of the paper.

Claire, to her overwhelming delight, is going to help Deirdre at the store and Sam has promised to take Phoebe ice-skating at Chelsea Piers, a place I have an outsized distaste for and do anything I can to avoid. The endless blocks of bowling lanes, hot dog venues, video game parlors, all with lights flashing and music blaring at ear-shattering decibels, strikes me as a Las Vegas for urban children, dizzying in its sensory overload and over-the-top prices.

"I don't know." It is so rare that I have free time alone that I haven't been able to settle on an option, I'm that out of practice. "I thought I might go into work for a little while after I drop Claire off."

"Why on earth would you do that?"

I have been trying to get Sam to understand how precarious it feels at Merdale, how I cannot seem to grasp their language or their motives, but each time he has offered up some rote bromide and changed the subject. Uncertainty has always left him deeply discomfited, and though I have tried through the years to make him understand that if I express confusion or self-doubt it does not mean that I expect him to fix it or that more long-standing chaos will ensue, it hasn't sunk in. Sam wants, needs me to be sure of myself and in many ways that has served me well, forced me to act more confidently than I otherwise might have. But there have been just as many times when it has left me feeling mute and misunderstood.

Still, he has been on his best behavior, making every attempt to listen—and I do not want to press it, not now as we are knitting back together.

"You're right. I'll probably just come home," I say.

He nods and gets up to dress. As he moves past the coffee table the newspaper scatters.

"What's that?" I ask, noticing a manila folder that looks vaguely familiar.

Sam picks it up. "Nothing."

I look more closely at the folder. "That's our financial records."

"I just wanted to go over some things."

"What things?" We usually tackle this odious task together once every few months. To lessen the pain, we have made something of a ritual of it, splurging on a far better bottle of wine than is our standard wont, squabbling over whose purchases are the least necessary, giving up, making up, regretting the price of the wine by the time we are done, anxiously swearing to cut back.

"I wanted to know where we stand these days. With the market the way it is, I thought we might move some things around."

"So where do we stand?"

"Knee-deep in quicksand."

I groan. "Thanks for the reassurance."

"Anytime. By the way, I realize this news isn't exactly going to break your heart, but I'm going to drop the Wells thing."

"When did you decide that?"

He smiles. "Oh, around two a.m. Seriously, I've been thinking about everything you said. I've got Simon breathing down my neck. And I just don't think I'm going to find what I need. Not in time, anyway."

"I'm sorry, Sam. I know how much work you put into it."

They are small gifts, his concession, my empathy, but they are what we have to give, they are everything.

"Don't forget Phoebe's mittens," I call after him as he rises to leave the room, the folder tucked beneath his arm.

"Huh?"

"For ice-skating."

"It's indoors. It's not going to be that cold," he says dismissively. In the enduring scheme of our marriage, caution is my department.

"She hasn't been skating since last winter. She needs them for protection when she falls." One of the things I love best about Phoebe is the blind optimism she has in her own athletic ability despite all evidence to the contrary. That's not to say it doesn't make me insanely nervous at times.

"All right."

"What time do you think you'll be back?" I ask.

"I don't know, three, four. Where are they?"

"Where are what?"

"The mittens."

It occurs to me that he is not really asking for their likeliest location but prompting me to find them for him. I consider telling him to look for them himself but I don't. The first attempt at ferreting out last winter's accessories from the jumble of mismatched gloves, hats and scarves is an iffy proposition at best, especially for one with little experience in this type of archaeological dig. "I'll get them," I tell him.

After Sam and Phoebe leave, I find Claire in her room trying on everything she owns while semi-pornographic rap thrums from her computer's tinny speakers. Clothes fly through the air; leggings, tunics, miniskirts drift like colorful parachutes and land in crumpled heaps on the floor. Nothing is right, nothing is good enough. The rawness, the gnawing dissatisfaction and uncertainty of being thirteen is painfully evident as she races back to the closet. I am torn between the impulse to laugh—the inanity so familiar and so futile—and to soothe.

"Try the pink shirt," I suggest.

"I already tried that."

"Claire, Deirdre is expecting you. You don't want to be late for your first day on the job."

"I can't go looking like this." Tears of frustration and despair pool in the corners of her eyes, a vestige of the childhood she is so desperate to leave behind. She whips off her skirt and top.

Silence is clearly my best strategy here. "Five minutes," I say as I turn to leave.

"I wish you'd just let me go by myself," she spits out as she slips on a pair of skintight jeans. "You're so overprotective. Why don't you trust me?"

"I do trust you," I reply. "Not that this week was the best example of it." I am still annoyed that she forgot to call when she and Phoebe got to school the other day.

Claire frowns. Her fury that I had the middle school dean track her down shows no signs of abating.

I soften. "I thought it would be nice to have a chance to catch up with Deirdre."

"We're going to be working, Mom." She glares at me, incensed at the possibility that I might monopolize her precious time with Deirdre.

"Don't worry, I have no intention of staying," I reassure her, as I head into my own bedroom to get dressed.

It is a gorgeous early fall day, the air sharp and crystalline when we finally leave the apartment. "Let's walk," I suggest. We have always been at our best when engaged in movement or activity, freed from the constrictions and expectations of home. When Claire was three, I took her to her first movie and we danced together up this very street. Filled with a surfeit of joyous anticipation, she turned to me, her eyes wide with revelation, and exclaimed "I love you!" as if just discovering it. It was the first time she had ever said it as anything but a response to a similar proclamation from me, and my heart has never been the same.

I still see hidden beneath her early adolescence the infant's face that I once studied with such wonder-filled scrutiny. It is there, inside her, inside me, always.

We talk easily now of television shows and upcoming movies, the previous sartorial wrangling forgotten. I am careful to avoid any potential minefields, anxious to preserve the moment.

When we reach the store, Deirdre kisses us both hello.

"So how was the first week of school?" she asks Claire.

"Fine."

"Did you scout out the boys at St. Bernard's yet, or Dalton?"

Claire smiles, admitting that she has. I look at her, surprised. It never even occurred to me to ask.

"So," Deirdre continues. "Any cute ones?"

Claire grimaces. "The nice ones aren't cute and the cute ones aren't nice."

"At least you're learning that early. It took me years. I'd love to tell you it gets better, but it doesn't. My advice is to go for smart and funny."

"Really? I thought your MO was more along the lines of borderline personality and unattainable."

Deirdre swivels to me.

"Sorry." I turn to Claire. "My advice is no dating at your age."

They both glance over at me and decide the best course is to totally ignore my existence.

Deirdre assumes an authoritative voice with Claire, flattering her with the no-nonsense way she details her responsibilities for the day. Claire listens closely, wanting above all to please and impress Deirdre. We leave her neatly folding a stack of boatneck cashmere sweaters—a skill I was unaware she possessed—and go into Deirdre's small office in the back. She sits down at her desk, cluttered with fabric swatches and dog-eared fashion magazines, catalogues and a startling array of unopened mail. I take the seat opposite her.

"Have you been avoiding me?" I ask.

"Of course not. I've been busy." She fiddles with the loose knob of her desk drawer. "I don't know. I guess I needed some time to think."

"Think about what?"

"It's been intense, okay?"

"What has?"

"Jack. Ben. Everything."

"I'm listening."

She pauses. "Whenever I talk to you about Ben you get this look on your face."

"What look?"

"Disapproval."

"That's not true."

"Yes, actually it is. I don't blame you. I'd probably disapprove, too. But it's there."

"Sorry. I just want you to be happy."

"And you don't think Ben can do that for me?"

"I don't know."

She sighs. "Neither do I."

"What's going on?"

"Maybe my seeing Jack bothered Ben more than he'll admit. Whenever he feels me slipping away he does something to pull me back in. Thursday night, he managed to get us a table at the River Café. I think he did a photo shoot of the chef at one point. Anyway, we had this incredible bottle of wine and you know how romantic it is there . . ."

"I've never been."

"You should go."

"I should do a lot of things. Go on."

"Halfway through dinner he told me sort of, maybe, that he'd thought about what I said and he's not as interested in having a 'rotation' of women anymore."

"Sort of? Maybe?"

"He was a little vague on details," Deirdre admits. "I didn't really press him."

"What caused his sudden change of heart?"

"I don't know. Jealousy? Don't get me wrong, I wasn't totally buying it. I know Ben too well. And he didn't say anything specific about us. But at least what he did say, or imply, was different from anything he's said in the past."

"The past meaning earlier this week?"

"See?"

"Sorry."

"What if he means it this time?" Deirdre searches my eyes for an answer we both know I cannot give her.

"Where did you leave it?" I ask.

"We didn't. It drives me batty. We had this fantastic night together and I haven't heard from him since."

"It's only been two days."

"I know. And he has his kids this weekend. He still hasn't told them about us, so I'm sure I won't hear from him till Monday." She plays with her hair, takes a deep breath. "You want to hear how pathetic I am? I've calculated his every-other-weekend schedule for months ahead. I don't make plans for weekends he doesn't have the kids, even though he doesn't always ask to see me then. And I tell myself not to feel bad on weekends he does have them if he doesn't get in touch. Of course, he has no idea of any of this."

She waits for me to lecture her, but I don't. I know that desire is not something we can control; too often it disappears when we wish it wouldn't and refuses to vacate our hearts when we would give anything to be free of its yoke.

"It's so hard to go from the kind of intimacy we had on Thursday to a total lack of communication," she says. "Relationships are supposed to make you feel less lonely, not more, right?"

"That's the general idea."

"I had this revelation last night while I was waiting like a pathetic teenager for the phone to ring. I mean, I guess I've known it all along but . . . Ben will never be my ICE person."

"Your what?"

"My In Case of Emergency person. I was reading this article about how you should program your emergency contact info into your phone, that hospitals or whatever look under ICE. And it hit me. Ben will never be my In Case of Emergency person."

"You deserve that from someone," I tell her.

"I know. But it's not that simple. He's so close to being what I want." She shakes her head. "In a funny way, I think seeing Jack reminded me of who I was before I got so scared."

"Scared of what?"

"Being alone. I found myself lying about aspects of my relationship with Ben to him. I was too embarrassed to admit what I'm putting up with. Even I can see that's a sign something's wrong. It's funny, all the things I didn't want before seem so appealing to me now."

"What things?"

"Belonging to someone. I've never really had that. Or maybe I did, a long time ago, with Jack. But I was too young to appreciate it. How was I supposed to know it would be so hard to find again?"

"What happened with you two the other night?"

"Nothing. Everything. I don't know."

"Did you sleep with him?"

"That's not the point."

"Excuse me? Of course it's the point. It's always the point."

She ignores this. "What's Alice like?"

"The only time I've seen her was at their wedding five years ago and I doubt we exchanged more than three words."

"He's not happy, you know."

"Did he tell you that?"

"He alluded to it. Look, I know he's married. Maybe whatever is between us is nothing more than a bad case of nostalgia. And maybe I'm just looking for something or someone to give me the strength to break it off with Ben, which I seem incapable of doing on my own. I get all that. But maybe it's something else, something more." She exhales loudly. "God, I'm driving myself crazy. And I'm sure I'm driving you crazy, too. Let's change the subject. Are things better with you and Sam? No more ridiculous worries about an affair?"

"No. I'm over that."

"Thank God. What was going on?"

"It was just work stuff. We're both in pretty tough spots job-wise right now and we're taking it out on each other. It's scary. We can't afford to live on one income, much less none."

"Is it really that bad?"

"Worse." It is impossible for Deirdre, who has never experienced genuine financial pressure, to fully understand the bone-deep anxiety it can cause, no matter how much she thinks she does. In the back of her mind, she always knew she had family to fall back on, something neither Sam nor I have. "I just thought by this point, at this age, we'd be more secure." I pause. "You know what I think the five sexiest words in the English language are?"

"You look thin in that?" she suggests.

"I'll take care of it."

"Technically that's six."

I frown. "I'm totally onboard with the whole fifty-fifty thing but it would be nice to hear Sam say that just once. Anyway, I have a favor to ask."

"Shoot."

"I'm on this insane benefit committee at Weston. I offered up Rita Mason but that's not about to happen. I can't go in and face those Park Avenue she-devils empty-handed. My children would never get another playdate. Any chance of you coughing up something?"

"Of course. What would work for you? A gift certificate?"

"It's a start. Maybe I could put it in a basket with some other things."

"I love you but you've got to move past the wicker stage of life. No one really falls for that padding in a basket routine."

"Thanks. You're making me feel so much better."

"You should ask Ben," she says, brightening. "I'm sure he'd donate a portrait session. And that's actually worth something."

"I can't do that," I protest. Nevertheless, a sense of hope invades me. The combination of art, commerce and media Ben personifies would go a long way with Georgia to make up for the looming Rita Mason fiasco.

"He'd be flattered. Give him a call. He's hanging out in town this weekend with his kids. I think he said something about having tickets to the Children's Film Festival."

"If you're sure . . ."

She nods. "Absolutely. He's a good guy. Underneath it all, he's a good guy."

She begins to rise. "I should probably get back out there."

I begin to follow her, but just before we reach the door, my BlackBerry bings from the lint-coated depths of my bag. I have to crouch on the ground and empty out half the contents to find it.

Deirdre peers down at me, amused. "Are they tracking you down on weekends now?" she asks.

"I wouldn't put it past them."

I open the message, read it quickly and put it away.

"Well?"

"It's not Merdale," I reply. "It's nothing."

"You did not look like it was 'nothing.' "

"There's this guy," I say tentatively. "Someone I met with about work. We've been e-mailing."

Deirdre looks at me closely.

"It's not like that," I protest. "He wants to talk to me about signing with Merdale. He's been slammed a bit in the press recently and he has a big deal coming up that he doesn't want squelched."

"So?"

"He wants to discuss it over a drink."

"What did you reply?"

"I haven't yet."

"Be careful, Lisa."

"It's completely innocent."

"Nothing between a man and a woman is ever completely innocent," she says and closes the door behind us.

THIRTEEN

This is so much cozier, isn't it?" Georgia Hartman glances around the living room of her East Side town house, with its double-height windows swagged in great billowing silk curtains that fall in puddles to the highly polished wood floor. The fireplace is unlit but its very existence offers the promise of warmth, of future comforts. The end tables are dotted with silver-framed photos of the multitude of Hartman children on their multitude of exotic trips, the couches and chairs are punctuated with embroidered throw pillows of vaguely ethnic origin, as if to proclaim that the Hartmans are so much more interesting, so much artier and less predictable than their neighbors with their chintz and their ormolu. Unlike some of the Weston families' apartments I've picked the girls up from, there is no hint anywhere of Louis-whatever (faux or real, I can never tell) or the ultramodern furniture that looks as if it might stab you if you don't sit down just so. Rather, it is expensively tattered in the way that only generations of money can accomplish and others spend far too much time and effort trying to imitate. I suspect some of them buy bags of dog hair from a hawker on Madison Avenue to scatter about the way others buy fake designer bags on Canal Street.

Nevertheless, I wouldn't exactly call the Hartmans' home cozy.

"Our whole apartment would fit on their second floor," Phoebe observed after sleeping over with a bunch of girls last spring. With ample space to spare, I refrain from adding.

She went on to report that the Hartmans had a dumbwaiter downstairs; in the morning the help put freshly ground coffee and the newspaper on it and sent it up three flights to the master bedroom.

"Big deal," Sam replied. "We have two dumbwaiters." He ruffled both girls' hair. At that moment, they would have traded us in for replacement parents in the blink of an eye. Preferably ones in possession of better real estate.

"As you know, the conference room at the school was booked by the diversity committee," Georgia explains, "which is just as well, as far as I'm concerned. Let them have it. If we are going to do this every week we might as well make it nice, right?"

It is evident that what is a dreaded obligation to me is the main event of the day for these women. Only Samantha, Class of '91, who had been so optimistic about consolidating her social position and has been outmaneuvered by Georgia's insistent if faultless hospitality, is less than pleased at the prospect of becoming a regular in the Hartman home. Personally, I would prefer it if the meetings were held at Weston, where escape seems at least nominally easier to accomplish. Besides, if I'm going to break or spill something, if I'm going to say the absolute wrong thing or emit an embarrassing noise, I'd rather it not happen in Georgia Hartman's living room.

The small talk about the first week of school moves on to the difficulty of convincing reluctant older children to go to country houses on weekends—they have parties, social obligations, sports meets of their own. Needless to say, this is not exactly a pressing concern of mine. There is some debate about what age you can start leaving them in town alone. I make a note of the mothers who think sixteen is appropriate so that I can remember never to allow my daughters to go to the unsupervised parties that are sure to follow. It does seem that the further north in real estate and income you go, the further south the behavior of the offspring sinks. Last year, Claire came back from a bat mitzvah at the Pierre and told me that two kids threw up on the dance floor after sneaking the adults' drinks when they weren't looking. "And Heidi hooked up with eight boys." I tried not to overreact, which might preclude any future reports from the front. "What does 'hooked up' mean?" I asked carefully. Claire hemmed and hawed, I doubt she even knew. "Do you mean blow jobs?" I pressed. "Eeww, that's disgusting," she shrieked, and went running from the room.

While the others continue to deconstruct the country house dilemma, I glance around the room, taking mental notes on the seemingly casual placement of tables, chairs and knickknacks, all of which manage to seem both inevitable and surprising. It is not the size of Georgia's town house I covet or the gads of money it implies—both are too far out of reach to even really contemplate—so much as her innate knowledge of what to do with it all when I can't seem to arrange a living room one fifth the size. Whatever gene allows you to visualize and then realize a home like this is woefully missing from my makeup.

I balance my coffee cup on my knees, refrain from taking a much-needed sip for fear the saucer will tumble gracelessly to the floor and pray for the small talk to continue. Except for Deirdre's $500 gift certificate, I have come here this morning empty-handed. I didn't have the heart to tell her that her generosity would be overshadowed by other chi-chi'er designer wardrobe offerings, to say nothing of the $10,000 visit to the celebrity derm, donated by "Anonymous" as if the offering itself would brand the giver as a Botox junkie, or the week at Bikini Bootcamp in Tulum.

Like a brilliantly trained conductor, Georgia stills the room with barely a flick of her birdlike wrist. Drawing all the attention to herself, she speaks in soft cadences so that everyone has to lean forward to hear. "I thought we could go around and get a quick update on the auction items before moving on to locale and entertainment," she suggests. "Tara, would you like to start? Where are you with the stay in Beaver Creek?"

Tara regards Georgia curiously. One perfectly groomed eyebrow raises slightly. "What do you mean?"

"Is it a go?"

"Of course." The idea that she might have to check with anyone is anathema to Tara. After all, isn't the whole point of being so fabulously divorced precisely that you never have to get anyone's permission again? She turns her attention back to the almond biscotto she has been slowly nibbling the edges of, indifferent to Georgia's charms.

If Georgia is at all perturbed—even the mildest show of insubordination is such a rare occurrence—she is far too well bred to let it show. Without missing a beat, she surveys the rest of the women, all of whom have secured everything they said they would, plus more; the Academy Award tickets now come with a preshow makeover by Angelina Jolie's hairstylist, the Ralph Lauren shopping spree is accompanied by tea with the designer's wife, there are backstage passes to Broadway shows and sit-down dinners with TV news anchors, there are courtside season tickets and private tours of the Metropolitan Museum. An air of self-satisfied pleasure permeates the room.

Georgia turns to me. "I was thinking," she says, "it's wonderful that Rita Mason has agreed to cook a private dinner for twenty, but . . ."

I freeze. I don't remember uttering the word "agreed." I sure as hell don't remember Rita Mason uttering it. Of course, that would have required my actually asking her, which I didn't. Any chance of that happening bit the dust when Mick Favata implied how unhappy she is with me. Surely the last straw would be requesting a favor for my daughters' school, an act that I'm sure she would claim was a form of extortion, surely a fireable offense. I had every intention of informing the committee that Rita had to cancel due to a "scheduling conflict" before announcing the Ben Erickson portrait session. The only problem is, despite leaving two messages, I haven't heard back from Ben.

"I've begun to think about the gift bags," Georgia continues. "We have some great items but it would be terrific if you could get us, say, a hundred and fifty copies of Rita's book to stick in? It would add a wonderful heft to the bag."

I can't help but imagine how Rita Mason would react if I told her that her book was only desired for its physical weight.

"Yes, of course." I begin to tabulate what one hundred and fifty hardcover copies will cost—since the only way they're going to end up in that bag is if I pay for them myself.

"So," Georgia says, "shall we move on to other matters?"

"I have some good news," Samantha pipes up in the raspy voice of a not-so-secret chain smoker. Despite her devoted use of Altoids and Chanel 19, traces of tobacco cling to her. "Absolut has agreed to provide the alcohol gratis. All they want is a tiny bit of signage in exchange."

Georgia smiles sweetly, the delicate papery skin around her mouth creasing in vertical C-shaped lines. My one consolation is that she is not the type to age well. "That's wonderful, Samantha. But I'm not sure a benefit for a scholarship fund should be sponsored by a liquor company. Not quite the message we want to send, don't you agree?"

Samantha, chastened, offers one meek "but" and doesn't finish her sentence. Visions of her social ascendancy lay in tatters on the polished floor.

"I suggest that we go back to the Cipriani down on Wall Street for the night," Georgia says, moving on briskly. "They've been so good to us over the years."

"And the lighting is so flattering," Rachel Weinstein points out.

The women all nod approvingly. Most restaurant recommendations come with a rating of the lighting along with the merits of the food. In a clinch, lighting wins out. I mean, how much are you going to eat, anyway?

After some discussion of menu choices and pleas to have the band not play quite so loudly this year (the only flaw in last year's event), the meeting finally winds down. Georgia walks to the front door and hugs us each good-bye as if we are guests departing a wedding. When it is my turn, she leans in and whispers, "I'm sorry about Claire. You understand, though. I had no choice."

At the mention of my daughter's name I stiffen. I have absolutely no idea what she is talking about.

"The other day?" she prompts. "When I reported her for being off-premises? Didn't the school call you?"

In fact there was a message from the head of the middle school but I didn't bother to return it. I figured it had something to do with the tardiness of our tuition check.

"I'm so sorry, Lisa. I just assumed you knew. I was on safety patrol," she begins.

I nod. Every parent at Weston has to sign up for one safety walk a year, a regimen instituted after a spate of muggings in which Weston girls had their iPods stolen by groups of non-Weston kids. Each parent is assigned a "buddy," given an enormous neon orange sandwich board, a walkie-talkie and a block to patrol for the two hours that the children are most likely to be heading home. Last year, my day fell in the middle of February. My buddy wore her orange sandwich board over a full-length sable coat, making us a walking bull's-eye for PETA if nothing else.

"I had just started," Georgia continues, "so it must have been around two-fifteen when I saw Claire and another girl . . . outside. In the Starbucks. Three blocks from school."

She stops short, waiting for me to absorb the import of this.

Eighth graders are not allowed to leave the Weston premises before three thirty p.m. until March, when they are granted their "privileges" and can go out for lunch or whenever they have a free period. Though they daydream about it as incessantly as a prison break, I dread it, knowing I will have to explain to Claire that she can't afford the sushi the other girls favor for every noontime meal.

Georgia waits for me to commiserate over my wayward daughter's infraction or at the very least exonerate her for reporting Claire. Neither of which I have the slightest intention of doing.

"Thank you for telling me," I manage to get out.

I say good-bye and walk out onto the quiet, tree-lined street.

I'm not sure who I am more angry with, Claire or Georgia. Suffice it to say I'm not particularly crazy about either of them at the moment.

"Can I drop you someplace?" I look up to see Tara standing next to a sleek black town car. When she sees me hesitate, she adds, "I may look like the enemy but I'm not."

I acquiesce and slide into the warm, dark interior. "Thank you."

After giving her driver my office address, we ride for the first block in total silence and I begin to regret my decision, no matter how convenient.

"She's a total bitch," Tara remarks in her husky voice as we stop for a red light. "Don't let her get to you."

I glance over at her, nonplussed. "Georgia?"

Tara nods.

"Her precious daughter Vanessa? Hospitalized for anorexia last year. Twice. No surprise. Georgia started giving her diet pills at ten. A chubby kid didn't fit her image."

"Really?" I'd always thought theirs was the type of thinness that comes from good Yankee genetics and years of horseback riding, not cabbage juice fasts and Pilates. I thought it was natural, for God's sake—and all the more alien and impressive for it.

Tara's magnificent honeyed head remains completely still. "She hates me, too, you know. All of them do. They want me on their committees but they won't invite me to their precious little dinner parties anymore."

"Why not?"

"Are you kidding? A divorcée with a boob job? It doesn't get any scarier than that. The only reason they're even the slightest bit nice to me is the money."

"Why do you go? You don't need them."

She shrugs. "Because it amuses me and irks them."

It occurs to me that Tara Jamison might actually be lonely. I suddenly remember a conversation about her that I overheard on a class trip last spring. "I heard she was on JDate," one of the mothers had said. "And she's not even Jewish."

There is a long pause before Tara speaks again. "Maybe I should go back to school," she says quietly.

"Do you know what you'd like to study?"

She shakes her head. "No, that's the problem. As soon as I decide on one thing I change my mind and want to do something else. I just get kind of paralyzed."

"Listen, if you ever feel like talking or, you know, getting together, I'd like that," I tell her.

She regards me steadily before a gentle smile forms. "Thank you."

I nod. "I could use a friend at Weston, too."

It is just past 10:30 when I get out of the elevator at 425 Park Avenue and head through the glass doors, stepping carefully around two workmen who are engraving "Merdale" across the entryway. Hoping to reach my desk unnoticed, I take a longer route so I will not have to pass by Favata's office.

But it is as if he can sniff me out. He is lurking just outside the locked closet where we store samples of our clients' goods—the pricey French cosmetics, the kitchen appliances and pocket electronics we bring to lunches with editors and messenger to their assistants in the hopes of printed coverage. We keep one person on staff whose sole job is to count up the number of mentions each month.

"Good morning." Favata's bulldog eyes narrow slightly. I see a few boxes still in their original wrapping sticking out from behind his leather binder.

"Good morning," I reply. "I was meeting with a client," I add hastily, instantly regretting that I feel the need to explain my whereabouts to him, which not only tacitly acknowledges his position as being above mine but makes me appear guilty of some indeterminate slacker crime.

"That's fine," he replies. "But it's important for me to get to know our clients personally. From now on, I'd like you to inform me of any appointments ahead of time. I'd like the option of accompanying you."

"Of course." I turn and head down the hall. I glance back once and see Favata awkwardly balancing his armful of goodies as he stops at the desk of a junior copywriter with double-D breasts where, I've noticed, he can often be found hovering.

Safely inside my office, I scan the morning logjam of e-mail. There is still no word from Susanna Carter in London, just an endless stream of meeting requests and a particularly annoying chain about a surprise birthday party for someone in the art department that required eleven sallies. I am in the process of deleting the first ten when Petra buzzes to tell me that Ben Erickson is on the line.

"Ben, hi, how are you?" I greet him with far more enthusiasm than I ever have in the past. He still holds out some hope of salvation, at least as far as the Weston benefit is concerned.

"I'm well, thanks. I'm sorry I didn't get back to you sooner. I was in a godforsaken corner of Connecticut with no cell phone service all weekend and didn't get your message until this morning."

Either Ben is lying to me because he didn't want to call me back—knowing his aversion to phones, this is not impossible—or he lied to Deirdre about being in town with his children all weekend. Nothing in his confident, easygoing manner hints at the slightest prevarication, though, which makes it all the more disturbing.

"Oh? I thought you were in the city with the kids."

"No." He doesn't explicate further, he is far too experienced for that. Having a "rotation" of women will do that to a man.

"So, you mentioned in your message you had a favor to ask for the girls' school?" he asks.

"Yes. Look, I know you have your own kids' school and . . ."

Ben's children, Beryl and Jake, go to a downtown private school densely populated with the offspring of Hollywood East, a onetime second-tier option now renowned for the number of movie stars seen dropping their children off every morning, as proudly as if they alone had discovered and trademarked parenthood. The six-foot-four actor famous for his political correctness and for his very hot, very young wife who never misses a hockey game is a particular favorite of the paparazzi. Applications have recently been skyrocketing.

"Go on," he prompts.

"Weston has this annual benefit to help with scholarships," I add, hoping to spin this as an appeal to his conscience rather than a way to save my butt. "I was wondering, you are probably far too busy, but is there any way you could donate a portrait session?"

"Sure," he answers so quickly I'm thrown off course.

"Really?"

"Of course. I'm all in favor of anything that mixes up the gene pool."

"I'm not following."

"I don't doubt private schools offer a superior education, but one of their main purposes is to introduce likely marriage prospects to each other. It's one of the last uncontested holdouts of class. Anything that stirs that particular pot is fine with me."

"Our kids are not even fourteen yet, I doubt marriage is foremost on their minds."

"No, but it's in the parents'."

"Don't you think that's hopelessly old-fashioned?" There is an edge in my voice that has nothing to do with Ben's theories on elite education and everything to do with his lying to my best friend.

"Yes, since you asked, I do think it's hopelessly old-fashioned. I also believe that it's true."

"Almost all the transfer kids Weston took last year came from public schools," I inform him. "Twenty-five percent of the school gets some kind of financial help."

"And the other seventy-five percent procreate and rule the world."

"Weston is all girls. They are certainly not procreating with each other."

"I believe they start mixers with the appropriate boys' school when the kids are still in diapers, no?"

"Didn't you go to prep school?"

He laughs. "Precisely. And I married someone I met there. She and her pals are good at talking to other billionaires and AIDS orphans in Africa. Unfortunately, anyone in between leaves them stumped. I'd like all of our children to be a little more open-minded. If donating a portrait session helps rattle the walls a little, I'm happy to oblige."

I wasn't seeing the donation as an act of subversion or a reaction to Ben's failed marriage, but I'll take it any way I can get it. "Thanks. I appreciate it."

"Just one request. If you could specify a six-month window for cashing it in, that would be helpful. I never know my travel schedule."

"Of course."

I begin to type an e-mail to Georgia sharing the good news even while Ben and I speak. I consider adding a postscript informing her that I spied her daughter Vanessa gorging on Milano cookies. At ten a.m. Three blocks from school. But I manage to refrain.

After exchanging a few more pleasantries with Ben about our children's lives, I thank him once more and hang up.

I am relieved by his consent, of course. But the last person I want to be beholden to is Ben Erickson, with his opaque heart and his little white lies. I contemplate calling Deirdre to tell her that he was not in the city with his kids this weekend as she thought but I don't want to hurt her. I know, too, that I would risk becoming the target of her ire and her disappointment rather than him.

Instead, I pick up the phone and call Jack.

"Finally," he says. "Did you talk to Deirdre?"

"Yes. I saw her on Saturday."

"And? What did she say? Do I have a chance?"

"Yes."

"But?"

"Move quickly," I tell him.

FOURTEEN

The enormous chandelier, a steroidal display of descending glass particles, shimmers disconsolately in the late-afternoon light. Though the gathering has been under way for close to an hour there remains an air of awkward anticipation rather than any real sense of festivity. People who just a few minutes ago were determined to mingle and introduce themselves, bonding over their shared good fortune at being here, have retreated to their own cliques, no longer trying to hide the divide that separates the guests. The Merdale people have marched into town—and won. Now, two weeks later, they are here to celebrate—or flaunt—their success with clients, potential clients, representatives from the Philadelphia and New York offices and a few lesser representatives of the business press.

I stand near the rear of the room fake-talking with someone from the marketing department while I stare warily out. Any nod to "merging cultures" or "taking the best of both companies" lasted all of about two minutes. Unlike other ambitious newcomers to Manhattan determined to learn the city's byways, and assimilate, Merdale exudes the brio of the triumphant and unapologetic provincial. The days of New York's unquestioned superiority are over. The conquering visitors have a thing or two to teach us.

Robert Merdale circulates on his wafer-thin loafers, his satisfied face glowing as he leads his dewy-eyed minions through the room, glad-handing, backslapping, while the few remaining holdovers from Steiner smile anxiously from the sidelines, trying to look as if they are thrilled, or at least at ease, with the turn of events. The only people who appear truly relaxed are the reporters, happy for an excuse to get out of the office and enjoy free alcohol before sundown.

I watch Favata slice through the crowd like a land shark. He cannot approximate the social graces of the others but he makes up for it with sweaty, testosterone-laden drive. There are those who manage to cloak their ambition in self-deprecation, those who can quell it with Ativan or justify it with constant rereadings of Machiavelli, but Favata is incapable of any of these accepted strategies. His jagged rawness is both off-putting and effective, an accidental weapon. Rita Mason, making the rounds by his side, towers over him, a prized possession.

Favata gives me a surprisingly enthusiastic greeting, though it is obviously not for my benefit. When he touches my arm it is all I can do to keep from screaming "cooties!" the way the girls used to.

I say hello to him without attempting to match his fervor, and turn to Rita. "I tried one of your recipes last night," I tell her, with what I hope approximates enthusiasm. "The roast chicken with thyme. It was delicious." Needless to say, there is not one iota of truth in this. I hardly recognize myself anymore.

She regards me with the jaded apathy she assumes comes with being in the public eye for longer than she has. "I'm sorry you've decided not to work on our account," she replies.

This is news to me.

"I explained that you decided to concentrate your efforts on our beauty clients," Favata interjects.

Considering beauty accounts comprise, oh, maybe ten percent of our client list, this is a highly unlikely scenario. Certainly an unwanted one.

"I'll miss you," Rita says, her eyes growing limpid on cue. I've heard rumors she wants to branch out from cooking to a talk show of her own. Showing sympathy for the downtrodden must be one of the talents she's been rehearsing in preparation.

"I'll miss you, too," I assure her.

She and Favata begin to turn to speak with an advertising columnist from a trade rag. Only when Rita is safely out of earshot does Favata take half a step back and lean into me, his cantankerous voice low and threatening. "By the way, Lisa, Susanna Carter was let go from Harcourt's London office last week. Be careful. You are playing a very dangerous game."

Alarm quickens my pulse but before I can reply the room begins to hush. All attention is turned to the podium, where Robert Merdale is lowering the microphone to his diminutive stature. "Welcome," he begins to a round of applause, "and thank you for joining us in what will surely be the beginning of an exciting new stage in our growth."

I hardly hear a word of what follows, the blood is thrumming too loudly in my ears.

"What was that about?"

I turn to see who is whispering in my ear, his warm breath so close I can feel it steal down my neck.

David Forrester is standing an inch behind me, his hands in his pockets.

"What are you doing here?" I blurt out.

"Now there's a friendly greeting for you."

"Sorry. That's not what I meant. I'm just surprised."

"I called your office and your assistant told me you were here. You might want to teach her to say you're in a meeting without quite spooning out all the details next time, though personally I'm glad she did. You've been so cagey about returning my messages I thought I'd better take matters into my own hands. Judging by the look on your face, it's a good thing I did."

"That obvious?"

"I've seen happier people at a funeral. What did Mick Favata say that got you so spooked?"

"You know him?"

David nods. "You didn't tell me he was working at Merdale."

"Does it matter?"

"It might."

The people to our right shoot us a dirty look, despite the fact that we are whispering. Their leader is speaking, we might at least show some respect.

David leans in closer. "We seem to be making ourselves rather unpopular. Do you have time for a quick drink? It will be easier to talk about this someplace else."

"I can't leave in the middle of Merdale's speech." I hesitate, though there is nothing I'd like more.

"Of course you can. No one will ever know. Come."

Before I can protest, he takes me by the hand and leads me around the outskirts of the room until we make it to the coat check. "I know a place nearby," he promises.

The street is just beginning to darken as we step outside. I take a deep breath, relieved to be away from the watchful eyes and murky motives run amok in the hotel ballroom. David touches my elbow to point me in the right direction and we begin walking west.

"I'm not sure if you just rescued me or doomed me," I remark.

He smiles. "I may not be an M and A guy but I've watched my fair share of acquisitions. There's always a shaking-out period," he tells me as we wait for a light. "You're being watched. You want to impress them. You have to learn a whole new culture. It's nerve-racking but I'm sure you'll be okay."

I strongly doubt that. Favata's threat echoes in my head, though sharing this particular piece of information is not in my best interest.

Two blocks away, David steers me toward a discreet gray awning. "In here," he says. We make our way past a glamorously disheveled couple with matching sun-streaked bed hair and the attractively weary eyes of the young and dissolute. They barely look up from their cigarettes as we pass.

Inside the clubby wood-paneled bar small groups of well-appointed men and women are ensconced on brocade settees and wing chairs with ironically old-fashioned cocktails before them. They all seem to be the same age—midthirties—as if the city as a whole has decided that this is the perfect nexus of experience and promise, barring anyone else from appearing in public. The only empty place to sit is a deeply cushioned emerald green couch against the far wall. We make our way there and settle in a few inches from each other. I sink more than I'd expected and struggle awkwardly to pull down my skirt while David watches with some amusement.

We order drinks from a waiter with a chiseled jaw and piercingly blue eyes who appears far more interested in David than in me. I'm quite aware that this is a genetic predisposition rather than a choice but it does nothing for my fragile ego nonetheless.

An uncomfortable silence ensues as we adjust to the quiet of our new surroundings, to our proximity. Our legs brush up against each other as I shift position and then separate.

"So, aside from the always delightful Mr. Favata, how is it going with the Merdale people?" David asks.

"Fine."

He laughs. "You are a very bad liar. A quality, I might add, that I appreciate in a woman."

"And not in men?"

"That's a separate conversation. Have they offered you a contract?"

"No. But I never had one with Carol either."

"That was different."

"I'm beginning to realize that."

"Then you must realize that there's not going to be room for both you and Favata."

"Are you trying to make me nervous or is it just happening naturally?"

"Sorry."

"Favata is only consulting," I insist.

"That's just a fancy term for unemployed. There hasn't been a consultant in history who isn't angling for a corner office, full benefits and an equity position."

"Shoot me now," I mutter.

David laughs. "I'm sure we can find a more appealing course of action."

I look over at him as he pushes his wire-framed glasses higher on the bridge of his nose. I can feel the dented armor I've been clinging to begin to slip. "He's taken me off all accounts except for beauty," I admit.

"Is that so terrible? They usually have a lot of dollars to throw around."

"Until an hour ago, I oversaw almost all clients. He is totally ghettoizing me."

"That's just his opening salvo. Be careful of Favata. He is completely lacking in scruples."

"So I've been told. What exactly is your history with him?"

"He represented a company we were bidding against a couple of years ago. Nothing wrong with that, I've always believed that as long as you play fair you can be on opposite sides during the day and have drinks at night. It's a circular world. But when his client ran into some trouble, Favata got desperate and began to spread rumors about us that were patently untrue. It cost us a lot of money. He went out of his way to damage my reputation personally, which I did not appreciate."

"If I'd been handling your PR that never would have happened," I inform him, only half joking.

He smiles. "That's why I'm here. Or one of the reasons."

I try to ignore the flush rising over my face. "I have given your eco-fund some thought."

"Go on."

"I'd start by naming an advisory board of people with impeccable environmental credentials, maybe someone from Greenpeace and that organization fighting deforestation out west, the Wilderness Society. I'd aim for about seven in all. Then I'd announce that a portion of the fund's profits will be donated to specific causes."

"Interesting. I like the advisory idea."

"You don't sound convinced."

"Lisa, you're right on target and needless to say I would love for us to work together. But I have to be honest with you, the only way I'm going to sign on with Merdale is if Favata is gone."

"There is nothing I'd like more."

"I knew we would have things in common."

I take a large sip of my wine. "I don't think there's anything I can do about it, though."

"You have to outsmart him."

"I'm not sure I can. He has more practice at this sort of thing."

"I'll help you," David offers. "The chance to even the score with Favata doesn't exactly make me unhappy."

"Remind me not to get on your bad side."

"I can't imagine that happening." His smile is slightly crooked, a little boy's grin in a very grown-up man. "Seriously, Favata is a bully. And I don't appreciate bullies. I have some experience with his type. If you need advice, I'll be happy to be your rabbi."

I laugh. "You are just about the least Jewish person I have ever met."

"You're right. I grew up on a failing farm in Pennsylvania. Well, most of them are. Failing, that is. And my family is Baptist. But for your information, when I came to New York I decided to be Jewish, at least figuratively. It seemed the smartest way to go. What I meant by rabbi was adviser, go-to person."

"I get that. I didn't need a translation."

"Of course."

"While we're on the subject of personal history, you never answered me about the three things that weren't true in your e-mail," I tell him.

"What would you like to know?"

"Were you serious about wanting to teach one day?" As much as anything else, this has stayed in my mind. I've always had a weakness for do-gooders. I suppose it excuses him to me in some way. Then again, I am surely the only person in New York who thinks David Forrester needs an excuse.

"Yes, as a matter of fact I was."

"Why?"

He smiles. "Don't you think it's a noble profession? Or is it that you don't believe I have anything to offer?"

"Neither. I'm just curious."

"Because it doesn't fit in with the image you have of me?"

"I'm still forming the image."

He considers this. "All right, yes. I had a teacher once who changed my life. I always thought if I could do that for someone else it would be a worthwhile thing. Payback, if you will."

"I believe the term is 'giving back.' "

He laughs. "I have been on Wall Street too long."

"Who was the teacher?"

"Growing up, it was automatically assumed I would take over my family's farm as soon as I graduated high school. I didn't really see an option, my grades sucked, my family had no money. But I had an English teacher who for reasons I have never quite figured out believed in me. She drove me to the local community college and enrolled me. It was my ticket out."

The couple next to us leans over to kiss, their arms wrapped around each other's necks, distracting me.

"So. You're the PR person," David says when my eyes turn back to his. "What do you think, good story?"

I flinch at the sudden twist. "That depends."

"On what?"

"On how much of it is true."

"Does that matter?"

"I'd like to think it does."

"Fair enough," he replies. "Now you owe me."

"Owe you what?"

"A deeply personal story that explains who you are to me."

"In fifty words or less?"

"In as many words as you like. I've got time."

"Can I get back to you on that one?"

"I'm counting on it."

I can feel David watching me, how I sit, how I move my hands. It is the first time in so long that I am not an employee, a wife or a mother, that I am at least in part still undefined to someone. I feel the brief thrilling rush of being alone in a distant land, open to possibilities, free from responsibilities, far away from real life.

"There's something else," I say quietly. "About Favata."

"What about him?"

"I don't know exactly. He did something in London. I can't seem to nail down anything specific. All I know is that it had to do with sexual harassment. I got the name of someone who was there, Susanna Carter, and e-mailed her for information. I'm not sure if she's the one he supposedly harassed or if she knows who is."

"What did you learn?"

"Nothing. She never wrote back. The creepy part is that Favata came up to me at the party and told me she had been fired. How did he know I'd even tried to contact her?"

"He's probably reading your e-mail."

"That's disgusting."

"Yes, but it's perfectly legal and more common than you think. From now on don't use company e-mail for anything you don't want read. In the meantime, let me see what I can find out about this London business for you, okay?"

Maybe it is the wine, maybe it is David's self-assurance when I have been so barren of it lately, but the idea that someone might actually be able to help me is balm to a wound I did not know the depths of until this moment.

"Okay, yes," I agree. "Thank you."

"That's settled then." The chiseled waiter with the lovestruck eyes is watching us expectantly. "Do you have time for another drink?" David asks.

I look at my watch and shake my head. "I should get home."

"To your husband?"

"Yes."

"Lucky you. Or I should say, lucky him."

I feel my cheeks grow warm once more as I nervously shred the wet, disintegrating corners of my paper cocktail napkin. "What about you?"

"You probably know this—Google has pretty much obfuscated the need for the biographical getting-to-know-you moment—though I suppose it's polite these days to pretend you know less than you do. Anyway, I'm divorced. It was just last year. I'm still getting used to it."

"I'm sorry."

"Thank you. I am, too. It was inevitable, I guess. We fell victim to the great marital Catch-22 of Wall Street. She married me because I made a lot of money and then she resented me because making all that money meant I was never home. Now I can be home more—and she's gone. Funny how that works."

The couple next to us have stopped kissing and are now sitting with their fingers entwined, their heads bent, staring in erotic fascination at their own hands.

"I really should get going," I say again.

"Should or want to?" David asks.

I laugh lightly. "You assume there's a difference."

"I've learned the hard way what a mistake it is to assume anything," he assures me.

David pays the bill and we walk out to the street together. While I wait beneath the awning, he steps out and hails a cab. He holds the door open for me and leans in before closing it. "The story about the teacher? It is true, for what it's worth."

I smile.

"I'll let you know what I find out about Favata's escapades in London," he promises, and taps the cab's roof to signal to the driver to go. There is something in that simple gesture, effortlessly in control, masculine, that makes me feel taken care of, protected. I sink into the backseat and shut my eyes, riding most of the way home in darkness.

It is exactly seven o'clock when I walk in the front door and find Sam in the kitchen pouring pumpkin ravioli from a pot of boiling water into a colander. I hang up my coat and kiss him hello.

"How'd the party go?" he asks as steam pours up onto his face.

"Merdale claims it was a wedding but it was really more of a wake. At least as far as my career is concerned."

"I'm sure it's not that bad."

I look at him and let it go. "Shall I dress the salad?"

He nods and we work quietly side by side.

I do not tell him about my drink with David Forrester, not during dinner, not later when he sits beside me in the living room and we stare at CNN pretending to follow the news out of the Middle East, not as we climb into bed and kiss each other good night.

I'm not sure why, but I don't.

FIFTEEN

If I thought Jack would be checking in regularly for emotional weather reports, spurred on by the anxious imperatives of the newly infatuated, or at the very least by the desire to say Deirdre's name out loud, I was mistaken.

I have not heard from him in the past two weeks.

Though part of me is relieved—the less I speak with him, the less I have to dissemble with Deirdre—I can't help but feel vaguely put out. From the uncomfortable but undeniable exhilaration of being his emissary, I have been relegated to—nothing.

I have no idea of Jack's progress.

I have no idea what is happening.

I can only assume Jack is following my "move quickly" directive. He is not a man of inaction. Then again, either or both of them could very well have thought better of the whole idea, chalked their desire up to the fleeting urges of a sodden night, to an atavistic longing for a time when navigating the gray areas was not the only approach to life. They could have decided that their union was better left in the past and should not be forced, could not be made, to traverse the intervening years or erase the missteps and disappointments that followed.

Deirdre has canceled our weekly breakfast—twice. She has answered my messages, but only when she knows I'll be out or too busy to speak for more than a minute or two, surrounded by children or co-workers. If someone calls during dinnertime once, it's a mistake; repeatedly, it's a strategy.

The last time we spoke was when I phoned earlier in the week to tell her that Claire would not be able to work for her at the store Saturday.

"Is she sick?" Deirdre asked.

"No, she is being grounded for cutting class and leaving school against the rules."

"As I remember, we cut our fair share of classes, too."

"First of all, we were in college. Second of all, I'm not paying thirty-three thousand dollars a year for Claire to sit in Starbucks and text the girls at the next table."

I realize how stodgy I sound. It is not just to Deirdre that I quote the astronomical tuition on a regular basis. I have become that nightmare parent who reminds her children at every opportunity what their education is costing and warn that they damn well better make the most of it. I am the one who becomes irate when I hear that the teacher showed a movie in class that seemed totally unrelated to any topic they were studying. I grumble that they have far too many vacations. Last year, when they had a day of silence in support of gay and lesbian rights and not one of their teachers said a word in class, it was all I could do to keep from hitting the oh-so-politically-correct roof. I mean, couldn't they at least have talked about the issue at hand? (Sam accused me of being reactionary but I reminded him that I am in full support of gay rights. An entire day of the kids doodling in the margins of their notebooks and learning nothing was what I objected to. We remain divided on this one.) In particularly masochistic moments, I have contemplated figuring out Weston's per diem but have so far refrained. There are some things it is better not to know.

"Can't you find some other way to punish her?" Deirdre asked. "I really could use the help. Janine, my usually brilliant store manager, seems to have made the deadly mistake of falling in love in the last week or so. Every time she hooks up with someone new she's so damn distracted sales take a nosedive. The only thing worse is when they break up. Besides, I love having Claire here."

"There's nothing I'd like more," I replied. "Among other things, if she's grounded, it means I am, too. They don't really tell you that in Parenting 101. But the only discipline that works with Claire is finding out what she wants most and taking it away from her. What Claire happens to want most is you."

"Would that were true for everyone."

"Huh?"

"Never mind."

"Trust me, I wish there was another way," I tell her. "I was hoping we'd have a chance to catch up."

"I know. Me, too. I miss you."

"I miss you, too."

Now, at two p.m. on Saturday afternoon, I watch with no small degree of envy as Sam and Phoebe get ready to leave the house.

"Why don't you just go out for a walk," Sam suggests. "You can leave Claire alone for a few minutes."

"Because she's proven to be so responsible lately?"

He shrugs. "Suit yourself, but I think you are completely overreacting." His impressive ability to avoid getting his hands dirty with the mechanics of discipline is an ongoing source of friction in our marriage. Just once I'd like to be able to reverse roles. There is not the slightest indication that this will ever happen.

After he and Phoebe leave I wander aimlessly around the apartment, straightening up the living room, creating new and somewhat neater piles without actually putting anything away. I glance at some magazines and contemplate giving myself a manicure before deciding that it is a job better left to professionals, a particularly easy task these days as there seems to be one on every street corner.

I check my BlackBerry, which now, on David's advice, has a personal e-mail account as well as my Merdale one, and see that there is a new message from him. "I doubt you'll need my advice over the weekend, though I'm always happy to offer it on matters big and small. For instance, you have yet to ask me where you can get the best thin-crust pizza in New York, a topic I have rather strong opinions on. Should the burning desire strike you, here's my number in the country. Have a good weekend, D."

Pizza is just about the only thing I haven't asked for David's guidance on lately. Favata has been finding new ways to try to trip me up and humiliate me on a daily basis. There was the meeting with the CFO in from Philadelphia that he told me started a half hour later than it actually did, the beauty exec he asked me to take to the theater knowing full well she would send her secretary instead, there is the ongoing sense of insecurity he has fostered. Whenever a shadow passes by my office door, I am convinced it is HR coming to escort me from the building.

With each fresh assault I have turned to David, who bucks me up and strategizes as if he has nothing else to do in the world. When we are not planning counterattacks to Favata's every move, we trade snippets about our lives, the emotional weather reports that cyberspace makes so easy, too easy perhaps, speeding up, changing the very nature of intimacy. Our e-mail goes in flurries, two, three a day and then nothing, leaving me with a vaguely empty feeling, a flatness that had not existed before. Sometimes I purposefully do not answer right away to put off the agitation that comes with waiting for his reply.

Already, he has become a habit.

In the meantime, if he has discovered anything more concrete about Favata, he hasn't shared it with me.

I read his message again and put the BlackBerry away.

Claire is in her room sulking. Along with the low-level throbbing of music seeping out, there is a pointed banging around of drawers that I am determined to ignore. Earlier, she spent half an hour petulantly rummaging through the front hall closet looking for her favorite scarf, leaving half the coats on the floor before I yelled at her to pick them up.

I am standing in front of the freezer surveying the ice cream options—I have tried everything from knitting (which lasted less than half a day) to hot baths to get a handle on my unfortunate habit of eating out of boredom, with depressingly little success—when the intercom goes off, making me jump. Looking into the little video monitor—the closest our building will ever get to a doorman—I see Deirdre smiling into the camera.

"What are you doing here?" I say into the speaker.

"I'm happy to see you, too. Will you buzz me in?"

I nod, though of course she cannot see me, press the button to let her in and go to wait by the front door.

Deirdre walks in carrying a bag of Tate's chocolate chip cookies, Claire's favorite before she swore off sugar, butter and various edible evils, though I doubt she will inform Deirdre of this. The cookies are obviously a bribe. Deirdre can't stand the idea of anyone being mad at her and wants to make evident that she had nothing to do with Claire being banished from the store. I could have spared her the effort. She has long since won any popularity contest by default when it comes to Claire.

"I come bearing supplies," she announces. "I assume my presence isn't against the rules?"

"Not if I get to keep you to myself. Why aren't you at the store? Is everything okay?"

"Everything's fine. Are we so old that spontaneity isn't even an option anymore?"

I look at her suspiciously.

"Okay, 'fine' might be the wrong word," she admits. "Let's just say things are transitional."

At the sound of Deirdre's voice, Claire comes dashing out of her room. "Hi," she exclaims with a surfeit of relief and pleasure. Like all teenagers, she is certain the visit has something to do with her, though she can't quite figure out what.

"How is my favorite prisoner?" Deirdre asks, ignoring my scowl. "I hear the food they serve here is wretched. I brought you a care package from the outside world."

"I love these!" Claire exclaims, taking the proffered cookies and biting into one as if she has been on a hunger strike.

"I thought you didn't eat those anymore," I remark petulantly.

Claire glances at me as if I'm demented and returns her full attention to Deirdre.

"I shut the store for the day in your honor," Deirdre tells her.

"Really?"

Deirdre smiles. "No, not really. But it wasn't as much fun without you."

Claire positively glows.

I glare at Deirdre—talk about undermining me—and she relents to my parental authority. "Let me be clear, I am in full support of your mother. You must not cut classes, smoke, drink or cheat on tests. Are you taking notes on this?"

Claire laughs, flattered that Deirdre would even consider such glamorous sins in the realm of possibility.

She hovers around for a few more minutes—adamantly, stubbornly—while Deirdre probes her about *Teen Vogue,* Claire's Bible. I listen with growing impatience as they dissect each page of the current issue from memory, culminating in a debate on whether or not it is acceptable to tuck jeans into slouchy boots or if that is so last year. Three minor celebrities have been photographed sporting the look but they are West Coast and it seems a little dubious.

"Don't you have homework?" I finally interrupt.

"I finished it," Claire replies sulkily.

"Then go find something else to do. In your room, please."

Claire finally slinks off, adding the enforced banishment to the growing ledger of crimes I have committed against her dignity.

"She is supposedly being punished, not courted today," I admonish Deirdre.

"Sorry. I was about to add that blow jobs really do count as sex to the list of no-no's but I figured I'd wait until next year for that."

"Thanks, you're a real champ."

"I aim to please."

"I'll be sure to send you the bill for her stay in the juvenile delinquent home."

"I believe it's called rehab these days."

"Same difference. So, what's up?" I ask as we settle into the living room.

Deirdre kicks off her shoes and curls her feet beneath her on the couch. Slowly, she steadies her gaze on me. "Have you talked to Jack recently?" she asks hesitantly.

"Not in the last couple of weeks. Why?"

"Promise me you'll just listen without judging?"

"Is that what you think I do?"

"Sometimes."

"All right."

"I should have told you all this before. I wanted to. But I didn't want a lecture. I couldn't have handled it."

"You still haven't told me anything," I remind her.

She sighs and finally begins. "That night, the night the four of us went out to dinner? After you and Sam left, Jack and I went out for a drink. It was so good to see him again. I don't know how to explain it. It was like everything else just fell away. The connection was still there." She pauses, looks at me. "We couldn't stop talking. For the first time in so long I didn't feel like I had to hide who I really am. We recognize each other. I think someplace along the way I forgot that two people may actually want the same things, that it doesn't always have to be a contest."

"Go on."

"When the bar closed, we weren't ready to end it. We went back to his hotel room." She says this quickly, with a touch of defiance, and waits for my reaction, but I am careful to betray none. "It was good," she continues. "More than good."

"I'm not sure I need the details."

She ignores this. "There was the familiarity of rediscovering each other but it was also new, which is a pretty goddamned amazing combination." Deirdre shakes her head, laughing slightly. "Of course, true to form, I completely freaked out."

"What do you mean?"

"I left at four a.m. Tore out is more like it."

"Why?"

"I'm not really sure. Maybe waking up together would have made it seem too real. Or maybe I was scared it wouldn't feel real in the morning. If Jack was going to get a sudden attack of guilt or regret, I didn't want to be there to witness it. But the thing is, it is real."

"How can you be sure? It was just one night. And there was a lot of alcohol involved."

"No, it was more than that. I thought that's what it might be. Just a onetime thing. A trip back. You know, tying up loose ends. I thought it would be . . . contained."

"But?"

"We've seen each other since. He's been called back to Manhattan three times for the job. And it's been just as good each time. Better." She smiles at a private memory and then turns back to me. "He's going to leave Alice," she says definitively.

"Did he tell you that?"

"Yes. It has nothing to do with me. It was over before this."

"Deirdre, I want you to be happy, I want that more than anything, but don't you think this is all rather sudden? You can't totally transform your life because of a few nights together."

"I told you, his marriage was over. He'd already decided to move to New York before this. I had nothing to do with it. And it's not like I've been overwhelmingly happy lately."

"I didn't realize you were so miserable."

"I didn't say I was miserable. But don't you see, Lisa? I have a chance, a real chance. I wasn't sure I was going to get that again. I'm almost forty. I want children. Desperately. Sometimes when I walk in the park and see little kids playing my womb aches. I tried for so long to tell myself I could sleep with Ben while I looked for something more but I don't seem to be capable of that. For the first time in my life I don't want to hedge my bets. I want to give this thing with Jack a shot. A real shot. That's all I promised Jack, that if he moved to New York I would give it a chance."

"If?"

"When," she corrects herself. "I'm sure he's going to get the job. They're down to dealing with the fine print."

"What about Ben?"

"Ben is never going to change. I went to him the other night and told him I needed some kind of an answer from him about our future. I wasn't asking for any guarantees, but I wanted him to say he would at least try it my way. I've certainly spent enough time trying it his. At a certain point don't you just have to shut your eyes and jump in? For all of Ben's flouting of convention, it seems to me he's the one most scared of taking a risk."

"What did he say?"

"Nothing. It was so frustrating. He couldn't say yes and he couldn't say no. I realize he might not have wanted to hurt my feelings by spelling it out but at one point I completely lost it with his stonewalling. I didn't care what he said anymore, I needed him to tell me something. You know what his reply was? That after all this time I should be able to understand him without words. Can you believe it? I don't even understand him *with* words."

I do not point out that there is a difference between not understanding and not wanting to understand. "You have to hand it to him," I remark. "He managed to distill a millennium of male wishful thinking into one line."

"He actually asked me how long the 'serial monogamy thing' would have to last."

I can't help but laugh. "What did you answer?"

"That I didn't think he would be going into it with quite the right attitude." She leans back and hugs her knees to her chest. "For years, I've been bouncing back and forth, trying to figure out a way to make it work, but he stays exactly the same. I never thought I'd still be doing it at this stage in my life. I assumed I'd be settled by now." She looks at me. "Ben will never want children with me. Even if he did, the chances of him sticking around to raise them are minimal, to say the least. Jack is different. He'll be there in a way Ben can't be."

"He will be your ICE person?"

"Exactly."

"So that's it?"

"Yes. I told Ben it was over, but I'm not convinced he believes me. I've done it too many times before." She smiles wryly. "You remember the first time I broke up with him? When he told me he was seeing other women?"

I nod.

"I think he respected me for saying that wasn't good enough for me. Of course, I pretty much blew that when I went running back to him. In some convoluted way, I've been trying to win back that respect ever since. If not from him, then from myself."

"Did you tell him about Jack?"

"I didn't go into details. Hell, he'd probably be just as happy to go on seeing me anyway."

Deirdre leans back and when she speaks again, it is almost as if she is talking to herself. "Don't you think I know that another woman would have been out the door ages ago? Don't you think I wish I was that other woman and wonder why I'm not? It's like desire for him is somehow imprinted on my DNA. Maybe I've stuck it out with Ben all this time because I'm the real commitment-phobe. But I can finally break that pattern now. With Jack. I can choose a different kind of life." She picks up her necklace, a thin gold chain with a small heart paved in diamonds. "He gave me this," she says, with an almost shy pleasure and pride.

I look at the heart resting in her hand. "It's gorgeous."

She nods. "It is, isn't it?"

"You're sure about all this?" I ask.

"Yes." She smiles. "I think. All I know is that I'm going to try not to screw it up this time. Lisa, I need you to be happy for me. I need you on my side."

"Of course," I reassure her.

"Maybe the next time Jack comes to town the four of us could have dinner again," she suggests, hoping to re-create a past we never really had. "It would be so much fun."

"All right. I'll talk to Sam."

"Good." She smiles, relieved. "Can I tell you a secret?"

"What was the rest of this, something you're posting on the Internet?"

She laughs, leaning closer, almost whispering. "The last time Jack was here? When we had sex?"

I groan. "Do I have to know this?"

"We didn't use birth control."

I rear back. "Deirdre."

"Relax. What are the chances of something happening so quickly? But it's a start. For both of us."

"I don't know what to say."

"Don't say anything, then. Please."

We move on to debate whether there is really such a thing as flat-heeled boots that don't look hopelessly frumpy with skirts (a pipe dream Deirdre insists that at some point I simply must give up), the merits of Emergen-C versus Airborne and whether or not you can lose more weight if you stop exercising—of course you have to stop eating as well, a minor point, though still worthy of consideration. But it is all just background noise to Deirdre's news, reconfiguring the past, reimagining the future, changing the geometry of what it appears will once more be the four of us.

After Deirdre leaves, I look in on Claire, who is lying on her bed reading a bodice ripper cloaked as history that she got out of the school library.

"Everything okay?" I ask.

"Fine." She looks up at me and almost smiles before remembering that she is thirteen and I am the enemy. "Oh, by the way," she says, "I found your phone in the bottom of the coat closet when I was looking for my scarf before." She gets some satisfaction from this, vindication no doubt for all the times I've scolded her for misplacing hers.

"Thanks. It must have fallen out of my coat pocket."

"It's on my desk."

I pick it up and leave her room.

As soon as I am safely out in the hallway I lean up against the wall and look down at the foreign object in my hand.

It is, in fact, a disposable cell phone, the kind you pre-pay for so that there will be no record of calls made, no inconvenient bill sent home, no evidence.

And it isn't mine.

SIXTEEN

When I was much younger, before marriage, children, there were days when I found it difficult to leave my bedroom, when my skin hurt if exposed to air, my eyes squinted painfully under the assault of daylight. They would descend, these days, and then vanish without warning, without apparent cause or cure. I kept them private.

And then they simply stopped. There was Sam, the girls, there was the rampant busyness of tending to young children with their overlapping demands and the exhaustion that could rock through your marrow at the end of the day and still leave room for happiness. Above all I was not, I was never, lonely. The memory of those bedroom days faded, like a sharp pain you once experienced but no longer feel and so don't quite believe ever truly existed.

Until now.

Everything is dim inside of me.

All Saturday night and Sunday I say little, do little, eat little. Talking is an effort. I tell Sam and the girls that I'm not feeling well and then grow angry at how easily they accept my explanation, how blind they can be. When she was younger, Phoebe would become agitated if I wasn't well, literally yank me up, force me to stand if I had the flu or a stomach bug. Now my withdrawal simply adds a low-level off-kilter air to the house. No one tries to make me rise.

I lie in the bedroom for most of the day, the lights off, and think about that phone.

I rack my brain but I cannot come up with any other explanation. It must be Sam's.

When Deirdre calls to tip me off about a sample sale I do not mention my resurrected suspicions. She would either deny them or assure me, with that great feminine faith in the omnipotence of communication, that Sam and I can work things out if we only talk, go to a marriage therapist, whatever. I thank her for the sale info, hang up and go back to staring at the ceiling.

By early evening it has become accepted wisdom that I have some sort of twenty-four-hour bug and I do nothing to enlighten my family. Rather, I admonish them to wash their hands frequently to keep from catching it. I listen to them arguing about whether to order in Chinese food or Thai or pizza for dinner and burrow deeper into the quilt. Sam checks on me every now and then and I assure him I need nothing, want nothing. I pretend to be asleep when he comes to bed. I'm not ready for confrontation.

I will stay here, lying in the dark, for as long as possible, forever if I can. Limbo is preferable to an alternative too painful to contemplate.

On Monday morning, I sit in my office paying little attention to the swirl outside my door. I have had Petra pull all the beauty accounts and am staring at them without absorbing a single word when Favata walks in without knocking.

He sits down, picks up a magazine from my desk, studies the celebrity post-baby weight-loss cover and then drops it. After glancing around and finding no other distraction he finally begins to speak.

"How are you making out with Tessa Caldwell?" he asks gruffly.

"All right. I think her writing is improving."

"Do you?" There is a sideways glint in his eye. "Do you really? I find that surprising." He leans forward on his stubby, chubby elbows. "Regardless, you've dragged your feet on this long enough."

"I don't understand."

"I thought I had made it clear that I expected you to fire her."

"But . . ."

"I've covered for you with Robert, Lisa. But enough is enough. Call HR. Today."

He leans over, picks up the magazine he had been glancing at and leaves my office with it tucked under his arm.

It is all I can do to keep from throwing my tape dispenser at the back of his head.

Instead I get up, shut the door and sit back down at my desk, burying my head in my hands, my eyes and throat burning.

Just what does he mean, he's covered for me?

I bite my lip in anger until a salty taste fills my mouth.

The setup is clear, even if a course of action isn't: I can throw Tessa under the bus, which may or may not save my job. Or I can fight Favata on it. In which case Tessa and I will both in all likelihood lose our jobs.

I dig my nails into my palms as my mind spirals in an ever-tightening knot of anxiety, fear and resentment: I can't quit, I need the job, If Sam leaves me, If I leave Sam, If my world falls apart, My world is falling apart, Sam is having an affair, I need the job, I can't quit.

There are times, I realize, when you simply cannot do the thing you most want to. But I seem incapable of movement, of action in any direction. Here. At home. Anywhere.

I don't know how long I sit at my desk, fighting back tears, ignoring the pinging of my e-mail.

Finally, resigned, I pick up the telephone and dial.

After two rings, a woman answers. "Hello?"

"Is David Forrester available?"

"I'll check. Who shall I say is calling?"

The assistant is just doing her job but I'm ready to kill her. I give her my name instead.

"Lisa, what a nice surprise," David says when he picks up.

"Is this a good time to talk?"

"I'm heading into a meeting but I have a couple of minutes. Are you all right?"

"No. I'm about as far from all right as you can get." I tell him about Favata's edict.

"He's obviously setting you up to look bad in front of Merdale," David summarizes when I have finished. "If you balk, he'll claim it shows a lack of loyalty to the new order. And if you fire this woman he'll be able to get more of his own people in. Not bad."

"I'm glad you're impressed by what an asshole he is. I thought you were on my side."

"I am on your side."

"Then tell me what I should do."

"I have people waiting for me in the conference room. If you can meet for lunch, we can hash it out then."

"Today?" It takes so much energy to remain upright, so much sheer will to go on pretending to be stronger than I am that I'm not sure I can withstand his scrutiny.

"Yes, today. The way you describe it, you don't have much time on this."

"Of course."

"Good. I'll have my assistant make a reservation and e-mail you with the details. Lisa?"

"Yes?"

"Sit tight. We'll work this out together."

"Thank you."

Despite everything, I feel a brief sliver of hope. It is too fragile, though, and vanishes before I can get to know it.

The gray-carpeted main dining room of the Japanese restaurant is suffused with the discreet hush of money, the tables set far apart to enable deals to be brokered with polite circumspection. I search the diners in their sober suits, their heads bent in concentration over menus and whispered negotiations, and finally spot David seated at a corner table in the rear almost hidden from view, scrolling down his BlackBerry.

He rises as I approach, his eyes steady while mine skitter nervously from his face to the room and back to his face. I offer my hand to shake but he leans over to kiss me hello, leaving my arm stranded in midair.

"I hope this was convenient," he says as I sit down.

"Yes." He must know it is only blocks from my office. "Thank you for doing this on such short notice. I didn't know where else to turn."

"I take my job as rabbi very seriously."

I smile, suddenly shy in his physical presence after the intimacy of our e-mail. Floundering in the uncharted space between the two, I reach for my glass of water and end up spilling icy liquid all over the table before David catches it.

"Oh God, I'm sorry."

"Don't worry. I find a little bit of klutziness charming." He hands me a napkin and we busy ourselves blotting the table. "Most of the women I run into these days are all so polished. I like it that you're not."

I groan. "That's one of the most backhanded compliments I have ever received."

"I didn't mean it to be. I really do like that about you."

"All I ever wanted was to be one of those polished women," I confess.

"Trust me, you don't."

The waiter silently removes the mound of wet linen and gives us fresh napkins.

"Can we start all over again?" We unfold the napkins on our laps. I square my shoulders. "How was your weekend?" I ask with exaggerated formality. We need to back up, ease into each other. "You were at your country house? The Hamptons?"

He smiles, playing along. "No, it's too social for me there. I'm something of a recluse by nature."

"I find that hard to believe."

"Granted you'd have to define *recluse* as having a house in Columbia County rather than the South Fork."

I laugh. "Try again." Two and a half hours north of Manhattan, Columbia County has become the destination of choice for artists with money, moneymakers who prefer to be around artists and filmmakers who pride themselves on knowing the local farmers by name rather than waiting on endless lines at Citarella. Of course, the price per acre for all this authenticity has tripled over the last few years, something the weekend residents can both bemoan and take to the bank. "We must have different definitions of *recluse,*" I tell him.

"You're right," he agrees. "Every time I think I'm doing something original it turns out to be just another cliché. Of course, the only way to be truly original when it comes to real estate is to live in a place with no running water and rats the size of steer. I'll settle for the pretense of originality."

When the waiter reappears, David pauses to speak to him in Japanese before turning back to me. "Can I order for you or would that be presumptuous?"

"I'd like that."

The two men engage in an enthusiastic conversation that involves much deliberation and eventually nod their heads in mutual approval.

"I'm impressed," I remark when the waiter leaves.

"Cheap trick," he replies. "I used to travel to the Far East quite a bit. I ordered a selection of things not on the menu, by the way, along with the more standard yellowtail. I realize you are having the day from hell, but that's no reason not to eat well. Quite the opposite."

"Day from hell is putting it kindly. I seem to be having the month from hell."

"How about if we start with today's problem. Is she any good?"

"Is who any good?" I have completely forgotten why we are here.

"The copywriter Favata wants you to fire."

"Tessa. No, not particularly," I admit.

"I see."

"That's not the point," I protest.

"The female reticence to fire people has always baffled me. I understand that you feel bad, that's natural, no one likes this kind of thing, but your emotions should not be the guiding force. If someone is incapable of living up to expectations, making excuses for them will only hurt you in the long run. It always comes back to bite you. Under normal circumstances, I'd tell you that, because you essentially agree with Favata, you should go ahead and fire her, no matter how difficult it is."

"But?"

"In this case, stalling might be a better option. Favata wants to get more of his own people in there. It would be to your benefit to hold him off if you can. We just need a little more time."

I am struck by his use of the word *we*. "Time for what?" I ask. "For them to come up with new ways to torture me?"

"I am getting close to something. About Favata," he adds.

"What?"

"I can't go into details yet. I need to get some proof first. But if I'm right it goes a lot deeper than sexual harassment. And it will get him out of your way for good."

"You're being very cryptic."

"I'd like to be sure before I say too much more."

"Is it filthy, will it totally destroy him?" I ask hopefully. "Was he caught having sex with a donkey in a dominatrix outfit?"

David laughs. "This is a new side of you. I think I like it. Sadly, there were no hooved animals or whips involved, at least as far as I can tell."

"Damn. You know," I add more seriously, "one of the things I don't get is if he was accused of sexual harassment, why did Merdale hire him?"

"I can name at least five male executives who have been charged with harassment, even abuse," David answers. "They apologize, pay up, go to rehab or take a couple of anger management classes and get their old jobs back. If they were good. If not, all bets are off. I don't need to tell you it's still an old boys' network."

"You have no idea how depressing that is."

"I didn't say I like it. I hate it as much as you do."

"I wonder if his wife knows anything about this."

"Probably not."

I play with my chopsticks, the pale wood smooth and slippery in my hands. "Can I ask you a question?" I say quietly.

"Of course."

"Why do men cheat?"

"It's not that complicated. All they really want is for a woman to tell them how big and strong and brilliant they are. Wives have an unfortunate tendency to stop doing that."

"There has to be more to it than that."

"You'd be surprised. I'm not convinced women are any better. They want someone to remind them how beautiful and sexually attractive they are."

"Has anyone ever told you that you have an overwhelmingly cynical view of relationships?"

"Biology is cynical."

"What about free will, responsibility? Doesn't that play any part in the equation?"

"Of course. I didn't say I think any of it is inevitable. But you asked about motive. In most cases, motives are quite simple. It always comes down to money, sex, ego or addiction. All you have to do is figure out which."

"Were you faithful?"

The corners of his mouth turn up. "Talk about getting right to the point."

"Never mind. I didn't mean to pry."

"It's all right. Let's just say my marriage broke up due to a series of unfortunate events." He pauses. "No. I wasn't faithful. I'm sorry."

"You don't need to apologize to me."

"What I meant was, I'm sorry that it happened. For any number of reasons. One of which is that I realize it diminishes me in your eyes. I wouldn't make the same mistake again, by the way."

"Good to know," I say dryly.

"Lisa, what's this all about? I get the feeling we've moved way past Favata. Are you all right?"

I shrug.

"I can be a good friend. If you'll let me."

I push a single grain of rice about the tablecloth with my thumbnail. "Everything's fine."

He stills my hand with his fingertips. "I don't believe you," he says gently.

I look down, feel the warmth of his touch seep in, and all the hurt I have been struggling to quell begins to rise up. I try to push it back but tears break through the thin membrane of propriety. Now, in this sedate expense-account restaurant with a man I barely know, I feel the onslaught and am powerless to stop it.

He gently brushes away the first tears from my cheek. "Lisa?"

"I'm sorry, I'm so sorry," I manage to get out.

"What is it? Please, let me help you."

I shake my head.

"No job is worth this," he tells me.

"It's not the job."

"What is it then?"

I look up into his eyes, open and kind and waiting, and I give in, give in to my need to tell someone, give in because I have no defenses left and he is holding out the promise, the temptation of comfort. "I think my husband is having an affair," I say.

"Sam?"

I nod.

"I see." David's face registers very little. "Are you sure?"

Sitting with our sushi untouched before us, I tell David everything. It streams out of me, from the late-night phone calls to the lies about Chicago ending with the disposable phone I found on Saturday. Maybe I need a little of his clear-sightedness. Or perhaps it is simply protection I crave. Deep down, there is still a part of me that believes men are able to do that, take care of things. All I know is that I don't want to think anymore, I'm not even sure that I can. I want someone else to do it for me.

While I speak, David leaves his hand on mine, steady, sure.

"What did you do with the phone?" he asks when I am done.

"I threw it out. It was like having something contaminated in the house. Besides, Sam can't very well ask where it is." Tears well up in my eyes once more. "David, you have to understand something. I love Sam. I've spent virtually my entire adult life with him. We have children."

"I know that. And I hope you can work this out."

I take a deep breath, beginning to regain some composure.

"Have you checked his finances?" he asks carefully.

"No. Why?"

"Men often start moving things around to protect their assets if they are planning to make a move."

"Sam's not like that. He's . . ." I am about to say "honorable," it is what I have always believed. I don't finish the sentence.

"Don't do anything until you have consulted with a lawyer," David tells me. "I can give you some names if you'd like."

"Oh God." It is suddenly so real.

"I'm not saying what I think the outcome will be. I'd just like you to be prepared."

How do you prepare yourself for heartbreak, I wonder. Or betrayal.

"I can't be as coolheaded as you," I reply, resentment creeping into my tone. Maybe I don't want his advice after all. "I can't plot out every step before I take it."

"I'm sorry. I didn't mean to sound like such a hard-ass. Believe me, I'm not. I may be a great strategist when it comes to business or giving advice about other people's lives, but I crumble with the best of them when it comes to romance. Once your heart enters into the mix, it's all improvisation. I'm just trying to help. It's hard to see you like this."

"I know that. I'm sorry."

"Don't be. I'm glad you told me."

"Are you?"

"Yes," he says. "I am."

He smiles and then he leans over, gently moving a loose strand of hair from my eyes, and presses his lips softly to mine.

SEVENTEEN

I glance at the clock. 6:07.

I shut my eyes and try to fall back to sleep for twenty minutes until the alarm goes off, but the noise from the kitchen is growing more purposeful. The papers hit the table with a dull thud, cabinet doors swing open and squeak shut again.

I pulled away. That is what I remind myself, what I have been reminding myself of all through the restless night. I pulled away from David's kiss.

But not before I felt the lingering imprint of his lips on mine, not right away.

This is how it happens, a touch, a kiss brushed off and then not, and suddenly you are there, in a foreign country you swore you would never end up in, it was for other people, not you, not your husband, not your marriage.

We weren't supposed to be that couple.

I shake my head. I moved my lips away from his, embarrassed, confused, but not unmoved. It was not David I pulled away from but myself.

Is that how it happened for Sam?

I have been conjuring images incessantly for days, nights now, visions of faces, of bodies, hers, his. Who would he desire, who would he give in to or pursue? Men's tastes, even my own husband's, are often inexplicable.

All I know is that she is not me.

A drawer slams vehemently shut in the kitchen. I hear the silverware rattle.

There is no way I am going to fall back to sleep.

Though Sam has wandered the apartment at dawn with increasing frequency, ravaged by insomnia, he has always been careful not to wake us, tiptoeing around on bare feet. The clatter seems purposeful, intended to rile me.

I turn on my side, taken with the guilt-ridden notion that he somehow knows about David's kiss and that is what he is banging on about. But how could he?

I sink back into the memory once more, his lips, the way I parted with him on the street corner with barely a good-bye, sadly, reluctantly, but resolutely turning my back, walking away.

Which seems to be a whole lot more than I can say for Sam.

Furious, I give up on the prospect of sleep and head into the kitchen. Despite what David advised—do nothing, say nothing until you are fully prepared—I am hell-bent, finally, on confrontation.

Sam is standing with both hands pressed against the counter, his back to me, his shoulders, beneath a worn gray T-shirt, hunched over. "I don't fucking believe it," he mutters, to himself or to me, I'm not quite sure. He turns around before I have a chance to say a word. "Look at this," he demands, thrusting the front page of the *Times* business section into my hands.

Annoyed at being thrown off course, I take the newspaper from him, searching impatiently for whatever it is that has upset him so much. It's impossible to miss. Just below the fold there is a photograph of Eliot Wells with the headline:

LEXIMARK FOUNDER BEING INVESTIGATED
FOR PRE-DATING STOCK OPTIONS. SPECIAL
PROSECUTOR CALLED IN.

I glance at Sam before reading further.

"I knew it," he says bitterly. "No one believed me, but I knew it."

"No one," of course, includes me.

I am slammed up against it, completely blocked. I realize that he couldn't have known my intention when I stormed into the kitchen, couldn't have planned this, but still.

Sam looks over my shoulder at the headline once again. "I'm fucked," he proclaims.

At this particular moment, I don't give a rat's ass about Eliot Wells, but I have to say something. "At least it shows Simon your instincts were on target."

"A lot of good that does me."

"You gave it your best shot. There will be other stories," I say feebly. Comforting Sam is not exactly high on my priority list.

"This is a goddamned disaster," he reiterates.

"Don't you think that's a bit of an overreaction? You had no choice. You were told to drop the story. No one can hold this against you."

"You just don't get it," he says irately. "You have done nothing but second-guess me from the beginning. You never made the slightest effort to understand what I was trying to do."

"That's not true."

"Yes, as a matter of fact it is. All you cared about was how my going after that story might affect you."

He slams his mug down, spilling coffee across the tile. I watch as brown liquid swims into the grouting. "I need to go in to work and make some calls." He leaves the room before I can say anything further.

I pour myself some coffee and sit down, staring at the table.

The girls, needless to say, manage to sleep through all of this. When they finally realize Sam's absence halfway through breakfast, I tell them he had to go in to work early and they return to their cereal, unconcerned. It is hard for me to gauge how much of the turbulence they have picked up on, if it is sneaking into their psyches in ways yet to be discovered or if it has barely made an impression on their naturally self-involved thoughts.

Yesterday, when we were talking about the upcoming parent-teacher conferences (children are asked to be present at Weston, their voices must be heard), Phoebe blurted out how sorry she felt for poor Rebecca Klennan. "Her parents' divorce is so bad they refuse to go to the conference together so she has to sit through it twice," she said.

"That sucks," Claire agreed. They began to list the girls who would suffer a similar fate—the ranking of parental discord obviously a popular topic in the cafeteria these days.

I try not to cry in front of them.

I clear their breakfast dishes, hurry them along, get ready for work.

I put on makeup, leave the house, swipe my MetroCard, avoid all eye contact.

All through the sleepless night, between reliving David's kiss and Sam's lies, I thought of David's edict—ferret out the financial facts, arm myself. Be smart, be deliberate. When I get to work, I consider calling our financial adviser, the polite but stern man who helps us try to figure out whether we should be saving for college or retirement because clearly there is not enough money for both, but I cannot face him. It is ironic that just at the time you should be most sensible you are the least able to be.

I pull out the spreadsheets I was working on before I left last night and try to concentrate on them instead. Every minute or two I glance at my computer, at my phone. There has been no e-mail from David, no message since I turned and walked away.

The silence has taken on a physicality all its own, snowballing, pulling everything into it, dense, thick, pressing in on me. I should be relieved by it, or at the very least not surprised, but I am neither. I try to imagine what David is thinking, if he is embarrassed or feels rejected, if he assumes that my walking away meant good-bye. Which it did and it didn't.

The silence, the not-knowing eats at me. I briefly manage to convince myself that I owe him an explanation or apology, that he is being a gentleman and leaving it up to me to get in touch or not, my choice, my move. This is, I realize, a convenient if specious excuse for reestablishing contact. But that doesn't mean it isn't true. Vacillating, I begin to type an e-mail but don't know what to say. I leave the e-mail open, blank.

At ten thirty, I look up to see Tessa Caldwell standing in my doorway. "Do you have a minute?" she asks hesitantly.

This is all I need. "Can it wait? I'm kind of busy right now."

She takes a step closer. "It's important."

I have no choice. "All right, come in."

I have formulated a tentative plan to put Tessa on probation for a month to buy myself some time but I haven't had a chance to run it by HR. I have no idea what to say to her now.

"I brought you the rewrites on the Elan account," she says, handing them to me as she takes a seat.

"Thank you." I glance down at them, stymied about how to proceed.

"I know I've been a little slow on the uptake lately," Tessa continues. "I appreciate your being patient with me. I owe you an explanation." She breaks into a wide, self-satisfied grin. "I'm pregnant," she announces.

Tessa is in her late thirties, single and of debatable sexual persuasion. This is not exactly what I expected. It is also an excellent piece of news. The surest route to a major lawsuit and a slew of damaging publicity is to fire a pregnant woman. Tessa has just bought me—and herself—nine months. I congratulate her heartily.

As soon as she is out my door I go into Favata's office.

"Can I help you?" he asks gruffly.

"I just spoke with Tessa Caldwell."

He looks a bit surprised. "How did she take it?"

"I didn't fire her. I couldn't."

"What does that mean?"

"She's pregnant."

Favata puts down his pen and stares at me as if I have personally inseminated her just to spite him. Finally, he nods. "I see." He turns to his computer and begins typing. I have been excused.

Back at my own desk, the person I most want to call to tell about the Tessa denouement is David. It seems crazy that I can't. I try to put it aside—it is for the best—and begin to rewrite three press releases myself, a task usually left to someone lower on the totem pole, but I am too distracted to concentrate on anything but what is missing.

There is no reason we can't be friends. I am blowing this all out of proportion. He is just waiting for a sign from me. Before I can talk myself out of it—or examine my motives too closely—I pick up the phone and dial David's number.

"Lisa." I can hear the relief in his voice. "I'm glad you called. I wasn't sure you wanted to talk to me."

"I'm sorry."

"I'm the one who should apologize to you. I was out of line. I certainly didn't mean to upset you more than you already were."

I don't know what to answer, I don't know what I want. To be asked so that I can say no and mean no but be asked again nonetheless. To keep my options open even as I deny them. To avoid finality, a closed door.

"You're not going to believe what happened with the copywriter," I tell him, my voice too bright as I move purposefully, clumsily away from us.

We turn the details this way and that for far longer than they merit, trying to reassure ourselves that we are back on familiar ground, though of course we are not.

Eventually there is nothing left to say about Tessa Caldwell.

There is a long silence.

We listen to each other breathe. I play with the phone cord.

"David? The list of lawyers you mentioned," I say quietly. "Can you send them to me?"

"Of course. If that's what you want."

"I'm not sure what I want."

Neither of us speaks.

"Lisa, I'd like to see you," he says.

I take a long time before answering. "I need some time to figure things out."

"I understand. Whatever you need. Will you call me when you are ready?"

"Yes."

"Or if you need anything at all."

"I will."

There is nothing left to do but hang up.

For the rest of the morning I go through the endless stream of papers that Favata is sending my way, the mind-numbing P&L statements, the expense accounts returned with queries written on every item.

It is midafternoon when Petra tells me that Jack is on the line.

"Deirdre told me she saw you on Saturday," he remarks after we exchange hellos.

He is mining for details, as avid as any sixteen-year-old girl to relive the minutiae of his courtship. It is natural, I remind myself, that he should want to speak to me of Deirdre. Romantic exhilaration, like confession, demands an outlet, and there is probably no one else he can open up to. One of the more annoying qualities of the newly in love is their conviction that happiness is contagious when so often, despite ourselves, the opposite is true.

"I don't know how to thank you," he goes on. "For everything."

"I really didn't do anything, Jack."

"That's not completely true," he says, as if he is paying me a compliment.

"Deirdre told me you almost have the job wrapped up."

"Yes, that's one of the reasons I'm calling. I have to be in town next week for some final negotiations. I'd love to take you to lunch."

"That's very nice, but you don't need to do that."

"I'd like to. Plus," he admits, "I have an ulterior motive."

"Oh?"

"I was hoping you could help me."

"With what?"

"Deirdre's birthday is coming up."

"An event she would very much like to forget."

"I was wondering if you could come with me to pick out a gift for her. Something special."

"Do you have any ideas?"

"All I know is I want to show her how serious I am."

"I think she realizes that."

"I just don't want to blow it."

I have been ignoring the blinking light while we talk but now Petra knocks and comes in despite my motioning for her to wait. "It's important," she whispers.

"I've got to go," I tell Jack. "I'll be happy to go with you. Just shoot me the details."

"What is it?" I ask Petra impatiently as soon as I hang up.

"It's Claire. She says it's an emergency."

EIGHTEEN

I grab the phone. "Claire? Is everything okay?"

She stammers, gasping as she tries to take in air, trapping the words in her throat.

"Claire? What is it?"

"It's Phoebe. She was with me and then . . ." Tears fill the empty spaces.

"And then what?" Panic crescendos through me.

"I can't find her," Claire cries. "I can't find Phoebe."

"What do you mean, you can't find her? Didn't you come home from school together?"

"I turned around and she was just . . . gone." Claire's voice is mottled with fear.

"Where are you?"

"Union Square."

"What on earth are you doing there?"

"I'm sorry."

"Stop apologizing and tell me what happened."

"We were going to Forever 21."

"You were going shopping?" Forever 21 is the mecca of choice for cheap designer knockoffs and trendy disposable baubles. The flashy, trashy inventory changes so rapidly that every teen in New York seems to feel the need to scout it out at least ten times a month.

"We were just going to stop on our way home from school."

"It's not on your way home. At all." I realize this is not exactly the most salient point at the moment.

"She was right beside me and then I turned around and she wasn't. I'm sure she's fine, right? I mean, she's just lost. I've been looking all over Union Square."

"Did you tell a policeman?"

"No."

"See if you can find one and tell him what happened. Then stay where you are. I don't want you wandering off looking for her by yourself. Do you hear me?"

"Yes."

"Go to the statue of Gandhi in the park and wait for me. Do not move. I'm on my way." I hang up and grab my coat, racing through the hall, pressing for the elevator, moving as fast as I can.

Phoebe is fine, she has to be fine. Children get lost. They get found.

I press the elevator button again, and again.

I remind myself of all the times she has wandered off in the past (it was always Phoebe, never Claire; sweet, distracted, untethered Phoebe, less nervous by nature than Claire, who had a tendency to glance back repeatedly, never allowing too much distance to grow between us). There was the time we had to have the guards lock down the entire Children's Zoo in Central Park while we ran through the caverns screaming her name, what better place for a kidnapper, a pedophile. Fifteen minutes later (it felt like hours, days, a lifetime) we found Phoebe calmly looking at the seals, oblivious to the commotion going on around her. She hadn't even noticed that there was no grown-up in sight, that she had unloosed herself. There was that time on the beach in Montauk.

The elevator finally comes and I squeeze in.

We found her, I remind myself, we found her every time.

Still, I wonder if this is one of those moments that changes your life forever, rips it in two, turns it into before and after. If this is it.

As soon as I reach the ground floor I dial Sam's office, but he isn't there.

I reach him on his cell as I am getting into a cab and tell him what happened. "I'll meet you in the park," he says. "Lisa, you know Phoebe. We'll find her." I strain to hear him over a noisy background.

"Where are you?" I ask.

"I'll be there in ten minutes, fifteen tops. I'm leaving now."

As the cab lurches through midtown traffic, I call home despite the fact that Phoebe lost her set of house keys two months ago and we haven't gotten around to replacing them. There is no answer.

"Hurry," I plead with the driver, "please hurry." I want him to leapfrog over the hoods of other cars, drive on the sidewalk if need be.

I jam some bills into his hand as he pulls up to the park and slam the door. My eyes roam frantically from left to right as I head into Union Square, past tattooed NYU students clustered in groups and white Rasta skateboard boys and nannies leading toddlers to the bucket swings, past a card table of kittens in cardboard boxes with hand-painted adoption signs and a blanket stacked with Xeroxed screenplays for sale. A part of me thought that I would discover Phoebe the second I got out of the cab, as if she were simply waiting for my arrival to materialize.

But I don't see her anywhere.

The air goes out of me.

I spot Claire standing by the statue, huddled in her navy peacoat, her eyes darting anxiously. "Daddy just got here," she tells me when I reach her. "He's talking to that policeman."

I look over at the two men and see them shake hands before Sam heads back to us. He kisses me quickly hello.

"What did the policeman say?" I ask.

"They are going to get a patrol car to circle the block but that's pretty much all they can do at this point. In the meantime, I want you two to comb the park and ask everyone you see to keep an eye out. Lisa, do you have a picture of Phoebe with you?"

I shake my head. Ever since the advent of digital cameras, my wallet has been barren of photos, all of them remain parked on our home computer, unprinted. I am a terrible parent. If anything happens it is my fault, the negligent mother who doesn't even keep pictures of her children in her purse.

"All right, do the best you can to describe her and tell them if they see anyone who fits the description to walk her over to the statue and wait for us. This is our meeting spot, okay? Be back here in ten minutes. And stick together," he admonishes.

"Come." I take Claire's arm and we begin to walk on the southern outskirts of the park. Just across from us, Fourteenth Street is a dizzying eddy of men hawking fake designer sunglasses, smoky kebab carts, people pouring into the subway kiosk, shoppers making their way out of Whole Foods laden with cloth bags, a maw that could swallow anyone whole, especially an eleven-year-old girl. I begin to grow nauseous.

"Okay, tell me again, where was the last place you saw Phoebe?"

Claire points a few yards ahead, just across from Forever 21. "We were crossing the street but when I got to the other side she wasn't there. Mom, I thought she was right beside me." She looks up at me. "We're going to find her, right?"

"Yes."

We walk a few more feet in silence and then stop at the spot Claire has indicated, turning 360 degrees while we call Phoebe's name. But there is no response, there is nothing, just a blurry sea of faces who have nothing to do with us. A few people turn to regard us with an impassive curiosity but it is someone else's story, not theirs, and they hurry on.

We begin walking again, weaving around a hunched-over junkie frozen mid-nod, when Claire's cell phone rings. We both stop dead in our tracks.

Claire grabs it from her pocket, opens it and looks at the number displayed. She flips the phone open to talk.

"My mom is here," she says quietly.

"Who is it?" I interrupt.

"Deirdre." Claire hands the phone to me. "She wants to talk to you."

"Why is Deirdre calling you?"

"I called her."

I look at her quizzically—it will have to wait till later—and put the phone up to my ear.

"Is everything okay?" Deirdre asks. "Claire left a message for me at the store but I was out. I didn't get it until now. She said it was an emergency."

"We can't find Phoebe."

"What do you mean, you can't find Phoebe? Where are you?"

I explain the situation while Claire and I resume walking, Claire calling out her sister's name, my eyes roaming while I speak.

"Do you want me to come?" Deirdre asks.

"No. Look, I need to go."

"Call me as soon as you hear anything."

"I will." I hang up and catch up to Claire.

"Why did you call Deirdre?" I do not look at her while I talk, I am looking for Phoebe.

Claire's narrow shoulders shiver as she fights to hold back the sobs that are gathering within. "I'm sorry, Mom. I'm so sorry. I knew how mad you'd be. I never should have come here. I'm sorry."

Her face is so contorted, so tragic, that all I can do is wrap my arms around her. "Let's just find your sister."

As we round a bend of trees, the statue peeks into view. It has become my talisman, my hope, as if somehow Phoebe will know this is our meeting spot.

But Sam is standing there alone, shutting his cell phone and putting it back into his pocket.

"Nothing?" I ask.

He shakes his head.

I shut my eyes, feel a sudden vertigo that makes the pavement fade to nothingness beneath my feet. Sam pulls me to him and I bury my head in his shoulder, the shape of his body, the smell of his wool coat so achingly familiar. His scarf, an old navy fringed cashmere one I gave him a million Christmases ago, brushes against my cheek. I clutch him tightly.

"We're going to find her," he says. "Phoebe has done this before."

I nod, wanting so much to believe him. "Now what?"

"We keep looking."

"What about the police?"

"Nothing so far."

"Can't they do anything else?"

"It's only been forty-five minutes. They can't file a missing persons."

I shudder at the words, so stark and gruesome, how could they have anything to do with us? "What about an Amber Alert?"

Sam shakes his head. "Claire, are there any friends of Phoebe's you can think to call?"

"I don't know any of their numbers."

"What about Rory?" I ask. Rory is Phoebe's best friend from camp, a would-be dancer who eats yogurt with a fork, letting it drip through the tines, slowly licking the remains and calling it dinner. She lives on the Upper West Side, she goes to a different school, I don't even know the last time Phoebe spoke to her, but at least it's something. I am just about to call information to get her parents' home number when my cell phone rings.

"Hello?"

"Is this Lisa?"

"Yes?"

"This is Brian DePaul."

I can't place the name, though it sounds vaguely familiar.

"Your downstairs neighbor?" His face swims through the murk, the opera lover with the night-for-day hours and the strange cooking odors seeping from his front door, a bony, solitary man nearing fifty who always used to complain about the noise the girls made while he was trying to sleep. At three in the afternoon.

"Yes?" I say impatiently. I can't imagine what crime against his delicate sensibilities we have committed now. Nor do I particularly care at the moment.

"I seem to have your daughter," he says archly, as if we have carelessly misplaced her.

"You have Phoebe? Is she okay?"

"I'll put her on."

"Phoebe, are you all right?"

Her voice is calm and even, soaked in maturity. "I'm fine, Mom."

"Thank God. How did you get home?" I am barely listening, all I hear is the echo in my head, she is safe, she is safe . . .

"I bent down to tie my shoe and when I looked up Claire was gone. I couldn't find her anyplace. So I walked home."

"By yourself? How did you know the way?"

"Mom, I'm not a moron." The degree of our alarm is incomprehensible to her, the terror of things she has never heard of unimaginable.

"We'll be right there. Can you put Brian back on?"

"Okay."

She hands the phone over.

"I don't know what to say. Thank you."

"It's a good thing I was home," he replies tartly.

The giddy residue of panic as it subsides silences all three of us as we find a cab and head home to claim our wayward daughter.

On the way, I phone Deirdre to let her know that Phoebe is all right.

"I'm so sorry I wasn't there when Claire called."

Sam puts his hand on my knee while I listen, watching my face.

"Everything's okay now," he says quietly after I hang up. "We're all okay."

We find Phoebe sitting in Brian DePaul's living room, where every surface is draped in Indian silks, lace and gauze, the elegantly fussy lair of a semi-shut-in. She is serenely eating ginger snaps from a tarnished silver platter, poised as if attending a tea party. It is only when I take her in my arms, feel her body pressed tight to mine, that I feel the truest relief. "Let's go home."

Later, after the recriminations and teary apologies have left us all depleted, we tuck the girls into bed, kiss them good night, turn at the doorway to be sure they are still there, aware with every movement of the normality of the evening, the blessing of it. We are all in place, safe, nothing has changed. I am so very thankful that the day has turned into an anecdote and not the end.

Closing the door to Phoebe's room one last time, I walk out into the hallway where Sam is standing, waiting for me. Our eyes meet and he takes me in his arms. He is the only other person on earth who will ever love my children as much as I do, the only person who will ever truly understand.

Sam goes to take a shower and I sit in the near-silent living room. I can almost hear the girls breathing deeply in their separate worlds of sleep. As I sink into the faded couch I am filled with an overwhelming sense of fragility, of how vulnerable we all are, how close we have come to flying apart, fragmenting.

And it terrifies me.

I am not at all sure that dissolution is what I want.

There are women who do nothing, who shrug off or ignore men's fickleness even if they can never quite forgive or forget, women who make a conscious decision to look the other way, wait for it to pass. There are marriages that come out the other side. I have always been judgmental of them but I am less so now. It is an option, after all.

I'm just not sure it is an option for me.

The list of lawyers is folded in my wallet.

I look up to see Sam standing in the doorway, getting on his coat.

"Where are you going?" I ask, taken aback.

"I left work in such a hurry," he says. "I need to go clean some things up."

"Now?"

"It was a rough day, Lisa."

I listen as the door closes behind him.

NINETEEN

A week later, news of my lax parenting has spread uptown. It is written on my forehead, it is oozing from my pores: I am the mother with the regrettable habit of misplacing her children.

First Claire, caught out by Georgia three long blocks from school.

Now Phoebe's escapade in Union Square.

I'm not quite sure how every woman in Georgia Hartman's living room this morning knows of it but they do, I can smell it. Like a game of telephone, the details have surely grown more baroque and damning with each retelling. No doubt half of them believe Phoebe was rescued from the clutches of a child predator just as she was about to be dragged over the George Washington Bridge. And the other half believes something worse.

I look around the room for help, but the only possible source, Tara, is a no-show. In a manner completely out of proportion to our real relationship, I miss her.

The topic of this morning's benefit meeting is the auction catalogue—but beneath it all I can feel their sideways glances, a stew of maternal censoriousness and condescending sympathy at the hardships I must endure raising two juvenile delinquents.

It is all I can do to keep from screaming, My kids are the normal ones.

But of course we have different definitions of the term.

My normal does not include being captain of an international fencing team in your spare time, having a college adviser at age twelve to help develop extracurricular passions (plain old interests are no longer deemed good enough) or being the youngest congressional aide on record. My kids do not attend Exeter/Yale/Harvard during the summer break for extra classes. They go to camp. A Y camp at that. With positively no educational value. Except that they love it. And yes, my kids wander off sometimes. But in my heart of hearts I believe that children who never stray, who never test boundaries, will develop raging drug habits and a midlife crisis at twenty-two. Of course, I could be totally wrong. Their kids could easily be running the world while mine are nodding out on street corners.

"Lisa?"

I snap out of my internal rebellion to find Georgia staring at me. This proclivity to drift off in the middle of conversations, to get lost in the poorly lit grottoes of my own anxiety and indecision, is a new development. I need to be more vigilant.

"Yes?"

"Did you bring the picture?"

"The picture?"

"Of Ben Erickson's studio?"

I stare at her for a moment before I remember what she is talking about. Georgia, not content merely to list the many impressive offerings in the catalogue, has decided that each should be accompanied by a photograph to "personalize" it, perhaps even making the catalogue itself a collector's item. Not just any stock publicity picture will do. No, Georgia has volunteered (or ordered) her oldest daughter, Vanessa, to do all the photography herself. The fact that this will be incontrovertible proof of Vanessa's "passion for photography" on her college applications is a mere side benefit, one that the women assembled are too polite to mention though each is secretly peeved she didn't think of it herself. (The way I figure it, Vanessa has nothing to worry about. Both Georgia and her husband, as well as one set of grandparents, all went to Princeton. How hard is it going to be? The word *legacy* was invented for her.) When Georgia first brought up the idea, I hedged, certain that Vanessa would pester Ben for an internship he has no desire to grant or a recommendation he would surely deny. It is bad enough that I am holding him to his promised donation despite his split with Deirdre. I certainly can't unleash Vanessa Hartman on him.

"I'm going to his studio this morning," I reply.

"I wish you'd reconsider." Georgia's sugarcoated smile is brittle, cracking in the corners. "Vanessa would be more than happy to do it."

"I understand, but Ben is very private. He doesn't allow strangers in his studio."

"So you've said. I didn't realize you two were such good friends."

"We've known each other for years."

"Yes, of course. Let's move on, shall we?"

I force myself to pay attention while the meeting progresses to paper stock, print runs and whether it would be possible to have one edition autographed by each of the better-known donors. Samantha, Class of '91, salivating at the connections this could augur, quickly volunteers to have her daughter do that.

It is ten a.m. when we are finally done. A slow, steady autumn rain, chilly and unforgiving, has begun to fall as I head out of the Hartman town house. I told Favata I would be doing department store research on one of our cosmetics companies and would be in by eleven, which doesn't leave me much time with Ben. I get out my four-dollar collapsible umbrella, open it, and curse the fact that I accidentally took the one with two spokes missing.

By the time I get out of the subway and make it to Ben's studio on West Twenty-fifth Street I am totally soaked. The smell of wet wool clings to me as I brush water from my coat and take a deep breath before pushing the buzzer. In all the years we've known each other, I have never been alone with Ben. As I ride up in the industrial elevator, scratched and dusty, my throat is suddenly dry. All of the conversations, the innuendos, all of the times I have urged Deirdre to leave him feel as if they are staining my skin.

If nothing else, the etiquette of the situation is oblique to me. Do I mention Deirdre, pretend I know nothing of their breakup, offer some form of—what?—sympathy?

Upstairs, a shaggy-haired young man in a black T-shirt and jeans, a single tattoo of thorns wrapped about his muscled forearm, opens the door to the vast studio.

"Are you Lisa?"

"Yes."

"Hi. I'm Owen. Ben's assistant. Come in. He'll be right with you."

Owen smiles pleasantly, an off-center toothy grin destined to shatter girls' hearts, and continues to pack up huge battered leather trunks with wires and clamps, lights and lenses. "He doesn't exactly travel light," he remarks without looking up.

"Where are you going?"

"I'm not. Ben is. India. *Vogue* is doing a story on an ashram outside Delhi and asked Ben to shoot it. Have you been?" he asks as casually as if it is Brooklyn.

"No."

"Me neither. I offered to go, but he prefers to use local people as assistants. Seems an iffy proposition," he remarks.

"He's going to have a field day getting all that through customs," I remark.

"We ship it over ahead of time. All he has to bring is a small carry-on bag."

Owen closes up one trunk and starts on the next while I step around a cluster of tripods leaning in the corner like folded-up tin men and go into a large open area, which has soaring white walls and a hammered-tin ceiling. At the far end of the room is a bare stage shadowed by a gray paper backdrop, rolls of colored screens, silver umbrellas and wooden stools of varying heights. An enormous African mask hangs on the wall beside it.

"It is supposed to offer protection but it has always seemed rather menacing to me. Then again, maybe instilling fear in others is the best protection there is."

I turn to see Ben walking toward me.

"You're drenched," he says as he leans over to kiss me hello. "Let me take your coat."

He steps behind me and gently lifts the shoulders as I struggle out of the dank, clingy sleeves. When I am finally free, Ben hangs it on an antique brass coat stand in the corner a few feet from his bicycle, an old gray clunker with a bent wire basket hanging from the handlebars. I would have thought he'd have some fancy spider-thin Italian number or a mountain bike with 102 gears—Ben, the connoisseur of people and objects, with his fine discriminating eye and his artist's appreciation for anything well made.

He notices my reaction and shrugs, smiling. "They get stolen every two or three months so I've stopped investing in them," he remarks, with none of the outrage or frustration others might evince but rather an easygoing acceptance, as if the city's flaws and favors are equally intriguing. Ben's confidence, his innate cool and unapologetic faith in his own taste and judgment, leave me feeling hopelessly conventional.

"You've never been here, have you?" he asks as I take in the studio.

I shake my head. "I can't thank you enough," I say as he leads me through the three-thousand-square-foot space. "You didn't have to do this."

"Not at all. I've been bullied enough times by the benefit committee at Jake and Beryl's school to know what it's like."

I can't imagine Ben being bullied by anything or anyone.

"I'll admit this catalogue thing is a new twist, though," he adds as we step around a ball of thick black electrical cords. "What exactly do you need?"

"Oh God, I don't know. Anything will be fine."

Ben laughs, his narrow face creasing. "Let me give you a tip. Pretend to know what you want, even if you don't. It makes the person posing far too insecure when there is no evident plan. Someone needs to be in control. It might as well be you."

"Is that your technique?"

"One of them," he acknowledges. Beneath his amused demeanor, there is an old-world wiliness, an assumption that anything can be bartered, and an undeniable relish in the process.

"This must be torture for you," I worry out loud as I pull out the digital camera I've brought, an old model twice the weight of the newer ones.

"Not at all. Amateurs often come up with far more interesting images than the hackneyed ones we professionals perpetrate. Fewer preconceptions, I suppose. Though I have a feeling you've come armed with a few about me."

I look away nervously.

He steps closer to me, his voice even and gentle. "Lisa, I realize the awkwardness of the situation, okay? But whatever happens between me and Deirdre, it has nothing to do with you. I'd like to think we're friends."

"Of course," I reassure him, relieved.

Friends and lovers, attached and unattached, are seemingly fungible delineations to Ben. Still, I can't help but imagine that his reaction might be a bit stronger if he knew of my machinations.

"Come. Tell me where you want me to stand. I'll do anything you want except for one of those hokey things where I'm holding a camera and looking pensive."

Needless to say, this is precisely what I was going to suggest. I glance around, desperate for some meager inspiration that will not totally embarrass me.

"How about here?" Ben asks, rescuing me from my own discomfort. He moves just to the right of two white couches in a makeshift sitting area. "The light is good and you can get the tripods in the background for all that local color the benefit ladies go for."

"Perfect." I hastily raise my camera.

Ben buries his hands in the pockets of his black jeans and turns so that his face is at a three-quarter angle. His handsomeness is one of hollows and planes, more intriguing because it is not obvious. As I study him through the viewfinder, his deep brown eyes look directly at me, unwavering. Despite his preternatural stillness, there is something tightly coiled in him, an edgy magnetism. It is impossible not to see the temptation, the lure of him.

I click the shutter twice and lower the camera.

"That's it?" he asks. "If I were you I'd take a few more just to be on the safe side. I'm sure the last thing you want is to have to come back here."

"Am I making it seem that painful?"

"Not at all. I just know how easy it is to make mistakes. Unfortunately, by the time you realize that you don't have what you need it's often too late." He walks over to the seating area and perches on the arm of the couch. "Let's try this. Move over to the right a few feet. There, that's good."

I smile. "I thought I was the one who was supposed to have the plan."

"Sorry. I'm not used to relinquishing control," he says, laughing just enough to soften the admission.

I take a few more pictures, following his direction. "I've always wondered, do you have an idea in your head of what the finished image will be before you begin?" I ask, kneeling down as he suggests.

"I try not to. My job is to expose what I discover in a person without editorializing."

"That's hard to do with some of your subjects, isn't it?"

"Not really. It's what makes it interesting."

I cannot decide if Ben's genuine lack of prejudice is open-minded or betrays the libertine's desire to taste and experience everything if his refusal to pass judgment means there is no right and wrong in his world.

"I seem to recall you can't believe anyone with a shred of sanity would sit for me," he adds teasingly.

"Did I say that?"

"Close enough."

"Well, consider it a testament to your talent," I reply.

"A likely story."

Finally, I have taken enough pictures to satisfy Ben.

"Owen said you were going to India to shoot an ashram?" I remark as I put away my camera.

"Yes, I'm leaving on Monday. A celebrity ashram, if you can imagine. According to *Vogue,* inner peace is the must-have accessory of the moment, though I believe they are selling it, subliminally at least, as a beauty treatment as much as anything else. When we were discussing the assignment, they made a point of telling me how everyone there had these fabulous complexions and how nice it would be if I could capture that on film along with the more sensual yoga positions."

I laugh. It is much easier to dislike Ben when I am not in his presence.

"Come, I'll show you out."

As we walk past the coffee table, my eye is caught by a stack of eight-by-ten black-and-white photos, fanning out across the glass. They look fresh, almost wet.

And they are all of Deirdre.

I turn away self-consciously.

"Do you want to see them?" Ben asks. "I just developed them last night."

He picks up the top picture, studies it as if seeing it for the first time and passes it to me. Deirdre in bed, sleeping, oblivious to the camera, her hair spreading out across the pillow like a darkened web, a sheet barely skimming her bare shoulders. Her lips are parted and there is a smudge of makeup beneath her eye, a study of flaws and vulnerability. I look at the next one: Deirdre, perched on the window seat, wearing only a shirt, hugging her knees as she looks down at the street below.

"What do you think?" Ben asks. I'm surprised by the question; he is by nature so unconcerned with others' opinions.

"They're very different."

"From what?"

"The images I've seen of yours. They're so much less removed."

"Yes, well, Deirdre and I do know each other rather intimately."

I pick up the last picture: Deirdre caught midact in her nervous habit of picking up her hair, letting it fall, her beauty almost lost as her face takes on the asymmetry of anxiety.

"Do you know the most boring thing in the world to photograph?" Ben asks as he looks over my shoulder.

I shake my head.

"Perfection."

"What is the most interesting?"

"Duplicity," he says.

"To catch someone in the lie and lay it bare. To expose the difference between who people present themselves as and who they really are. That's the moment you wait for. The tricky thing is that you don't always know if you've captured it until you see the film."

"Everyone has a face they present to the world. That doesn't make them a liar."

"Maybe not," Ben replies. "But it is a very thin line."

TWENTY

I have taken to walking to work most mornings now, hoping to exhaust some of the tension within, repeating to myself over and over, You can't quit, no matter what they do, you can't afford to quit. Sometimes I listen to that old Lesley Gore song "You Don't Own Me" on my iPod as I make my way through the midtown streets.

This morning, though, I dress carefully and put on heels. I have promised to meet Jack at lunchtime to go shopping for Deirdre. Though we haven't settled on a locale I assume it will be in the vicinity of Fifty-seventh Street or Madison Avenue, maybe Bergdorf's or Bendel's for a fantastically extravagant bag—alligator, perhaps, or a little something from Chanel, half a year's tuition fashioned into a quilted leather satchel. I'm not particularly looking forward to the expedition. It's not that I am jealous exactly, but the vicarious thrill of shopping for another woman goes only so far, even if Deirdre is my best friend.

"You look nice," Sam says, coming up behind me as I put in earrings and kissing me on the back of the neck.

I feel my muscles tense.

I'm not sure if the flinch is an internal cringe evident only to me, like the rumor of lines one sees in the mirror months before they are visible to others, or if he senses it.

He steps away, answering my question. "I don't know what's up with you lately but this ice maiden routine is wearing pretty thin," he remarks, irritated.

"Sorry."

It is only slowly dawning on Sam, the marital war of attrition we seem to be engaged in: There is favorite cereal not replaced, the back turned just a split second sooner than usual. Like most men, he is terrified of female anger—so much less linear, so much harder to comprehend and combat. He assumes it will subside, particularly as he cannot pinpoint a specific cause. He thinks he can wait it out. He is clearly losing his patience, though.

I know that my avoidance cannot last forever, but for now it is all I have the will for. I am waiting for the moment when my anger outweighs my fear.

Halloween decorations are going up all over town; the cardboard ghouls and king-sized bags of tooth-destroying candy that even Claire hasn't outgrown dot every drugstore window. The girls have settled into school and neither has strayed again from course, at least not that I know of. Deirdre and I managed one breakfast last week, though it was rushed. She did not mention Ben at all—for the first time in their checkered history I see no evidence of longing or regret. She speaks only of the future: her future with Jack. Four days ago she called to say he had gotten the job in New York.

"What about Alice?" I asked.

"He told her."

"Told her what exactly?"

"That their marriage is over. He's filed for divorce."

"How did she take it?"

"Well, it wasn't exactly a surprise. She was having an affair for over a year, what did she expect? She's not going to contest it."

"Did he tell her about you?"

"I don't know," she says. "I don't really see what difference that makes."

Jack is tying up loose ends, packing up his life in Boston, planning a fresh start.

Sam turns away from me and stuffs his wallet in his pocket. “You’re sure you don’t mind about tonight?” he asks. He has checked with me twice to make sure I don’t object if he meets with a source about the story he is doing on a bank foreclosure cover-up. “I can see if I can switch the meeting.”

“It’s fine,” I tell him. “I’ll be home by seven to let Marissa go. I don’t want you to miss your deadline.”

“All right. Thanks. I’ll be home as soon as I can.”

He pecks me on the cheek and walks out with the girls.

As soon as I get to work I pull out the spreadsheets I should have brought home over the weekend but didn’t. There is a budget meeting in forty-five minutes and I need to go over the billing and expenditures on my accounts, or what’s left of them, one last time. I run my forefinger down the columns, rehearsing my explanations, and try to anticipate the questions I might be asked. Numbers are not my strong suit and Favata will do everything to make that painfully clear to everyone in the room. I have not taken a deep breath in weeks. Everything is tightening around me.

When my e-mail pings I’m tempted to ignore it, but I can’t.

It’s from Georgia: “You never got back to me with the estimated value of the Ben Erickson portrait session. We need it for tax purposes.”

Damn. I’d forgotten all about it. I call Ben’s studio and he picks up himself on the third ring.

“You sound breathless,” I remark after we say hello.

“I know. It’s insane. My flight’s not till six p.m. but I still have a lot to finish up. *Vogue* keeps tacking on things they’d like me to shoot. They have a sudden penchant for orange. Anything orange. If I hear one more editor telling me what her vision is, I’m going to chuck the whole thing.”

“How long are you going for?”

“Just a few days.”

I tell him of Georgia’s request.

“I don’t care—put down whatever works for you,” he replies.

“The IRS will love that.”

"Okay, say ten grand. Fifteen if the person who gets it is an asshole."

"Ten it is."

I wish him a good trip and hang up.

At five minutes to ten, I gather my notes and, glancing back once to be sure I haven't forgotten anything, head out of my office. Petra still isn't in and as I pass by her empty desk I quickly rummage through the unsorted pile of invites, junk mail, magazines, letters and gray interoffice envelopes that were dropped off this morning. I am almost at the bottom of the pile when I come across a large white envelope addressed to me, with "Confidential" written neatly on the bottom.

I slide my thumbnail under the flap and open it, glancing quickly at the cover note. "No evidence of sex with donkeys but this is pretty major. Favata didn't just harass the woman, according to the police reports he beat her up pretty badly. This should be all you need. David. PS: I've been honoring your do-not-call edict but I hope you are well." I pull out the next sheet just enough to see the official insignia of the Hospital of St. John and St. Elizabeth, London.

"Ready?"

I swivel to find Favata standing directly behind me.

I nod, hastily dropping the envelope back onto the pile of mail—as if the mere fact of my holding it will awaken his suspicions—and follow him to the conference room, where three men and two women, all with calculators positioned in front of them, are already seated.

For the next two hours, I listen as they go through each account's P&L. I am the highest-level holdover from Steiner and it is my job to defend what Merdale increasingly sees as an inexplicable quagmire of mismanagement and missed opportunities. This is made all the more unpleasant by my sense that, despite their tsk-tsking, they are enjoying their show of fiscal superiority. The only thing that makes it at all bearable is knowing that the white envelope from David is waiting for me. I look at their smug faces and for the first time in weeks I don't feel completely powerless.

While they rattle on, I fantasize about my next move, debating whether I should take the hospital records directly to Merdale and get Favata fired or use them as leverage to secure a large payout, though the idea of having to keep silent about what Favata did is disagreeable at best. My favorite option is to hand the whole packet over to the press and let them ruin him, which is exactly what he deserves.

When the torture session finally adjourns, I hurry out and head back to my office. Petra has at last arrived. "Morning," she calls out cheerfully. It goes without saying that she offers no excuse or apology for her tardiness.

"Good morning." I glance down. "Do you have the mail?"

"I sorted it and put it on your desk."

I go into my office without another word.

I put down my notepad and begin to riffle through the stack of letters, slowly at first and then with an increasing sense of urgency.

The letter with the hospital records isn't there.

I take a deep breath. I must have missed it, that's all. I carefully go through the pile again.

Nothing.

Frantic, I look in my in-box, under my notebooks, on the floor beneath my desk.

The letter has vanished.

"Petra," I call out.

She appears in my doorway. "Yes?"

"What happened to the rest of my mail?"

"What do you mean?"

"I thought I saw something earlier. It was marked 'Confidential.' "

She shakes her head. "This was everything that was dropped off this morning."

"You're sure?"

"Definitely."

"All right."

Alarm pounds against my temples, constricts my throat. I must not panic. This is fixable. Surely David wouldn't have sent me the only copy.

I dial his number.

"He is in a meeting. Shall I have him return your call?" his assistant asks.

"Yes, please."

I look through every pile and paper on my desk one last time, furious with myself for leaving the letter on Petra's desk. I look through my trash, year-old files. Finally, already running late, I grab my coat to meet Jack.

He is waiting for me on the corner of Park Avenue South and Twenty-first Street when my cab pulls up. Though he has sworn me to secrecy, he has chosen a meeting spot dangerously close to Deirdre's store. I've racked my brain trying to come up with a shop that could have lured him here rather than to the Upper East Side but have come up with nothing. Then again, it is not outside the realm of possibility that even a newcomer to New York might know some hidden cache of luxury that I am not privy to. This thought does nothing to cheer me up.

Jack is rocking back and forth impatiently, his hands buried in his pants pockets. When he sees me, he breaks into a broad smile and kisses me hello.

"I'm a little surprised by your choice of neighborhood," I remark as we stand together on the corner. "Is there some incredible little jewelry shop hidden on a side street here?"

"Not that I know of."

"Did you have a plan in mind?" I ask skeptically. I want to get this over with and get back to my office as quickly as possible.

"You'll see."

"This is supposed to be Deirdre's surprise, not mine," I remind him.

"Come. It's just half a block away."

I check my cell phone, telling Jack it's "just a work thing," and follow him up the street.

We stop when we get to a newly minted apartment building with the German starchitect's name written in a thin script across the entryway, branding the imposing glass tower and all who enter with its imprimatur of taste or insecurity or both.

I look at Jack questioningly. There is no store in sight.

"I bought an apartment," he says, grinning. "I'm about to buy it, I should say. I wanted you to see it. I don't know all that much about Manhattan real estate. It's the first one I looked at but it seems perfect for us."

"Are you out of your mind? You're buying Deirdre an apartment for her birthday?"

So much for thinking Chanel would be extravagant.

"No, it's not Deirdre's birthday present," Jack reassures me. "Not exactly, anyway. Though I am thinking of having a surprise party for her here. Promise me you won't say anything."

"Of course not. But Jack . . ."

"Look, I'm going to need a place to live when I start at Loring, Marcus," he interrupts. "Of course, I'm hoping Deirdre will move in when she's ready. Her apartment isn't going to be big enough down the road. But I realize that might not happen right away and I'm okay with that. Just look at it with me, okay?"

I am only somewhat mollified.

We walk through the rather daunting lobby of glass and steel and the aggressive neutrality of ecru washed across the textured walls, the couches, even the lilies on the concierge's desk. Surely there is a dress code for the building's inhabitants, barring any hint of color or extraneous detailing. The real-estate agent has left keys for Jack and we ride up to the eleventh floor, where he opens the apartment door to reveal an enormous space of freshly painted white walls and parquet floors. Sunlight streams through the curved glass windows that take up the entire length of the immense living room, the spires of midtown Manhattan sparkling in the mid-distance.

"What do you think?" Jack asks eagerly.

"They must pay partners in corporate law firms a helluva lot of money."

He smiles. "Let me show you around."

He leads me through the chef's kitchen, with its Viking range and Sub-Zero refrigerator, to the master bedroom, with a view of Madison Square Park. He shows off the walk-in closets, the his-and-hers sinks in the bathroom, thoughtfully designed for parallel lives, obfuscating the need for messy overlap, a veritable luxury in a city where elbowing for space too often begins at home. I'm sure if more people had them Manhattan's divorce rate would plummet.

"I have major real-estate envy," I admit.

"Come."

I follow Jack into a spacious second bedroom, where he leans up against the window seat, perfect, no doubt, for a child curled up with a book.

"Well? Be honest. Do you think Deirdre will like it?" He fidgets nervously, alive with excitement and uncertainty.

I hesitate. It's not just how different this is from her downtown loft. I am suddenly alarmed by the too-muchness of it all, the pressure of such overweening expectation, all this space waiting to be filled with a future not yet secured.

"Lisa, what is it?"

"Nothing."

"Tell me," he insists. "If there's a problem I want to know about it."

"The apartment is fantastic, Jack. I'm just worried that it's too much too soon."

"What do you mean?" he asks defensively.

"Maybe you should have talked to Deirdre first," I suggest.

"You don't think she's going to like it? Is it too hard-edged, too modern?"

"That's not what I mean. She could very well love it, I don't know. All I'm saying is she might want to feel she has more of a say in it."

It has occurred to me that Deirdre will see the apartment as a trap rather than a gift, view Jack's grand gesture as an ultimatum rather than an offering. I cannot help but remember how she resented his unyielding insistence all those years ago that she move with him to Cambridge, how she ran from it.

Jack shakes his head. "I'm not a fool. I know Deirdre isn't going to just up and move in right away. She can take as long as she wants. But Lisa, we are going to have a life together. We are going to start a family. She wants that, too. I know it. In the meantime, I need a place to live."

I can't really blame Jack for his impatience. So few of us get the chance to rewrite our own romantic history, to go back and play it differently, get it right this time, to replace the regrets that haunt for a lifetime with the future you were always meant to have.

"I'm sorry. I shouldn't have said anything. It's a wonderful apartment."

"It is, isn't it?" He glances around the empty room, then looks at me, smiling. "Come, my little wet blanket, I'll take you to lunch and listen to your cynicism for as long as you'd like."

"I am not a cynic," I protest.

"In that case, you can give me decorating advice."

"I'm even less of a decorator. Jack, I'd love to have lunch but I really have to get back to work," I tell him. "We'll celebrate next time you're in town."

He grins, he is already living here, he has already furnished the days and nights to come in his mind. "Deal."

I leave Jack walking jauntily up Park Avenue South and grab the first cab that comes along, pulling out my cell phone as I climb in. There are two messages from David. I call him back as the car lurches forward.

He picks up right away. "Lisa, I've been trying to reach you. Are you all right?"

"No. David, I lost them. Or someone took them. I don't know what happened." The words rush frantically out, I do not even try to hide my panic.

"I'm not following. What did you lose?"

"The hospital records. Everything you sent me."

He takes a deep breath. "Calm down."

"How can I calm down? I'm terrified. What if Favata has them?"

"Can you meet me after work today?"

"Yes, anything. It's going to be okay, right?" I ask.

Our connection is broken before he can answer.

TWENTY-ONE

David is seated in the back of the dark and clubby bar we went to after the Merdale cocktail party, drinking a scotch. We haven't seen each other since the Japanese restaurant and there is a decided awkwardness as we embrace, unsure what the tenor, the boundaries are.

As I slide in beside him on the velvet couch I notice the manila envelope by his side and am relieved that he has brought along a copy of the records.

"Thank God you have them," I exclaim, feeling calmer already.

David glances at the envelope and nods distractedly. "It's so good to see you, Lisa. I've missed you."

I nod, pleased, flattered, but unable to admit I feel quite the same, to him or to myself. "It's good to see you, too."

"What can I get you to drink?" he asks.

"Just a glass of wine. I don't have that much time. I have to get home to the babysitter."

He motions to the waitress. The blue-eyed lovestruck waiter from our last visit is nowhere to be found.

"When you said you might have dirt on Favata I never thought it would turn out to be something like this," I tell him after I have ordered. "Maybe I'm naïve, but it's shocking to me. I knew he was a skank, but what kind of man beats a woman up so badly she ends up in the hospital?"

"Not the kind of man you should be working with."

"Not the kind of man anyone should be working with. How could Robert Merdale not have known this?"

"It was two years ago. In England. Favata did a pretty good job of covering his tracks."

"Not to look a gift horse in the mouth, but how did you get ahold of all this?" I ask. "Aren't hospital records confidential?"

"Many things are confidential, until they're not."

"You are an evil genius," I tease.

David plays with the ice in his drink. "Sometimes, even if you are looking for something, it's disappointing when you find it."

I look at him quizzically. "You sound like you are having second thoughts. You can't feel protective of a man who hits women."

"I don't. Favata deserves everything he gets."

"Then what?"

"Nothing." He takes a sip of his scotch. "Tell me, how have you been, Lisa? Aside from this."

"I don't know," I answer quietly. "All right, I guess."

"Did you call any of the lawyers I sent you?"

I shake my head. "Not yet. I need more time." I smile sadly. "I keep waiting for a sudden attack of clarity, but I'm as confused as ever. Whatever I do or don't do will have such huge ramifications, not just for me, but my daughters."

David nods.

"What made you finally decide to leave your marriage?"

"It was decided for me."

"Maybe that's easier."

We look at each other, then away.

David finishes his drink. While he signals for another, I pick up the manila envelope and begin to open it.

He turns sharply to me. "Lisa, don't."

"C'mon, I'm dying to see it. I didn't really have a chance this morning."

"Please. Not now." He reaches for the envelope but I twist away from him and slide my thumb under the flap before he can stop me.

"I'm sorry," he says so quietly I can barely hear him.

I can barely hear anything at all.

There are no hospital records inside.

There are three photographs.

I look at the first one. It doesn't register. I know these people but not in this configuration, they are so ingrained, so familiar and yet not. I look closer, as if they will somehow shift into a pattern, a context I can recognize.

It is a photograph of Sam and Deirdre in the café two blocks from Aperçu. Their heads are almost touching, his hand is on hers. You can feel the breath between them, their faces, their lips are that close, you can almost hear the whisper.

Nausea rockets through me.

It's not possible. They don't even like each other.

I stop breathing, flip to the second picture.

Sam and Deirdre embracing on a street corner, their arms around each other's waists. I can tell by his overcoat and navy fringed scarf that it was the afternoon Phoebe got lost in Union Square.

The last photograph was also taken outdoors. They are clearly arguing. I know both of their faces so well, I can see the vitriol in their expressions, in the tilt of their bodies.

I drop the pictures back on the table.

A cool sweat films my face, the back of my neck, blackness encroaches on my peripheral vision, leaving me dizzy and weak.

"I'm so sorry," David says softly.

I can hardly see as I push my chair away, race to the bathroom, dashing into the first empty stall to throw up.

I sink onto the cold tile floor, my head buried in my hands.

It is not possible.

Sam and Deirdre.

All the times she assured me he would never have an affair, told me to stop asking him.

All the times he lied.

The two of them, together, against me.

What an idiot I am.

Their faces swirl dizzyingly before me, but I can't fit them into place, they fly apart and then rejoin: sitting at the café, their heads almost touching. Embracing on a street corner. I lean over the toilet and throw up again. There is nothing left but bitter acid. I heave so loudly that the woman in the next stall comes and crouches down beside me, and asks if I need help. I shake her away.

I gradually stand up and make it to the sink, where I rinse my mouth and face with cold water. I stand stock still, staring into the mirror. I don't recognize myself, I don't recognize anything. The contours of everything I thought I knew have shattered.

I have no idea what to do.

There is only one thing I know for sure, sharp and hard and clear, one absolute, and that is pure rage at David. It drives me forward, leaving no room for anything else and I grab on to it, ride it.

I cannot feel my legs moving, there is nothing but this. Before I know it, I am standing over him. "Why did you do this?" I demand furiously.

"I'm sorry, Lisa."

"You had no right."

"You deserve better than this. As painful as it is, you deserve to know the truth. I wish someone had done that for me when my marriage was falling apart. It would have saved me a lot of torment and guilt."

I grab my coat. Whatever it is he has to say, I don't want to hear it. "I need to get out of here."

He begins to rise. "Let me take you."

I turn angrily to him. "No. You've done enough."

"I can't let you leave like this." He reaches over to touch me, but I push him forcefully away and race out.

As soon as I am outside, the anger that guided me, gave me purpose for those few brief moments, dissipates.

I lean up against a building and slowly sink down until I am kneeling on the ground. It is as if every word I have ever known has been stripped of its definition. I am left without language, without meaning, it is all just gone.

A moan escapes but no one stops, no one looks.

I try to sift through the past, all of our pasts, together and apart, but the threads elude me. Nothing meets up, nothing makes sense.

I have never felt so alone.

I slam my fist into my thigh over and over, the pain, the humiliation made tangible, but it doesn't help.

I cannot stay here, I cannot stay still, the pressure within boils over, demanding movement, propulsion. I rise, light-headed, and begin to walk again, fast, without direction, as if I can outpace the tumult within.

At some point I realize my cell phone is ringing. "Home" flashes on the screen.

It is Marissa. It takes me a few seconds to remember who she is.

"Yes?" I hear the misplaced anger in my voice but cannot stop it.

"It's seven o'clock," Marissa says with a questioning tone.

"And?"

"I was supposed to leave now."

Christ. "I'm sorry. Please, can you stay and give the girls dinner until Sam gets there? I'm tied up."

Marissa reluctantly agrees and we hang up.

I grip the phone tightly as I keep walking. I must have gone ten or twelve blocks before the next horrific piece edges into my consciousness: Jack. Jack with his hopes and his second bedroom, Jack, equally betrayed. I dial his cell phone. I cannot stand to be alone with this much anger.

At first, all I can do is say his name.

"Lisa, what is it? Are you okay?"

I don't know where to begin. I wish he could somehow learn it all by osmosis so that I wouldn't have to put it into words, tell him, wreck it all, every last shred. But he is in this, too, he deserves to know. And so I tell him of the photos. The two of them. Behind our backs. This was all going on behind our backs. God only knows for how long.

"I don't fucking believe they did this again," he spits out, beyond anger.

"What do you mean, again?"

"Sam and Deirdre."

"What are you talking about?"

"He never told you, did he?"

"Told me what?"

"The affair he had in college while you were in London . . ."

"Yes?"

"It was with Deirdre."

I reel back. "That can't be."

"I saw them," Jack assures me.

"You saw them?" Perhaps if I repeat it enough it will begin to sink in.

"Yes. I was away at a tennis match. When I got back to campus it was after midnight, but I thought I'd surprise Deirdre. I went to her room." He stops suddenly, the hurt, the shock still fresh after all this time, I can hear it in his voice. "They were drunk. Not that it matters. But they were. Naked. Together."

My entire life has been a lie.

A truck drives noisily by, clanging against the pitted street.

"Why didn't you tell me?" I demand. "You knew this for all these years and you never told me."

"I turned around and left. They never knew I saw them. I never said a word. I thought if we didn't talk about it, it would be as if it never happened. I kept watching them for evidence that something was still going on but I never saw anything again. I would have said something if I had."

"You lived with it all this time?"

"I loved her," he says simply. "I would have done anything to keep her."

"That's why you were so adamant about Deirdre moving to Cambridge with you, isn't it? You didn't want her anywhere near Sam."

"Yes. But then the two of you got married and I tried to forget it. It wasn't my place to tell you." I lose him to a silence. When he speaks again, there is a venom in his voice that shocks me. "Fucking bitch. She's not going to get away with this again. Not this time."

He hangs up before I can say another word.

I am left alone once more. With this.

Everything in tatters, everything gone.

There is no one left to turn to.

Sheets of fury and resentment, shame and embarrassment layer on top of each other. I don't know where to go, what to do.

And so I walk.

I walk as the night darkens to blackness and chills me deep within.

I walk as my cell phone rings and rings.

I walk, my brain a riptide of hatred and loss, confusion and revelation. Every now and then I look up to discover that I've drifted to a completely new neighborhood before succumbing to the chaos of my own psyche once more.

I'm not sure what time it is. I'm not sure how I got there.

But when I next come out of my trance I find myself outside of Deirdre's building.

No one comes or goes. There is no movement.

I dip back into the shadows and I wait.

PART TWO

TWENTY-TWO

It is close to midnight when I slip my keys in the door and slowly turn the lock. My hand is quivering—from the cold, from exhaustion, from a rage that is not yet spent—and it takes three tries before I can open it.

Inside, the apartment is black, silent, coated with sleep.

I kick off my shoes and leave them by the front door to pad barefoot down the hall. I look in on Phoebe first, cocooned inside her quilt. She always folds it in half lengthwise and wriggles within, safe, enclosed, another smaller blanket wrapped around her head. For all of her daytime adventurousness she prefers to be confined in sleep, swaddled. I lean over, kiss her warm, soft cheek, the only part of her still rounded with the last reminder of baby fat.

I leave quietly and go into Claire's room, heavy with the scent of the powdery perfume she bought with her allowance last week, Claire fumbling at femininity, those tentative early steps when you spend hours staring into the mirror trying to figure out your potential attractions, though real sexual longing, the catalyst for all of the efforts and insecurities, is still vague, viewed from a distance, at least for a little while more. I rest my lips on her silky tangled hair, breathe her in.

What will their worlds be like tomorrow?

Sam is sleeping, snoring lightly. I managed to send him a text an hour or two ago telling him I had to work late and not to wait up. Still, it surprises me that he took me at my word, that it is so easy for him. I have no idea what time he got home or when Marissa left. I shut off my phone as soon as I pressed "send." I look down at him, the contours of his body, the way he has tucked a blanket between his knees, all so familiar. Everything I believed about him, every assumption, was based on a false foundation; the past I thought we had been standing on was illusory.

I lean over, my fists clenched.

I want to pummel him, to bash my knuckles into his impassive, untroubled sleeping face until he starts, wakes, sees me, finally sees me as I now see him. I want him to know that I know.

I stand there, leaning over him, trying to breathe.

He doesn't wake, doesn't sense me.

I do not have the language, cannot summon the words that would give voice to the depths of my wounds and my infinite anger, and I will not risk waking the girls with what will surely rise far above a whisper.

I do the only thing I can do—I walk away from him.

When I do confront him, I need to be in control, to be cooler, harder than this.

Tomorrow, after the girls go to school and we are alone.

Until then I will, quite literally, lie in wait.

I take a pillow and blanket to the couch, where I stare at the car lights flickering across the windows, unable to sleep. My brain is fragmented, I can no longer hold on to any emotion for more than a few seconds before it is supplanted by another. It seems a lifetime ago that I was sitting in that bar with David, though it is only, what, seven hours? Time has slowed down, fractured. My mouth is dry but I do not have the energy to get up for water. I pull the blanket over my head. Like Phoebe, I want a layer between myself and the world. Maybe if I burrow deep enough it will all just fade away.

I must have drifted off somehow. The next thing I know sounds from the kitchen begin to creep into my consciousness. It takes me a moment to remember where I am before the knowledge of last night smashes into me, a thud that will not stop. I sit up, shake the numbness from my fists I had clenched even in my sleep. I can hear the girls rustling around in their rooms, beginning to get ready for school. I don't want them to find me here, waking up half-dressed on the living room couch, I don't want to have to come up with explanations yet for a fissure it will soon be impossible to hide.

Sam is in the kitchen making breakfast. I cannot fathom how I can look at him with any degree of false equanimity, I can no longer pretend even for the girls' sake. Before Phoebe and Claire emerge I sneak back into my bedroom, close the door and strip off the rest of my clothes. I take a shower, letting the hot water pour over and over me for as long as possible, trying to run out the clock.

I hear Sam knocking on the bathroom door. "Are you okay?" he calls out.

I don't answer. I soap my legs, my arms.

"Lisa?"

I do not want him to open the door, I do not want to see him. "I'm taking a shower."

"I realize that. But you've been in there forever."

"Can't you get the girls ready?" I retort. "Just this once?"

I cannot hear his hiss of aggravation but I'm sure that it is there.

He stays there—I can feel him, it makes me grit my teeth—for a minute more and then he leaves me be.

Fifteen minutes later, I come out, wrapped in a robe, just as the girls are shimmying into their coats.

"Mom overslept," Phoebe proclaims happily, as if she is storing up ammunition for a future argument.

I lean over, kiss her. "It happens to the best of us, sweetie."

"You never let it happen to me."

"I've told you, it's my job to annoy you as much as possible. That includes making sure you get to school on time."

I turn to Claire, who pulls out her MetroCard and waves it in front of me before I can ask for it.

She is just slipping on her thirty-pound backpack, festooned with political buttons and miniature fuzzy animal key chains—even her bag is caught between two worlds—when the doorbell rings.

I look quizzically at Sam, who shakes his head, as confused as I am. It is only 7:30 a.m. No one has ever come by at this hour.

Sam runs his hand through his sleep-matted hair and steps up to the front door. "Who is it?" he asks.

"Detective Larry Callahan. NYPD."

Sam glances at me for an explanation but I have none. All four of us are here, accounted for, safe. There is no reason to panic.

I watch as Sam tentatively opens the door. "Can I help you?"

The detective, a tall, wiry man with washed-out, almost colorless hair, freckled hands and an impassive face, shows Sam his badge before sliding it effortlessly back into his coat pocket. "Is Lisa Barkley here?"

I tighten the sash on my bathrobe. "I'm Lisa. What is this about?"

"Can I come in?" Detective Callahan asks. His voice is deeper than his thin body might lead you to expect, as if he had purposefully lowered it as a young man to lend a sense of heft and authority his physical lightness had denied him.

"Of course."

He steps in and, glancing around, notices the girls standing in the doorway watching him.

"These are our daughters, Claire and Phoebe."

Callahan offers up a professional smile that puts no one at ease. "Nice to meet you," he says, with the formality of one who is not used to dealing with children and would prefer to keep it that way.

The girls nod shyly. It is obvious that Callahan is not going to say anything further in their presence. The five of us stand there, directionless, stumped.

Sam snaps out of it first. "All right, girls. You'd better get going or you'll be late for school."

They button their coats and submit to our self-conscious goodbye kisses, glancing back at the stranger in the foyer.

"Don't forget to call when you get off the bus," I admonish as they head out.

The presence of a police detective forestalls the standard eye-rolling and they dutifully agree.

We watch as they press for the elevator, wait for it in silence, get in. Only then does Sam close the door.

It is just the three of us now.

"I'm sorry to barge in on you this way," the detective says.

"What is this about?" Sam asks.

The detective turns to me, his narrow eyes, beneath their pale fringe of lashes, blinking as if he had just gotten something in them. "Are you acquainted with Deirdre Cushing?"

"Yes, is she all right?"

"I'm afraid I have some rather bad news."

A coldness begins to snake down my spine. I can see Sam standing up straighter as well, instinctively bracing himself. There is still room for denial, though: whatever it is won't be, it can't be, that bad. Perhaps it is a different Deirdre Cushing, not ours.

"She was found dead early this morning," the detective says.

I gasp, a loud gurgling sound I don't recognize escaping from someplace deep within.

"What do you mean?" Sam asks. "What happened?"

"We don't know yet. Her next-door neighbor came home around two a.m. and found Miss Cushing's front door open. She knocked to tell her and when there was no answer, she went in. She found Miss Cushing lying on the floor." Callahan reports with a lack of modulation, his tone a marriage of sympathy and procedure.

"You're sure it's her?"

"Her neighbor identified the body."

"Was there an accident?" I ask. My voice sounds far away, child-like and tinny, disconnected from my body.

"We don't know exactly what happened yet," Callahan says. "There were no signs of forced entry and nothing appears to be missing. But it does appear there was a struggle. We'll know more after we get the autopsy results but the medical examiner places the time of death between approximately nine and eleven p.m."

Blackness encroaches, all that is left is a tiny pinhole of refracted light.

"Ma'am? Maybe you'd better sit down." He's done this before, of course, worse—told mothers they had lost their children, asked husbands to identify mangled bodies. He is practiced at breaking bad news and knows the signs of a fainter, knows, too, that part of his job is to note the response. I can feel him watching me with a detached concern.

Sam leads me to a chair in the kitchen. I stare down, it seems like a totally foreign object to me, I can't quite remember what chairs are for. He gently guides me into it just as my legs give way and then sits beside me, both of us lost.

"How did you know to come here?" Sam asks.

"We looked on Miss Cushing's cell phone for a family member to contact. Your wife is listed as her ICE person."

My throat constricts as if I am being strangled, I can't get enough air. Sam reaches for me, making a soothing sound, ssshhhh, that seems as if it is coming from another room.

Callahan waits until I have gained a modicum of control. "Does she have family we should contact?" he asks.

I am her family. Or was. Or thought I was. Until last night.

"Her parents are both dead."

"I see. How well did you know Miss Cushing?"

I stare at him, too woozy to speak, his words, his question swimming about me.

"They've been best friends since college," Sam replies for me.

"I realize how difficult this is for you," Callahan says. "But we could use whatever help you can give us."

"Of course," I manage to get out.

"When was the last time you saw Miss Cushing?"

I shut my eyes and see us, the two of us. "We had breakfast last week." The Gramercy Park coffeehouse and the organic oatmeal and her talk of Jack and all the while she was lying to me.

"I'm sorry, I couldn't quite hear you."

"Wednesday. I had breakfast with her last Wednesday."

The detective is writing everything down in a little spiral pad. I am conscious of my words going straight to the paper.

"Have you spoken to her since?" he asks.

"Yes, a few times."

"Yesterday?"

I stare at him.

"Ma'am?"

"No, I didn't speak to her yesterday," I mumble.

"And you didn't see her?"

"No."

"All right. The last time you saw her, did she say anything that might have indicated she was in trouble?"

"Trouble?"

"Of any sort. What about boyfriends? Was she seeing someone?"

Fucking bitch, Jack said. I hear the venom, the pure hatred. "She's not going to get away with this. Not this time."

I shake my head. It's not possible.

Callahan is studying me. "Ma'am?"

I glance over at Sam, his head bent, entranced by his fingertips, the side of his cheek pulled in between his teeth. *She was seeing my husband,* I think. But just as quickly a sense of shame and embarrassment overtakes me, as if Sam's affair reveals a flaw on my part. The instinct to protect, to keep our dirty laundry private overwhelms logic, honesty, it puts it all on hold. I need to talk to Sam first, alone. The omission is a split-second decision. I regret it even as I execute it.

"Jack Handel," I tell Callahan. "She was seeing Jack Handel."

"Is there any reason to believe they were having problems?"

Fucking bitch, Jack said.

"Yes, there might have been." I pause, trying to find words to convey Jack's state of mind and his anger without admitting the cause. I have dug myself into a hole that I cannot see my way out of. Layers of the mistake are already piling over me. "They had a volatile relationship."

"Do you have an address for him?"

"He's in the middle of relocating here from Boston. He was looking at an apartment in the East Twenties but he hadn't bought it yet. I have his cell phone number."

Callahan writes all this down and then looks up again. "What about his place of work?"

"He's due to start at Loring, Marcus next week."

"Is there anyone else you can think of?" Callahan asks.

"What about Ben?" Sam asks me.

"He's in India."

"Do you have a photo of this Jack Handel? It would help if we had something to show to Miss Cushing's neighbors, find out if they saw anything. Her building has no security cameras or doorman," he adds disapprovingly.

I nod. The four of us at Jack's birthday dinner, squeezed in, inebriated, a night on the brink, we were just about to tip over, our smiles lopsided and too wide, each of us with our longings so close to the surface, so hidden from view. "I have a picture from last month but it's still on my computer. I'll need to print it out. I don't even think I have paper."

"You can e-mail it to me. We'll print out copies." He gets out his card. "You'll call if you think of anything?"

"Yes."

"We'll be in touch."

"You'll keep us apprised as soon as you learn something?" Sam asks.

"Of course. Thank you for your help."

While Sam sees Callahan out I put my head between my knees, rocked by torrents of nausea, my bowels churning.

When he comes back, he gently rubs my neck. "I'm sorry, Lisa.

I'm so sorry. I know what Deirdre meant to you. I can't believe this is happening."

I push his hands away. I cannot stand him touching me, it repulses me. "I should have told him," I spit out. "I should have told him everything."

"Told him what?"

"About you and Deirdre."

TWENTY-THREE

Sam takes a step back. "What do you mean?"

"How could you, Sam? How could either of you?"

"Will you calm down? I have no idea what you are talking about."

I stare at his unshaven face, guarded, alert to danger but impenetrable, wearing his stubborn ignorance like an amulet, giving me nothing, and I feel a sudden and fierce hatred mixing with the anguish and disbelief. I pick up his coffee mug from the table and throw it at him, missing. We both watch as it shatters on the wall behind the counter, shards of the blue and white ceramic raining down.

"Don't tell me to goddamn calm down," I hiss. "I saw pictures. Of the two of you."

"What pictures? You're not making any sense."

"How long were you having an affair with Deirdre? How long were you lying to me? Tell me. I really want to know. Tell me."

"What on earth makes you think I was having an affair with Deirdre? That's insane."

"Is everything a lie, all of it, our entire life? God, you two must have thought it was funny, what an idiot I was. I can just imagine."

"Are you crazy? I was not sleeping with Deirdre."

"Stop lying. For once, will you just stop lying? I told you, I saw pictures."

"What pictures? Lisa, I have absolutely no idea what you are talking about."

"There are photographs of the two of you together."

He stops, takes this in. I watch as he readjusts his position, internally, externally.

"You were following me?" he asks, unsure what is called for, offense or defense.

"No. I wasn't. I didn't think I had a reason to."

"Then where did these so-called pictures come from?"

"Stop talking to me like I'm one of your goddamned interviews." His stonewalling infuriates me. "They are not so-called."

"You didn't answer me. Where did they come from?"

"That's not the point. A friend of mine. You don't know him," I answer impatiently.

"Just what is it you think you saw?"

"You and Deirdre together." In the café, their heads touching, the whisper between them. On the street, their arms around each other. Arguing. "More than once," I add.

Sam closes his eyes, there is no place left for him to go. "All right," he says, so quietly I can hardly hear him. He is talking to himself really, psyching himself up before diving off a precipitous cliff. "All right."

We are here, then. Finally here.

"I'm sorry." He exhales and begins to speak as if there is nothing left, no way around it. "Yes, Deirdre and I were seeing each other. But it's not what you think."

I remain motionless, waiting, careful not to make any sudden movement or sound that might put him off his confession.

"I certainly wasn't sleeping with her," he continues.

"What were you doing, then?" I ask bitterly.

"It's complicated."

"I'm sure it is."

He begins pacing back and forth across our tiny kitchen.

"Stop that. You're driving me crazy," I snap at him.

He sits down at the kitchen table, inches from me, and looks directly into my eyes. "I borrowed money from Deirdre."

"You what?"

"I needed fifty thousand dollars."

"Good Lord. What kind of trouble were you in?"

"It was just a bridge loan. I was going to pay her back in a couple of weeks."

"I don't understand." My head is spinning as I try to grasp the meaning of his words, they are so garbled and unforeseen, so foreign and detached from anything I expected.

"Last month, when I was reporting that ill-fated story on Eliot Wells, I heard rumors of a start-up he was going to back, Uni-Prophet. They were keeping it hush-hush until all the financing was set. It was by far the best idea I've heard of in a long time. It will change the nature of online marketing."

Sam looks at me with a fragment of all that obstinate, glittering hope I'd seen six years ago, but I don't care about that now.

"When the piece on Wells didn't pan out," he continues, "it freed me up to talk to the start-up guys. They offered me an opportunity to buy in on the ground floor. The upside would have been huge, but no one would give me a loan. I knew that as soon as Wells announced his involvement, the money would flow in and I'd be able to pay the fifty grand back, but I had to move quickly."

"Where does Deirdre fit into all this?"

"I had no place else to go and she has the money. Had the money," he corrects himself. We both flinch. We haven't absorbed it, it doesn't yet bear the horrific weight of reality. Once we enter that universe of grief there will be no turning back. It is just seconds away.

"I'm not getting any of this," I say. "Why would she give you that kind of money? Why didn't either of you tell me?" It is one more incomprehensible riddle added to all the others that have turned the last twelve hours into a funhouse distortion of everything and everyone I thought I knew.

"I don't know, maybe she felt guilty about what happened six year ago." Sam looks at me intently. "You have to understand, she didn't do it for me, she did it for you."

"What do you mean, she did it for me?"

"She thought all of our problems stemmed from our financial pressures. You all but told her that. She was trying to help. She figured you had too much pride to take money from her. If it makes you feel any better, she hated lying to you. The only reason she agreed was that it was just supposed to be for three weeks. Unfortunately, it didn't quite turn out that way."

I can absorb only pieces of this, stray facts that make their way through the confusion and ever-widening ache.

"You weren't having an affair with her?" I need to hear it again, need to hear it until it sinks in.

"Of course not."

With each word Sam utters, a new wound forms. Deirdre, Deirdre in her apartment, hurt, battered, I can't use the word *dead* yet, can't even think it, but it is everywhere inside of me, inside this room.

Two thoughts collide in my head, overtaking each other, separating, joining: Sam was not sleeping with Deirdre; Deirdre is gone.

In the moment of regaining my husband I am losing my best friend for good.

It pierces through me, a knife-edged lesion that makes me double over.

"Why didn't you tell me you needed money?" I ask when I am finally able to speak again. "Why didn't you come to me when this all started?"

"I was going to. But Merdale took over and you were worried about losing your job. The timing couldn't have been worse. You never would have been willing to take the risk even if we had that kind of money." He looks at me. "Would you have?"

"I don't know." Neither of us believes me.

"You blame me for losing the money six years ago," Sam goes on. "You've never come out and said it. And I appreciate that. But it's true."

"That's not fair. I never blamed you."

"No? Anyway, I wanted to make it up to you. Prove that I could do it. And this was different. It was a sure thing."

"There are no sure things. You of all people should know that."

"At least let me tell you what it is," he pleads.

"Not now." I do not care, I will never care.

"All right, but you have to understand that the only reason I did any of this is that I believed it would be the solution to all of our problems."

"What problems?"

"What do you mean, what problems? Don't you think I know how stressed you are about money? How unhappy you've been lately? Do you think I like watching you go to a job you hate every day? I get that I'm not making enough money, you've made that quite clear," he says bitterly.

"I've always been proud of what you do. Whatever decisions we made, we made together."

"I know that. But I got the feeling that you were beginning to wonder if it was worth it. If I'm worth it." There is a raw anguish in his face that makes me look away. "You make fun of all those Upper East Side matrons but deep down you're constantly comparing our lives to theirs."

"I don't want their lives."

"No, I don't believe you do. Even so, it's hard not to feel small around them, not to question your choices." He touches my hand. "I felt you slipping away. Don't you see? I was trying to make things better for you, for us."

"How could you think all I cared about was money?"

"Not all. I never thought all."

"You were gambling with our future." It is at once an observation and an accusation.

"Not with, on," he says. "I was gambling *on* our future."

We stare at each other, frustrated. Between *with* and *on* there is an oceanic differential we may never be able to cross.

"Is Deirdre's money gone?" I ask.

"No. It's just going to take longer to get back than I thought."

"What happened?"

"The exposé on Wells, that's what happened. The minute all the accusations about him pre-dating options was in the news, everyone got gun shy. The VC guys went running for the hills. Wells was supposed to be the big draw to get other investors to go in. Suddenly that wasn't looking as likely. The start-up isn't off, it's just going to take more time to get sufficient funding."

"I can't believe that you kept all this from me," I say. "If you had just come to me we could have talked it out."

"And if you had said no? That would have been it."

"So rather than risk it you worked around me?"

"Yes. Maybe that was wrong, maybe I shouldn't have done it that way, but that's what happened."

I raise an eyebrow. "Maybe?"

"Okay, yes, it was wrong. I was wrong. I'm sorry. But I was trying to fix things. I didn't want to lose you," he admits.

"You were never going to lose me."

"No? These last few months, you seem to resent everything I say or do."

"You're the one who's been so preoccupied, pulling away. Lying to me."

He doesn't reply.

"When were you going to tell me all this?" I ask.

"I wanted to come to you with good news. Something concrete. I wanted you to be proud of me, not give you something else to worry about. I love you, Lisa. I've always loved you. That has never changed."

I rise, pacing myself now. It is too much to untangle all at once, too much to grasp, how far we have drifted, what strangers we have become, misguided interpreters of each other's desires and fears.

I shake my head and begin to cry, the realization that has been hovering on the edges, held back by shock, crashing through now, carrying with it an infinite pain. I cry for Deirdre, for my inability to apologize to her for my own worst thoughts, for the phone call to Jack that I never should have placed, for all of our missed and faulty conclusions, all of our best intentions gone awry, a knotted ball with no beginning, no end. It is too late to matter anyway.

"Say something," Sam implores.

My head is spinning. I am about to turn to him for comfort, I am leaning into believing him, maybe even forgiving him, at some point forgiving him, when I remember the rest of it, Sam and Deirdre's affair in college, and I am filled with doubt once more.

TWENTY-FOUR

There is a long silence as the sediment shifts, settles, unsettles, resettles.

"What about you and Deirdre in college?" I ask, numbly.

"What about us in college?" Sam asks, his eyebrows knit in bewilderment.

"You slept with her while I was in London."

He looks up, stunned. "That's ridiculous. What gave you that idea?"

"Jack told me he saw the two of you."

He shakes his head in disbelief. "That's impossible. There was nothing to see."

"Are you so sure about that?" I challenge.

"What exactly did Jack tell you?"

"He said he came back from a tennis match late one night and went to Deirdre's room to surprise her. He saw the two of you in bed together." The words come out slowly, there is so much internal bruising.

"I don't know what Jack saw. Or what he thinks he saw. But I never slept with Deirdre. Not really."

"What the hell is that supposed to mean? That's like being a little bit pregnant. There's no such thing as 'not really' when it comes to sex."

"Oh God, Lisa, it was all so long ago." Sam runs his hands through his hair, his eyes shut tight. Deep horizontal lines crease his skin. "It was a mistake. A horrible, drunken mistake. But it was one night. And we didn't go through with it. We couldn't."

"You expect me to believe that?" I glare at him. "I'm going to need more than that."

"I had just gotten that famous letter of yours from London. I thought you were breaking up with me."

"Why would you think that?"

"It seemed as if you were questioning everything. Me, us."

"That's what we did at that age."

"I didn't."

"Go on," I say.

"I ran into Deirdre at the pub. She and Jack had one of their fights and he was off at some tournament. She was upset, I was missing you. We starting talking, drinking. You remember what it was like."

He looks over at me, hoping that I've heard enough to get the gist and he will be excused from offering up the details.

I do remember what it was like. All those nights in the dingy campus pub, the floor sticky with beer, the inconstant couplings and uncouplings, all that talk, all that specious reasoning when you are nineteen and it is late and you think there is some sort of answer waiting just beyond your fingertips and regret is still a lifetime away. The rush of cold when you finally leave at closing time, standing just outside the door as you listen to the locks slide into place, rocking back and forth on your toes in the clean crunchy snow, waiting for whatever will come next.

"What happened?" I ask flatly.

"I don't know. We were both hurt and looking for comfort. After the pub closed we ended up back in Deirdre's room. Just to talk. And then one thing led to another. The point is, we stopped. I know that's no excuse, not really. But we both realized what we were doing. And we stopped. Whatever Jack saw, that's all that happened. It was just drunken fumbling. If he had ever asked Deirdre, or me for that matter, we would have told him the truth." He stops, leans back. "This is why Jack always hated me," he says, one more revelation in a room already too filled with them.

"How come you never told me about that night?"

"What would have been the point? It would only have caused unnecessary pain. I told you. Nothing happened."

"Something happened. A barrier was broken." I pause. "You both knew something I didn't."

"Deirdre and I never spoke of that night, we never mentioned it again. It felt like someone else who did it. It felt like someone else even at the time." He tilts his head. "Why are you asking me about this now? When did Jack tell you all this?"

It is my turn to take a deep breath, hesitate. "Last night."

"You saw Jack last night?" Confusion plays across his face. "But you told the detective . . ."

"No, I didn't see him. I called him. After I saw the pictures of you and Deirdre."

Sam shoots up. "You told Jack that you thought Deirdre and I were having an affair? Are you out of your mind? I can't believe you would do something like that before you even talked to me."

"You have no idea what it was like, seeing those pictures," I reply, feeling that staggering desolation once more. "I had just spent the afternoon with Jack. He was buying an apartment for the two of them, he was planning out their whole future. I had to tell him."

I stop short. The tenor of that call, the sickening realization of what I may have unleashed, begins to hit me, slowly at first, then fully. "Oh God." I shake my head, it can't be. "I never should have called Jack, it was a horrible mistake."

Sam sits back down, rubbing his temples. When he looks at me it is with different eyes, his tone eerily calm, as if he is speaking to a child having a tantrum. "What exactly happened last night?" he asks. "What did Jack do after you talked to him?"

"He was furious. Beyond furious. He thought it was a repeat of the past. After I told him he hung up on me. I have no idea what he did or where he went."

"And you? What did you do?"

"I walked. I didn't want to come home. I was too angry to talk to you and I knew the girls would still be up. I couldn't imagine going through the motions of pretending everything was okay in front of them."

"You walked for all those hours?" he asks skeptically.

"My world had just been blown apart. I couldn't see straight. I don't even really remember getting there, but I ended up at Deirdre's."

"You told the detective you didn't see her."

"I didn't. I stood outside her building for a long time, but I just couldn't bring myself to go up. I couldn't face her. Eventually I started walking again. I stopped and had a glass of wine at that place on Seventeenth Street, Bar Jamón. Then I came home."

"You went to everyone, Jack, Deirdre, everyone before you even tried to talk to me."

"There was more at stake with you."

The ache grows stronger, pressing from the inside out, drenched in loss and regret and a sadness that will never dissipate. Deirdre is gone.

I can feel my insides being hollowed out.

I start to say something but Sam hushes me. "I need to think for a minute." He bends his head between his hands. I watch his back rise and fall with his breathing.

"All right, let's back up," he says, clinging to the last shreds of control. "You still haven't told me about those pictures. Who the hell would have done something like that?"

"It was all a mistake. A misunderstanding."

"Yes, so you've said. But that doesn't explain how it could have happened to begin with."

"There's this guy, I met him through Carol. She wanted me to try to land him as a client. She thought it would help me with Merdale. We starting meeting about that and we became friends. He was giving me advice, helping me deal with what was going on there. We talked."

"I'm sorry, but I don't see how you go from trying to sign a new client to having your husband followed. You'll have to enlighten me a bit more than that," Sam insists. "Does this guy have a name?"

"David. David Forrester."

Sam rears back. "David Forrester did this?"

"You know him?"

"He didn't tell you? No, he wouldn't," Sam says dryly.

I shake my head, I am falling farther and farther down a bottomless well. "How do you know David?"

"I was doing a story on insider trading a couple of years ago. His name kept coming up. He managed to shut it down before I could nail him. I don't know what he threatened people with. Or who he paid off. He did everything he could to destroy my credibility. You don't remember any of this?"

I vaguely recall something along those lines, but I'm not sure Sam ever told me his name. Perhaps he did and I wasn't listening.

"I still don't get it," Sam continues. "Help me out here. You're meeting with Forrester supposedly about business and the next thing you know he's putting a tail on me. There are a few holes in your story."

I hug my knees to my chest. "I never asked him to, if that's what you think."

"You must have said something. That kind of thing doesn't happen out of the blue."

"I told you, we were friends. I was going through such a rough time. You and I were hardly speaking to each other. It felt like we were living in separate rooms. It's not as if I simply decided one day to blurt out every detail of my personal life to him for no reason. You were acting so strangely," I remind him. "I couldn't figure out what was going on. There were all those lies. I needed someone to talk to."

"What lies?"

"Your trip to Chicago."

"I explained that."

"There were other things."

"What other things?"

"I found your phone."

"What phone?"

"Your disposable phone. Claire found it in the coat closet."

"I never had a disposable phone. Why would I?"

"To call—whoever."

"I don't know what Claire found, but it wasn't mine. Even if you believed all this, why would you tell Forrester of all people? Were you sleeping with him?"

"No. Sam, it wasn't like that."

"Yeah? What was it like?"

This is what it was like, I think: David made me feel attractive, made me feel a sense of possibility, isn't that what all seduction is, however false or aborted, and I fell for it, just a little but yes, I fell for it, because I was lonely, in some gut way so deeply lonely, because we weren't making love the way we used to, because everything between us was so flat and distanced and I thought you had deserted me. But all I say is, "I thought we were friends."

"Where are they?" Sam asks finally.

"Where are what?"

"The photographs."

"I don't have them. David does."

"That's fucking great. He's just the guy you want messing with your life. You don't know him. You have no idea what he is capable of."

"I'm sorry," I repeat.

Even that one warm flush of flattery I allowed myself to feel at his attentions was rooted in a lie, the attraction manufactured at will. It was never about me at all.

"I've never heard Jack so angry, Sam. If I had any idea something like this could happen . . . Oh God, what did I do? This is all my fault, all of it."

"Let's remember that we don't know what happened yet."

"No matter what happened, Deirdre is gone," I sob. The ache spreads through every cell, stealing the last bit of oxygen from my lungs.

"Lisa, you are going to have to tell Callahan about your phone call to Jack," Sam says softly. "You are going to have to explain this all to him."

"I can't," I protest.

"I don't like this any more than you do. It doesn't exactly make either of us look good. But the minute David Forrester hears about Deirdre or reads it in the paper, those pictures are going to be all over the goddamned place, starting with the police. He'll make sure of that. You need to tell them first, you have to control the story."

I don't move, neither of us does.

"Call him," Sam prods grimly.

I stand up, splash cold water from the kitchen sink on my face, the back of my neck, sit back down. Sam hands me the phone.

"Mrs. Barkley," Callahan says as soon as I get through. "I was just about to call you."

"Oh?"

"Are you sure about the name of the law firm you told me Handel was starting at?"

"Yes. Loring, Marcus. He's been made a partner."

"They have no record of him. No one there has ever met with him."

"That's impossible."

"They have no reason to lie." There is a pause before Callahan speaks again. "Handel's cell phone hasn't been used since early evening yesterday. The records indicate the last call received was from you. Can you tell me the nature of that conversation?"

"Yes." I catch my breath and I tell him of my call to Jack, of my mistaken interpretation, of Jack's rage and my regret. "I should have said something to you earlier," I apologize, "I wasn't thinking. I was just so . . . shocked."

"We are going to have to talk to both you and your husband,"

Callahan says flatly when I am done. Everything is different now. "And I'll need David Forrester's contact information. We'll have to get those pictures from him."

"Of course."

Callahan gives us the address of the precinct house and hangs up.

TWENTY-FIVE

It is close to one a.m. when I finally crawl into bed and lay beside Sam. He shifts slightly to accommodate me but makes no move to touch me. We cannot comfort each other. At some point, I hope, we will both be able to understand and forgive. But not yet, not tonight.

"Any luck getting through?" he asks without lifting his head from the pillow. His voice is hoarse with exhaustion.

"No."

I've been trying to reach Jack all evening, desperate to tell him that I was wrong, he was wrong, about everything. I need him to assure me that he hasn't done it, of course not, how could I ever think such a thing about him.

I suppose, too, on some level I believe that if I can just get through to him I can head off something that has already happened.

Jack never picks up his phone.

I pull the sheets tight to my chest, curl into the fetal position.

If only I had ripped the photos up, thrown them in David's face, or gone to Sam first. If only I hadn't called Jack. But no matter how much I replay it, I cannot change what I have done. It will be with me forever.

I can tell by Sam's uneven breath he isn't sleeping, not even close.

I turn on my side, pull the pillow beneath me.

All I see is Deirdre. How she must have looked when they found her.

And before. In the moments before.

Grief, sharp and fierce, has taken its place in my heart, my head. I can't believe I am never going to talk to Deirdre, never going to see her again. I go over our last breakfast. It was just so ordinary, it was just us. It is unimaginable to me that that was the last time I am ever going to see her. I cannot picture my life without her.

I shut my eyes, feel contractions of the deepest sorrow.

I don't notice the crying coming from outside our door until it escalates, a stepladder of pain.

Sam turns to me. "It's Claire."

"I'll go."

I hurry down the hallway to her. When Claire was two, three, she suffered from night terrors. I would find her wide-eyed, sweaty, barely able to see me. No amount of comfort would calm her, pull her back into the world. Only when she had thoroughly worn herself out would recognition gradually begin to dawn in her eyes, only then could she be soothed. It hasn't happened in years.

Claire's forehead is hot and damp when I touch it, smoothing the hair from her face. She'd been gnawing one strand in her sleep, working it over until it is a wet snarl, and I gently free it from her mouth. She wakes enough to see me but not to speak. I lie down and curl my body tightly around hers. I'm the Cheerio and you are the spoon, she used to say. I let her cry now, her narrow back and ribs trembling with grief. I don't tell her it will be okay, I just stroke her head, kiss the back of her neck, feel once more that most unambiguous of loves.

Her body finally stills but I do not get up. I lie motionless in her single bed, staring at the filmy white curtains she has tied back with colorful ribbons and scarves, while she melts into sleep.

Both girls peppered us with questions when we told them what had happened, increasingly suspicious and frustrated when all we could reply was, We don't know. We just don't know. Claire grew ferociously angry, taking what had happened to Deirdre as an act of violence propagated against her personally. She became inconsolable, locked herself in her room. Phoebe clung more than I can remember her ever doing, her innate bravery crushed. For the first time she sensed that danger that can creep through any door, there is no guarding against it.

I wonder if they will ever feel truly safe again and the sadness that they might not, that it is one of the things lost last night, falls atop all the other sadnesses ratcheting through my heart.

As I lie there, bits and pieces of my conversation with Sam float back to me; I pick through them, choose one, turn it over and over, trying to assimilate it and form a new mosaic of who we were, who we are.

There was a time when we were happy, purely happy, there must have been.

The relief we had at finding each other, reclaiming each other again after that early separation, the night I told Sam I was pregnant with Claire, and two years later with Phoebe, those times of course. But it is the smaller, incremental moments that return to me, the instances when recognition and desire take you by surprise, the evening we made love on the kitchen floor after a dinner party if only to put off cleaning up, our first parent-teacher conference, when the nursery school director spent forty minutes deconstructing the way Claire held scissors and our suppressed laughter burst out in torrents on the street until tears were streaming down both of our faces. We were on the same side once, completely on the same side, I'm sure of it.

We chose the world we live in, I know that. We wanted it—we were young and confident of our ability to take what was good and challenging and worthwhile in it and not fall prey to the prejudices, the greed and poisonous envy. We thought we were better, stronger, surer than that. And maybe we were.

Nevertheless, it feels as if the city itself has wedged its way between us like a blade, separating us from each other, from our truest selves.

I try to remember when exactly the fumes of my money anxiety seeped out and infiltrated Sam, mushrooming beyond anything I meant, a funhouse mirror of my own worst impulses and insecurities. I try to remember when the distance grew so great between us that we were both too scared to try to traverse it with words, terrified of what we might hear. Or say. Instead we fell victim to guesswork, the most dangerous proposition of all when it comes to love.

I will at some point forgive Sam for that fumbling misguided night with Deirdre, I will believe his claim that it was not consummated, though I will always wonder if Deirdre thought of it every time she saw me. It is the not-knowing, the being left on the outskirts of my own history that will be hardest to forgive. I realize that we all have different versions of our lives, I just thought ours were closer.

Claire's soft breath brushes up against my neck as I lay there trying to make sense of it all.

It is near dawn when I crawl back to my own bed.

Sam opens his eyes slightly. "Are you okay?" he asks quietly, touching me now, gently, tentatively, with his fingertips.

I shake my head no but it is too dark for him to see.

TWENTY-SIX

In the morning, while Sam fixes the girls breakfast, I call Merdale and leave a message informing them that I will not be in. Though I don't say it, I know I will never go back there. If Favata has the missing hospital records he can do with them what he will.

There are three missed calls from David Forrester and one e-mail from him on my BlackBerry asking me to please get in touch, but I have no intention of ever speaking to him again.

We consider keeping Claire and Phoebe home from school but decide instead that it is important to maintain routine. If nothing else, there is the hope that their classes will distract them from their own imaginations and distress. It is impossible not to hold them just a bit longer before they walk out the door, though, not to want to pull them back.

"Call," I remind them as they disengage.

Claire pulls out her cell phone to prove that she has it.

They are standing by the open door, ready to leave, when I remember. "Honey, do you know that cell phone you found in the coat closet?"

"Yes."

"It wasn't mine. Or Daddy's. Do you have any idea where it came from?"

She shakes her head.

"You're sure?"

Phoebe looks over anxiously at her sister being grilled before speaking up in a quivery voice. "It was mine."

"What?"

"You wouldn't let me have one, so one of the kids in school got it for me."

I stare at her incredulously. Every time I underestimate the sophistication of the world she inhabits, the awe-inspiring navigational skills of its children, I am dead wrong.

"I'm sorry," Phoebe says. "I don't see what the big deal is."

Sam and I look at each other and let them go.

When Claire calls thirty-five minutes later to say they got to school safely she hands the phone to Phoebe. "I love you, Mommy," she whispers so that she is not overheard, embarrassed. "I'm sorry I didn't tell you about the phone."

"I love you, too. More than anything in the universe."

At five minutes to ten, Sam and I walk into the large white brick precinct house on Twenty-first Street and ask to see Detective Callahan. "He's expecting us," Sam tells the uniformed officer stationed at the front desk.

He motions to us to step to the side while we wait for him. I glance nervously around at the "Wanted" posters with their sketches of androidal faces rendered in black and white and the sign on the far door that reads "No Guns Past This Point."

Callahan appears a couple of minutes later. "Thank you for coming." He is only slightly less formal in a tie and shirtsleeves, as if we have come to his home this time, which of course we have. He stands perfectly erect, his posture disciplined against the tall man's temptation to stoop.

"Of course," Sam replies. "Anything we can do to help."

We follow Callahan up a narrow staircase to the detectives' department on the second floor. He leads us through the maze of old-fashioned mismatched desks past a holding cell where a post-drunken young man is clutching the bars, staring silently out at us. There is a low-level hum of ringing phones and conversations, a fax machine spitting out paper and the clacking of computer keyboards. "Have you spoken to Jack?" I ask as I step around an overflowing wastebasket.

"We haven't been able to locate him yet. There's been no movement on his cards and he still hasn't used his phone. We've been trying to reach his wife as well to see if he's made contact but we haven't gotten through to her."

"They're separated."

"So you've said. Anyway, we've tried her home and the university where she works, but no one seems to know where she is."

When we reach the far end of the room, Callahan slows to a stop and a woman wearing a double-breasted navy wool pants suit, her deep-red hair pulled back into a tight ponytail, appears beside him. She is just shy of pretty, her strong jaw and broad shoulders closer to handsome, though she is lucky with her hair, the type of red that is burnished and smooth rather than frizzed, a source of pride rather than a lifelong bane.

"This is Detective Gibbs," he informs us. "She's helping out with the case."

Gibbs smiles reassuringly at us. She is in her midthirties, with pale milky skin and nails bitten down to raw stubs. "I'm sorry about your friend," she says as she shakes both of our hands.

Before we know exactly how it happens, it is so subtly accomplished, so balletic and rehearsed, Sam and I are separated.

Gibbs talks softly as she guides me into a small interrogation room, as I once did to ease the children in doctors' offices, dentists' chairs.

"Can I get you some coffee?" she asks as she closes the door behind us.

The floor, the walls, the chairs are all variant shades of industrial gray. There is a small two-way mirror on the far wall with a shade pulled crookedly up above it. The cabinets and shelves that line one side are filled with papers and office supplies, a utilitarian element in a space meant to intimidate, to cause discomfort.

"I'm fine, thanks."

We sit down across the narrow rectangular metal table from each other.

"I understand you and Deirdre were roommates in college," she begins, her elbows on the table, both hands playing with a thin silver chain necklace, sliding its charm back and forth like a seesaw until there is an irritated red skein left on her skin.

"Yes."

"This must be incredibly painful for you." She shakes her head. "I lost touch with my college roommate. We were best friends and then who knows what happened. Now we see each other once a year and pretend we're closer than we are."

I nod without speaking. I am waiting for the rhythm, the parameters to be established. I am not sure whose side she is on, or even if there are sides. I haven't slept in two days and my skin is tingling. The artificial light has taken on a strange neon-tinged blurriness. I don't trust myself, I don't trust her.

"Still," Gibbs continues, "even the memory of that connection is stronger than most of the connections I have now. I don't know why that is. Maybe there are just too many things later on, jobs, relationships, responsibilities, everything becomes diluted." She leans forward. "But from what I understand you two remained close?"

"Yes."

"I'm impressed. How'd you do it?"

It strikes me as a curious question, as if she expects me to reveal the secret formula to a complicated magic trick. "We were best friends," I reply, a reductive catchall for more than twenty years of our intertwined lives, too simplistic and yet true.

"How often did you see each other?"

"We had breakfast almost every week. We talked."

"I envy you, having someone like that in your life. That kind of continuity is so rare these days. Anyway, we printed out the pictures you gave Detective Callahan to show to Deirdre's neighbors," Gibbs says, pulling them from the leather binder she has brought in with her. "You never know what someone might have seen. It's a small building, just six lofts." She takes the first one out: the four of us at Jack's birthday dinner.

"We also got these photographs from your friend Forrester." She uncovers David's pictures of Deirdre and Sam. She studies the top one before passing it to me, Deirdre and Sam on the street, touching, close. "Deirdre was a beautiful woman," she observes.

I can feel tears forming in my eyes and try to will them away. "She is. Was."

She turns slowly to the next photograph until all three are splayed before us.

I regard them with different eyes now, the words that I had imagined Deirdre and Sam saying, the purpose of their touch altered, though the closeness, the proximity cannot be. No matter what I know to be true, the images form a disturbing geometry that is hard to explain away.

"Deirdre and your husband look so, what would you say, intimate?" Gibbs remarks.

I shift uncomfortably in my seat. "It's not what it seems," I insist. "I told Detective Callahan that. Sam borrowed money from Deirdre, that's what they were meeting about."

Gibbs picks up the photo of Sam and Deirdre in a café, their heads almost touching. "It's easy to see how you might have misinterpreted them. I know how I'd feel if someone showed me pictures like this of my husband. I understand you saw these for the first time the evening Deirdre died?"

"Yes. I've explained all this to Detective Callahan."

"That was when, about six, seven p.m.?"

"I guess."

"Your husband and your best friend. The two people you were closest to. Do you know when the pictures were taken?"

"Within the last couple of weeks."

Jamison studies the top picture. "I love her necklace," she says, almost to herself. She looks up at me, touching her own necklace. "Do you know where she got it?"

"It was a present from Jack."

"If I had something like that I'd never take it off," she ruminates.

"I don't think she did."

Gibbs leans back. "So. What did you do?" she asks. "When you saw the pictures?"

"I called Jack. I shouldn't have. I know that. I'd give anything to take back what I said, anything." Guilt pushes my voice up an octave, rushes it.

"Which was what, exactly?"

"That I thought Deirdre and Sam were having an affair."

"How did he respond?"

"He was furious."

"Did he threaten her?"

"No, not exactly."

"What does that mean?"

"He was upset."

The room is overheated, the air stale. I can feel my skin grow damp beneath my wool sweater.

"Do you remember his exact words?" Gibbs asks.

"He called her a bitch. He said she wasn't going to get away with it," I admit.

"That certainly sounds threatening to me. Can you give me a sense of their relationship? Was there any history of violence?"

"Not that I know of."

"Did Jack tell you where he was when you spoke to him?"

"No."

"And you have no idea where he went after that?"

"No."

She stacks the photos up neatly, aligning the corners just so. "What did you do after talking to Jack?"

"I walked. I just walked for miles. I was trying to clear my head."

"I see. Here's the thing, Lisa. May I call you that?"

I nod.

"One of Deirdre's neighbors claims she saw a woman who looks like you outside of her building last night around eight o'clock."

"I did go there. I was going to talk to her. But in the end I couldn't do it. I wasn't ready. I wish I had."

"Why?"

"Because she would have explained. She would have made me understand how wrong I was. She would have told me the truth."

"So you didn't see her?"

"No."

"And you didn't see Jack or anyone else going in?"

"No."

"How long were you there for?"

"I don't know."

"Then what?"

"I had a glass of wine at Bar Jamón."

"What time was that?"

"I don't know. I was upset. Watching the clock wasn't my first priority. I suppose around nine thirty or ten."

"What time did you get to your apartment?"

"I guess around eleven or twelve."

"And your husband was already asleep?"

"Yes. Am I a suspect?" I ask incredulously.

"We're just trying to piece this all together," Gibbs assures me.

"Don't you think if I knew anything, if I saw anything, I would tell you?" Outrage pierces through the exhaustion. "I loved Deirdre."

"No one is accusing anyone of anything," Gibbs says evenly. "But sometimes people don't know what they've seen. Obviously, it is crucial that we find Jack Handel."

"All right." I lean back, only slightly mollified.

"Let's back up for just a minute. What made you decide to have Sam followed to begin with?"

"I didn't know about it. Talk to David Forrester. He can tell you."

"Yes, we have spoken with him and will continue to. I understand Monday night wasn't the first time you two had been together?"

"What does that have to do with anything?" I demand.

"I'm just trying to understand," Gibbs replies evenly. "Even if you had no idea that Forrester was having your husband followed, you did confide in him there were problems in your marriage."

"Did he tell you that?"

"I'm asking you," Gibbs says.

"I may have."

"In fact, you told him you thought your husband was having an affair."

I don't answer.

"Where was Sam last night?"

"Working late. He had to meet with a source for a story."

"Does he do that often?"

"He's a journalist. It's part of his job."

"Of course. Did he happen to tell you the name of this source?"

"No. He keeps his sources confidential. If he didn't, no one would trust him enough to talk to him."

Gibbs looks at me as if that is the most naïve thing she has ever heard. This doesn't seem like the time to launch into a constitutional argument, though.

"We've been going through Deirdre's e-mails looking for leads. You're right, your husband did borrow money from her. It seems that she was quite annoyed with him for not paying her back. In fact, she was threatening to tell you this weekend if he didn't. Their last exchanges were rather heated."

"Can I see them?"

"I'm sorry. No. They are part of an ongoing investigation. What time did you say he got home last night?"

"I didn't. He was already asleep when I got back," I reply indignantly.

"I see. By the way," Gibbs says, "the medical examiner has told us Deirdre had sex in the hours before she died. What I'm having trouble figuring out is, if Jack was so furious with her, as you say, so sure he had been betrayed, why would she have had sex with him?"

"She must have told him the truth about the pictures, about Sam, that he had borrowed money from her and that's all it was."

"It's one of the things we will have to ask him."

"When you find him," I remind her.

"Yes. When we find him."

The walls of the small room are closing in on me. I try to inhale but the air catches in my throat.

"I'm sure you're very tired," Gibbs says. "It's been a rough thirty-six hours. We'll stop for now." She rises and begins to lead me out. "In the meantime, it would be helpful if you could remember where you walked the other night after you left Deirdre's, if anyone saw you."

I stare at her blankly. No one sees anyone on the night streets, no one wants to. We look away, all of us.

"One last thing," she adds as she holds the door open for me.

"Yes?"

"Borrowing money from someone doesn't necessarily preclude the possibility of having sex with them, does it?"

TWENTY-SEVEN

When I get out of the room, Callahan is standing alone in front of his desk, restlessly flipping through a large tattered Rolodex without looking at it, a diversion he readily gives up as soon as he sees us. He and Jamison exchange glances before Callahan turns to me. "Your husband is waiting downstairs for you." His sympathetic air of yesterday has been replaced by that of a disappointed teacher, as if we have somehow not lived up to our potential. He had thought better of us.

"Thank you."

"We'll be speaking," Callahan says as I turn to make my way back through rows of desks cluttered with computers, phones, crumpled candy wrappers and piles of papers to the staircase, my eyes focused straight ahead.

Downstairs, Sam has his back to me, staring out of the smudged window in the reception area, his fingertips drumming a staccato rat-a-tat against the glass. He starts when I touch his back.

"You ready?" he asks impatiently, barely turning to me.

"Yes."

"Good. Let's go." He pushes open the heavy door and we head out onto the street, lined with diagonally parked police cars nosing their way onto the pavement like sharks.

"Where to?" Sam asks as we begin strolling aimlessly up the block.

"I don't know."

We have walked out into a different city than either of us normally inhabits, one of quiet streets and strollers, meandering college kids, men and women with laptop computers and big ideas and nebulous jobs, a parallel, more leisurely universe that goes on without us on weekdays between eight and six while we are someplace else entirely. We look around and have no idea what to do. We are no longer inhabiting our own lives.

"Let's get some coffee," Sam suggests, and for a few blocks, this gives us a direction, a goal. We hardly speak, a silent if mutual agreement to wait until we have settled someplace. The residue of the police station still clings to us.

We head to a coffeehouse on the ground floor of a nineteenth-century brownstone that we used to frequent on winter weekends when the girls were younger, snowy days when this would be our only outing, an escape from the apartment, from the bickering and the dishes and the toy-strewn floor, from the inertia that left us loopy but seems so luxurious now. The girls would get mugs of hot chocolate, a dense soupy mixture that made anyone past puberty ill but was manna to them, and we would sip cappuccinos, which seemed at the time a uniquely adult, almost guilty pleasure, a reward. If we were lucky and had timed it just right the girls would nap when we got home and Sam and I would make love in that syrupy afternoon way, one ear always primed for a restless child.

As we make our way down the three worn stone steps into the darkened room a wave of dizziness washes over me and I take Sam's arm to steady myself. I feel constantly in danger of losing my balance, tipping over, dissolving.

"Why don't you find us a table and I'll get our drinks," Sam suggests.

While he goes up to the counter to order, I glance around the room filled with tiny round tables and clusters of chairs in random and chaotic order. I squeeze past a man in a puffy bright red down vest, his gray tousled head buried in an alternative paper favored by people half his age and two hopped-up models trying to figure where to put their impossibly long legs. They glare at me when I trip over their size eleven feet.

I find a table in the far corner next to a group of three young mothers balancing babies, bottles and lattes as they gossip and catch up. They seem a continent away from me, these midday women, all three slim and long-haired and chicly disheveled, tired perhaps, but with so much ahead of them, so much yet to be determined. One of them catches me staring at her and, embarrassed, I pretend to be looking over her head for my husband, so handsome still, though if you look closely there are blue rings under his eyes, my husband in his khaki pants and wool coat, lost in thought as he carries our drinks to the table, oblivious of the women. We are in our own tunnel now, everything else is just a rumor of the existence we once had.

The table rocks as he places the cups down. The foam threatens to spill over the edges and yet somehow, defying gravity, doesn't.

"So," Sam says, stirring in two sugars, an indulgence he rarely allows himself, "that was rather smooth of them."

"What was?"

"The way they separated us."

"They were only doing their job."

"Their job is to find Jack and stop wasting time dicking around with ridiculous insinuations."

I lick the cinnamon-flavored froth from the back of my spoon. "What kind of 'ridiculous insinuations'?"

Sam frowns. "Callahan had the gall to ask me if I knew where you were Monday night, what time you got back."

"What did you tell him?"

"That you were walking around, upset. Mistakenly upset," he emphasizes. "And I wasn't sure what time you got back. I thought around ten, ten thirty."

"You didn't tell them I went to Deirdre's?"

"No."

"Why not?"

He takes a cautious sip of his cappuccino, unsure how hot it is. The foam is never an accurate indication and it is dangerous to be too cavalier. "I didn't know if you would have wanted me to."

"Why wouldn't I?" I ask, taken aback.

He studies me and then shakes his head. "No reason."

"Well, I told them."

"All right. I'm sure it's fine."

I lean forward and the table rocks again. "I don't need you to protect me. I'm not hiding anything, for God's sake."

"I know that, Lisa. I didn't mean anything by it. It was just instinctive. Jesus, I can't think clearly anymore. Something about being in that room was so unnerving. Maybe it's just a knee-jerk reaction to authority or to being questioned, but it got under my skin. I resent how they are handling this. We're trying to help, they should be able to see that."

"They asked me what time you got home Monday night, too."

"Of course they did. Why else would they have tag-teamed us? It's outrageous but until they find Jack we seem to be all they've got. They need something to report to their boss so it looks like they're making progress, no matter how bogus it is."

I'm not sure if I completely believe this. I'm not sure he does. I'd be asking us questions, too, if I were them.

"Did you give them the name of the person you were meeting with?" I ask.

"You know I can't do that. The piece is on a potential bank cover-up that could have high-reaching implications in the mortgage business. Shocking as this might seem to them, I actually think it's an important story to get out. Aside from that, if I go against my word not only would my source lose his job, I'd destroy my reputation."

"These seem to be extenuating circumstances."

"I am not going to break every rule of journalistic integrity to make their lives easier."

"You could at least tell them where you met. Someone must have seen you."

"We met outside on a park bench. He didn't want to be seen. That's kind of the point, isn't it? I gave them Marissa's number to verify what time I got back."

I can't help but smile. "That should be interesting." Marissa, with her fluid relationship to time, who is still convinced that real artists are beyond such petty bourgeois concerns. She somehow hasn't gotten the memo that they have their own PR agents now, ever-increasing rents and alarm clocks, that even inspiration is working on a tight schedule. "They'll be lucky if she remembers you came home at all."

Sam smiles, too, and there is a flicker between us, a recognition of things only we share.

We become quiet again, almost shy of each other.

"Gibbs told me that Deirdre had sex before she died," I remark carefully, playing with my drink to avoid his eyes. It feels so invasive to be talking about Deirdre like this. I am not yet used to the way death obliterates the normal boundaries of privacy, how everything becomes fair game.

"Yes, so I hear." Sam leans forward on his elbows and the table sways. He looks down angrily at its spindly legs before he turns his attention reluctantly back to me. "They asked me to take a DNA test. Just to rule things out, they said. They seemed to use that term a lot."

I can feel, beneath the tingling weariness, that my heart is racing though I make every attempt not to betray that.

"I refused, by the way," he adds.

"Why?"

"I want to talk to a lawyer first."

"Do you need a lawyer?"

"It wouldn't be such a bad idea. For either of us."

"Sam?"

"There's nothing. Nothing I haven't told you. We should get some advice, that's all. That's what people do. In fact, I don't think we should speak to them again without lawyers present."

"I suppose," I say halfheartedly.

It makes sense, but I can't help but worry that asking for a lawyer will taint us, make the detectives even more suspicious. I understand rationally that looking out for your own interests is not a shameful act, that you don't win points for being unwilling to make waves, but it goes against my nature. It is one of the things I have always counted on Sam for, his ability to take whatever action he deems best regardless of external opinion, while I have a tendency to tie myself up in knots.

"I'm sure the police know more than they're telling us," Sam says. "There must have been other clues in Deirdre's apartment."

I stare down disconsolately at the brown dregs at the bottom of my cup, tears forming in the back of my throat.

"There's something I keep thinking about," I say quietly. "About Deirdre. For all of our closeness, we never really talked about what we would want."

"Want?"

"You know, religious beliefs, last wishes."

There were no churches or synagogues either of us frequented, no rites we upheld beyond present-giving at holidays. The most spirituality either of us engaged in was chanting in Sanskrit at the yoga classes we sometimes took on Saturday mornings. Neither of us had the slightest idea what we were saying. "Has it ever occurred to you that for all we know we could be chanting 'Death to all Americans'?" Deirdre asked as we rolled up our mats one day. I have no idea what she believed happens after you die. That kind of speculation is for the very young or the very old. It's not that we thought we were immune, we just assumed we had time.

"I want to do the right thing, I want to do what she would have wanted." I am crying now. The young mothers are trying not to look over at us but they can't help it. "But I have no idea. How could I not know? I should know this."

There are so many things I long to ask Deirdre, to say to her. I will never have the chance again.

"I keep wondering what it was like, if she was scared, if she felt pain."

"Lisa, you can't think that way."

"How can you not?" I ask tearfully. Her face, her crumpled fallen body has been before me every second since Detective Callahan walked through our front door. "I'm not sure I can do this," I murmur.

"Do what?"

"Any of it. Live with it. With what happened."

A few feet away, the mothers fumble in their diaper bags for money, juggling sippy cups and toys and tissues as they rise and make their way slowly out.

"We'll make it through this," Sam promises. "Somehow we'll make it through this."

"Ben still doesn't know. I've left messages for him on his cell phone. I'm sure it works internationally, he travels so much, but he hasn't called me back."

"Did you tell him what it was about?"

"I couldn't very well spell it out. Can you imagine? But I said it was important. Maybe they confiscate cell phones at the ashram."

"When is he due back?"

"I don't know. I suppose I could try to get ahold of his assistant to find out, but I don't really see the point. He'll be home soon enough. And then he'll be where we are."

"Well, not exactly."

"No, not exactly. Still, they were in each other's lives one way or another for a long time."

"Not Deirdre's wisest choice."

"It doesn't matter anymore."

Our drinks are gone, the room is emptying out of its late-morning customers and not yet filling up with lunch people. "Now what?" I ask.

"I thought I'd go into the office for the afternoon," Sam says. "Is that okay?"

"Yes." I can't think of an alternative plan. Just what are we supposed to be doing? We have no guidelines for a day like this. The very notion of plans, a future, has lost all meaning.

"I want to make some calls about UniProphet to see if there's any progress."

"On what?"

"UniProphet. The start-up." He looks at me with some frustration. "You know, if you would just hear me out, maybe you would understand why I was drawn to it."

"All right," I say, with little enthusiasm. It seems so beside the point to me, though not to him, even after everything, not to him.

"Good," he says before launching in. "Okay, here goes. For years everyone from Amazon to tiny mom-and-pop sites has been trying to target what products to push to their users judging by their previous purchases, but no one has figured out how to do it with any degree of success. There are too many variables. The best rate anyone has managed to achieve is about ten percent accuracy. But these guys have come up with an algorithm that combines all sorts of data no one has used before. They have the highest rate yet of figuring out what people are most likely to be interested in buying. Do you have any idea how many companies will pay big bucks for the technology?"

His confidence seems willfully naïve to me and it strikes me again how even the smartest of men can be blinded by their faith in their own business acumen despite all evidence to the contrary.

"What do you think?" he asks, wanting something I cannot give him, approbation, exoneration.

"I don't know, Sam. I can't concentrate on it right now." I was hardly listening.

"All right, I understand. This isn't the best time." He cannot hide his dejection, though.

"I'm sorry. All I can think about is Deirdre."

He nods. "What are you going to do this afternoon?"

"I'll pick the girls up from school. Maybe take them out for an ice cream or something." I want them near me, that's all I know to do, keep them close, watch for fault lines, help piece them back together.

We rise and, careful not to knock into the table, we begin to gather our things, slip our arms awkwardly into our coats.

"I'll bring these to the counter," Sam says, picking up our empty cups.

"I'll meet you outside."

I am halfway out the door when my cell phone rings. I pull it out of my bag and glance at the number but I don't recognize it.

"Hello?"

There is a pause on the other end of the line.

"Hello?" I say again.

"Lisa, it's Jack."

TWENTY-EIGHT

Jack. Where are you?" I ask frantically as I rush out of the coffeehouse, where the hissing of the espresso machine makes it difficult to hear.

"In Boston."

"Why haven't you called? I've left a hundred messages on your phone. Everyone's looking for you."

"I know." His voice is a hollow shell, everything alive is gone from it. "I just talked to a detective in New York. Some guy named Callahan."

I lean up against a parked blue Toyota, trying to catch my breath, gather my rattling thoughts.

"What did Callahan tell you?" I ask cautiously. Every word is loaded.

He breathes deeply, his exhalation barely muffling a sob.

"Not much. Except that Deirdre is dead." His voice shudders, then completely breaks. The pain is still fresh for him. It has not yet settled into the steady omnipresent ache that it is and always will be for me.

Or so he would like me to think.

I clutch the phone tightly.

"I can't believe it," he says slowly. "You read about these things. But it's always other people, not you. Not the people you love. I just don't understand, how could something like this happen to Deirdre?" Her name expands in his mouth.

"What exactly did Callahan say?"

"He wouldn't give me many details. Who could have done this?" It is a lament, really, and I have no answer.

"There was no sign of forced entry. They assume she let whoever did it in."

"Jesus."

Beneath the interminable silence that follows I can feel the beat of protest sounding in us both, It cannot be, it cannot be.

I snap out of it. He is no longer "friend," I don't know what he is.

"Jack, what happened Monday night?"

"What do you mean?"

"After we spoke. What did you do?"

He doesn't answer.

I switch the phone from my right hand to my left. I hear his words, will hear them always, "I don't fucking believe they did this again. . . . She's not going to get away with this again."

I steel myself, afraid to push him, unable not to. "Did you see Deirdre on Monday night?"

"Is that what they think?"

"No one knows what to think."

"No, Lisa. I didn't see Deirdre. I couldn't. You have no idea how devastated I was after you called me."

"Actually, I do," I remind him coldly, irritated by his solipsism, the assumption that his suffering is greater than mine. "I told Callahan about the phone call, the pictures."

"I see." He swallows. "It seems the police should be talking to Sam then, not me." His anger is visceral, pointed.

There is still so much he doesn't know.

"Jack, I was wrong. I never should have called you. I never should have said anything until I talked to Sam. It wasn't what we thought, what I thought. I made a terrible mistake."

"What are you talking about?"

"Sam borrowed money from Deirdre. That's what they were getting together about. There was never an affair."

"Who told you that?"

"Sam."

"And you believe him?"

"Yes. The police found e-mails between the two of them. It was always about money."

He doesn't make a sound.

"Are you still there?" I ask.

"Yes. Where is Sam?"

"He's here. With me. Jack, why didn't you return my messages?"

"I didn't get them until this morning. I didn't have my cell phone. After I talked to you, I was so upset I threw it on the ground and it shattered. I just left it there." His voice lowers, intensifies. "I couldn't get the image of the two of them out of my head."

"What did you do after we spoke?" I ask warily.

"The last few weeks I really believed that Deirdre and I were finally going to be together after all these years. I was totally blindsided. Everything came crashing in on me."

"Jack, what did you do when you got off the phone?"

"I got in my car and drove. I didn't even realize what I was doing until I was halfway up to Boston." A sob escapes, washing away his narrative. "This can't be happening. Lisa, I would have come sooner, I would have called if I'd had any idea. We just got back a few minutes ago."

"We?"

"I'm at Alice's house. Our house."

"What?"

"I didn't know where else to go."

"The police need to talk to you."

"Yes, I know. I'm coming down this afternoon to meet with Callahan. I'm heading to the airport now. I'll get the first shuttle I can."

I hear him swallow.

"I loved her," Jack says. "I always loved her. No matter what."

I do not answer.

"Can I see you? After I talk to Callahan."

I hesitate. "I'm not sure that's such a good idea."

"Please," he presses.

"Call me when you're done and we'll see."

I flip my phone shut and look up to see Sam studying me.

"Jack?" he asks.

"Yes."

"Where the hell has he been?"

"Believe it or not, with Alice."

"Just out of curiosity, they're still legally married, right?"

"Yes. Why?"

"How convenient for him."

"What are you talking about?"

"A wife can't testify against her husband."

"Sam, don't you think you're jumping ahead about a million steps?"

"Maybe. But keep in mind Jack happens to be one of the savviest lawyers around."

TWENTY-NINE

At ten minutes before three I stand outside Weston, waiting for the girls.

I am an interloper here, a visitor to the country of mothers who pick their children up every day. This is their territory. They stand together in clumps, a few with strollers, keeping one eye on the blue doors and the other on each other as they talk. The nannies have positioned themselves a few feet closer to the entrance, ever mindful to appear more vigilant than actual parents. They know all too well the dangerous game of telephone mothers are more than happy to engage in if one is not deemed up to snuff. One of the school's security guards stands poised to lead children into the private minivans that we, too, used until this year, spending thousands of dollars to have Phoebe and Claire shuttled downtown to a waiting babysitter. Behind them, the street is clotted with cars despite all the recent e-mails and letters sent home advising, begging, threatening against it. In homeroom last week, Claire's class was asked to share their funniest bus or train stories. More than one girl admitted she had never been on public transportation. "That's not possible," I protested when she reported this to me, but Claire just rolled her eyes. For all their political correctness, Manhattan's private-school parents surely have their own circle in eco-hell for their contribution to greenhouse gases.

I glance eagerly at the school doors. I crave them, my own children. I long to hold them close, to smell and to touch and enfold them, to batten down the hatches behind us.

I spot Georgia at the center of a group a few yards away and smile politely, hoping that will be sufficient interaction to satisfy any social obligations. I do not have the energy to engage. I am willing to cede to her, cede it all, anything she wants, if only I don't have to talk. Unfortunately, I see her extricate herself from her crowd and begin to make her way over to me wearing a look of great solicitous concern.

"Lisa, hi. Is everything all right?"

"Yes, why?" I ask cautiously. She cannot know about Deirdre, there is no way, and yet. The city has a message system all its own, an underground railroad trafficking in gossip and salacious news, hidden, lethal and decidedly hazardous to underestimate.

"We don't usually see you here."

"I have a job," I remind her, gritting my teeth. Or used to, I think.

She nods dismissively as if this is some crazy whim of mine. Women like Georgia cannot conceive of the notion that not everything in life is a matter of choice. I cannot help but wonder, though, if that will change as Wall Street bonuses vanish and layoffs escalate even in the upper echelons.

"Of course," she says. "But I assumed you were swamped at work since you missed the benefit meeting this morning. Or perhaps you weren't feeling well?"

"Apparently neither seems to be the case," I reply tartly. I realize that my attitude is not helping matters, but I cannot stop myself. I can feel the pent-up resentment bursting out, impossible to stanch.

"That's too bad. There is something I wanted to talk to you about."

"Oh?"

"Yes. I'm confused. We all were, to tell you the truth. When Vanessa called Rita Mason the other day to arrange a time to take her picture for the catalogue she didn't seem to know anything about it.

In fact, she made it quite clear that she never volunteered for the dinner at all."

I stare blankly at Georgia. It occurs to me that she could very well have called to ask me about this when Vanessa first had the conversation with Rita. She preferred to wait for the opportunity to publicly humiliate me. No wonder she was so disappointed when I didn't show up this morning.

"Rita changed her mind," I reply. "There was a scheduling conflict. I thought I had told you."

"I see. And is Ben Erickson really donating the photo shoot or is there a scheduling conflict with that as well?" she asks sweetly.

I stare at her. "You know what, Georgia? Screw you. Screw you and your two-bit committee."

Her face freezes. Slowly, ever so gradually, her perpetual half smile begins to sink down her perfect face. It is the first and only time I have ever seen Georgia Hartman speechless.

My pulse is still racing as I watch her storm off to her posse, which immediately begins to roil and stir, shooting outraged looks in my direction. I'm fucked, my children are fucked. Already regret is nibbling at the edges of my defiance. I stand up straighter, bracing myself as the school doors open and girls tumble out in chattering clumps, calling out to each other, hugging as if they are about to part for months, pulling on coats as they stuff cookies into their mouths, the straps of their two-hundred-pound backpacks slipping off their shoulders, a cheerful chaos that makes me smile. I have a brief vision of a different life, one where I pick the girls up every day, take them out for treats and hear all their news, we have all the time in the world for each other. Of course, if I actually tried to accomplish that, we would end up destitute.

I see Phoebe immersed in conversation with two of her pals, a symphony of laughter and eye-rolling, surely directed at some poor teacher's incalculable stupidity. She suddenly notices me and I smile broadly, expecting to see a mirror image of my pleasure reflected in her expression. Instead she takes a step back, as if she doesn't quite recognize me. Finally, she regroups and smiles tentatively as if this is the reaction she knows that I expect and is offering it up out of kindness. She separates reluctantly from her friends and walks over to me.

"What are you doing here?" she asks suspiciously.

I lean down, kiss her. "I'm happy to see you, too."

"You know what I mean, Mom."

"Can't I pick you up from school if I want to?"

"Sure, but you never do."

I exhale, defeated. Children give you no leeway, none.

"I didn't go to work today and I thought it would be nice, that's all."

"Why didn't you go to work? Because of Deirdre?"

"Yes."

Phoebe stares at the ground, shuffling her feet. Nothing is as it was and my presence is a jarring reminder of that. Rather than a pleasurable surprise it is another disturbance. She glances back at her friends, at the world I have disrupted, and then forces herself to return to me, conscious of not wanting to hurt my feelings.

"It's okay," I tell her. "Go talk to your buddies."

She shakes her head, her lower lip tucked into her top teeth. She has gnawed a bloody red hole in it, an old nervous habit she had only gotten the better of after the pediatrician warned her that if she continued she would have permanent scars. She hasn't done it in months.

We are standing there, making awkward small talk as if we have just been introduced at a cocktail party, when Claire comes out with Lily. The minute she notices me she turns, whispers something to Lily, and strikes off alone in my direction. She has never been one to deal well with transitions and, judging by the look on her face, it is doubtful today will be an exception.

"Why are you here?" she asks as soon as she reaches me.

I groan. "Good Lord, why do I need to apologize for my presence? As I informed your sister, I felt like picking you guys up, okay? I thought it would be nice. In the future I will submit a request in writing."

"I was just asking," Claire replies sullenly.

"You're right. I'm sorry. I guess we're all on edge."

Both girls shrug.

I give it one last try. "How about going out for ice cream?"

Phoebe looks hopefully at Claire, who vetoes the idea. "I have homework."

"Since when does school take precedence over a hot fudge sundae?"

"Can we just go home?" Claire asks.

"Of course."

Deflated, the three of us ride downtown on the Lexington Avenue bus in a disgruntled, cranky silence.

As soon as we get in the door the girls peel off to their bedrooms. I hang up their coats—I don't have it in me to nag them today—check for messages and then go knock gently on Claire's door. "Can I come in?"

She opens the door wordlessly.

I touch her shoulders and if she doesn't fall into my arms, she doesn't shrink from me, either. She looks up, at once fragile and guarded.

"Are you okay, sweetie?" I ask.

She doesn't answer.

"I know you loved Deirdre. I did, too. She was my best friend."

Claire looks at me, waiting for something I cannot give her.

"There's nothing I can say that's going to make this better. But if you want to talk, I'm here. Always. You know that."

There are tears in her eyes and I can feel her shaking slightly. I kiss the top of her head and let her go back to her computer, where a close-up of a single pale pink rose fills the screen, a different flower every day, last week it was kittens, she is so young still, so sentimental.

I look in on Phoebe, who has climbed under her blankets with a book. She has always had the ability to submerge herself in stories, losing track of time, of any reminder of the outside world. I sit down by her on the bed and wait until she finishes her page before I speak.

"How are you doing?"

"Okay, I guess." Though she is deeply shaken, I suspect a part of her acknowledges that Deirdre belonged to Claire, that Claire's grief takes up more room, overshadows hers. "Did they find the robbers?"

I shake my head. "Not yet, sweetie." I envy her the world of black and white, good and bad, of simple explanations.

"But they will?"

"I hope so."

I stroke her cheek with the back of my fingers, kiss her, then gently tap her lip where a new red sore is already forming and remind her not to chew it.

There is a dividing line, a moment when you realize that you cannot make everything better, kiss every hurt away. I don't know who that realization leaves more bereft, parent or child. Once passed, though, it is impossible to return to the time before love's limitations have been rendered so painfully blatant, no matter how much you might long to.

Phoebe picks up her book once more and I withdraw into my bedroom, shut the door. My eyes, swollen and ragged from crying, fill once more. I let the tears trickle down the slope of my cheeks, too drained to wipe them away. I curl up, grasping a pillow tightly between my arms.

Jack must be in New York by now, talking to Callahan. I wonder if he is in the same gray airless room with its dusty linoleum floor, I wonder if Gibbs is there as well, with her thin gold chain and her innuendos. I assume they would call me if they had made an arrest, but I could be wrong.

It is a little after six when Sam walks in with two large bags of take-out food. I rouse myself to go out and greet him, kissing him hello without desire or relief.

"How are you?" he asks as we head into the kitchen and unpack the cartons of enchiladas, guacamole, tacos, fajitas, rice, beans, little plastic containers of sour cream and hot sauce. I know that he meant well, that he, too, is groundless, grasping at anything that might offer comfort, but the extravagance of it all irritates me. He pulls out a Tecate beer for himself and one for me. "Did you pick the girls up from school?"

"Yes, but I didn't exactly get the response I was hoping for," I admit. "Maybe surprising them wasn't the world's best idea, but I thought they'd be at least a little bit happy to see me."

"I'm sure they appreciated it on some level."

"I don't think they appreciate much of anything right now. How could they? They're stuck in this nightmare, too. I don't know what to do. Should I bring Deirdre up, should I not bring her up? I don't know what will help and what will make things worse. I feel so helpless." The ability to console my own children has been decimated along with everything else.

Sam touches my shoulder. "You're doing everything you can."

"But that's just it, there's nothing I can do. I can't change anything, I can't help anyone, I can't make us go back in time."

I shut my eyes, wrap my arms about myself, as if this will somehow keep everything within me from exploding into fragments, a splatter of grief and fear and regret that, once let out, I might never be able to rein back.

Sam holds me tightly until my breathing steadies.

"I don't want the girls to see me like this," I say quietly, straightening, though the barrier is fragile and may not hold.

I move slowly, underwater, putting a stack of napkins in the center of the table. "I promised Deirdre's store manager, Janine, that I'd go in tomorrow afternoon and help her sort through things," I tell Sam as I get out silverware. "She's totally overwhelmed. The police took Deirdre's computer and a lot of her papers. I don't know how much I can accomplish but I can at least sift through invoices and that kind of thing. It's going to be weird, being in there without her."

"Lisa, maybe it's not such a good idea right now. It might be too much. You're allowed to change your mind."

"No, I want to do it."

We turn to see both girls edging into the kitchen, eyeing the massive amounts of food with skepticism.

"What's all this?" Phoebe demands.

"I believe they call it dinner," Sam says.

"For a Mexican army?" Claire retorts.

"Stop complaining and eat a taco. Or twenty," Sam replies.

He passes around containers and the business of arranging plates of food distracts us all.

"How was school today?" Sam asks as he piles his taco with such a gravity-defying mountain of lettuce, cheese, chicken and sour cream that biting into it will be an insurmountable feat.

"Fine," both girls mutter.

"I suppose if I ask what happened, the answer will be 'stuff'?"

They look at him and decide to ignore this.

Instead, Phoebe turns to Claire. "What happened with Kara Fielding today?"

Sam leans over. "Now we're getting somewhere. I was wondering the same thing. What did happen with Kara Fielding?"

"She went off her meds and went nuts in the cafeteria," Phoebe deigns to explain.

"She did not go off her meds," Claire archly corrects her younger sister. "She had a reaction to some new antidepressant she's on."

Sam and I look at each other.

"How old are you?" he asks the girls. "Thirty, forty?"

Claire and Phoebe begin a vigorous debate about who is or is not on medication for ADD, depression and various other of the psychological ills that are so very much in vogue, while we listen, slack-jawed.

By the time we are done eating we have barely made a dent in the containers. The thought of closing up the grease-spackled cartons of food and putting them in the refrigerator repulses me and I throw them in the trash instead, though I am careful to hide the evidence from the girls.

"Are you scared of your own daughters?" Sam asks, amused, as he watches me cover the containers with other garbage.

"Aren't you?"

"They do seem to have a moral absolutism that we've lost along the way."

"I think I need the name of Kara Fielding's psychopharmacologist," I remark.

"For them or for you?"

"Can't we get a group rate and all live happily ever after?"

"It doesn't sound like that worked out so well for good old Kara."

"I'll take my chances."

He kisses me lightly and goes to catch the last few minutes of the evening news.

I am drying my hands when my cell phone rings.

"Well, that was suitably unpleasant," Jack says after a grumbling hello.

I drop the dish towel on the counter. "Where are you?"

"Twenty-second and Park Avenue South. I just finished with the police."

They let him go, then.

"Can you come meet me?" he asks.

"Why don't you come here?"

"I don't want to talk in front of Sam."

I lean against the refrigerator, exhausted. "I don't know."

"Please."

"All right," I relent.

Sam is in the hallway, listening, as I hang up.

"You're not actually thinking of going to meet Jack?" he asks incredulously.

"I won't be gone long."

"That's not the point. Just what is it you hope to gain, Lisa? You think he's just going to up and confess to you?"

"No," I reply unconvincingly.

He is right, of course, on some level, irrational as it is, he is right. Though I am not sure if I am looking for confession or expiation for my own role.

"You realize it might interfere with the investigation?" Sam warns me.

"Maybe you're right, maybe I think he'll say something or I'll see something in his face that will help me make sense of this, as crazy as that sounds. All I know is that I need to do this, okay?"

Sam stands completely still for a long while before speaking again. "I think you are making a big mistake, but go ahead if you feel that strongly about it. You have to promise to call and let me know you're okay, though."

"I will. But Sam, I really don't think you need to worry."

"I'm not so sure about that."

THIRTY

L'avventura, which opened to great fanfare two months ago, is nearly deserted, leaving its baffled owners to wonder how it came so close, garnered such publicity—and somehow just missed. They are all too aware that there is little chance of recovery—you only get one shot at newness before the city, impatient and unforgiving, moves on. As soon as I walk in they greet me with a discomfiting surfeit of eagerness and show me to the back, where Jack is already seated, playing restlessly with his unused silverware, aiming the knife blade between the tines of his fork and withdrawing it over and over again.

His face is etched with fatigue, his sallow skin tinged with a fresh stamp of age. It seems impossible that it was just days ago we stood in that vast empty apartment with its shining floors and second bedroom, Jack racing so avidly into the future, grabbing at it with both hands. He came so close.

"How are you?" I ask, a ridiculous question. The only language I know has been rendered insufficient. Still, I suppose there are gradations of grief, confusion, shock to be sorted through.

Jack searches my eyes. We are the people who loved Deirdre best. And we are the people who, at critical junctures, were the most mistaken. We see both of these things in each other's expressions.

He takes a sip of his drink, staring into the amber liquid while he speaks in a hushed voice. "I'm having a hard time accepting all this," he admits. "Sitting here with you or talking to the police a little while ago, I know that it's real but part of me keeps thinking it isn't, that it's all somehow an enormous mistake and any minute now everyone is going to figure that out."

"I know. It just doesn't seem to sink in. I don't think it ever will." I shake my head at that impossibility. "How could it?"

Jack looks down at the table. "For as long as I can remember, Deirdre has had a home in my imagination," he says. "No matter what happened or how much time passed, there was always the chance that we could still fix it, change it, that we would be together in the end. I know it seems crazy but some part of me always believed that, even during all the years we weren't speaking. And now it's gone. She's gone. Really gone this time. It doesn't seem possible."

I begin to cry softly. I don't know what happens to the space people you love take up in your heart once they are gone, if the muscle eventually closes over it or if the wound is always there, aching and raw. All I know is that it feels a million miles wide tonight.

I shouldn't have come here. I am drowning in it, seeing Jack, the past reflected in his face, all that we mangled, all that we lost, all that will never be.

"Callahan showed me the pictures of Sam and Deirdre," Jack says when I have blotted my eyes with my soggy napkin.

I nod wordlessly.

"You left out some rather crucial details when we spoke this morning," he continues, his expression harshening.

"What do you mean?"

"You didn't tell me that Deirdre had sex before she died." The set of his mouth betrays the grim satisfaction of having your worst predictions proven right.

"I didn't have a chance." My foot bangs into the table as I cross my legs, making a dull tinny sound.

"Did they ask you to take a DNA test?" I ask, trying not to betray the anxiety that is coursing through me.

"Yes, I took care of it right there. I have no reason not to. I gather your husband can't say the same."

Every cell in my body goes on alert. "What's that supposed to mean?"

"I didn't see Deirdre Monday night and I certainly didn't sleep with her. So just who do you think did?"

"I don't know, but it wasn't Sam."

"I'm willing to take the DNA test and according to Callahan, he's not. What does that tell you?" There is a concentrated meanness in Jack's voice that I have never heard before. It makes me come very close to hating him.

"He wants to talk to a lawyer first."

"They can get a subpoena. They can make him take it."

"Jack, you are way off base," I reply angrily. "Sam borrowed some money from her, that's all. The police verified that. Or didn't they bother to tell you?"

"They told me a lot of things," he says cryptically.

"You were mistaken about their relationship in college, too."

He regards me with a withering condescension. "I was there, Lisa."

"Sam admitted there was a bit of drunken fumbling, but they didn't go through with it. They realized what they were doing and they stopped. I'm not defending it or saying it doesn't bother me, but that's all it was."

"Your powers of denial amaze me."

"I trust Sam," I tell him defiantly. I'm not sure which one of us I am trying harder to convince.

"You're telling me that what I saw was just a matter of bad timing, that if I had walked in an hour later, everything would have been different?" he asks sarcastically.

"I'm not blaming you. I'm sure I would have come to the same conclusion."

"I know what I saw. Two people naked in front of me. I have carried that image around with me for years. I have tried to forget it. I have tried to forgive it. I have tried to accept it and move past it. I thought in these past weeks that I finally had." He laughs bitterly. "It turns out I was wrong yet again."

My anger and grief, confusion and distrust are a frenetic roller coaster and I veer from one emotion to the next at a dizzying pace.

"There's something I don't get," I say. "Callahan said Loring, Marcus has no record of you, that you were never going there as a partner. Did I have the name of the firm wrong?"

"No, you had it right."

"I don't understand."

Jack's shoulders slump, his defenses momentarily vanishing from view. "I needed an excuse, or thought I did," he confesses.

"An excuse for what?"

"Coming to New York that first time. I know turning forty is an arbitrary date, but it's a powerful marker, you can't escape it. All I could think of during the last few months was that I had to see Deirdre. I had to give it one last shot, I had to find out if there was any chance. In a way, it was keeping me from truly entering the life I had. There was no way I could move on, in any direction, without knowing."

"What does that have to do with Loring, Marcus?"

"I thought it would be easier if I had a reason to be here. It would take some of the pressure off, make it seem more natural. And then that first night, at dinner, Deirdre seemed open to it, to me. So I continued the story. It gave me an excuse to keep coming back while we figured out what there was between us."

"There was never a job?"

"There would have been. At some other firm. That wouldn't have been a problem."

"You were lying to Deirdre."

"I was making it easier on her. I didn't want to scare her off. I didn't want anything that could be interpreted as an ultimatum. I made that mistake once before. I was terrified," he says quietly.

"Of what?"

"Losing my last chance. Making a fool of myself."

He shuts his eyes and when he opens them again there is a lacquer of tears over his retinas. We are both more tired than we have ever been in our lives, and older, ancient. So much of what we were, what we wanted, is gone.

"Did you even give notice where you work?" I ask him.

He doesn't answer.

"You were covering all the bases, weren't you?" I marvel.

"Lisa, we're not in college anymore. The stakes are different, the investment is different. I was willing to uproot my entire life for Deirdre. I loved her. I've always loved her. But I needed to be sure first. The funny thing is I thought I was." He shakes his head. "I was living in a dream world. It's obvious she never felt the same, no matter what she said. All the time I wasted in some stupid fantasy of mine, I could have gotten on with my life."

"That's not Deirdre's fault."

He ignores this. "When you called Monday night, I realized what a mistake I'd made. It's like I was in some kind of fog and you brought me back to reality."

"But it was the wrong reality. I told you that. I'm sorry I called, more sorry than I've ever been about anything."

"I don't think you were wrong."

I frown, displeased by his accusations, his acrimony. "So you went running back to Boston without even talking to Deirdre?"

"Yes. All I could think of was what a fool I'd been, how close I came to throwing away the life I had."

"I'm surprised Alice was willing to give you the time of day."

"There was a lot we needed to talk about. That's why we didn't get any of the messages. We went up to the house we're building on the Cape. We needed to be alone, with no distractions, to try to figure things out."

"Alice is a very forgiving woman."

He shrugs and it suddenly dawns on me. "You never told her about New York, about Deirdre, any of it, did you?"

"I was going to."

"But you didn't."

"Not every detail. She knew we were having problems."

"I don't believe it. You know what Deirdre told me? That for the first time she didn't want to hedge her bets, that she wanted to give this a real try. She broke off her other relationships for you. And all the time you were the one making sure you had a backup plan."

"That might be what she told you but she obviously didn't break off all her relationships," he snaps. "Just ask the police. Better yet, ask Sam why he won't take that DNA test."

"I already told you why." My voice is shot through with doubts, though, doubts that hadn't been there before. I rummage through the list of men Deirdre had mentioned over time, some transient, some she had turned to repeatedly through the years on empty, restless nights. I thought that was over, I thought they were gone, but it could have been one of them, it must have been.

"Go on and stick to your defense of Sam as long as possible," Jack sneers. "Let me know how it works out for you. In the meantime, I'm going back to Boston."

"Callahan is done with you?" I cannot hide my surprise. I do not consider this particularly good news.

"He knows where I'll be if he needs me. He has no jurisdiction to keep me here."

"Just out of curiosity, what did you tell Alice about all this?"

"The truth. She knows that Deirdre was an old girlfriend of mine and that the four of us had gotten together recently."

"That's not exactly the entire truth, is it? She might not be as naïve as you seem to think she is."

"Why don't you worry about your marriage and let me worry about mine," Jack retorts, and motions for the check.

We part as quickly as possible on the street, anxious to put distance between all that we remind each other of.

When I get home, Sam is in bed reading a magazine. I climb in beside him and answer his questions about the evening in a shorthand that suits us both. I do not want to talk, I only want to prove

Jack wrong, about me, about Sam, about all of it. I want to douse it out, bury it.

I run my hand along Sam's torso and he rolls over, pressing his body to mine.

We have not made love since we heard of Deirdre's death.

But I do not find the solace or reassurance I am seeking. I do not find answers.

It is as if other people are inhabiting our bodies, there is a distance between our skin and our souls, a space that hadn't been there before. We are avatars of our past selves, going through familiar motions, passing through each other bloodlessly.

Sam falls asleep and I lie awake staring at the shadows on the ceiling, lonelier than I have ever been.

THIRTY-ONE

The air is sharp and bracingly clear, a premonition of winter without the cold murky sludge, deliciously false advertising for what is soon to come. I begin to walk slowly from my apartment building, filled with trepidation about going to Aperçu. The store was so much a part of Deirdre, a corner of her psyche and predilections made tangible.

I have gone only a block when I stop into the corner deli and grab an oversized chocolate chip cookie, justifying it as lunch. I eat the cookie as I walk, though it is disappointing, dry and cardboardy. I comfort myself with Deirdre's theory that if food doesn't taste good it has fewer calories. She had so many wacky convictions that I laughed at but adhered to nonetheless.

I am closing the cellophane wrapper around the last half of the cookie—even I'm not that desperate—when I hear someone calling my name, quietly at first and then more insistently.

I turn to see David hurriedly approaching. I reel, too shocked to organize a reaction, a plan. I want desperately to run and yet I don't.

I remain rooted until he is inches from me and then swivel purposefully away, unable to face him.

"Lisa, wait. Please," he intones.

I stop, turn to him. "Are you following me?"

"No. Well, yes. I've been trying to reach you for days."

I have not answered any of David's messages. I have been screening my calls to avoid him. I have sworn to Sam and to myself that I will never talk to him again. Beneath the very real anger, I have been wounded in ways that are not entirely comfortable to admit. Nevertheless, part of me has been waiting for this, despite everything, because of everything.

"I just want to talk," he says, his breath curling white in the air between us and then dissipating.

David looks at me with an uncloaked hopefulness, his eyes boring into mine. He brushes his fingers nervously through his hair.

After all the diatribes that have been spooling relentlessly through my head, the words fly away. I don't know where to begin. There are so many entry points of betrayal, resentment. "Do you have any idea what you've done?" I demand irately. "Do you have any idea the damage you caused?"

"I've spoken to the police. I'm so sorry about your friend. I had no idea that you knew the woman in the photograph. Are you all right?" He reaches to touch me but I move instinctively away. He lets his arm drop.

"No, I'm not all right. You destroyed everything. You had no right to interfere in my life."

"Lisa, I never meant to hurt you."

"Just what did you think was going to happen?"

"Not this."

"Why? Just tell me why you showed me those pictures."

"I know this may be hard to understand, but I was trying to help you," he says. "I went about it all wrong, I know that now, and I'm truly sorry. But I hated seeing you so confused, watching you cry that day in the restaurant. I overstepped, I get that. But I was trying to give you information that I thought you needed." He glances sideways at a truck unloading boxes on the pavement, then turns back to me. "I was clueless about what my wife was up to and I suffered for it. In my world, information is power."

"No matter who it wounds or how wrong it is?" I demand.

"No, of course not."

A mother pushing a baby in a stroller covered with a plastic wind protector makes her way around us. I watch as she stops for the light, checking on her child before moving on.

I know deep down that I am the one who grabbed on to those pictures and used them as a lethal weapon, unwittingly perhaps, but disastrously nonetheless.

I shift my weight from one foot to the other, trying to summon the will to meet David's gaze, the fury I feel both lessened and magnified by his proximity. I cannot get my bearings.

"Sam told me about your history with him. You never cared about me at all. You just wanted to get back at him." I am aware that I sound more scorned and bitter than I had intended, but it is too late.

David shakes his head. "You're wrong," he insists. "I'll admit that I was a bit more curious about you when I found out who you were married to. But then we got to know each other. I did care about you. I still do care about you. Very much. I never intended to cause you this kind of pain."

He leans forward with a sad earnestness that gives me pause, but I refuse to give in to him.

"Well, you did."

"Is there anything I can do to make it up to you?"

"No," I reply harshly.

He begins to speak but I do not want to hear it.

"I have to go," I tell him.

"Lisa, we're not done. Please. Let's just talk."

"No. We are done. Don't do this again, don't call me. I mean it. Don't."

He stands completely still, cocks his head, blinks. Our eyes meet for an instant before I turn to walk quickly and self-consciously away from him.

I do not know how long David stands there, I do not know if he is watching me. I resist the urge to turn around.

I race down the busy street, wending around people lined up at a coffee cart for caffeine and stale sugary donuts. I stare at them as if it is a ritual I have never seen before.

I cannot give credence to David's contrition or his rationales. They change nothing, excuse nothing. Still, it would be nice to believe he did care about me, that when he reached to kiss me it was attraction and not calculation. Because even if I didn't cross that line, I thought about it.

I shake my head and keep walking.

It is just before noon when I get to the store and all thoughts of David are pushed aside.

Though I tried to prepare myself, imagining how it will feel without Deirdre, the first steps inside are more agonizing than I'd anticipated. The imprint of her touch and her taste, her vision, is everywhere. I can almost smell her perfume.

Two young women of indeterminate age and indeterminate but surely highly creative hyphenated jobs are rifling through a rack of navy dresses—Deirdre always grouped by color rather than style—while they talk about a new wine bar set to open in the East Village next week. They have both been to advance parties there, it has potential, but once the hoi polloi make their way in, it could go either way. They engage in a detailed cost-benefit analysis of whether it is better to appear on the first night in case it turns out to be something or if that would in some way brand them as not quite in the loop, at least not the inner-inner loop. I watch as each pulls out a dress, scrupulously studies it, puts it back, and moves on while they continue their finely honed social calculations.

"Lisa, thank God you're here." Janine comes over to hug me and begins to cry. "I can't believe this, I just can't believe this," she says over and over again. There is no reason this should make me impatient. I have no right to measure her grief and entitlement to mourn against my own and find it lacking, and yet the fashion-girl theatricality of it irritates me. Which then makes me irritated at myself for being so ungenerous. I hold her, pat her back, and gently let her go. The two girls at the dresses glance over with only the slightest curiosity and move on to a grouping of Pucci-inspired blouses.

"The police were here for hours yesterday," Janine tells me. "They were asking all these questions. They took Deirdre's computer and papers, all these other things."

"What kinds of questions were they asking?"

"Who her friends were, men, who she did business with, you know. If there was anyone who hung around the store a lot. If she was ever gone for unexplained reasons. If she seemed upset recently. I told them everything I could, but Deirdre didn't share much about her personal life with me."

"I know."

"People keep calling. What am I supposed to tell them? What am I supposed to do about deliveries?" She begins crying again, she only wants to do what is right, she only wants to help, but . . .

"We'll figure it out," I reassure her.

For the first time in days, there is a clearly delineated path in front of me. I leave Janine up front and go to Deirdre's tiny office in the back. The blank spot on her desk where her computer had been is jarring but I take a deep breath and sit down, unsure where to begin. I pick up a file of unpaid bills but there is a hold on all of her bank accounts and they will have to wait. I turn to her bulletin board, touch the fabric swatches, wonder what she had intended for them. There are darkened rectangles on the cork where, I assume, the police removed scraps of paper, phone numbers. I go through the fashion magazines checkered with yellow Post-its, some with scribbled notes about the designers, stars drawn in red ink, question marks. I open her desk drawer, a cluttered mess of paper clips, nubs of pencils, slips of paper I cannot make out. I find the hand-drawn tulip that Claire gave her last Valentine's Day. I put it in my bag, careful not to bend it, it wrenches my heart. There are over-the-counter diet pills, the kind of pseudo-natural supplements that are advertised in the back of magazines, I didn't think Deirdre would fall for that, all those little harmless secrets we keep, exhumed along with the more prosaic detritus that goes to make up a day, a life.

I don't find anything related to Sam in the drawer. Not that I was expecting anything, I knew there wouldn't be, but still, I am relieved.

Every now and then Janine sticks her head in, asking if I need anything. She is palpably comforted to have a grown-up in the house, though I am clueless about so much and spend long intervals staring off into space. I wish I had paid more attention when Deirdre talked to me about the specifics of what she did but no one really listens all that closely to the ins and outs of other people's jobs. There are so many things she said that I try to recall now, so many lines I try retrospectively to read between. Too often what you deem to be inconsequential about another person turns out to be just the opposite.

Digging into Deirdre's file cabinet, I'm surprised to discover that she was far more organized than she appeared. Like women who claim they never diet but secretly count every calorie, she preferred to make everything appear effortless, to keep the hard work hidden from view. I try to remember if I ever told her I admired her but I doubt it. It is not the kind of thing you say.

The night Deirdre signed the lease on the store she came over to our apartment with two bottles of Champagne and we finished both off while the girls watched the Audrey Hepburn movies she brought them and Sam drifted in and out of the room. We sat at the kitchen table while Deirdre laid out her plans with all the giddiness, pride and anticipation she usually dismissed with a self-deprecating shrug, she was so exuberant that night. It really wasn't all that many years ago.

My eyes fill with tears.

More than anything I miss her. I simply miss her.

I miss most of all the small moments that seem like little nothings but prove to be indelible. The time Deirdre and I went out to dinner at some cheesy Italian restaurant in the West Village; she leaned over for a breadstick and her hair caught fire in the candle, or was it mine? I can't recall, all I remember is the singed acrid smell and our laughter. Her sadness at her father's death that she had never really made peace with him and the last of his mistresses, though they were together for nineteen years. The way she told me her womb ached.

This person, this friend, is being stolen from me bit by bit, lost to investigations and allegations as much as death. Mourning her seems a luxury I am not yet allowed.

I have heard nothing all day. It irks me that the police do not feel obligated to inform me of every twist and turn the way they would a family member, that we are all still under suspicion. There is, too, the question of the DNA, noxious and unavoidable as much as I try to put it out of my mind.

It is just before five. I promise Janine I will come in again tomorrow and get ready to leave. Before I do, I take advantage of my last few minutes alone and pick up the phone.

"Lisa, what can I do for you?" Detective Gibbs greets me.

"I was just wondering if you had any new leads." The phrase feels clumsy, it is not something I have ever said before, but my need to know takes precedence over any self-consciousness.

"Sometimes the most important thing you can do is eliminate false leads."

"What do you mean?"

"Jack Handel's DNA was not a match. And his wife confirmed that he was home in Boston at eleven p.m. Monday night." Gibbs pauses. "Lisa, we are going to have to talk further to your husband."

THIRTY-TWO

This is what you do: You pretend that things are normal. Long past the point of rationality, you keep on pretending. It is the only way to keep moving, to get through the day with any shred of sanity. You pretend there is not a black hole in the center of your existence. But you know all the while there will come a time when that is no longer possible.

The following morning I rise early and make the girls pancakes for breakfast. I watch Sam tease them at the table, gently ribbing them over supposed crushes and imaginary academic infractions, I see his tenderness. The rhythm of our family life goes on, as it should, as it must, unseen by others and yet more real to me than anything that takes place outside these four walls. I still believe this is the truest version of ourselves, of Sam. I must believe that.

The alternative is unthinkable.

It is teacher development day, one of the myriad holes in the Weston calendar, most of which are unnecessary if not indulgent, as far as I'm concerned, and the girls have no school. After Sam leaves for work, I let them watch DVDs while I shower and then lie down on my bed, fully dressed and made-up, staring at the ceiling. All I see before me are empty hours ahead, a shapeless day waiting for anything that might bring definition to this no-man's-land of grief and regret and bewilderment.

I am past paying attention to anything else. If Phoebe is eating ice cream by ten a.m. and Claire is trying to conquer the use of eyeliner despite my ban on makeup, so be it. None of it seems to matter.

A couple of hours later, I drop Claire off at Lily's, where they will put on outlandish outfits and then videotape themselves in endless scenarios that for some reason usually entail one of them ending up in a shrieking death grip. Phoebe has a birthday party at Mud Bath, one of a chain of do-it-yourself pottery stores that cater to restless rainy-day children and parents desperate for any craft activity that they do not personally have to engage in. In a brilliant bit of marketing, the store offers jug wine in the back so that parents can get quietly and happily sloshed while their kids make twenty-dollar mugs in the shape of cows and dogs. All across Manhattan, there are children drinking hot chocolate out of pink speckled pig heads, the ears long since broken off and lying on windowsills waiting forlornly to be glued back on.

When we walk in, the party is just getting started, the children's smocks already covered in ashy bits of clay. Phoebe takes her place at the end of a long rectangular table festooned with balloons and begins to work silently on a mug while the other girls chatter around her. I have always thought of Phoebe as a happy, self-sufficient girl and seeing her shrink this way among her classmates pulls at my heart. I stand a few feet away, surreptitiously watching, the interior life that I once found transparent abstruse to me now. It is impossible to know with children if a sudden change in demeanor is a temporary reaction, situational, or if it is the first glimpse of a seismic and possibly permanent shift, if this will be the new normal. She catches me looking at her and frowns with displeasure.

I admit my guilt with a helpless shrug, and turn to leave. Just before I get to the door, I run into Tara and her daughter, Isabel, on their way in. Isabel scampers off to the table without so much as a good-bye while Tara, barely noticing, turns to me.

"I heard about your dust-up with Georgia," she remarks coolly.

"Oh God," I groan. "I'm sure it's all over the school."

"Like a bad case of lice," Tara admits.

"I was having a crummy day. I never should have lost it that way."

"I've always thought if Georgia would just break down and eat something she'd be a lot less cranky. You shouldn't let her drive you off the benefit committee."

"I think she already has."

"If I were you I'd go to the next meeting just to see the look on her face."

I smile doubtfully. "Maybe."

We glance over at our children, reaching for jars of glaze, jostling one another as they try to hoard the best colors. Later they will each be given a paper ticket to pick up their creations after they have been fired a couple of days from now.

"I never remember to come back for these things," Tara admits. "Do you think there's a landfill somewhere out in Queens with thousands of abandoned pig and cow mugs?"

"If you want I can pick up Isabel's mug when I get Phoebe's," I offer a bit shyly. We are both aware that it is an overture.

"Are you sure?"

"It's no problem. I'll send it into school with Phoebe." The truth is, I have never forgotten to pick up one of these damn mugs in my life. That kind of nonchalance is totally beyond me. I envy it as much as I secretly reproach it.

"That would be great." She looks around, drained of conversation. "Well, I'm sure you have to get back to work," she says hopefully.

"Yes, I ran over here on my lunch hour."

We say good-bye and I walk out as if I have someplace to go.

I didn't intend to lie, certainly not working isn't exactly a mark of shame with this bunch, but I do not have the energy to deal with explanations.

Though I don't miss my job, at least not the perilous minefield it had become, I have no structure to take its place, no distraction from worries and obsessions. I am left with just myself. I don't know what word on the street is about my departure from Merdale, if they are spreading lies to cover themselves or if they are pretending I simply never existed. I will find out soon enough when I look for another job. Just the thought of it, of sitting through interviews and pretending I want it, really want it, leaves me depressed and exhausted. But I can see no other option. Even with unemployment insurance I can't go long without working. I am almost forty. I will never be the next new thing, that is over for me. And I cannot afford to try new careers on for size, not at this point. Looking ahead at years, decades of work that no longer engages me but is necessary nonetheless is too discouraging to contemplate right now.

When I get to Aperçu, Janine is ringing up a woman at the register, carefully folding her multitude of purchases, two jersey wrap dresses, a short swingy tweed jacket, a silk blouse or tunic or minidress, the length is indeterminate, a scarf, between sheets of crisp pale-blue tissue paper. I try to calculate what the woman has spent, marveling that anyone has that kind of cash to blow on clothes. She walks out slinging the glossy shopping bag over her shoulder.

"She'll return half of it tomorrow," Janine remarks. "She always does. She once accused us of having a mirror that makes her look ten pounds thinner than the one she has at home."

She leans over, kisses me on both cheeks. For a short period of time, a third kiss appeared in certain circles but luckily it faded into the graveyard of other failed trends. Janine appears to contemplate giving it a comeback but thinks better of it.

"I tried to compile the list of designers that you asked for," she says. "I'm not sure if it's all of them, but it's close. I left it on Deirdre's desk."

"Thanks. I'll go have a look at it."

It feels a little less strange this time to walk into the office, hang up my coat.

I glance quickly at the designers list but it means little to me. I have never heard of ninety percent of them. There was so much Deirdre and I didn't have in common. It was one of the things we laughed about, finding our vastly different styles and fields of knowledge amusing, if at times baffling.

Within an hour I realize there is very little I can do here. When Janine comes in to drop off the day's mail, I pretend to be busy but I don't think she falls for it. I thank her and begin to rifle through the catalogues and bills. Already, there are invitations to Christmas parties from designers, some with personal notes to Deirdre written across the bottom: Hope to see you, Looking forward to catching up, It's been too long. They knock my breath away. I stare at them, queasy, until I can barely see straight.

I am almost at the bottom of the stack when I come across a nine- by twelve-inch manila envelope with Deirdre's name written in black Sharpie. There is something in the intimate scrawl that makes me hesitate. There is no return address. I turn it over and run my fingernail beneath the adhesive flap.

Inside there is a black-and-white photograph of Deirdre, the one I saw last week in Ben's studio, Deirdre wearing just a shirt, staring out of the window. There is no note, just the inky signature at the bottom, "xob." I put it down and look at the postmark on the envelope. Ben must have put it in the mail the afternoon he left for India.

My hands shake slightly as I hold the picture close and feel an ache in every organ. I trace Deirdre's outlines with my fingertips, the pensive look, satisfied or sad or both, it is hard to discern, the smudge of mascara beneath her right eye, the way she is hugging her knees, her hair spilling over her shoulders, the beauty mark she hated on her collarbone, these are the things you miss most, these are the specifics of loss and longing.

I shut my eyes, but a spectral replica of the image is imprinted behind my lids.

It seeps in slowly, a question, a realization.

I pick up the picture once more. The shirt Deirdre is wearing, with its variegated stripes and loose folds, is the one she bought at the sample sale that she invited me to after she told me that she and Ben had broken up.

No matter what she said, no matter what she told Jack, they never really had stopped seeing each other at all. I sit in Deirdre's office with my coat on, staring at the photograph, while the light outside grows dark.

Ben has not returned any of my messages. Whatever Deirdre was to him, or he to her, whatever the photograph says about the forensics of desire, it seems impossible to me that he doesn't know she is gone, that he is walking around, working, going about his life, assuming she is doing the same.

Despite all my misgivings about Ben, I cannot deny their bond any more than I can understand it. It is there, sitting before me on the desk in black and white.

I pick up the phone and call the photo department at *Vogue*. After telling at least a dozen interns, assistants and junior editors that I am a family member of Ben Erickson's and there has been an emergency, I finally reach the photo director, who is singularly unmoved by the words *family* or *emergency*. "If you've left messages for him I really don't see what else I can do," she informs me snootily.

"Can you at least tell me when he is due to return?" I ask, frustrated.

"All right," she sighs, as if this is a herculean task. "I'll check the call sheet. He was going to do a pretty quick turnaround. I'm pretty sure he flew in this morning."

I listen to her rustle around.

"Huh. Looks like he called in and said he needed the day. He'll be back later tonight. That's twice in one trip he changed his ticket. First class to India. Do you have any idea what that costs?"

"He changed his flight out, too?"

"Seems he missed it. He got a later one that night. I wish these photographers would realize that the anything-goes days of the past are over."

"You're sure he missed his flight Monday night?"

"Yes," she replies impatiently. "That's what I said, isn't it?"

I thank her and hang up while she is still railing about the slump in advertising and draconian budget cuts.

I stare down at the photo before me.

Ben, with his bruising fingerprints, his fickle heart and his questionable moral compass and the sex that Deirdre told me hovered on the edge but never crossed over.

What if, just once, it did?

I pick up the phone and call Detective Gibbs. "There's someone you need to talk to," I tell her.

THIRTY-THREE

There is the chance, of course, that I am wrong, that Ben doesn't even know of Deirdre's death. All through the night, I feel a creeping guilt about my phone call to Gibbs, the way I led her to Ben, then pushed, then shoved her there when she didn't seem to quite grasp the import, the likelihood of it all. I got the disturbing feeling that the strength of my convictions made her suspicious not of Ben but of me, my motives.

His name, it seems, was not new to her.

They have been doing their job after all.

"You're saying they were still dating?" Gibbs asked. It seemed such an anachronistic word, too flimsy for Deirdre and Ben's inexorable pull to and away from each other. "What about Jack Handel?"

"I don't know."

"Would you say Erickson is a jealous man?"

Questions, more questions, as if she wanted to purposefully diminish what I was trying to tell her.

But I refuse to give in to doubt.

Lying in the dark, Sam sleeping beside me, I go over and over the conversation in my head, the case I built for Gibbs's benefit, for my own. I told her of the bruises I had seen, the erotic aggression that worried Deirdre, puzzled her, gripped her in ways I will never understand. Deirdre, with her mischievous glint, her fierce desire to be claimed, her provocations. I am betraying her, giving pieces of her away, pieces I held tight until now, pieces that I preferred not to examine too closely, but I have no choice.

"Did you ever see bruises on other parts of her body?" Gibbs asked, more interested.

Sam shifts slightly, pulling the sheets into a tightly held bunch.

I imagine a phalanx of policemen greeting Ben in customs, taking him away.

I imagine this being over.

Sam said little last night when I told him of Ben's presence in New York, his face grim as I described the subterranean tendencies I had never told him of before, out of loyalty to Deirdre. He has never liked Ben, never trusted him, sensing a certain shrewdness he found distasteful. He is willing to believe the worst. Though he was measured in his response, he, too, would like this to be over, attention turned away from us, from him.

At ten the next morning, I put together a bag of juice packs, water, fruit roll-ups; I give the girls knee pads and jerseys for the school sports day on Roosevelt Island. I have begged off, pleading a headache, but the truth is I do not want to be distracted from the concentrated act of waiting for news, for affirmation, for confession or formal accusation.

I kiss the three of them good-bye.

"You'll call if you hear anything," Sam says as he buttons his coat, shepherding Phoebe and Claire out.

"Of course."

I close the door behind them and feel their absence in the newly silent apartment. I go back into the kitchen, scrape the uneaten breakfast into the trash, load the dishwasher. I straighten the newspapers, turn the radio on, flip impatiently around the dial, turn it off. And still, only twenty minutes have gone by.

All through the morning, as I attempt to stay busy, going into the girls' rooms, picking up clothes, trying to organize the flotsam of their lives in a way that they will not vociferously protest as soon as they get home, I wait for a sign, for word that doesn't come.

An hour goes by, two. I long to call Gibbs to find out if they have brought Ben in, what he has said, what he knows. I cannot help but worry, too, that they have told him of my role.

Instead, I reread old e-mail from Deirdre, short notes filled with typos about where and when to meet, her detailed list of everything she ate that day—she had a compulsion to confess whenever she thought she went overboard—the chain letters she was oddly susceptible to that promised good karma if you passed them on within thirty seconds. Silly things. We saved everything that really mattered for conversation. These snippets are the only concrete record I am left with.

When I have finished them all, I sit staring at the computer screen. On impulse, I click on the file labeled "finances" but there is nothing there I haven't seen before. I keep going down the list of documents. Some of Sam's are password-protected and will not open.

Before Gibbs got off the phone yesterday she said that she had one more question. "On another topic, we are trying to track the money Sam borrowed from Deirdre. It's a complicated trail but our people believe the entire amount might be gone. Has Sam discussed that with you?"

"I don't know anything about it," I told her.

I am not sure if she was looking for information or imparting it.

I cannot help but feel that the detectives are condemning us for the messiness of our lives as much as anything else. Certainly when Callahan and Gibbs chart our steps in such a logical and linear manner it seems impossible that we did not see our own mistakes in the making. There were so many times when intervention would have been possible. But we were asking all the wrong questions. We were misreading all the clues.

The trajectory of any life, laid out across a table, reduced to jottings in a pad, would no doubt seem both damning and inane, our imperfections difficult to justify despite our best intentions.

At least that is what I would like to believe.

I shut off the computer.

I cannot sit still any longer, I have waited myself out.

I am just about to call Janine on a pretext I haven't quite decided on when the intercom goes off. The loud ringing, designed to be heard in every corner of the apartment, startles me. I put down the phone and go to the white video monitor in the kitchen that the children have named Oscar for reasons I no longer remember. I press the button that allows me to see whoever is downstairs.

I step away, my breath beginning to fray.

The buzzer goes off again, more insistently. He will not let it go.

I take a deep breath and let Ben in.

While I wait for him to come up, I glance around the apartment for backup, for anything to buttress me, but I am completely alone.

I hear the elevator door open and his footsteps in the hallway. Before he can knock I open the door.

Ben walks quickly in, disheveled, stubbly, visibly distraught. He looks at me, his eyes bloodshot, exhausted, jet-lagged, and heads into the living room without saying a word. I follow him, watching nervously as he paces back and forth, tense and wiry. When he finally turns to face me I see a fury that makes me take a step back.

"Why didn't you tell me?" There is pain in his voice, but more than that, an anger sharp and spiked.

"You talked to the police?"

"Yes, I talked to the fucking police. Two detectives were at my door before nine a.m. this morning." He rests his hands on the back of a chair to steady himself. "Why didn't you tell me about Deirdre?" he demands again. "I can't believe I had to hear about this from goddamned strangers."

"I'm sorry. I left messages for you while you were away."

"You could have told me what it was about, you could have tried harder."

"I didn't know what to do. It wasn't the kind of news you leave on voice mail. You could have called me back," I add defensively.

Ben turns to me with a cold, hard steeliness. "What the hell did you tell them?"

"What do you mean?" I can feel the blood rush to my face.

"What did you say to the police about me and Deirdre?" He stops, shakes his head in rage and confusion. "You have no idea the kinds of things they were asking. I had nothing to do with her death. I didn't even know about it until this morning. I still can't believe I'm even saying these words. I can't wrap my mind around it. And then to have these idiots standing in my home accusing me of being involved somehow, spewing some bullshit about rough sex. Where do you get off telling them something like that?"

My legs are shaky, weak. "Those weren't my words."

"They had to come from somewhere."

"They asked me who Deirdre was involved with. That's all."

Ben looms over me.

"Can we sit down? Please," I implore him.

He doesn't move.

"Whatever happened with me and Deirdre was between us. You have no right to judge it. You have no right to judge me."

"I'm not."

"Of course you are. You always have. Don't you think I know that? Don't you think Deirdre knew it? And now you seem to have done a pretty good job of convincing the police that I was somehow involved. How dare you? How fucking dare you?"

"The police are questioning everyone, Sam, Jack Handel. It's not just you." I will say anything to get him to back off, to leave. "It's an investigation. I'm sure they're talking to everyone Deirdre ever knew."

Ben slows down, somewhat appeased. "Is that what they told you?"

"Yes."

His shoulders slump and he collapses on the edge of a chair facing me, burying his head in his hands before looking up. "I can't begin to take this all in," he says quietly. "The last time I saw her . . ." he stops before he finishes the sentence, either because he can't or because he thinks better of it. He looks directly into me, his eyes narrowed and focused and opaque. "She was very much alive when I left her apartment."

"When?"

"Monday."

"What were you doing there? I thought you two had broken up weeks ago."

"It wasn't that simple. There were things we weren't finished with yet."

"What things?"

He smiles slightly and then sinks into sadness. "Each other."

"She told me that it was over."

"Did it occur to you that Deirdre didn't always share everything with you? You know why she didn't want you to know we were still in touch? She thought you'd disapprove. She didn't want you to be disappointed in her."

"Did she tell you that?"

"She didn't have to."

I flinch. "I know one thing," I retort. "She was ready to be with someone who could make a real commitment to her and clearly that wasn't going to be you. Couldn't you have just left her alone? She had a chance at being happy. After all you put her through, couldn't you let her have it?"

"Who are you to decide what would or wouldn't make Deirdre happy? You assume that what works for you automatically would have worked for her."

"If she was so damn pleased with you, why did she break it off?"

Ben leans back, runs his hands through his hair. "Deirdre didn't know what she wanted. She knew what she was supposed to want but that's not always the same thing."

"She wanted a family. If you really loved her, you'd know how important that was to her."

"You don't get to decide what my feelings for Deirdre were," Ben replies angrily. "Love comes in all different iterations. Because I don't define it or expect from it the exact same thing you do doesn't give you the right to judge how much I cared about Deirdre. Or to judge her decisions either, for that matter. Deirdre was a grown woman. She was quite capable of deciding on her own who she wanted to be with."

"Do you have any idea how much you hurt her?"

"I was always honest with Deirdre about what I could or couldn't give. I never lied to her."

"That doesn't make it all okay."

"I realize that. But she was responsible, too. Maybe we wanted different things, but that doesn't make one of us the good guy and one bad. You see relationships as having only one possible useful outcome, marriage, and anything else is deemed a failure. But Jesus, how many people get married because they think that's what they should do, because it's expected of them? You think they're so happy?"

"That's not the point. You strung her along for years."

He ignores this. "Look, I know you wanted what was best, or what you thought was best, for her. And I know that she was drawn to the life Jack was offering her."

"She told you about him?"

"Yes." He looks up at me. "Maybe she even loved him. But that didn't mean she stopped wanting me. Or that I stopped wanting to be with her." His face is crooked with pain. "I don't want to argue with you, Lisa. I'm trying to make sense of all this. A few hours ago I didn't even know Deirdre was gone."

"Why did you go to see her Monday night?" I ask cautiously.

"There was something I wanted to tell her. Something I wanted her to know before I left for India."

"What?"

"I found out that morning that my divorce was finalized."

"You want me to believe that after all your years of arguing that monogamy is a bourgeois pipe dream you had a sudden change of heart? Did she fall for that?"

"That's not what I'm saying. That's not what I said to her. I wanted her to hold off and give me a little time to think. Maybe I was tired of how I was living, I don't know. I wasn't promising her anything. I was asking her to wait, that's all."

"You just didn't want her to be with Jack. She was finally leaving you this time. You'd do anything to sabotage that. It was all about your ego."

"That's not true. If I really believed that was what she wanted, if she was completely convinced that was right for her, I would have let her go without a fight."

I don't believe him. He is lying to me or to himself.

"What makes you think she wasn't sure?" I ask.

"Because of how we made love that night," he answers simply.

It is a long while before I speak again. "It was you, then," I say so softly I'm not sure he even hears me. It wasn't Sam, it was never Sam, it was you. "Did you tell the police that?" I ask.

"Yes," he answers. "I didn't really have a choice. You made sure of that."

THIRTY-FOUR

How do you reclaim what you never admitted you had lost?

Ben is scarcely out the door before I race to call Sam and tell him of Ben's admission, barely able to mask the swell of adrenaline and relief—it was not you, it was never you. Sam listens intently, asking a few questions, waiting for me to finish. If he feels vindicated, he gives no evidence of it. But then, he cannot say "I told you so" to a question I never dared to ask out loud.

"I will never understand why she chose to be in the same room with that man," Sam mutters.

"You don't know what she chose. You're coming dangerously close to a blame-the-victim argument," I warn him. "For centuries men have gotten away with that 'she was asking for it' gambit. I thought we had moved past that by now."

"You're right. I'm sorry. I'm certainly not about to defend Ben Erickson. Do the police think that he was the last person to see her alive?"

"I don't know. I assume so. I haven't spoken to Gibbs or Callahan. I'm a bit surprised they didn't hold him for further questioning."

"I hate to say it, but having sex is not a crime. They'll need more than that. With Ben involved, it will be a high-profile case when it breaks. They're going to make sure to dot all the *i*'s and cross all the *t*'s."

In the background I can hear the cries of the playing fields, a cheer rising up, petering out.

I hesitate. "At least this lets you off the hook," I say tentatively. "With the DNA test, I mean."

"Maybe."

"What do you mean, maybe?"

"Callahan still wants the name of the source I was meeting with and I'm still not giving it to him," Sam replies. "Hopefully this will get him to back off. Look, Phoebe is on the soccer field. We can talk more when we get home."

He hangs up and I sit very still.

I know that Sam is right, at least in part. Whatever edge Ben pushed Deirdre to, emotionally or physically, she was obviously drawn to it. As Ben made painfully clear, Deirdre kept parts of herself and her desires tucked away from me. I'm not sure whether it was my perception of her or her self-image she was trying to protect. I cannot estimate how much she left out and I filled in with my own prejudices and expectations. Realizing the discrepancies does not make me miss her any less, though. Friendship, it seems, is not contingent on full disclosure. Perhaps quite the opposite is true.

There is one more call to place, though admittedly it does not come from my best instincts. Sam may not admit to feeling vindicated but I cannot resist the urge to set the record straight. Jack was wrong. About the past, long gone and immediate, about his flawed assumptions constructed out of fragments. I understand even as I dial his number that what releases me from doubt and turmoil—it wasn't Sam with Deirdre that night—will not do the same for him. Jack may have had the wrong man, but it doesn't change the fact of Deirdre's betrayal. I will never know, none of us will, whether her interlude with Ben was a final indulgence before she bid him good-bye or an avowal of their ongoing affair, if she planned to break it off with Jack or, after a flicker of weakness, steer headfirst into a future with him. We don't get to see how the story ends.

Jack listens in begrudging silence while I tell him of Ben's visit, his version of that night. If I expected him to offer an apology for his accusations about Sam, he makes no move in that direction.

"Let me know when the police come to their senses and arrest Erickson," he says brusquely.

"Jack, I'm sorry," I offer quietly. I can afford to be more generous now. My husband has been returned to me in full. "I know this must be so difficult for you."

"It's over, it's the past," he replies coolly, quick to minimize his hopes and his disappointments, his own feverish anticipation of attaining what he had always longed for. I understand that it is far easier to get over a romantic failure if you diminish it, but the rapidity of his about-face stuns me nevertheless.

When Sam and the girls get home, covered in mud and grass stains, I listen to the roundup of soccer scores, the accusations of unnecessary roughness, the teams they almost beat but didn't. The exertion seems to have done both girls good, the concentration and sheer physicality required for play pushing aside the unhappiness of the past week. With their red cheeks and tangled hair and excitement, they seem almost like themselves again. I am glad of it even as I realize how tenuous it might be.

While Claire and Phoebe shower and get ready for dinner, Sam opens a beer and we go to sit in the living room.

"I called Gibbs after I spoke to you," I tell him.

"Oh? What did she have to say?"

"Not much. She basically told me she didn't have the authority to share anything further about the investigation. I couldn't get any more out of her about Ben. She did say that they are ready to release Deirdre's body. The cause of death will be listed as a head injury, what did she call it, a subdural hematoma."

"Did she say if it came from a fall or a blow?"

"I didn't ask. Do you think it matters?"

"Just curious."

"I can't imagine Ben intentionally hurting Deirdre," I admit.

"It could be that whatever they were doing got out of hand."

"No matter what happened, I don't understand how he could have left her there."

Sam takes a sip of his beer, then rests the bottle on his knee, running his forefinger around its circumference.

"People do strange things when they panic, things they may regret. Sometimes they just can't see a way back from them," he says.

"That doesn't change anything. It doesn't excuse it."

"No." He finishes the rest of his beer in one long gulp. "Have you made a decision about a place for the memorial service yet?"

"Yes. The Quaker Meeting House on Fifteenth Street, the old red brick one with the white columns. Deirdre once went to a wedding there and the simplicity appealed to her. It's the only place that feels even close to right."

"Is there anything I can do to help?"

"No. I'll make calls and tell people to get in touch with whoever they think should be there. I want to do it as soon as possible, for everyone's sake. I spoke to someone at the Meeting House and he said there was an evening open next week."

"Sounds good." He leans over to kiss me. "I'm going to go take a shower."

He rises and is almost to the doorway before I call after him.

"Sam? I've been meaning to ask. Is there any chance that we're going to get that fifty thousand dollars back?"

"The jury's still out. The VC guys are not buying in with any major commitment and without more capital there's no way to staff up properly. They're scavenging around but everyone is in a cautious mood. In the meantime, I will continue to cling to the masthead for dear life until they figure a way to outsource magazine writing to India."

I watch him as he turns and walks down the hallway.

We will recover. We will stitch ourselves back together, mending the rip, and if the seams will never be invisible, the fabric permanently flawed, it will be a whole cloth nevertheless. I'm almost certain of it.

After we eat, we skip the news and spend the rest of the evening watching bits and pieces of old movies, paying little attention, until it is time to tuck the girls in.

We go to sleep side by side.

But Sam's insomnia has not abated; he is restless and twitchy, unable to get much rest. The next morning, though it is Sunday, I hear him in the kitchen making coffee at six fifteen. I do not ask what is eating away at him in the night: We are still standing on jagged pieces of land separated by a quake, it is understandable.

He spends the day at his computer while I take the girls shopping for winter coats.

By Monday morning, after another sleepless night, Sam is bleary-eyed and snappy.

I join him in the kitchen before the girls get up.

"Are you all right?" I ask.

"Fine. I just need to finish this story on the bank mortgages. Simon is losing patience and the police badgering him isn't helping any."

"What do the police have to do with it?"

"They called him over the weekend asking him a bunch of questions including the name of my source. I thought they'd leave it alone by now but they haven't."

"Does Simon know who it was?"

"Of course not. I don't get why no one seems to understand the definition of *confidential* these days. Anyway, Simon assured me he'd back me up, but it's not winning me any points, I can tell you that. He is obsessed with the word *increasingly* lately. Every article has to have it as a justification within the first two paragraphs. As in, Simon is increasingly interested in downsizing our staff."

"Is that true?"

"Yes. He's hired an efficiency expert to spend a month on premises and then submit a report. No efficiency expert has ever come to the conclusion you're doing everything right and there is no money to be saved. If nothing else, they have to justify their own fees. This guy is determined to figure out why it takes half the number of people to get out a magazine in Europe than it does here."

"Why does it?"

"I'm not sure. I'd prefer to think we have higher journalistic standards rather than that we are bloated and self-indulgent but I may be in the minority. Even if I'm right, I doubt it will matter. Head count is the mantra of the day."

"I am going to get a new job, you know," I assure him.

"I'm not worried."

I raise one eyebrow.

"Okay, a little worried," he admits, smiling. "But not about you."

After Sam leaves I break down and call a headhunter who has come highly recommended.

"I would love to talk to you about the 'Lisa Barkley' brand," she assures me.

Despite my distaste, I make an appointment for eleven thirty the following day. I get out my résumé, update my history of employment and try to come up with answers for the inevitable question of why I decided to leave Merdale. I rehearse saying, "I am looking for a new challenge," though in truth a challenge is the last thing I want. I've had more than enough, thank you very much. I don't suppose, though, I can walk in and say, At this point, what I'm really looking for is an easy ride.

Aside from a quick trip out to buy stationery to print my résumé on and another when I realize I am out of ink, I have an overwhelmingly unproductive afternoon. I wander the apartment, conscious of all the useful things I could be doing, but I don't even bother to fool myself that any of them are about to happen.

There has been no further word. If the police are coming any closer to arresting Ben, I see no sign of it. The dearth of any discernible progress baffles and then worries me, the solution I had been so sure of growing fuzzy around the edges, elusive.

On Monday night, Sam stays late to finish his piece. I order in food, put newspaper down on the living room floor and rent a dippy romantic comedy. Phoebe, Claire and I watch it while we eat, an illicit girl party. They are surprised by my lack of discipline—it is a school night, after all—but they don't question it. They are weighing the signs of domestic aberrations, looking for clues. There was no milk in the house at breakfast, I did not scold them for leaving their beds unmade. It is beginning to make them both nervous. I vow to myself to be more attentive.

I am half-asleep when Sam comes home past midnight and assures me that everything is fine, he filed his story, go back to sleep, I didn't mean to disturb you. I drift off while he washes up.

The next morning, I dress carefully for the interview and make the girls hot chocolate. When Phoebe and Claire make their way into the kitchen, I try to convince them that they also need to eat something, but they both insist the hot chocolate fills them up far too much to contemplate anything else. I let it go. At least it's protein. And calcium. Things could be worse. Rumor has it that a few of the girls they know have Pop-Tarts for breakfast, though considering the nutritional compulsions most of the parents in their set display, this could well be an urban myth.

They don't protest when I tell them that I will ride part of the way on the Madison Avenue bus, leaving them to go the last twenty blocks alone, and the three of us walk out into the dank gray morning together. When the bus comes we find seats in the back and I ask them both what classes they have. I can never keep it straight. Is Tuesday a good day with art and gym, or a bad day with math and science? They answer as patiently as they can before Claire pulls out her iPod and Phoebe doodles on the cover of her history text.

When we reach Sixty-sixth Street I kiss them both good-bye, though they shudder at the mortifying public display of maternal affection, and rush off the bus before the doors slam in my face.

I have decided to follow Tara's advice and go to the benefit meeting this morning, knowing that if I continue to avoid Georgia I will have years of torture ahead of me. I figure my best course of action is to take the high road and pretend the whole thing never happened, which, I suspect, will have the added benefit of depriving

Georgia of the satisfaction of overtly cutting me. I have stashed an Ativan for courage and Tara's daughter's pig mug in my bag.

Six women have already gathered in Georgia's living room when her maid lets me in. A fire is lit against the chill and they stand a few feet from its warm radius, chatting amiably in indecipherable voices. As soon as they see me, all conversation comes to an abrupt stop. Georgia turns, noticeably shocked by my presence. She quickly regroups and walks toward me.

"Lisa, I'm surprised you made it this morning," she says, smiling acidly as she approaches.

"Really? I've only missed one meeting," I remind her.

"I meant under the circumstances."

"What circumstances are those?"

"Surely you must know. It's all over the papers today."

"What is?"

"I just assumed, seeing as he is such a good friend of yours." She turns and walks to the mantel while the other women watch in utter silence, hanging on her very move.

"Didn't you see the *Post*?" she asks, handing me the tabloid folded to page three.

"We don't get the *Post*," I tell her. Sam reads the business column online and I have no interest in the gossip pages, where Georgia and her friends turn up on a regular basis, tabulating each other's mentions like baseball scores.

"Well, I'm sure you'll be interested in this."

I look at her and then glance down at the paper.

CELEBRITY PHOTOGRAPHER ARRESTED

Ben Erickson, the noted celebrity photographer whose work has appeared in *Vogue*, *Vanity Fair*, *The New York Times* and numerous other publications, was arrested at his TriBeCa home last night for the alleged murder of clothing boutique owner Deirdre Cushing, 39. Cushing's body was discov-

> ered seven days ago in her East Side apartment. The medical examiner has determined the cause of death as a trauma to the head. A police detective involved with the case told the *Post* that DNA evidence as well as Erickson's own account place him at the scene of the crime on the night Cushing died. "They had sexual relations before her death, his skin was found beneath her fingernails and bruises consistent with Erickson's fingerprints were found on her body," says the anonymous source. Erickson and Cushing dated for the past two years and police have reason to believe that she had recently broken off their relationship. Asked about speculation that Erickson will mount a "rough sex" defense, a police spokesman replied, "That is up to his lawyers." A spokesman for *Vogue* confirmed that Erickson had been on a recent assignment for the magazine but declined further comment. A bail hearing is set for tomorrow.

I let the paper fall to my side, aware of all the eyes trained on me. No one makes a move.

Beneath Georgia's expression of faux concern, I detect a note of triumph.

Only Tara Jamison steps forward to break the silence, resting her hand gently on my shoulder. "I'm sorry," she murmurs quietly. "Did you know her?"

"She was my best friend," I say.

THIRTY-FIVE

Dusk settles outside the enormous hand-blown windows of the nineteenth-century Meeting House. Inside, the dusty scent of old wood and services gone by fills the unadorned room with a sense of calm.

Sam, Phoebe, Claire and I sit a few rows back, watching as the simple white pews fill with the men and women who populated Deirdre's life. There are the familiar faces of those she was close to and people I've been at parties with over the years whose names I've long forgotten, an aunt I never met, customers from the store, other single women, her weekend women, Deirdre sometimes called them affectionately, gym buddies, men I vaguely recall her dating, acquaintances from other eras and other neighborhoods, all witnesses to a Manhattan life, compartmentalized and varied and so rarely gathered in one room.

Only Ben and Jack are missing.

Sam and I debated about whether to bring the girls but finally decided in favor of it. They deserve to be included in whatever comfort ritual can bring. I look over at them sitting solemnly by my side, stone-faced, uncertain what to expect or how, precisely, to behave, at once so grown up and so achingly young. I touch them both reassuringly. I told them that there would be sadness in the room tonight, and perhaps tears, but that we were gathering to celebrate Deirdre's life and there should be joy as well. I try to remember that myself as the last people filter in and the doors close behind them.

It is just after six p.m. when the man I had first spoken with about the service walks to the center of the room. Slightly stooped, with thinning hair and a graying goatee, a tweed blazer and wide-wale corduroy pants, he clears his throat and begins to speak in a gravelly voice, his pronounced Adam's apple bouncing up and down.

"Hi. I'm Tom Madison from the Society of Friends. We are honored that you chose to remember Deirdre Cushing here with us tonight. For those of you who have never been to a Quaker service, I'd like to give you a brief introduction. At our Meeting, we practice what we call 'unprogrammed worship.' Instead of proscribed ceremonies, we believe that the Spirit of God lies in each of us. Anyone may speak up when they are moved to do so. I invite you to rise and share a memory or thought about Deirdre whenever you feel the Spirit."

Tom Madison's crinkly eyes roam the room before he sits down without further ado.

A thick, self-conscious silence descends as people stare at their hands resting in their laps, glancing surreptitiously about, shifting positions as discreetly as possible. Outside a car alarm sounds in the distance, then stops.

No one wants to go first.

I feel vaguely responsible, as if I am the hostess of a party in the midst of flopping, one of those interminable events that never quite establishes a rhythm.

My leg begins to fall asleep.

Someone's stomach grumbles.

I sneak a look at my watch. Eleven minutes of absolute silence have gone by.

I hear a rustling and look over to see Janine rising shakily a few feet away, resting her hands on the pew in front of her to steady herself. Her voice quakes as she begins, is stopped by nerves, begins again. I want to go up and kiss her, I am so grateful.

Everyone in the room glances at her hopefully.

"Okay, um, I'm not sure if this is the kind of thing, all right, anyway," she stutters, then steels herself. "Deirdre was the most stylish woman I ever met. I mean, you all know that. She was my role model. Totally. I always thought she could do anything. Except for one thing: drive."

Groans and laughs of recognition go up around the room, encouraging Janine to continue.

"As many of you know, Deirdre didn't get her license until she was thirty and she never really drove anywhere after that. She was the only person I know who sent Christmas cards to every single cabbie in the Hamptons. Anyway, last year she decided she had to get over her fear and she hired this guy, Sammy, to give her lessons. Every Wednesday afternoon, Sammy would pull up in front of the store, Deirdre would get in and they would take off at about three miles an hour.

"She did fine the first few weeks when they tooled around Manhattan," Janine goes on, "but when Sammy told her he was going to take her on the FDR Drive the next week she totally panicked. I've never seen anyone so nervous. Of course, she canceled and never drove again. You know what she said to me? She said she decided she didn't have to conquer all of her fears, just some of them." Janine chokes up, collects herself. "The thing is, I thought it was really glamorous of her not to drive. I mean, I didn't know people like her growing up in Ohio." She looks nervously around the room and sits down.

The silence returns but it is more companionable now, filled with recollections instead of awkwardness.

Elaina, one of Deirdre's fellow single friends, stands up next. "I don't know if it was one of her fears but one thing I'm sure of is how much Deirdre hated to be bored. She'd do anything to avoid it. One time when she was in between boyfriends, she sent the exact same note to eighty-seven guys in one fell swoop on Match. Seriously. I'm not exaggerating. She said she wanted to shake her life up. I can't remember if she actually read each guy's profile or if she chose them randomly. I think she figured her odds were pretty much the same either way. The thing that gets me is that when they kicked her off the Web site she wrote this indignant letter saying they had no right to judge how many potential soul mates she had."

The stories pile up, the armful of dresses brought over unbidden to a friend recovering from pneumonia, the time she passed out on MacDougal Street on the fourth day of a diet that consisted of six plums a day, the way she still took books out of the public library because she liked the way they smelled. Some speak of her love of children, her penchant for roaming the Metropolitan Museum for hours whenever she was sad or confused or needed to clear her head, her dedication to a charity that donated business clothes to homeless women to wear on job interviews, her independence. Most of all they talk of her humor and her deep, essential kindness.

I gather these stories in, hold them tight, those I know and those I don't, I savor them all. But I do not rise to speak, fearful that if I try, my knees will buckle beneath me. In some ways, tonight, in this soaring room with its closed doors and its mourners, is the first time I have come close to believing that Deirdre is truly gone and no amount of wishing or magical thinking will alter that finality. It leaves me faint.

I will never see most of these people again.

The city will continue to whirl around us, rending us apart, uniting us, treating us to chance encounters and unexpected heartbreak. It is Deirdre who carried Manhattan and all its heady promise with her to that upstate campus where we first met, Deirdre who gave me both the confidence to come here and the will to stay. It was her lasting gift to me.

Tom Madison reaches to shake hands with the person on his left and then his right, signaling that the Meeting is over.

As we file out into the courtyard Sam asks the girls where they would like to go for dinner. Except for a late-afternoon snack, none of us has eaten.

"Posto," Phoebe proclaims, her favorite spot for thin-crust pizza and lemonade you mix yourself with liquid cane sugar.

For once, the girls don't squabble and we head out onto Rutherford Place, where the trees of Stuyvesant Park are outlined against the darkening night, its stone fountains turned off for the season. We are a few feet past the Meeting House gates when I hear someone call my name.

I turn to see a woman I noticed sitting in the back pew hurrying up to me. She looks vaguely familiar but I can't quite place her.

"Lisa?"

"Yes?"

"I'm Alice. Alice Handel." She is thinner than I remember, her pretty, once round face now anxious and distraught. She reaches for my forearm. "I need to talk to you."

THIRTY-SIX

"Alice, of course." It has been five years since I last saw her at her wedding to Jack on a sultry Cape Cod summer night, Alice in a simple deep V-neck satin gown that floated from her slim figure, her blond hair loose, tendrily, her face glowing, that's how I remember it, all that freshness, all that shimmer. The woman before me is still lovely, but a palpable weariness has dimmed her complexion, painted shadows where none had been.

"Please, it's important," she insists, holding on to my arm.

Sam, who has been watching from two feet away, steps forward. "Go ahead," he says. "I'll take the girls to dinner."

I look at him and nod, not at all sure what I am getting myself into.

Alice watches impatiently while I kiss Sam and the girls goodbye, telling them I will meet them at home.

It is only when they have begun to walk off that I turn my attention back to Alice.

"Is Jack here with you?" I ask.

"No, I came alone. He doesn't know I'm here. Is there someplace we can go? Someplace private? Please."

"Of course. My apartment is a few blocks away. Why don't we go there?"

"Yes, fine."

As I lead the way, Alice walks quickly, her head down. We speak little. Whatever she so desperately needs to talk to me about consumes every ounce of her concentration, it is all she has.

We ride up in the elevator in silence.

Once inside, I turn on the lights.

"Can I take your coat?" I ask as I slip out of mine and hang it up.

"That's all right, I'll keep it on."

I show her into the living room. "Would you like some coffee or tea? A drink?"

"I'm fine."

I consider pouring myself a glass of wine, which I could sorely use, but am reticent to drink alone.

We settle onto opposite chairs, Alice perched at the very edge of hers, glancing around nervously, chewing the inside of her mouth in agitation.

"You were at Deirdre's service," I remark.

"Yes." Alice looks down at her lap.

I nod. It is impossible not to wonder about our predecessors in love, to compare ourselves to them, searching for similarities, hoping for flaws, wondering, too, what they can tell us about the person who is now ours.

Tears begin to fill Alice's eyes but she doesn't bother to brush them aside, she just lets them fall. She is a universe away.

"Are you all right? Can I get you anything?"

She shakes her head. "I always knew Jack loved her," she says, picking up a thought midstream. "I knew it when I married him, even though he said he hadn't talked to her in years. I thought it was the past but as soon as we were married they got back in contact. I tried to ignore it. I told myself it didn't mean anything, that he had picked me. The thing is, he never really chose me at all."

"He married you."

"I was a distraction he hoped would work, but that's different from love."

I'm uncertain what she wants from me, affirmation or refutation. "I'm sure it was more than that," I tell her.

She looks at me vacantly, wrapped in resignation, there is no fight left in her. "Did you know that Jack saved everything Deirdre ever gave him? He kept a box stashed in the back of a closet with all these pictures of her from college, notes she had left him, movie tickets. All these souvenirs of their affair. He thought I didn't know about it, but I saw him with it sometimes. I used to look at them myself when he wasn't home, trying to figure out what hold she had on him. But I never said anything. Then, in the last few months, everything began to change. Jack changed."

"What do you mean?"

"He started making trips to New York he never really told me the purpose of. There were middle-of-the-night phone calls. He wasn't always where he said he was. It was getting harder and harder to pretend it wasn't happening even though I kept trying. It's amazing how much you can delude yourself if you want to."

"I know," I say quietly. "Jack told me you were having troubles," I gently posit. "In your marriage, I mean. He thought you were seeing someone else."

Alice looks at me incredulously. "He told you that? That's ridiculous. He knows that's not true."

She stands up and goes to the window, staring at the street below for a long while. "When Jack came home that night and told me he wanted to give our marriage a fresh start, I was so happy. You have no idea how relieved I was. I didn't ask him why the sudden renewed interest. I didn't care. It was everything I'd been hoping for."

She turns to me defiantly. "You know what? I was happy when I heard Deirdre had died. I know she was your friend and I know that's a horrible thing for me to say, but it's true. I thought for the first time I'd have Jack to myself. I thought we'd finally have a chance."

She sits back down, studying me to see how deep a wound she has inflicted.

I am suddenly so very tired.

"Alice, why did you come here tonight?" I ask.

She looks off into the mid-distance, speaking in a trance. "I heard him come in that night. He thought I was sleeping but I heard his key in the door. I heard him take a shower in the downstairs bathroom. The next morning when I found him sleeping on the couch, I didn't say anything. He was back, that's all I cared about."

"What are you saying?" I ask, confused.

"When we got back from the Cape the next day, the police called to tell us about Deirdre. While Jack was being questioned in New York they talked to me, too. They asked what time Jack had gotten back Monday and I told them eleven. That's what he had told me. Maybe it was true. I don't know."

"But you do know," I say.

She plays with a ragged hangnail, unable to look me in the eyes. "I looked at the clock, it was close to three a.m."

"Why didn't you say anything?"

"I wasn't in the habit of questioning him. He was with me, that's all I cared about. Then the DNA results came back and they exonerated Jack so it didn't seem to matter."

"I don't understand why you're telling me all this now."

"Last night, when Jack thought I was asleep, I saw him crouched in his study, weeping, holding on to that stupid box of mementos. I realized he was never going to let her go. Even after Deirdre died she had this unbreakable power over him. I was never going to win, it was always going to be her. I could lie to myself, I could lie for him but it was never going to make a bit of difference."

I can see him sitting in the dark, Jack with his pieces and his pictures, thinking he could compartmentalize his feelings for Deirdre, keep them hidden away, contained, manageable. He had done it for so long, almost done it.

"What happened?" I ask dully.

"I decided to wait until he went back to bed and then throw the box away." Her eyes are half closed. "I realize it was just a symbolic gesture, that it wouldn't really change anything, and I knew Jack would be furious when he realized what I'd done, but I didn't care.

It was bad enough trying to compete with her when she was alive but I had no intention of spending the rest of my life trying to compete with a ghost."

"Did you get rid of it?"

"No." Alice stops speaking. She digs her hand into her pocket and pulls something out, holding it in her tightly clenched fist so that I cannot see what it is.

Finally, she opens one finger at a time.

Lying in the palm of her hand is the gold chain with the diamond heart that Jack had given to Deirdre.

"This is hers, isn't it?" Alice asks.

I nod.

"I knew everything in that box. I know that sounds sick, but I couldn't help it. This wasn't in it before Jack went to New York that last time. It wasn't there before she died."

I hold out my hand and she slides the necklace slowly into it. The light catches the diamonds. I bring it closer. Staining just a quarter inch of the delicate chain I see what I am certain is dried blood.

THIRTY-SEVEN

I look back up at Alice. I cannot organize my thoughts, everything is out of order. I don't know where to begin.

"Why did you come to me instead of going to the police?"

"I don't know. Maybe I was hoping you would tell me I was wrong." Her voice cracks. "I've been pretending for so long. Not seeing, not knowing, becomes a habit, a way to live. Sometimes it seems like it's the only way to live. But I saw the newspaper clipping on Jack's desk and I realized that when it came down to it, I couldn't live with myself if I let someone else go to jail for what he did. It's the last bit of self-respect I have left."

"You have to tell the police," I say.

Alice's shoulders sink. "I know."

I get up, stand still until the light-headedness passes and then walk to my bag to get Gibbs's card with her cell phone number out of my wallet. I take the phone into the kitchen to talk.

When I come back to the living room, Alice is curled in her chair like a tired child.

"Detective Gibbs wants us to come to the precinct house to meet her," I tell her.

"Now?"

"Yes."

Alice looks up at me, depleted.

"You're doing the right thing," I reassure her.

"I'm turning in my husband," she replies bitterly. "How can that be the right thing?"

"You have no choice."

"Of course I do." She unfolds her legs, her arms. "It's not really proof of anything, anyway."

"You wouldn't be here if you believed that."

I write Sam a note telling him I had to go out, promising to explain later, and grab my coat while Alice rinses her face with cold water in the bathroom. She is buying herself time, one last stand against a future she doesn't want to enter.

The police station has a quiet, desultory air at night, most of the desks empty, the remaining officers gathered in the corner doing their duty, waiting for something bad to happen. It usually does. There is no one in the holding cell. Gibbs leads us to the back, where Callahan is waiting for us.

"Thank you for coming in, Mrs. Handel," Callahan says with a cool formality.

"Alice, please."

"All right, Alice."

We sit in the small gray room and Alice sips the coffee Gibbs has brought her, holding the cup in both hands to warm herself, though the heat is on. The radiators making a creaking rasp at unpredictable intervals. I jump each time, though the detectives don't seem to notice, having long ago absorbed it into the syncopation of their days, their nights. I wonder if it infiltrates their dreams.

"Lisa gave Detective Gibbs a rough idea of what you told her this evening," Callahan says. "Of course, we'd like to hear it from you. Before we begin, I need to ask you one question. Does your husband have any idea that you are here?"

"No. I told him I was visiting my sister in Rhode Island."

"And if he should call there looking for you?"

"Linda will cover for me."

Callahan relaxes, ready to get down to business. "All right. Let's start at the beginning. What time did your husband come home that Monday night?"

"Around three a.m."

"But you told us before it was eleven p.m."

"Yes."

"Which is true?"

Alice looks from Callahan to Gibbs in frustration and shame. "I'm telling you the truth now. It was three a.m."

Callahan leans forward. "Why are you changing your story now?"

"I should have told you this before, I know that, okay? I didn't think it was that important. And then when your tests showed that Jack wasn't with Deirdre that night, it didn't seem to matter."

"Our tests only showed he didn't have sex with Deirdre that night," Callahan corrects her.

Alice cringes. It still pierces, her husband and another woman, bandied about so casually.

"Go on," Gibbs encourages.

"I heard that you had made an arrest and I thought it was settled."

"But here you are," Callahan says.

"Yes."

"Alice, Lisa told us you found a necklace. Can I see it?" Gibbs asks gently.

Alice pulls it out of her pocket and puts it on the table.

Gibbs turns to Callahan. "It does appear to be the one Deirdre was wearing in the photographs."

"It is definitely the one Jack gave her," I confirm.

Gibbs picks it up carefully with a pen, the chain dangling down like a golden snake, and places it in a plastic bag, though surely there are already so many fingerprints on it I can't imagine why one more set would matter. "We'll send this to the lab. In the meantime, what are the chances your husband will discover it is gone before tomorrow?"

"I don't know," Alice admits. "He might."

"Your husband is a very smart lawyer. Don't you think he would have washed the necklace if he thought it might be incriminating in any way?"

"She said it wasn't there before Deirdre died. What other explanation could there be?" I demand.

"He probably assumed no one would find it," Alice answers more calmly. "He thought that box was secret all these years."

Callahan turns back to Alice. "What do you think your husband would do if he realized the necklace was gone? Do you think he'd suspect you had taken it and brought your suspicions to us?"

"I don't know," Alice repeats. She begins to tremble, the reality of being in a neon-lit interrogation room in a New York City police precinct just beginning to dawn on her.

"What I'm asking is," Callahan continues pointedly, "do you think he'd take off?"

"Take off?"

"Run."

Alice stares at him. "This is crazy, this is all so crazy." She looks at him with the worst kind of wonderment. "We're talking about the man I'm married to."

"We realize that," Gibbs says soothingly. "We're just trying to figure out the best way to proceed. We don't want to risk Jack eluding us but we will need to establish probable cause to get an arrest warrant."

"I don't know what he'd do. I don't even know who he is." She is crying now, sniffling loudly.

I find a crumpled tissue in my bag and hand it to her. The detectives wait while she blots her eyes, trying to compose herself.

Callahan turns to Gibbs. "Call Boston. Tell them to pull Handel in for questioning and hold him for as long as possible."

"All right." She gets up to leave the room.

"What happens now?" I ask Callahan.

"If the DNA of the blood on the necklace matches, we have a pretty good shot at getting an arrest warrant and having Jack brought to New York. It's not a slam dunk, but your testimony about his state of mind that night and Alice's timeline should be enough to get the process going." He pauses. "There's one other thing. The medical examiner found a mark on Deirdre's neck consistent with a necklace being yanked off. None of our searches turned it up. Until now."

"What about Ben?"

"That depends. Assuming this pans out, the charges against him will be dropped."

An hour later, we are done. Alice and I stand on the chilly side street, both of us looking down at the ground disconsolately.

"Are you all right?" I ask.

"I can't imagine ever being all right again." She wraps her arms around her chest, looking down the street, away from me. "I just want this to be over."

"I know."

Even as I say it, I know that can't happen. The past is never really over. Our interpretation of it may shift like a kaleidoscope, it may inform us or lead us astray, it may bring comfort or delusion, an excuse to hate or a reason to love. Some of us race too quickly to try to escape it, some of us cling so tightly it blinds us to the present. But one way or another, it is always with us.

"Do you want to come home with me?" I ask.

"No."

"Where will you go?"

"Up to my sister's. She's expecting me."

I put Alice in a cab that will take her to her parked car near the Meeting House and watch as the taxi drives off. I had thought that perhaps she would turn and find me watching after her, but she doesn't look back.

I turn and head home, walking as quickly as I can.

I slip my keys quietly into the front door and stand completely still in the foyer. I hear Sam in the kitchen, boiling water for tea, I hear Phoebe on the phone and Claire playing music while she studies for a bio test and I drink it all in, relish every sound.

I walk up to Sam and put my arms around him, burying my head in the crook of his neck, breathing him in, his touch, his scent, his very being so familiar and so unknown. It is the only place I have ever truly wanted to be.

At ten o'clock the following morning, Detective Gibbs calls to tell me that Jack has been arrested.

EPILOGUE

A thousand tiny white lights twinkle in Cipriani's amber banquet hall, draping the balcony overhead in glittering scallops, snaking through the delicate bare white branches of the centerpieces, the simplest form of magic. The hum of between-course chatter, animated by cocktails and vintage wine and the all-too-rare conviction that you are in the right place at the right time, drifts in the air about us, laced with satisfaction and bonhomie. Outside, the city is covered with February's first big snowfall, crusted over with a dangerous icy shell, but within the warm, fragrant dining room the women are wearing strapless dresses and strappy sandals, defying the seasons with their gaiety.

I lean against the knobby lattice of the high-back chair and look over at Sam, who has migrated two seats away, so handsome in his navy suit, his face confident and engaged as he speaks with three men who have come to pay court, to curry favor or mine for insider tidbits. Sam, amused, flattered, but not taken in, glances over their shoulders at me, the irony lost on neither of us, and I smile back. In one small corner of one small world, he is the man of the moment. Since his piece broke last week on the Merdale cover-up and all it implies about the nasty undercurrent of sexual harassment coursing through corporate America, he has been on two network talk shows, had his exposé discussed in newspapers, blogs and radio programs across the country and gotten a surprisingly generous book offer.

An envelope filled with Mick Favata's damning records landed on Sam's desk three weeks ago without a note, though we both knew who it was from. It was David's parting gift to me, and to Sam, his way of trying to apologize. He had kept a copy after all. Perhaps David does have a latent sense of outraged morality, however situational it might be. In my best moods I am willing to give him the benefit of the doubt, though forgiveness is a different matter. After numerous interviews and a quick trip to London to verify the facts, Sam blew the lid off Favata's violent attack against the woman in his office (there were others as well) and Robert Merdale's willful cover-up. It turns out my flighty assistant wasn't so flighty after all. Merdale had her keeping an eye on me all along and gave her a sizable bonus when she hijacked the London reports from my mail and turned them over to him. Favata was gone from the company within days. Merdale is busy making apologies and reparations to various women's groups as publicly as possible. Some clients have jumped ship but not all.

The story couldn't have come at a better time. Simon, convinced by the efficiency expert's ruthless report, had come to the conclusion that Sam—older, more expensive than those just coming up—must go. Firing Sam before he turned forty next month would save the magazine from one of those pesky age-discrimination lawsuits that are rampant these days. UniProphet's future was also looking bleak, the money Sam had borrowed from Deirdre in all likelihood gone for good. Despite all their fancy beta tests and inflated promises, when UniProphet actually put it into action, it simply didn't perform up to expectations. They, like others before them, discovered that past behavior is not predictive of future actions with anything more than ten percent accuracy. The other ninety percent remains idiosyncratic, unknowable, forever subject to last-minute, inexplicable changes of heart. There are no algorithms that forecast with any certainty what any one of us will want in the end, though people will surely continue to try.

On stage, the auctioneer from Christie's, a brittle woman in a severe black cocktail frock and hair lacquered into immobility, clears her throat to gain everyone's attention. As the bidding begins, Sam returns to his seat beside me.

"Have I told you that you look beautiful?" he whispers.

I smile. "The dress is going back tomorrow."

"Ah, the privileges of ownership," Sam teases. "Anyway, it suits you."

"The dress or the privilege?"

"Both."

The dress, a lapis silk halter, is by one of the young designers I found earmarked in Deirdre's magazines. I suppose I am still seeking her approval, perhaps I always will. In matters great and small, we wanted to make each other happy. So often we did. Those are the times I choose to remember.

Deirdre's diamond heart necklace is lying in the back of my top dresser drawer. The police returned it to me after Jack pleaded guilty to manslaughter 2. When confronted with all of the evidence, including a witness from Deirdre's building who had finally come forward, Jack admitted that he had gone to her loft that night, arriving soon after Ben had left, the residue of their lovemaking still written all over Deirdre's face. Jack claimed that they had argued and she had pushed him first. He was trying to restrain her when she slipped, landing on her head. He swore that she was alive when he left, leaving the door open so someone would be sure to find her. He settled out of court for a four-year sentence. I was shocked that that was all he got, but Gibbs explained that the case remained largely circumstantial. There were only two people in the room that night, she reminded me, and one of them is gone. Ben was issued a formal apology the following day and all the charges against him were dropped. Though he has said he has forgiven me, I doubt we will ever speak again.

Deirdre left everything to me in her will and I was set on closing the store until Sam convinced me I should try to run it. I will never have Deirdre's taste and discernment when it comes to fashion, nor am I looking for the sense of identity she found in Aperçu. I am gaining something entirely different—freedom. I can make my own hours and pick the girls up from school two or three days a week. Though they have yet to admit it, I believe that they are pleased with the arrangement. Sometimes, when they don't have too much homework, we go out for ice cream, all the minor domestic skirmishes put aside as we dip into our sundaes that taste so much like a holiday. On Saturday afternoons, Claire helps me in the store, though Phoebe, after trying it once, finds it too boring for words. She has taken up swimming with a newfound passion and spends the time at practices while Sam sits on the other side of a glass wall, looking up from his newspaper to watch her do a flip turn and flash her a thumbs-up.

All around us paddles rise and fall. There is enthusiastic bidding for the first-row season tickets to the Knicks, for the Ralph Lauren shopping spree and the seats at the Academy Awards, a giddy roaring splurge of money changing hands, friends outdoing each other with great good humor and affable competition. It is all for a good cause, after all.

When the week at Tara Jamison's house in Beaver Creek comes up I smile over at her, seated across the table with her date, a dark-haired, six-foot-tall lawyer nine years her junior, the topic of much gossip, disdain and envy tonight. When we meet for coffee now and then, Tara still talks about going back to school, though she has made no concrete move in that direction. Maybe next week, or the week after that.

The auction goes on: the party for thirty children at Dylan's Candy Bar, the walk-on part in an upcoming HBO series, the visit to the celebrity dermatologist all add to the impressive grand tally. When the week at a famous director's six-bedroom house in Mustique comes up (he has a daughter in the fourth grade), Georgia Hartman, sitting three tables away, raises her paddle high into the air. The opening bid is a bargain at six thousand dollars. Though it wasn't on her to-do list of countries it is too tempting to pass up. Others feel the same: paddles rise in swift succession as the price goes up in increments of two thousand dollars.

"Must be nice," Sam mumbles in my ear.

"Must be," I agree.

I am not jealous, though, not really. There will always be moments when I envy people like Georgia for their ease, their freedom from financial worry, the calculations they do not have to make, but I am at peace with my choices. I have what I want most. I always did.

When the bidding hits ten thousand, Tara raises her paddle with a slow-motion laconic grace. "Twelve thousand," she says in her husky alto.

Georgia, surprised, shoots her a harsh look. Not to be outdone, she pushes the bid to fourteen.

It is down to just the two of them now, though Tara has not so much as acknowledged Georgia with a glance, which only annoys her further. She keeps her eyes steadily focused on the auctioneer. When the price hits sixteen thousand dollars, Georgia's husband puts his hand firmly on hers and holds it down on the table until the auctioneer says, "Sold." Tara has won.

"Congratulations," I say, leaning over.

She shrugs. "I can't stand Mustique."

"I don't understand."

Tara smiles. "We can't let women like Georgia win. Why don't you take it?"

"I couldn't do that."

"I insist. Consider it a thank-you gift."

"For what?"

She smiles but doesn't answer, distracted by her date, who has leaned over and is enthusiastically nuzzling her neck.

The last item of the evening is the portrait session with Ben Erickson. The minute his name is mentioned an excited murmur fills the room. Since his arrest and subsequent release in the death of that boutique owner whose name no one can quite recall, Ben's glamour has only magnified. He has never been more coveted, personally or professionally. Though his donation had been given an approximate value of ten thousand dollars in the catalogue, the bidding is spurred on by the scent of danger, sex, talent and celebrity that clings to him. The father of twins in the eleventh grade wins with a final bid of twenty thousand dollars and his wife glows with visions of the imminent social success such close proximity to the photographer is sure to convey, if only for the gossip value.

"I know Ben," I whisper to Sam. "He'll never go to their dinner parties."

"Worse," Sam says, "he won't airbrush her precious portrait. She'll end up stashing it in some closet and pretending the whole thing never happened, though her husband will undoubtedly make that impossible. C'mon, let's get out of here before the rush."

We get our coats and make our way down the slippery steps to the sidewalk. The narrow winding cobblestone streets of old Manhattan and the shining towers of the new are all deserted now. We pull our collars tight against the bracing winter air, all alone in the dark and silent city. "Thank God we escaped," Sam says, reaching over to kiss me.

I smile. We are so very lucky and we are old enough and smart enough and shaken up enough to know it. We know, too, how careful we must be.

"Let's go home," I say, slipping my arm through his.

"Yes, let's."

ACKNOWLEDGMENTS

I would like to thank Greer Hendricks for her friendship, invaluable editing skills and sharp insight, as well as the entire terrific team at Atria for their ongoing support. I deeply appreciate Suzanne Gluck, who has always been there, and Erin Malone at William Morris. Shana Kelly provided an early read that meant so much. To my family and my longtime friends, the women who provide a safety net, a sounding board and much laughter: Eve Bercovici, Diane Burstein, Karen Fausch, Diane Gern, Judy Glantzman, Penelope Green, Janice Kaplan, Sally Koslow, Julie Pinkwater, Rebecca Sanhueza, Lynn Schnurnberger, Lesley Jane Seymour—thank you. For his years of friendship, advice and loyalty, thank you to Adam Glassman. My heartfelt appreciation goes to The Writers Room for providing a sanctuary in the city. And most of all, to my daughter, Sasha, you are the best part of every day.

ABOUT THE AUTHOR

Emily Listfield lives with her daughter in New York City. This is her seventh novel.

www.emilylistfield.com